MESSAGES FROM THE DEAD

SID JOHNSON

Published 2006 by arima publishing

www.arimapublishing.com

ISBN 1-84549-146-7
ISBN 978-1-84549-146-8

Printed and bound in the United Kingdom

Typeset in Garamond

swirl is an imprint of arima Publishing

arima publishing
ASK House, Northgate Avenue
Bury St Edmunds, Suffolk IP32 6BB
t: (+44) 01284 700321

www.arimapublishing.com

Overture

So here's how it started. I wanted to know who was in charge round here. I wanted to know whether this 'I' chap I'm forever asserting in speech actually stood for anything substantial, something more than his body. Or was the body in fact the *only* consistency, a leaky carrier for an ocean of driftwood, a sticky tangle of lost threads, a clutch of straws matted together by occasion, location, coincidence.

But the harder I looked, the less I saw. Could it be, I wondered, that persistence of identity, the assertion of me, was actually a matter of ego-driven effort, in large part reliant on patchy memory for content, and pride and fear for its protection and promotion?

"Pompous rhetoric," thought Richard, without words.

"Fist fulla fer-a-py, Doccy Dick'd sor-tim," sang he.

That's Rich. My Rich. *Our* Rich.

Before long my thoughts began to float, more as moments than objects. Once firmly-held opinions revealed themselves as mere sensation, reactions to a world now strangely on the outside, superficial seasoning to a cobbled cast of facts and memories, who thrived and died like characters in soap opera. Does plain causation outsmart free will more often than we'd care to admit, I wondered? Brains rumble like a dodgy stomach … and we call ourselves King.

Nevertheless I was enjoying the search. In fact, far from being put off I was hooked. I wanted to know more about these faceless mysteries soaring around my empty heart. I allowed my personality to drift, I became a coach trip tourist who's decided never to go home. "What value consistency, if one is consistently wrong?" I yawned through sleepy eyes, as the world whizzed by.

"Got to leave your mark," said the man he called dad.

"But I'll show you how *not* to leave a mark," he replied, years later, without words. "I'll show you a proper ride, a genuine thrill-spiller, that's if you got the bottle, and at four pints an hour I'm quite a bargain, you'll see."

As the sun beat down through my glass pillow I wondered where the genuine risk takers had gone, the frontier heroes ready to explore some proper rough country, the real world, the world *inside*. Let's ride the foamy waves of a cerebral theme park, said I, challenging all to join me on this life-long white-knuckler, with not a safety harness, team leader or big wheel in sight. For surely there's too much to explore in this immense ocean to lay anchor at some fixed character, some proud personality, teetering like a tower of dirty plates.

Dear Reader, you simply must let go, otherwise we will not get on. For I have every intention of breaking in and rummaging through your deepest darkest drawers so it would be so less messy if you let me in first. You must make this intruder feel at home - in fact we must trash your pad together, it's the only way. And please don't reach for the phone. There are no Mind Police. That's just Cold War paranoia. This is pure no-go.

Richard knew all about no-go areas, took a lot of organisation keeping the place clean, keeping it clear of the filth. "All I wanted was a bit of peace and quiet." That was his excuse, apparently. He doesn't talk about it much, no-one does, about anything, you'll see. Detail and dialogue will not be our strong points. But that must have been some night all the same. Year Zero, the day the clocks went back, right back to square one. Quiet, yes, but no peace and certainly no justice, we'll have none of that nonsense in this story, and that's a promise.

SID JOHNSON

Our foundations may have been nurtured long before we secured our philosophical privacy, but it's never too late to cast those toe-curling family kisses aside. If those moustachioed aunts and uncles are still hanging around then it's time they drank up and were on their way. And if they ignore the warm hand of reason then simply offer the cool hand of violence. Host simply must turn bouncer - I fear this is gonna be a long long night.

There's always room in Richard's head. "Small gaff, but surprising what you can do with it mind," he might say, if he was ever to throw a party - one where people actually turned up. "Oh, and the drinks are free, totally free. Come on in. Suey'll sort you out. Have you met Uncle Ray and Auntie Nat?" There was a time when Richard's party was always banging. He dutifully did the rounds, made sure no glass ran empty. But then they left. They got bored. Which would be bad enough, but his guests weren't even *real*. Well, not as such. Can you believe that? But they always leave don't they Richard? And it's just you again, just you and your small empty gaff.

Things have gone awful quite these days eh Rich? Everything's all a bit hush-hush. What price peace eh? Just what *is* the price of peace and quiet these days? Apparently there are no ideas behind objects, no ideals behind reality and ultimately everything's on the outside. But if men don't cry, then just what *is* that noise keeping you awake at night Rich, as you shake and stare, in the cold and the sweat, the freeze and the fog?

But back to the search. I know it sounds pretty lame, but I was looking for myself. How else can I put it? And worse still, this 'I' chap appeared to be the only man capable of directing such an absurd mission. And so to calm his nerves I decided he would need protection, a piece of armour that said "I'm in charge", some sort of shield perhaps, or better still, some top quality stationery. "Step aside world," I snarled. "This mutha's gonna be taking some notes". And so the book, this book, was born.

They say everyone has one in them. But perhaps not all stories should be told. Sarah's saying nothing, again. She spends her days saying nothing. As every hack knows, there's only one way a story should start, and that's at the end, the best bit, the climax. The randy plumber can always call in the last scene. But I've decided she's getting no end – she'll be no jailbird jackass holding court with the boneheads. Oh sure, our Sarah has a book in her, and that's just where it's staying.

I calculated that in just three months I produced a novel's worth of words for my employer (feel that mate, sheer quantity that is), so I figured there was no logistical obstacle to 'writing a book'.

But how should it start? How should I start? Should I just write down everything, anything? Or should there be some method behind the madness? For I have often felt such an ambition to be just that, and never so keenly as when it emerges, blinking, into the glare of public scrutiny: "You're writing a book? How wonderful – what's it about?" demands Dinner Guest, with a smirk I welcome like heartburn.

However, being blessed with the knack of turning the juiciest gossip into something akin to the shipping news, I can usually find some sort of escape: "It's about what I reckon," I proffer, with an apologetic smile, trusting yet another one of my prize tumbleweeds to drink dry any excitement the moment may have contained. Although secretly I scold myself: "You must stop telling people – why can't you just make something up?"

But it began to take up so much of my existence that not to mention it would have been to lead some kind of double life, and I didn't want to bear that burden either, racing home like some chatroom pervert to the privacy of my neon lover.

So I explain that I read philosophy at university and then with a bit of luck their eyes cloud over and no more is said. Or even better they divulge their own hilarious views on my beloved subject – the customary batch of anecdotes which only serve to thicken the protective crust which formed long ago across this secret sea of gold. "Yep - that's me alright," I venture with relief, and a daffy shake of the head for good measure, just to acknowledge the fluffy clouds they've now set sail between my ears.

Sometimes I think Richard's not so bad. He has a philosophy on life, and he's entitled to it after all, one of the few birth rights we *can* all claim. In fact he'd probably enjoy a bit of Nietzsche that Richard: "Like I've always said – dog eat dog and churches are for poofs." But who's gonna eat *you* Richard? A pack will hunt him down alright, but I'm not giving away the ending just yet. I'm no hack, not today. This is supposed to be a book, right? All I'm saying is that one day our Rich is gonna wish he hadn't scared those rozzers away. But if I'm saying nothing, then neither, of course, is Sarah. Jaws wired shut, insides caving in, she sits in a tree gazing down on a field of poppies. The wind's blowing, this could be her defining moment. But she sees nothing.

But if their's was not to reason why, then soon enough neither was mine - for before long the beast was living and breathing on its own, method or no method, and in the squalid confines of my flickering hideout it was thriving, oddly whether I fed it or not.

I had no real reason to believe it would be the first of many and therefore treated it as an only child throughout - in my mind there is no sequel, there couldn't be. There may be further detail one day, more meat perhaps, but this heap of bones must represent absolutely everything and anything which came to mind. All life would be here, all of mine anyway. No minor inspiration would be left untranslated, all thoughts would be captured. Good, bad, yours, mine: on toilet rolls and beer mats, bus tickets and birthday cards.

And like some hunchback gimp I would present these scraps at my master's table the following day, where they would be devoured without pattern or trace. I can assure you, this dual existence was not played out in some metaphorical dreamworld. Anarchy became my method, my guide, an anti-brief born from a fear of planning. I was adamant there would be no pre-ordained structure - any lean form would have to fight hard against such tireless gluttony.

I delved deep into my insides. Fanciful ideas were stripped down to their component parts, which were then soldered to others in unnatural proximity, just to see what reaction might take place.

Like some fearless Frankenstein I felt I was indeed creating a terrible monster. And this creature was growing at an alarming rate. But it was not healthy. Crippled by clumsy amputation and drunken surgery, its wounds were left gaping, and I became both scared and excited in equal measure by what grew before me. For surely this beast was my mental manifestation, my very self reborn on paper - it could be nothing less. If we lived purely in a world of ideas then I was surely a creature of colossal grotesque, and ultimately suicidal, as contradicting forces eagerly sought each other's destruction.

Sarah lives on the smouldering slopes, too weak to climb, too scared to fall. A life on the rocks, gazing at the darkness, the void which happily devours her space and time like they were its last two meals. Sarah would have something to say to those scientists. She knows about the lies those liars tell us, and one day so will you. Because they all saw her and they all missed it. "Not all ideas have objects, not all existence is temporary. There are shadows which thrive beyond your petty probes and policies," she thought, as she shut the door on yet another barren interview. But she's saying nothing. "It's not the Good Lord that proves the scientist wrong," she thinks, without words. "It's the evil men do and the terror they leave behind."

Yet the project was borne from a desire to find consistency. While I would never interrupt any chain of thought I was desperate that the book itself would be no beatnik stream of consciousness. So one day, in a fit of sympathy, I left my beast to die, and instead thought about my life, about nothing, about me, and then returned, afresh. The book, I decided, would not be some philosophical Domesday Tome, a mere inventory of one person's thoughts – this was just not good enough, however well indexed.

I knew that with a project of this kind self-indulgence would be unavoidable, but it didn't have to win every battle. So I decided that no matter how tenuous, the world should be a better place for it. Like many before me I now set about searching for the good life. I was not worried whether I would get there, but at least I had a destination, of sorts, and if the journey was long and arduous enough it might just come to mean something, to someone.

"Bleedinell – don't they go _on_," thought Richard, staring out a rather animated bunch ('of tossers') across the bar, sitting down ('like bloody girls') and enjoying a debate ('about Jack Shit'). "It's about what I reckon," he hears one say, sheepishly. Tumbleweed? Nah! The woolly jumper is saved, as the pompous pack descends on the silence; howling, screeching, dribbling cack. "What you looking at?" thinks Richard, as the poor little lamb glances over with a grimace, both crooked and open. "Hold that gaze one more second big boy, I dare you."

Richard was drinking alone, this was his watering hole, this was his Monday, this was his thirst and this was his beer, action without reflection indeed. Not everything that moves does so for a reason, there _are_ no ideas behind objects. Richard always knew that and now so do I. I guess this was where it all started.

While resolved to the fact that inspiration must be fortified by organisation, I could never have guessed that such a _create-then-craft_ process would itself become part of the book. That the book would then come to generate its own ideas and settle down into distinct parts was something I could never have hoped for. Creating order from chaos, taming the wild, filling the gaps – I think this is when we are truly kings, at our most masterful, our most human. I loved it.

Richard and me, Richard and me. Welded together by some failing metalwork student, the bond may be strong but it's ugly. Like me Richard doesn't look back, like me he knows what things we cannot change, like me he knows his island. But that's where the similarities end. At least that's what I used to think. But things changed. _I_ changed.

Encouragingly, this structure came to resemble works of philosophers before me, and I tell you now, I make no bones about calling myself just that. I might be a bad one, but all that's needed to join this noble rank, to stand proudly alongside some of history's greatest minds is a wicked appetite for self-analysis and a relentless craving to simplify, compare and categorise the fruits borne from such bare-faced indulgence. So before we travel any further down my road, this might be an appropriate time to consider one of *the* defining debates of philosophy, on which this book is shamelessly built.

The classical theory of dualism contends that mind and matter are two distinct things. Its most famous advocate, Descartes, argued that because he could question the existence of everything *apart from himself*, then this self, this questioner, this *thinker*, boasted an existence superior to anything that might conceivably be abandoned to such scrutiny. "I think therefore I am," sang his catchphrase.

And before long he concluded that this 'I' was ultimately rooted in an alternative reality, one immune to the Degradation, Decay and Death with which he now characterised an inferior material world.

Richard knew about the Three Degrees alright. A rather pessimistic take on nature's blind ambition for constant change perhaps, but they about summed it up. But death is not the end – Sarah could have told him that. If only he'd known the truth before that night. Perhaps he should've listened more at Sunday School, for the Bible too tells us that death is not the end … Sarah knows this, and now Richard does too. Riches in Heaven says the Good Book. Is he? I wouldn't have thought so, not unless the door policy has moved on somewhat since I was a lad.

Dualists, known as 'rationalists', also believe we arrive in the world pre-armed with innate qualities, one of which is the ability to reason, and by reason alone can we discover knowledge that can under no circumstances be false. They claim we cannot hope to find such certainty via our senses, which can only ever detect temporary facts, fluctuating states of play which might easily be otherwise.

Contrasted with this school of thought are the 'empiricists', who discredit any knowledge which cannot be borne out by the senses and disregard this other-worldy self as an illusion, mere self-consciousness, the neutral buzz of existence, the seamless mental sensation of being alive, behind or beyond which there is nothing.

If forced, grudgingly, to choose, I might well accept this view. But I do so only by recognising, embracing, *rejoicing* in the fact that it is completely counter-intuitive. For if this book has taught me one thing, it is never to fear contradiction - quite the opposite. It reminds us we're only human after all. And who knows, when holes appear in the defences erected by man-made logic, maybe, just *maybe*, we will be permitted a privileged peek at life on the other side.

Now suitably immersed in such rich paradoxical spirit, try these two beauties for size. One: "What we believe, cannot be – yet what is, is unbelievable." The perennial problem for philosophy, for any *language*, is that it only really works in the mouth of a dualist. We can barely open our mouths without asserting an ego, an *I*, even though such behaviour may be mere evolutionary overspill. It may appear impossible, *unbelievable* even, to feel indifferent towards ourselves, our self, but dear reader we must, and we will.

Sarah would like two lives, two heads, and she knows which she would live in and which she would happily leave to rot. And she would welcome that sticky stench fermenting at her cheek. She would treat it as one might the bouquet

rising from the finest of wines, each measured nosefull reminding her that ...
Come on **Sarah. Stop that. You cannot have two heads, are you mad? But Sarah is definitely not mad: mad people are crazed, distressed, frustrated, and Sarah is none of these. But to be honest she's mot much of anything really, more an absence, barely held together by her mission impossible. Poor Justice, she too is absent, but these two are not together, for the not-world is a big old lonely place.**

And Two: genuine happiness can only be achieved by understanding, appreciating and *indulging* the dualist model, however misguided it might ultimately be. My worldview may be empiricist, but my goals are quite the opposite. I want adventure, passion and beauty. I want a soul and I'm gonna get me one, you'll see. While nothing in the world suggests to me that I will somehow survive my physical death, every waking moment still cries out that it somehow matters what happens while I'm alive.

Like all facts in this empiricist reality things might well have been different. Evolution might have taken an entirely different route, leaving us the waking dead, indifferent to pain, stumbling round a world blissfully bereft of good and evil. But it didn't. Instead we became hugely complex animals with hugely complex desires. And I believe that unless we fill this palace with beautiful things, it may collapse in on itself, reduced to nothing more than a hollow folly, a heartbreaking façade, a sickening tribute to some knotty tangle of hairless sinew.

Our brain strives for ultimate meaning behind a world which just won't give it, so we must give it something else. More of this later, much more, but I guess we're all just trying to get through this. The facts of life may render it meaningless, yet it certainly doesn't *feel* that way. So let's breathe some life into the lifeless, and while doing so perhaps be a little more grateful that the stark reality of the situation lies, for the most part, hidden.

"But surely such a majestic beast cannot have come so far for nothing?," cries the dualist dreamer. But I ask him to consider this: perhaps that potent pride which propelled us from the swamp may have fired too far. Maybe we have started believing the lies our words tell us, imagining purpose behind superiority, right behind might: in short, seeing things which just aren't there?

Yet in a more conciliatory frame of mind I can quite believe the empiricist and rationalist started off from very similar positions, and it was almost a matter of temperament that pushed them apart. As thinkers I guess we all start with ourselves and work outwards. It is *the* philosophical exercise, encapsulated by Descartes, to sit in a room, in silence, and take it from there. And if the rationalist sees some inside world, and believes it to be somehow superior to an outside, then, as a metaphor, as a *model*, I may well not disagree.

The empiricist might think the rationalist arrogant and the rationalist might dismiss his adversary as a hopeless cynic. But if this philosophical gulf can be reduced to mere name calling then we have truly gained some ground. And if we can rename cynicism as honesty, and arrogance as optimism, then surely we can feel and maintain both positions simultaneously. After years of philosophy I've never felt the need to choose, and neither I suggest should you.

Let me introduce you to Ratty and Emma, two friends (of each other that is, certainly not me) who have decided to ponder life's big question: Of what can we be certain?

Richard's never asked himself such a question, but he would if you suggested it, so please, don't bother. Don't start him off. Sarah won't either, for apparently now her life *has* a purpose. Seems things are moving. What was that she read somewhere? That we need projects, and through these projects we create meaning? Well there you go then. "If that's all one needs then my life certainly has meaning," she concludes. She vaguely remembers some other bollocks about creation and beauty and giving something back to society, but now was not the time to get bogged down in detail. Her mission says "Kill All Reds" apparently, whatever that means. It's just a shame she will never win. We can't all be winners after all. Deal or no deal.

Their first answer might recognise an inner world, a private world of thoughts, one which they are more often than not happy to call 'I', even if they might struggle to deconstruct the concept in the high humidity of a philosophy seminar. Their second might realise they have considerable freedom and control over their bodily movement, including speech, while in a mysterious way holding somewhat less power over the path their thoughts take.

Having cleared these hurdles in tandem Ratty and Emma might, with growing confidence, take on a few more. This philosophy lark's a piece of piss they think. But if they were to look back, their decision to start the race at all was definitely a turning point. This is going to turn out real sad by the way. I probably shouldn't say so much, but if there's one thing I hate more than suspense in real life, it's suspense in fiction.

A third answer might accept an outside world, one of matter and movement in which their bodies exist and move, one with which it can interact and change.

For after a lifetime at school we are at least aware that the movement of matter in this physical world is *significantly* predictable. While at the outer limits of science we are told things might not be quite so simple, when it comes to our daily navigation through life, we do so armed with a comprehensive knowledge of, and confidence in, the world's predictability. Fire hurts so we don't touch it. If I drop this vase it will travel towards the centre of the earth, a direction we call down, and probably smash if it hits a hard surface – the law of gravity says it will do that.

But we also know there is another sort of force which can also make things move, make things change. Alongside the world of sturdy objects, which only move when we push them, there are plants which grow and die – and more amazingly there are animals! Matter, yes, skin, bones and fur, for sure, but behaving in a way which cannot be predicted from a knowledge of Newton alone.

I've come to detest dogs. Deep terror rises as their slimy jaws bark hate at me. I swear, these monsters, these descendants of evil, should not be in the home unless stuffed. The potential for pain, my pain, is never more than seconds away. And yes, I hate the owners too, these dealers in dread, these airhead terrorists, bathed in the glow of my living nightmare. You just know Richard has a dog and you just know his pooch is the dog's bollocks, head honcho in the Canine Union of National Terror.

I still remember when he looked over that night, Dick and Dog, for I could only see them as one and the same. Funnily enough I didn't fear Dick's Dog then, but that's only because my eyes were on owner, not pet. At least I think that's what happened, it was certainly something. Something moved.

Random energy, like lightening, earthquakes, volcanoes – these are the true thrill spillers, the genuine risk-makers – dogs have it, Dick has it, and I was transfixed. I still remember when he saw me, old D&D, across a crowdless bar. Too much energy, there. Far too much.

So we see other beings blessed with a life force, just like us. But once we see life, we see Death in its shadow, and we understand …

The biggest cause of death is life. We could have escaped the scythe if only we hadn't been born, but once we live, we die. Nature reminds us every day, creatures whose lives begin and end in 24 hours, and we just know we're all part of it. That's why the Ancients built those huge stone triangles, I guess we've always tried to survive our death in some way. And no culture is immune, with its temples and cathedrals, its motorways and malls. We don't want to die so we live among things that never will. But deep down, as each second hand brushes away another grain of sand, we know the pyramid is dying too. Father Time may take his time, but let's face it, he's got something of a monopoly in that area.

But one thing none of us *ever* admit is that this relentless catalogue of death and destruction doesn't stop with those melting monuments. The Earth is approaching middle age now and soon enough the whole place will be too hot to handle, just like those facts of life we prefer to leave hidden. We consume and discard, we eat and we shit, but we will never die, we don't do death us humans, we *hate* it – we hate it in ourselves and we hate it in others. It's just so damn rude.

But death is just the beginning, says the priest, and here Sarah would agree. Death is just the beginning because the crying never stops. I think Richard would like to die, he'd give up on that ghost like a shot if he knew how. Coz he's not all that where it matters – hard shells always betray a softness within. Armour is only made for those who need it after all, and I bet that Richard, that Knight of the Freezing Fog, plays host to some sickly sticky newborn rat, blind pink, as near to death as birth. That's the time to get them you know. Every mamma puss knows that.

Ratty has a son and I just bet you know who it is. Well look here, smart arse, *he doesn't*, and that sort of a shock could kill a man, so we're all keeping schtum on this one, got it? Ssshhh! Here he comes. Keep him in the dark. His son must never shine. Believe me, one more secret will hardly over-season the plot.

So where are Ratty and Emma now? Are they still racing together? Of course they are - it's the same world isn't? The same damn world which couldn't give two arses how two arses see it.

But I fear their paths are about to diverge.

Poor Ratty, this is his story:

Ratty didn't do death much. In fact death rattled Ratty alright. But his was no spiritual fear of what might come after. He simply liked life and fancied he'd rather miss it if it weren't there anymore.

Ratty liked science too, from a distance, and like a good citizen obeyed Newton's laws to the letter, as if they were his own. He liked the fact that even though there was decay, and even destruction, little by little the Royal We was starting to override all that muddle, and carve out a better life, a better world. And as shiny factories arose from the ashen spires of superstition, he saw signposts pointing to a brighter future. Yes indeed, man was starting to sort this lot out. We were clearly the privileged species, put here to bring some order, *new* order. Huge diseases, real-life killers, were falling one by one. We were protecting ourselves against the ravages of nature, against the suicidal tendencies of life, of time, itself. "Well look at this! Splendid work indeed! Won't be long before you chaps have that tiresome mortality licked, eh?" (I said he kept a distance.)

But Einstein really ballsed it up for our Rats. I had to be the one to break it to him, although right now I wish I hadn't: "I don't quite know how, but apparently Newton's laws don't work all the time," I whispered. "Oh, and Rats (for I figured this was as good a time as any), you know Time? Well it bends mate."

How many bends in a circle? Sarah knows a thing or two about time, the calendar's deceit, the lying dying years ticking by, striking a sense of progress and achievement to this endless, never-bendless horror. For the crying will stop when the clock stops which is never, because Uncle Einstein couldn't keep it bloody shut could he. He couldn't resist spilling the beans. For if time bends, then it surely, if given time, will catch itself by the tail? Sarah has a mission now. One day she may turn off the orbital into the dead end she craves. But first Richard must join the traffic, and that's going to take some time, proper time, good old-fashioned reliable time. Not that modern bendy shit.

Ratty could hear Einstein's laughter echoing for what seemed like eternity, and fancied him quite the worst Uncle one could ever have. But Ratty could have had the last laugh, if he'd paid attention, for in time Uncle Clever Clogs himself would be proved wrong too.

But to be honest our Rats was past caring. In his mind science had long since strayed from the Path of Understanding and the whole enterprise was quite frankly forgetting its roots. A discipline once based in observation and test, was now becoming refuge to the theorist, the fantasist, now conveniently free from the burdens of corroboration which once weighed down their predecessors. And as their standard of proof slipped from definitely to likely to possibly (to Godly?) Rats walked off the other way, from fascinated to tolerant to yeah-whatever. This was when he changed.

"You're all missing the point," he begged. "You're looking in the wrong place. Move away from that microscope young man, for you won't find the universal in the minuscule. Don't waste any more of your beautiful brain on these crude changelings. Listen to your instincts. This didn't happen by accident. Nothing became something for a reason, and with *reason* can we be guided towards real truth. This recording of the physical world will carry on ad infinitum, a never-ending game played for eternity by whosoever cares to take part – but that's not truth out there. All you're doing is updating one fact with another, your beloved science is nothing more than the best version of events at the time of publication. Instead we should be concerned with eternal truths – facts which could *never* change – truths about life, its meaning, its purpose, *our* purpose."

And after an oh-so-meaningful pause, this King of the Drama Queens sat back, closed his eyes, and began:

"Of what can I be 100 per cent sure?", he asked, with a slightly annoying French accent thought Emma, who had, up until now, ignored her soup and listened patiently. But she soon grew weary as Ratty listed fact after fact, object after object, each followed by an increasingly pompous rejection: "Sand – non, the sun – non, the sea – non. *You*, my dear Emma – Non, non, non!

"For it appears I can doubt everything but my own existence. If I am thinking this thought, then the 'I' cannot be called into question, unlike Dear Ratty's growing paunch," he chuckled, patting his taut waistcoat. ("Third person," Emma groaned. "Always a bad sign.")

But there Ratty froze, unable to move, locked in his inner world with nowhere to go, not in this life anyway. "But wait," he thought. Another pause, this time genuine: "With a bit of imagination ......?" And off he went, Ratty the Great Drama, the great dreamer, floating around the grand halls of the mind. "For if I have no body then I cannot die," he laughed, soaring onwards and upwards towards the heavens. "Now this," he declared. "Now this is *real* life."

Through pure reason alone, safe from the ink-stained claws of science, he had found the key to his own existence. He had travelled back against the grain of space and time and discovered a tiny door into true reality. Stripped of its crust the 'I' had revealed its true being, as a beautiful soul, destined for greatness in eternity. And who looks after souls? "God does," chorus the circling Syrens, beckoning him through the clouds. "Yikes!" thought Rats. "Seems he *was* the main man after all. Wish I'd gone to church a bit more! But I'm a decent enough chap. I'm sure my name's still down."

But if Ratty had spared a moment more back on Blighty, had thought to open his eyes just once, he would have seen Emma like never before. Hands in hair, tears in eyes, looking for all the world like she'd lost the love of her life.

Poor Emma, this is her story:

Emma by name, cucumber by nature, far too cool. Emma doesn't mind death much. She doesn't dig it in a sick way, and she doesn't crave it in others, even herself. She just doesn't really think about it an awful lot. She reckoned that if it mattered that much it wouldn't happen so easily, so often. She knew her time would come but not in a fatalistic way (oh Emma, if only you knew, if only on that one dark night you hadn't ....) She knew all that talk of being called to the other side was mystical nonsense. She knew why people wanted to believe this – why they found the burden of existence too much to bear, Emma felt that more than most. But she was strong, she faced up to it. She needed no sick note. She liked games. She *wanted* to play, not look for a way out, a way of pretending it wasn't all so immediate, so here, so now. She took no directions from that Blind Sage called History, waving at the future with a white stick.

She had always been able to tolerate Ratty before, for theirs was a bond which cared not for surface similarity. Until now they had loved disagreeing *with* each other, but this was something different. By the look in his eyes, or rather, lack of it, Rats was on some sort of internal journey, the journey of a lifetime, *his* lifetime. But most importantly it was one to which she was clearly not invited. We all recognise when events have turned for good, she thought. I guess there are times when we all have to let go.

Our Emma was never all that into science either. She wouldn't have gone so far as to say it was pointless, she just wasn't frankly that good at it – but she was damn grateful others were. She had heard that Einstein had done it for dear old Newton, and she was kind of pleased with that, pleased that everything everyone had ever thought was now tinged with something new.

"Ours so *is* to reason why, but in the end we'll do and die."

Emma had coined this catchphrase all by herself and would delight in repeating it over and over. "After all there's only one thing worse than groundless pessimism, and that's groundless optimism." That was another of hers, another joke against the world, the wanky world of words which she escaped each night with a walk in the dark, just because she shouldn't.

"You're all missing the point," she thought to herself, imagining a parallel world where Fatty Ratty had been so occupied with his steaming soup that she had been the one to speak first.

"You're looking in the wrong place. Move away from that pulpit old man, for you won't find the universal in the Invincible. We must learn to mistrust our instincts. Nothing may just have became something in a way we will never comprehend, and we've just got to live with that I'm afraid. Don't turn to religion just because you can't answer key questions about the universe: don't fill gaps with Gods.

"Of what can I be 100 per cent sure?," she thought, with a slightly annoying French accent, smiling to herself. "This was going to be fun!" And she too sat and listed fact after fact, object after object, each followed by an increasingly pompous rejection.

Sand – "non", the Sun – "non", the Sea – "non". Me, dearest Emma – "Non, non, non!" And finally, just like that, she stopped.

"I can doubt everything *including* my own existence," she thought, aghast, now feeling very uneasy and actually rather queasy.

I see nothing in the world which needs me, yet see nothing in me which does *not* need the world, she fancied. If I am thinking this thought, then there are indeed thoughts in this brain of mine, but I don't know who made them anymore than I know who made the coins in my pocket. These thoughts may be mine for now, but only until I spend them, making space for new ones I'm getting tomorrow. So if these thoughts are not exclusively *by* me, how can they really be exclusively *for* me? Such mental mess coats the earth like mildew – it's how we communicate, it's how we understand each other.

Is, then, this thinking lark, this idea of *being*, merely the feeling of a brain rumbling, to which I should pay as much attention as an empty stomach? Sophisticated certainly, illusory perhaps, yet as predictable, as *controllable*, as the flights of dust in a storm?

And there Emma froze, locked in the outside world with nowhere to go. Suddenly the 'I' disappeared, her thoughts became *some* thoughts, more movement than object. Her opinions, her once precious 'points of view' became mere *locations* in time and space, co-ordinates personalised by mere circumstance, in a brain she's never seen in a head she never chose. Now she was truly nauseas.

"*Take me* unsightly sickness. Grab at the foot of my gut and tear *out* what you hold." Sarah knew her Shakespeare and she knew this wasn't it, but she felt it all the same, for the empiricists are wrong, they make stuff up. We *do* have an inside world, we all host a creature beyond the ravages of time and space, and this little terror never feels the slightest bit queasy.

Emma looked across at grinning swaying Ratty, and was envious: "If I am nothing more than matter and movement, a hairless baboon prowling the earth for food and sex, if my view of the world is as meaningless as the existence which spawned it, then why shouldn't I join him on his adventure? Better to be mistaken and happy, right?" she thought, without believing a single word of it. Words are such good liars. Those little buggers can't help themselves.

She was glad his eyes were tight shut. She sighed, the lump in her throat rendering her final goodbye a pubescent croak. She struggled to her feet and stumbled off in silence, the steely silence we wear like armour, the soulless resilience we all draw upon when something is lost, forever. Emma may have felt like she had lost Ratty for good, but she couldn't think about that now. Her loss was from the inside. What was once healthy cynicism, proud pragmatism, unrelenting doubt, had got the better of her. She was left with nothing, quite literally. Her empty stomach now churned.

A sad tale – but which to choose? Misguided or vacant? There's not a lot to commend either so we must find another way. Somehow we hopeless dreamers must let imagination be our guide, but never our escape. But more later. This is only the beginning. And while we're doing introductions I want you to meet an old friend of mine

Antoine is an anti-hero sitting in a café in Bouville. He's in a novel with no story, and to my mind the greatest ever told. Our unlovable rogue invites us to scoff at any sort of fixed future, one directed by the past, driven by the momentum of the present.

How scathingly he dismisses the entrance of the wise Doctor: "He keeps and uses his past and turns it into experience. Knows men like he made them. How I should like to tell the crackpot he's being duped. At the age of 40 they baptise their stubborn little ideas with the name experience. They explain the new by the old. They've never understood anything at all. Nothing new under the sun they say." [1]

I'm already feeling the warm of Camilles. I guess I've eaten there more times than I can remember. But who's this entering stage left? It's Emma and Ratty, right on cue, chilled by the cold air sweeping up Rue des Horlogers. They've sat themselves down, tempted, no doubt, by the smells of sauerkraut and cassoulet. Direction for now has a Director you see. Our chums might have left us but I haven't left them, for this is my story and I've decided to play Father Time.

Some might speculate that Emma and Antoine are something of a match, but in truth their relationship would never progress beyond the Platonic. Empty souls, like dead magnets, do not attract. When numbers go out to play, the zeros stand alone. In another world they might realise their vacant stares were lids locked tight on chests of gold. But ultimately they're no players. So there'll be no play.

"Nothing new under the sun they say." But Einstein was new, and how our Doctor loves to shake his head. With a wise old finger he motions over to Ratty, speculating on a kindred spirit who might like to take the seat next to his. "Won't you join me for a consoling glass of wine," he sings. "A couple of wise old birds looking back on a world more certain, when people knew their place, when you and I sat comfortably between our God above and the Godless below."

But Ratty will not go. When our heroic pair have finished their lunch they will leave one at a time. Antoine is not for us, he has stopped, he has remained in the comfort of the restaurant, locked with Dr Bore in someone else's story, a role he cannot escape. Part of me wishes I could have stayed with Antoine, perhaps become a new character in someone else's story, but I looked at his eyes, his stare, and I too saw a match, a parallel 'me' gliding through space, and a mirror was the last thing I needed.

Antoine drifted, his very identity merged with the outside world, his thoughts shed their thinker, ephemera with neither birth or destiny. "Now when I say 'I' it seems hollow .. A pale little memory of myself wavers in my consciousness, and goes out. The

---

[1] Nausea, Jean-Paul Sartre, 1938

consciousness is between these walls - perpetuating itself, nobody inhabits it anymore. It dozes, it feels bored, and this is the meaning of its existence. It is a consciousness of being superfluous."[2]

But our Emma is made of sterner stuff. She is going to tackle the human paradox head on: "Why does it feel the world matters when in fact it clearly doesn't?" This is the question on Emma's mind and it will stay there until she finds an answer. This, she figures, is a proper question, a decent question, not like that Big Bang bollocks.

Hopefully dear old Ratty is also made of sterner stuff. On another day he might have joined the bad Doctor, not as an act of camaraderie, but with Emma fading away I'm guessing he'd be keen to weave his new spun philosophy on any sympathetic ear.

For lunch with Emma had indeed been a bit frosty, a chill far sharper than offered by the winter breeze. He was worried about her. He wanted so much to tell her what he had discovered. But Emma wasn't all there - quite literally. He had heard her whisper goodbye, but had pretended not to hear. And through his tight-eyed tears had watched her shrinking figure stumble into the distance. Now it was just him, a scowling Frenchman and a bad doctor, and Rats too suddenly felt unease in Camille's.

He might have been looking at Richard, in another drinking hole in another country with another scowl at another stranger. But Richard is no Antoine and I am no doctor, good or bad. Still, that first time when our eyes met … I should have remembered those childhood trips to the zoo – "Don't stare at the Gorrilla," said the sign. "To do so is an act of aggression". I really should have read the signs. How did I fall for you Richard? Couldn't even be the hero in my own sodding story. I read somewhere they end up writing themselves. Is that what happened? I created a monster and stood there and watched, holding its watch as it fought me for air. But how did I fall for you Richard? I've said too much. This is no confessional, not yet.

Ratty was certainly scared of these strangers – his world was not theirs. And so he also left, to ponder his new thoughts in the chill of the Bouville breeze, this earthly element which couldn't touch him, not the real him. And soon enough he was smiling in his shell again, imagining himself soaring towards the clouds, detached from the sensations his extremities relayed. But boy was it cold.

"Hope Emma's okay," thought Ratty, out loud. But he couldn't cry anymore, not one tear. He stumbled off in silence, the steely silence we wear like armour, the soulless resilience we all draw upon when something has been lost, forever.

Regrettably we may need to visit once more the soporific confines of philosophical theory to understand better the dispute between our departed friends. But the ideas of necessity and contingency may well be the sharpest knives on a philosopher's belt, so would you bear with me while we get tooled up:

A is a *necessary* quality of B if B would *not* survive its removal, but A is only a *contingent* quality of B if B *would* survive its removal.

For example: a brain is a *necessary* quality of human life but an arm only a *contingent* one. Language could clearly survive without truth, but what about the other way? As good philosophers we are forever questioning whether that which keeps things apart is actually *less* important than that which might keep them together.

---

[2] Nausea, Jean-Paul Sartre, 1938

In Ratty's mind he could doubt everything but his own being. He could imagine a reality without all he saw before him – it could after all be a dream, a hallucination – and as he discounted, one by one, all the contents of the physical world he sank back into himself, *his* self, a reluctant actor who didn't need the part.

So in our terms he might have imagined that the physical world was a *contingent* quality of his self, one it did not need to survive. And if he could persist in some way without the physical world, then he must do so in another reality – but what might that be? For being a modest sort of chap he couldn't help but consider whether *he* was now a contingent quality of something deeper, something which might quite comfortably survive without him! What pond-life comforts had he sacrificed for the horrors of this new ocean? For while he felt more than a man, he still felt much less than a God, and somehow still just like Ratty, perhaps strangely more so than ever before.

Yet regardless of what new world lay ahead, life on earth had started to resemble a passing phase, a shrinking part of a growing whole, a chapter in a story, neither the first or the last. Well you take good care Ratty because I can hear who's just around the corner. Mercifully those tamborines shatter silence like a baby's scream.

But just what is Emma's problem? "Why can't you feel what Ratty feels Little Emmy?" (I only talk to her like this, privately, because I know she hates it. She's never liked me, and I'm nowhere near big enough to like *that* about her: "Antoine with drink" is how she describes me. Yeah, whatever. In the end I was there you see, in a way. Sitting right next to him. *Had* to be .. didn't I?)

"Horse shit!" she yells back at me, no more tears now, as trot turns to canter. Perhaps I should let her get this off her chest:

"I reject the conclusion because I reject the reasoning. You feel a human soul so strongly that you can't help but go a-huntin' for one. And that slavering pack of yours is so whipped up with faith and fear that sooner or later they're bound to sniff out some trail to chase."

(Yeah right, like you just came up with that. Been practising in someone else's story again, playing one off against the other? But what use moonlighting on a night without moonlight?)

"Surely our thoughts are a *contingent* part of nature. It could, and has, and will again, survive without them. But more importantly nature is a *necessary* part of us. I can show you a world without humans, but can you show me a human without the world?

"Look at our evolutionary journey from sea to land, from crouch to stand – what is common to it all? Nature, pure unadulterated physical nature. I wonder dear Ratty, does all life have some deeper reality waiting for it? Is there a wormy heaven awaiting those little wrigglers once they've shat their last? No? Not animals you say? So when exactly did we acquire our privileged access? Tell me Rats, just how erect did homo have to be to earn his security pass?"

Oh great. Not a friend in the world. Perhaps I've got it coming, or worse still, perhaps I haven't, as Oscar might say. By the way, did I tell you? No? Well, it's .. er .. just that me and Richard went for a drink the other day......

"Back again?" barked D&D. I remember now the pure fear of that first meeting, when our eyes met. Hardly Mills and Boon but definitely the start of something special.

(Special my arse. Go on. Do it! Special forces, special case, special needs more like ... that wasn't how it was and I know it. Don't believe everything you read, especially my bits. I'm a coward, Sarah will tell you, so would Emma, even Richard in the end. I'm lily-livered low life, a wretched retch of made-up trash, a gravy-brained gannet with no control or the courage to admit it. My bleeding arse. That wasn't how it was and I know it.)

I wonder what Sarah thought the first time she saw tricky Dicky? You see I probably should know, but this fiction business is getting me right down right now. It never was my thing. I'm much better at philosophy, you'll see. Quite a decent bloke by all accounts.

If Emma's rant seems more negative than Ratty's then perhaps that's because empiricism shouts loudest as a rejection of rationalism, and also because her best mate had just melted into his soup. It may just be the nature of empiricists to talk about the limits of humans, rather than their potential, and I guess this tendency has earned them their grumpy image. And while I'm the first to admit they could do with a decent slice of cheesecake, I'm not actually sure it was they who pooped the party first.

But all this talk of philosophy is making me concerned. I'm worried I'm putting you off, for believe me this book is no more about philosophy than is life itself. So if I sound like some frantic compere stringing out a lame tale while the first act remains stuck in traffic, then at least allow me to introduce the rest of the bill:

First up then is Morality, then Politics, then Truth, then Soul and finally Creation. And we also have a fine coach motivating each performer, one whose name may sound clumsy in theory yet brings fine rewards in practice - and that is Superform, our secret weapon, our sixth sense, and our greatest hope for victory.

But more of the Gaffa later.

So if I have one last piece of advice before we take to the field it is this: look for what we share, not what we imagine keeps us apart. Those curious foreign folk take a dump in the morning too you know, they really do. And they fall in love and forget jokes and tell lies and have restless nights and favourite meals and weird dreams. And we're all fucking petrified, every single one of us. But we must be strong nevertheless. On this rocky road we must be well prepared with a steadfast armoury: a cleared-out conscience and the ability to think without emotion should do us for starters. Good luck.

Part One

Sarah so wanted to show us all, to reach her goal, for her dream to come true, but I couldn't let it happen, and for that she will never forgive me. Yeah whatever. I've gotten so hard, right through to the core. Not proper hard, like the house on the rock, no siree. Not for me some noble vigour which brave souls muster against all the odds. What was the phrase? "That steely silence we wear like armour." Bollocks. We need new slogans for a new man. Consider instead the resilience of stale bread, pure rigormortis shot through with neglect. Hard as toast, that's me. They all hate me now, although I did stitch them up. I'm sure they'd much rather have gone their separate ways, but what can I say? I needed them. But did they need me? Of course not. Could they have survived my removal? Of course they could.

Yeah whatever. It's time everyone realised the brutal fact about fiction. I am God, I am Control, and in this dismal farce the Director's taking the lot. And perhaps I should mention, Richard will be hanging around for a good while now. Sarah's time will come, but I fancy that will be later.

She's got a mission to keep her quiet, but hers is a savings plan and just what does *not spending* look like? How can we tell when someone is merely waiting for the right moment? So if our Sarah comes across as being rather congenial, rather helpful, and you start to wonder just what all the fuss is about, remember her melting pot is a slow burner, a real winter stew. Everything she does and everything she doesn't is for one reason and one reason only. She'll let us know when it's ready.

My search for the good life can be split into two parts, which can be defined by asking two simple questions:

Question A: In what ways are we the same?

Question B: In what ways are we different?

Question A is concerned with pursuing Authenticity in the outside world, considering the civic needs we all share, and will act as our guide through Parts One and Two.

Question B is concerned with pursuing Beauty in the inside world, considering the philosophical privacy which keeps us apart, and will act as our guide through Parts Three and Four.

It was the summer of '59/'69/'79 and Del and Bel and Anne and Stan and Peter and Rita were finishing college, with bad friends Richard and Sarah (no rhyme no reason, they should've known something was wrong from the start. I told you she wasn't blameless. To live is to sin, right Sarah?) Imagine, please, some sort of scenario like that for if the Devil's in the detail then he must be awfully dull. Anyway, there they stood, full of promise, poised on the precipice, gazing with hope across a rich life to come, full of fun, friendship and fulfilment. That faking, fear and failure actually welcomed our octet to their graves was something they wouldn't have guessed at, but which of us ever do?

And yet how many of its promises does life actually keep? Far better off balancing on the brink I reckon, true brinkmanship is a skill we ignore to our peril. Perhaps perpetual students don't have it so wrong. "What are they scared of?" we jeer at those ageing hippies. But we all know what, of course we do, on those nights when we don't put ourselves to sleep properly, on those nights we forget to drink enough.

What use rulebooks come the darkness? Those nights spent sweating under our slate-tile canvas, as each scream we pretend not to hear pierces those staring eyes we feign to close. You just *know* there's a campsite beneath every city, you know we've changed nothing. We're just plastic surgeons smearing scum over gashes which never heal. What use rulebooks at night? What use rulebooks when terror can't read?

Oh by the way, of course Richard didn't go to college, he was ten years older and he worked there, and he finished when Sarah finished, okay? I'm not defending him. That's just the way they told it back in those early years, their little joke in the days when things could still be funny.

In what ways are we all the same? Sarah knows, same bodies, same babies, same game, same horror. Richard on the other hand barely understands the question and would love to pass. If pushed he would be hard pushed to remember the last time he had even used the word 'we', for the very concept presupposes a verb to follow, in which he and at least one other human did the same thing, together.

No, our Rich does things *to* people, *at* people, and even *for* people; but certainly not *with* them. "No way too gay." Richard doesn't conjugate 'nous', he jumps straight to vous (you plural, the rest of the world, poofs) and ils (they, the rest of the world, poofs). But I've seen his 'we', Dick and Demon, D&D, last thing at cider night, before he crawls to bed for some Suey sleep.

It never speaks of course, but there's some solace in that beast, his lover in violence. He loves that mutt. Even Richard can love. Not humans of course, that would be sick, proper cross-species sick (like that film we wish we'd never seen).

No wonder we drink, but I wonder why Richard does? Dutch courage I guess. Oh, and here's a good joke, there is another 'we' Richard certainly *does* do as he lies in his cider bed trying to get to Suey sleep. HAHA! As I said, I sometimes wonder why he drinks. But don't tell anyone I told you because there's only one other person who knows, and the last time she told someone …

"What sort of name is Justice anyway," thought Richard, without words, as he dripped away to the toilet, never to be seen again. That's how she tells it. I guess you're starting to piece it together now, I told you I was crap at this, but as I said before, there's only one thing I hate more than suspense in reality. And to top it all look who's back, like some straight-to-TV sequel. Who *is* that prowling in a Dick's clothing? What really happened that night? There was laughter, there were drinks, there was crying and then what? I'm not even sure Richard knows, although it appears Sarah certainly does.

Anyway, time will tell, it always does. That Great Healer's the biggest snitch of the lot. But I'm saying nothing for now.

In what ways are we the same? "The question contains an unverified statement, rendering it impotent until resolved," chorus our Richard and Sarah, without words, those no-rhymers who should have guessed there was no reason from the start.

Oh yeah, a minor detail. Richard shits blood - every time. But *no-one* knows this one, not even Sarah, so don't tell will you? Seems she might have a messy rival for her big finish - I'll take bets if you're interested but perhaps I'm talking

up the wrong horse? An inside tip tells me there's more to come and the bookies always win remember. Perhaps there's only one mission after all, a whole pack of Kill All Reds, whatever that means. Anyway, if I know Richard he'll figure he can drink his way through this crimson crap like a proper man. I guess none of us are getting any younger.

The purpose of Part One is to extract a morality solely from the observable human condition.

It will be guided in part by certain *reflexive instincts* we might seem to share with much of the animal kingdom – like pain avoidance and life preservation.

But it will also consider a more complex set of *gut feelings* - like empathy and fairness even - which while peculiarly human are no less physical, no less *natural* at heart. And our new morality will be both nurtured and justified by its earthly rewards, therefore side-stepping any recourse to self-sacrifice in return for a better after-life.

Sadly though, Mr Morality has rarely been dressed in such earthly garb, not since the Priest turned him Double Agent, luring him with a promise of new powers to peer into a quaking heart. They may have raced back in imaginary time and resold it as The Fall, but it was always The Rise, and to this day such trickery still manages to makes fools from the best of us.

Since that fateful elevation, Agent M was given licence to strut, his conduct to be revered, rather than realised. In his new uniform he was invited to scowl at our innocent urges towards self-interest, progress, and happiness, preferring to treat them now as enemies, rather than escorts, to be denied, rather than drawn upon.

In fact the more he rallied *against* human nature, the more he was seen to symbolize his new Master, ruling from a world far beyond our own. Which is a real shame, because I'm convinced Good needs no God. In fact he's far better off without him. I say why look further than the old adage, which can be said in two ways:

(1)   *Do* unto others as you would have them *do* unto you

(2)   Do *not* unto others as you would have them *not* do unto you

Such simplicity is nothing short of genius, for I think we all *feel* something about hypocrisy - the expectation of standards in others which people don't meet in themselves - that turns our stomachs so acutely, so *entirely*, that for a split second we might be forgiven for imagining that an idea of Fairness had been woven into the fabric of a Godly universe. Yet I believe this sort of intensity in our reaction actually reveals the opposite to be true, showing us that morality is grounded in real life, real feelings, real *guts*.

The first version of the adage is actually more appropriate for the second half of this book, more concerned with meaning than conduct, and will be invaluable as we explore Question B.

But for now be assured that it too will be justified by self interest, as it guides us towards the hidden economies of scale to be had, the value to be added, the efficiency to be *engrained*. It understands that teaching teaches, that we learn about ourselves when others learn from us, and that helping people forces on us a clarity, a *stature*, of thought we might otherwise have failed to attain.

It is the second version which is so key to our current business, a passive guide to our conduct in society at large, a civic contract, whereby I agree not to hit you in return for you not hitting me.

Until now we have split human life into two worlds: King Philosopher on the inside and the Beast, *his* Beast, on the door. Yet when we operate in our sophisticated civilisation, we do so wearing a third mask, and that is the mask of The Citizen, our representative in society, our public face (and unfortunately our weakest weakspot).

Whether this tricksy trio exist as a balanced recycling machine or a band of suicidal carnivores is down to us:

Ignore the King and our life soon has no meaning. Before long we're merely passing time, honing the consumer skills of the Citizen to satisfy in the depraved privacy of our feathery nest the relentless urges of the Beast. And then we die, bloated bleating wankers, a 70-year handjob scaling one pointless prick. Our epitaph: "I came, I came, I went".

But ignore the Citizen and our King quickly succumbs to self-indulgence. He needs *connection* or else he becomes a distant ruler of a distant land, overlooked by modern maps, bereft of visitors, exhibiting little form and zero function. And most obviously, ignore the Beast and you're nothing but a fool. Sex, drugs and sausage rolls may not be the meaning of life, but we say things *feel* good for a reason.

If I had to choose one I'd probably go for the Beast for I despise the fanaticism to which the other two can aspire. For this chap is the one still dancing when the Citizen has taken yet another early night and the King is just too damn wired darling. Philosophy can be so serious, such a damnable *duty*, and as for the good Citizen – his masticated monotony, his drips of dribble, spittling at the peripheries of ancient power games he dare not call by name. Far better sharing a glass with Rousseau, under the sun and the trees, the birds and bees ....? Words are such good liars. If only *any* of that was true, if only I believed even one tiny part of it.

Yet still, after years of pompous neglect I'm truly developing a genuine fondness for the Beast, and there's no-one better to level a beery burp at the boss now and then.

Ideally the attitude we're after from *The Citizen* is found in the genteel weekly rag, somehow driven by disinterested duty, perfectly happy with the odd fete and official opening, yet never really tempted by aspiration, perspiration or anything stronger than public spirit.

But if our King doesn't fill the time left free by such petty sobriety, a chap can become dangerously idle. Creeds of all kinds thrive when philosophers do nothing, and for the spiritually curious searching for more than a handjob, the Morality Mall may be too hard to resist. For this swarm of theorists are experts at exploiting such vulnerability, their poisonous patter selling self-sacrifice in the name of some established authority, some immutable Cause, be it divine or political, rallied by tambourine or drum. "Isn't it about time you joined," they whisper. "Isn't it about time you *joined in*?"

I kid you not, King Philosophy is essential not just for what he gives us, but perhaps most importantly for what he keeps out.

I've been careful to save plenty of time later on for religion, so I think now's the time to consider its biggest rival for Brainwasher of the Year. For while Part Two has enough on its hands dealing with systems and players on a global scale, his fearsome footmen still pack enough venom on the domestic scene to warrant some serious attention. It's time to put the political animal back in his cage.

I've become something of an raging radical in my old age. Not for any great positive reasons. No siree, the attraction of extreme liberalism lies in its pathological distrust of political morality.

And I am constantly amazed that it is not the politics of choice for all philosophers, for I would have thought respect and protection for the freedom and privacy of one's thoughts, and the championing of passion-free detachment in all public affairs would have been considered their most important preconditions of any good government.

Perhaps self analysis too often becomes self obsession, which in time turns to feelings of superiority. Seems some philosophers don't actually want too many people to do what they do, hastily stamping some inky-black privilege over a universal birth right, acting as if they were chosen, when all along it was they who did the choosing.

Many philosophers do not recognise my balanced triangle of the human condition. Instead they start with the King, and ask him to imagine a political world from the confines of that bubble, desperately trying to give birth to a political society somehow *shaped* like their pulsating idea. This is sheer arrogance indeed.

The battle for authenticity is fought in the streets, and the final battle for beauty, for meaning, will be fought in the silent confines of our own consciousness.

But don't ever imagine the two can come together, a glorious union realised in some Hegelian superstate. History's most catastrophic governments have placed ideology at their heart, while its most successful have hummed away in near-silence, its benign practitioners, its philanthropic engineers, barely discernible by their knowing nods, gloriously devoid of aspiration, and perspiration.

Existence precedes essence remember. The caveman had no need for politics, in fact the vast majority of human history existed quite happily without it. There wouldn't *be* political ideas if man hadn't happened upon the economies of scale wrought by living in towns and cities.

Ideology is a sociological bi-product of recent modern history, not some universal truth in a uniform. Yet we seem permanently stuck in some horrendous theoretical quagmire, sacrificing real lives for what should actually be a question of sensible crowd management.

In time a better government may emerge through the process of Superform, when after a prolonged period on the door we might consider he has earned the right to take on some new responsibilities. But I wouldn't hold your breath. The shadow thrown by medieval religion is far from fading, and to this day Government attempts to tell us how we shouldn't live our lives while on *our* side of the police line are still producing some of the most vile laws known to mankind, relentless legislation against behaviour in our private worlds of leisure and pleasure. Now I'm wondering, could such a blood-stained CV *ever* inspire the necessary degree of trust?

However I am well aware that even though politics is the lowliest of our little trio, it can come to dominate a life, whether imposed externally by dictatorship or fostered internally through ideological attachment. And I guess we're all team players at the end of the day, we all like to belong to something bigger. We look in the mirror and those buttons sparkle so bright we're blinded as to the meat rotting inside. Perhaps it's not entirely our fault: encouraged from birth to take good care of our uniforms, to take pride in that which set our community apart, force fed a diet of saccharine culture and fatty

SID JOHNSON

tradition until our guardians felt able to set us free to do their bidding. Perhaps we never stood a chance?

Senses of belonging via race, class, culture, nation, gender, religion, mask the true philosophical family of which we are all part.

Socialism may claim to cut through these vertically-hewn bands of brothers, ascribing a glorious commonality to all workers, but the way I see it, two wrongs don't make a right. You don't bring people together by cutting the cake the other way. Socialists love division as much as the monarchist, the capitalist and the fascist. It's the battle, the sticky struggle, the 'us-and-them' mentality which binds these jisms together. To my mind they share more than they'd ever admit.

Monarchists and republicans, owners and workers, even blacks and whites – they may be kitted out in opposing uniforms, but they're all in the same ballpark, playing the same stupid game. If you get off on the random circumstances of your birth then good for you. Quite frankly darling, I haven't got the time.

If there's any distinction to be made then it's between those who stand up to be counted and those who stand up to walk away. But perhaps I shouldn't wield my own cake slicer, for there's salvation for all in my non-religion - just don't wait until your dying seconds to convert, because I don't do much in the way of an after-life I'm afraid.

If we are to talk of brotherhood then it must be seared in the *mind*, not the church or the factory floor. We must be held strong by a shared privacy, not by hymn books or party songs.

We might like to believe we like people because we share their political make-up, but such academic accord cannot sustain *true* friendship, anymore than discord will kill it. Yet we flag-fearing fools still get up the next day and go to war with those who, under any other circumstances, we'd far rather share a drink with.

Take me and Richard. We all know familiarity breeds contempt, but that's not so. Familiarity is actually neutral, nothing but a catalyst for change. Feelings become stronger, one way or the other. It's a gamble. We *think* we want to see more of someone so we risk the lot to find out if we actually do.

Take me and Richard. ("Oh yes," thinks Sarah, "perhaps I shall" – and she could as well, she could be a one woman cluster bomb if her feelings (one way or the other) for her beloved Richard weren't quite so strong, but I'm pretty sure she won't take any chances - she really doesn't like me that girl. Familiarity has definitely bred contempt between us two.)

Take me and Richard. Now that's quite another story. I too wanted to test the strength of our little love nest – because once I'd met him I knew there was a future of sorts between us – I simply had to know more – indifference to those eyes just wasn't an option. So I tested it and to this day I still haven't got the results back. Strikes me that while none of us were looking love and hate met round the back for a quickie. Ask fascism and communism whether they stand at opposite ends of a spectrum, and their coy blushes and shuffling feet will tell you everything. Similarities always outweigh differences.

Take me and Richard. What do I see in him you ask? Richard the philosopher? Sounds ridiculous I know but lets look at the facts: Does he live in his own world? Yes. Does he think most other people are full of shit? Yes. When he has an idea does he pursue it in private but with passion? Why yes. Like love

and hate, like fascism and communism, like me and Richard, we all met up round the back while no-one was looking.

Talking of which, have you heard of the beer test? Of course you haven't because I made it up, and it goes something like this:

We often find ourselves in situations where we need to judge someone's character, whether for example it be on a macro level at the ballot box, or on a micro level in the workplace. I suggest you ask yourself this question: "Would you want to have a beer with them?"

I don't mean: "Would you like the opportunity to sit this person down and give them a piece of your mind?" I mean: "Would you like to have a beer with them, talk footie or TV, have a laugh, a game of cards perhaps, not be embarrassed to introduce them to your mates as a new friend? If they unexpectedly turned up at your party would that be a good surprise or a bad one?"

Sounds simple but give it a go. Apply the test to world leaders, religious leaders, people at work, people on TV, your friends, your family even. I've applied this to many a politician and the cross-party results are very surprising, unnervingly so.

I guess it becomes a question of trust and authenticity, character and humour. A question of bed times, rather than bad times.

It's a question which could also be used to illustrate the central concept of socialism. If you would rather go for a beer with someone in your position at work from another country, rather than with your boss in this country, then you're half way up the red carpet. For despite the national, cultural and linguistic differences, what's most important has appeared horizontally, not vertically. Sure you *could* sustain a natter with your boss about TV or sport, but at the end of the day you don't want to be seen sitting in a pub with him: it's boring, *he's* boring, embarrassing even. Far better to share a glass with Henri, for I guess we all laugh in the same language. Right?

But I'm not interested in breathing fresh life into socialism, or any other jism come to that. Ironically, it is the beer test which has actually weakened my interest in that cult, for I've met many people from the Left, committed enthusiasts, and count many of them as among the dullest people to walk this planet. I wish to God it wasn't true, but I fear the Right's got the best jokes. The lofty lefty lexicon of exploitation and empowerment, workers and owners, rights and wrongs, just doesn't connect with me anymore. I understand the language in an academic way, but it sounds so *historical*.

We all work in call centres now and our boss is the bloke who was sitting next to us last week. But yesterday he just got promoted with a new badge, an easier job and 50p more an hour. Good for him I say. You don't really expect me to stop going to the pub with him do you? And what's more, I wasn't lured into this job by some capitalist plot designed to crush my human potential. If I remember rightly I approached them, because I needed the money, to finance my real life, life *outside* work.

The trouble with the Left is that it treats work so *seriously*. It criticises the capitalist machine for exploiting our labour and treating us as dispensable robots, but it's the Left that defines man by his job. I don't imagine capitalism gives a flying fanny whether we take their work seriously or not, so long as it gets done.

Consider Baby Natasha and Baby Raymond, playing happily in the shade, in Time's shadow cast by that horror still to burn: Give a chocolate to Nat and two to Ray, with no explanation, and Nat feels hurt. *Instinct* tells her this is not fair – instinct tells her she should have the same. But consider again Baby Natasha and Baby Raymond, playing happily in the shade, a warm-blooded affection not yet cognisant of the warm blood yet to drip: Ray has been very good, and Nat very naughty, and they both know this. Give them a chocolate each and Ray feels in his gut that this is not fair, because human instinct tells us that if we put some effort in to life, then we should receive a greater reward than the man who puts in no effort at all.

If someone wants to spend all the hours God sends climbing the corporate ladder then good luck to 'em. Shocking waste of a life to my mind, but they deserve that air-con car don't they? For this is the way the Common Man thinks in the New World Order, and he's neither the exploiter or the exploited. While you're head's been buried in that textbook, Mr Right has caught up with the new reality, embraced the modern apathy, which is why he's so damn popular.

Surely socialism is about "fairness in the workplace", and if the Common Man *wants* the chance to work his arse off and win promotion, or to sit on it and do enough to fund his crack habit, or do one for ten years and the other for another ten, and that's *his* definition of fair, then that's what socialism should be trying to achieve for him. Right? Because if you're not there for the Common Man's idea of fairness then you're only there for yourselves, putting essence before existence, theory before reality, words before people. And in time, won't you're beloved socialism become fossilised, a curious imprint on the rockface of political history, an interest for academics who no-one wants to be seen dead in a pub with, even if for once they did stay up past bed time?

Which brings us back to the beer test – would I have a beer with Richard? Bit late for that question really. Would I have a beer with Sarah? Not bloody likely – not without witnesses anyway. Emma? Pointless, she hates me too. Ratty? Yeah – definitely. Could get rat arsed with Ratty I reckon. Gerald? I'd rather swallow crushed glass then a glass of red with Gerald.

And Natasha, his beloved, and Ray, and what about Nathan? Sorry, you haven't met that lot have you. Like I care, never been one for introductions. Richard passes the beer test with full marks. There's no need to ask why, we all know when a yes is a yes. So here we are, two lovable loners brought together by circumstance, and we'll stay that way until it blows us apart.

So you can shove your political theories up your arse. Life is a particular way. It may have been otherwise, but it's not. So let's find out how it *is*, not drone, dream and dribble about how it might be. Sorry to go on but the trouble with *theorists*, be they political or spiritual, is that their methods are self-fulfilling: they look only for pattern and, hey presto, that's what they find. But the logic is bogus, for if you act like God is all around you and the physical world is some temporary sinful appendage, then that's the world you'll live in. And if you prowl suspiciously round your office at work, condemning the fickle coffee machine as yet another covert agent of capitalist oppression then that too is the reality in which you will find yourself.

We like to insist that seeing is believing, but for far too many of us it's the other way round. In science we are told to speculate, test, observe and finally theorise. Yet with politics and religion we do it all backwards. As young privates we spend our days in incubation, being told how the world is, until we know it off by heart and can be sent charging over the top to fight for what's right in *their* world, one distorted by hand-me-down spectacles, smacked on our face like the brace fixing a young American's smile.

Theories must come last. They are summaries, temporal pattern-spotting from what we've seen so far, ready to *include* the new, not dismiss it. Any theory, whether scientific, religious or political, which could never be proved wrong is nothing more than a circular linguistic abstraction, and ultimately a lie. In fact, if no evidence could count against it, then that's all the evidence we need to steer well clear. Immutability is useless to humans. We need solid flaws.

Richard's started asking me about memory. He said something really important happened a few weeks/months/years back, but he's forgotten it. But the weird thing is he now knows what he's forgotten, because someone's told him. I haven't the faintest idea what he's on about. Have you?

Let's consider those instincts and feelings I touched on before: First up we have an inbuilt desire to avoid the causes of physical pain. They are bad without the need for further analysis, giving a pain-free life pre-reflective desirability.

And it seems we have a corresponding desire to preserve this life as something worth living. Again this is not the conclusion to some dispassionate analysis, it is a *given*, a truth we *feel*, a necessary condition of the only humanity we can ever know.

This obviously brings up questions of self-harm and suicide which can be dealt with swiftly. I see both as the very triumph of mind over matter, man over nature, of beauty over authenticity – nothing less than a wholesale rejection of the beast. But it needs a self-conscious Philosopher to do it – lemmings don't commit suicide, they are not depressed, they just jump off cliffs, happy or sad.

Consider this: we're about to end our life, we're on the edge and we're about to jump. Someone shouts "watch out!" and we turn to see a stone approaching our face at full speed. We duck, of course we do, we have no choice. Even at this dire moment the beast is victorious, and easily overrules the suicidal beauty at his side. But when all is calm we stroke the beast to sleep, and jump anyway.

A similar analysis can be applied to those who cause pain to themselves. We despise pain because we are *not* in control, because an element in the outside world is dominating our existence, suffocating our philosophical privacy, rendering us nothing but whining cattle. This is why torture works, because it rips our insides out for all the world to see. But self-inflicted pain is quite the opposite, in fact it is best called pleasure for the activity is about ultimate control, denying nature's instinct, tormenting our own beast, playing God. For even though these people might turn a private knife on themselves, they would still flee an armed attacker, for they are well aware that when it is not under control, pleasure-pain very soon becomes pain-pain.

Self harm is a very particular sort of pain – and one in which all of us, at one time or another, may have indulged. Whether it be sticking a clothes peg on our skin to see how long we can leave it there, swimming in a winter sea, ordering the hottest curry or pushing ourselves to the limit and beyond on the sports field. We're all micro-perverts pushing the boundaries of sensation, far closer to that fishnet-orange-gobbed hangman than we'd like to admit.

And of course, pain and life are connected, because we imagine that the causes of pain would, if allowed to continue unchecked, probably kill us. When we as a body and a mind avoid pain it is for a reason in each camp as it were: one, because the *sensation* is unpleasant to the body in the short-term, and two because our mind imagines its *cause* to be harmful in the long-term.

But why split them up, you ask? Well you try telling the wife who's grown used to abuse that the feeling of pain and real damage are inseparable, or the husband who's just woken from a dream in which a dead baby was hacking away at his legs with a chainsaw.

As if they needed any more introduction – I think it's high time we found out a bit more about our terrible twosome. I've told you about first meeting Richard's gaze, but what about Sarah? We've all heard about animal magnetism – perhaps that's what he's got, and in time more clichés would be appropriate for Sarah. "I've never felt like this before," she might have whispered truthfully, gazing into his gorilla eyes. "Please stop," she might have added, without words. Welcome to the epoch of high-cynicism, where nothing's funnier than misfortune, no-one lies like a leader and money is still the root of all evil, it's just that now we're chewing it like there's no tomorrow (why, it's the tastiest bit!)

I tell you what, irony really irons out the creases in a conscience doesn't it? When anything goes, everything goes. How have we become so blasé? How did pain and suffering come to matter so little? When did wrong become right? Can you remember? I can't. I guess in this postmodern world reality is just *so* last year darling.

So it's with carefree candour that I tell you about the brutal bond that is our Rich and our Sarah. Hey, I might have found them, but we're all making them. There's no tasting without baking in our kitchen Dear Reader, you must realise it's you who's giving them life. A book on a shelf keeps all its secrets, it's time you accepted your part in this.

We simply must become more affected, things must matter more, else it will all end in tears. And the thing is we won't care. In fact we'd probably laugh. Let's face it, full-on nuclear war couldn't tempt most of us from our bean bags. But it's just not good enough, this stopping has simply got to stop. We need a new superhero to show us the way, to fly fist forward into reality, the here and now, the horror.

But for now, for some, for Sarah, it is too late. It will end in tears because that's how it started, and she will never forgive me. What she'd never heard before somehow became the sound she had always heard, she could remember no different, now and forever more. Aaargh! Men. I don't feel sorry for her anymore, I'm past caring, but you *must* Dear Reader, there's more of you than me. I don't come out of any of this at all well, you'll see, but there's still time for you, it's only Part One after all. I know how this ends, but you, you *must* feel something.

I also believe we have an overpowering empathy towards our fellow humans, and while it is undoubtedly sophisticated, ultimately it is yet another mark of the Beast, and once asleep the King can again feel something, or nothing, as he pleases.

Consider this: a deathcamp guard is keeping a queue of inmates in order, shuffling mother and baby along, The mother slips, the baby falls, the guard shoots out his hand to stop its head splitting open - and then proceeds to guide both into the gas chamber.

Of course Richard loved the little mite at first, but after a while, well, say 24 hours .... "Dress 'em up in cotton wool don't they, not like that in my day.

Always leave your mark my dad said." But then a dilemma, for she may be small but she's still a witness, eh? Always cover your tracks Rich, victims can't be called to the stand in their own murder trial. Total immunity apparently, like Royals and mad folk. *Oh what a night!* Or at least that's what he was told. History can be so unreliable.

I believe the individual desire to avoid pain and death, and our empathy towards the suffering of those just like us, are enough on their own to give life an intrinsic value, without stepping anywhere near the minefield of human rights.

I think I could just about accept we have a right to that which we appear designed to desire, whether that be life, water, food, air or comfort (defined here as freedom from unwanted pain). But such rights are not embedded in the folds of the universe, like some twist in the lining, if we want human rights then we have to make them up and protect them ourselves, because the cosmos couldn't care how many babies we send to the gas chamber, it really couldn't.

Many of you may smart at the term "duty", and considering its shabby treatment at the hands of the Church and the Military I can fully understand. For we must have no interest in that distorted brand called *national duty*, which merely served as a cool enough means to protect an establishment to which people *already*, in peace time, gave so much for so little.

So if we are to use the word at all then it needs to be redefined, *reformed* even, and forced to confront the empathy we share, not some wretched bias towards whichever side of the border we were born on. Our new duty must be adhesive, not divisive.

To put the case more formally: might, then, we be duty-bound to protect, promote and participate in a system of public life which treats other people's journeys as we never tire on insisting they treat ours, with encouragement, respect and, most importantly, privacy?

And if some slobbering in-bred wants to put a light under his family silver spoon and suck all life and death towards him then so be it, but in doing so he loses all the rights to safety and security which only superform can deliver. And if we were to find this creature unawares, and alone, one night, then perhaps he will be reminded of just how random, just how *circumstantial* life really can be.

Wow! What a night … no not *that* one … another one, after then, way after then. Me and Richard became friends you know. I asked him to do a job and he got it done alright, and in that way it brought us closer together. He definitely did the business, and now we're partners, of sorts.

And it's true what he said, he *can* leave no mark. I saw our Nathan a month later and we chatted away, you know, about old times, the Monday Club and what a shame it had all finished, and some other stuff I can't really remember (he was always the easiest to ignore, even back then). And as I said, Rich did a nice old job, not a mark. One of his hands seemed to think itself somewhat superfluous, and a couple of inky holes had welled up either side of his nose, but from a distance they looked just like the real thing. I saw it happen as well, I'm sure you've guessed by now, I watched, I risked it, I took a chance he wouldn't remember any *facts*, just ideas without words, faces he could never name. But as we talked something began to stir in those stagnant sockets, some bubbles of air were rising from the deep – was he remembering, had he seen something in me?

But I fear nothing. For I am the last person our Nathan would suspect – and any association between the face of his old mate and that night will only serve to heighten his paranoia, or as dear Richie put it with one final sickening crunch: "Philosophise on this one." I told you, I've changed, but I feel no shame, just circumstances really. Me and Richard didn't fall in love, but we definitely fell into something, not my fault is it? I didn't decide on Monday Club HQ, I was not the chooser of that boozer – I only held his watch, I only watched your honour, … er, okay, I *did* pay, but as Richard told me you've got to for quality these days. And I can't deny it *was* a quality job. As I said, not a mark. Of course I'll get away Scott free, proper criminals always do. For as long as the rozzers are looking for a reason they'll never find me. They should read some philosophy that lot, then they'd realise that objects don't need ideas, actions don't need actors and violence certainly needs no motive (in fact the best rarely has). Ask Nathan, ask Sarah, ask Emma. I told you, I've changed, but I feel no shame, just circumstances really. Hardly the good life I know, but we're all sinners in the eyes of the Lord, right?

Somehow we must take our turn feeding the monster who we insist feeds us. And who knows – it might not turn out that bad. We all know the story of the four sons sent out to fetch a different vegetable for the supper pot, and the tasteless broth they were served as each kept back his find for himself.

Perhaps Hegel wasn't so far off the mark, perhaps we can conceive of some civic spirit, in which a proper participation will actually afford a superior happiness long lost to the West. Somehow we must separate duty from hardship, we must stop seeing virtue in sacrifice and effort. This is not about earning points for the after-life, it's about improving our now-life.

By stripping altruism of its selfish benefits the Priest has denied us the beautiful truth which operates at the heart of human endeavour. For if superform is to be believed (and turn your back at your peril, Nathan will tell you) then time spent with others will become a refreshing contrast to time spent on yourself, a cool way to recharge those batteries, to learn from other people's journeys.

For if we're so great, then do you know what? They just might be too, to themselves that is. And if having time for our inside is what life has evolved to desire then it's just plain ridiculous for preventable conditions on the outside to stop this happening. We can't search for beauty if we're searching for food.

But don't read this as some pity for the hungry, for I hold about as much respect for *religious* duty as I do for its nationalist sibling, that code of conduct which seems to care more for the sacrifice of the actor, than the outcome of the act.

Such folk rightly see the importance of public action yet they will tolerate no repayment, for they're convinced all wages will be paid on death. One might be tempted to think: "Great, free help for everyone," but this refusal to see heaven on earth means they rarely push for *systemic* change, preferring instead to shake their tins on the cold periphery ("small change for small change anyone?").

It's a tough question, but do charities play their part in an unequal society along with the free market? One creates the poor, the other helps them, but does either try to stop poverty arising in the first place? But worse still, I fear these people all too often help the needy for what it does for *them*. They become junkies of the selfless act, inhaling that stoic smack until it smacks of masochism. The Ministry of Self Indulgence long since declaring their inside world out of bounds, they flail desperately in a world of temptation, throwing themselves again and again at the greatest hardship, the bed of nails without which (and *with* which!) they would die.

Let us be more optimistic: remember your philosophy. Is poverty a *necessary* or a *contingent* quality of global society? Could society survive its removal, yes or no? No matter how loud you shake those tins, you can never drown out the scream of truth.

But if we did get rid of poverty, just think how many passages of the Bible would fail to make sense. People in need give the religious someone to help, so the last thing they want to hear is that there's actually plenty of food to go round and the end of poverty and suffering is a simple matter of improved management and good politics. "Just you dare," they cry, for in a world with no-one to help they might just be forced to look in the mirror, and that's far too scary.

The world's riches don't have to be doled out in such a patronising and heartbreaking way. God may be the only answer if you consider yourself helpless in the face of inequality, if you are convinced that poverty is a *fixed* cost of human society, but I think we can all do better, *much* better.

I've made you angry now, I can tell, I can hear you outside in the cold, shouting up at my window: "What sort of twisted twat sits in his warm room arguing that charities are wrong, you're just using word games to justify your own miserly apathy." Wowzers, easy now Reverend.

Cue Gerald, a great man who's spent a lifetime supporting charity fetes yet has always voted for low-tax Government, he needs that little bit extra for his beloved tin you see (*now* don't you see?!) And anyway, he can do with someone to pity on a Sunday afternoon, it helps him deal with the memories of last night's bath - you'll see.

But right now he's righteous and angry, angry with *me* the cheeky bastard **(you're time will come Gerry Boy, I'll make sure of that, and that's a promise)** "But at least we're out here doing something," he hollers from behind the Reverend, shaking a fistful of raffle tickets at me. "Are you telling me you can feed the starving millions tapping away on that computer with your head in the clouds?"

I can only reply that the philosophical journey is totally justified because it will reveal the proper role of politics, one that works with the brief that every human is *philosophically* equal and deserves an opportunity to search for meaning. But to do that he will need proper time and space, which can only be provided by a free basic package of physical provisions which endeavour to counter the random variations wreaked by circumstance, until we all have enough space to forget about politics altogether. Then perhaps we can dispense with this degrading Dickensian web of charity and pity once and for all.

But if you still feel a burning desire to dedicate your life to the happiness of others, while ignoring your own, then so be it lazy bones, but please don't expect it in others. Martyrdom is not for everyone, some of us have grown up a bit. And if you must live a life of self-sacrifice then piss off somewhere else and do it – and believe me, I *really* don't want to hear about it when you get back – that's one book we must all burn. In fact, I think you should have a good hard think about the life you're giving up, and make pretty sure you are doing some good for someone else, well actually for at least two people, because you're already one-nil down before you start.

I would urge suspicion towards such folk, but at times of more extreme anger I think: "How *dare* they waste their beautiful life". If it's evil for a dictator to sacrifice your life, then it's evil for you to do it too. If superform is about helping others to help ourselves then we can see that it's enemies are both the self-promoter and the martyr. It's a two-way process – you must give *and* take – else you become a freak of nature, a voluntary cripple limping along on one strong leg while its withered partner swings lifelessly by its side.

Helping others is easy, it's a piece of piss, we're really not that impressed. But finding time to help yourself, that's much harder. Looking in the mirror is the *true* test of character, requiring real honesty and courage, and a genuine love of life, of living. But like some half-cut smackhead lying in an alleyway waiting to die, I fear you may have given up on life my friend, you hate it as much as these words you're reading.

Not that everyone lying down in an alleyway waiting to die is a smackhead of course, I know that much now, now I've seen it with my own eyes. I held his watch, that damn watch, why can't I get it out of my head? But now I've remembered. Richard's watch had stopped, hands pointing upwards, frozen in time. Mind you I don't think he'd ever realised and I'd never point that out to him of course, what use time when terror can't read. Just what is happening to me? What have I got myself into? Perhaps you're right to hate me. Can't say *I'm* that impressed myself at the moment.

The rabble of fears and desires camped out in your average human far outweigh those in the beast, in both number and sophistication. And having in much of this world built a life which has all but removed physical pain, such mental states are creeping constantly to the fore. Cavemen weren't filled with the fear of God, not with sabre-toothed tigers up their arse.

The organic growth of language may have allowed us to form abstract and generalised thoughts, sticking reusable labels on ideas once lost in time with the event that caused them. But this meaning, this essence, which words seem to give to life, is nothing but a bi-product of the progress of humanity, a super evolved being who just can't stop himself getting better. Compared with other beasts we're shit hot, I'll not deny that, but all that stands between us and them is the distance we have travelled. We've crossed no boundary into another existence.

We may be brain over brawn, but it's nothing more than a bloodshot jelly snake, and haven't you noticed, animals have them too? But I guess we're stuck with it now, this glistening organ which quite apart from being totally creepy looking is far too big for the job. And as our physical life gets easier I'm afraid it's only going to get bigger, which means more thinking, more worrying, more therapy. By all accounts it should have stopped growing by now, when you consider the average usage required by the modern world. But I guess the decision to leave the branches, those first words, those first societies, required such a superhuman effort that despite the best efforts of dumb modernity such prehistoric momentum has yet to peter out. Perhaps we beer bellies could do with a bit of nuclear anarchy after all, just to wake us up a bit.

Talking about fatsoes, do you remember this little gem from the playground?: "Why do Americans have such big hats? To fit their heads in." I loved that joke as a child. Just what is it about that race of freaky deaks which so incenses us Brits? They absolutely love us, you know, but the feeling is *so* not mutual. In fact, let's leave Christians alone for a while and take a big ol' look at the big ol' Union of Saggy Arses (and if that means some of you are about to get it for the second time then I'm sorry, but that's hardly my fault is it?)

Those homesteaders didn't need so much therapy. Why? Because they were more mentally balanced than their descendants? No.

Because after they'd gone to fetch water, repaired their log cabin, hunted for food and educated their children they were, funnily enough, dead beat. Now the modern American might argue that their ancestors suffered from such an all-consuming lifestyle, and stumbled towards their death with a crippled brain *crying out* for a talk show session on the couch. But such reasoning is as watertight as a donut.

Therapy is the waste product of a society which has become so obsessed with physical comfort that someone forgot the brain.

They drive to see their neighbours on their lawnmowers you know – believe me, it's *true*! To my wholly prejudicial TV-based opinion it seems that for generations that nation's wealth has allowed and encouraged its citizens to stuff their faces while leaving their minds to rot in a flabby overprotected shell, and only now are they coming to realise the damage this has caused. Any American considering therapy is quite right to question how they can possibly be so unhappy while living in the richest country on the planet, but to conclude that an hour a week talking about themselves is the answer merely feeds the slobbering swine of self-obsession that already roams that corndog of a country.

But of course to the already bloated industry of therapists things could not be better. To watch their pet pooch prowl along those terrified tree-lined avenues each day must be a beautiful sight to behold, obeying the one command whispered in his doggy ear each morning: "Tell them it's good to talk, make them real paranoid, and tomorrow the world is ours."

The therapist won't tell you to stop paying him thirty dollars an hour you fool, you gotta do this yourself. Why not, just for one whole month spend the money on a one-off college course instead.

That doggy-lover isn't going to tell you to stop being so self-indulgent and consider giving something back to society, or invent a card game, or make some wine, or go to an art gallery, or get healthy, or stop giving a flying fanny what others think about you - for he'll never nick your nickels that way.

He'd much rather you paid minute attention to every second of your attitude towards others in the week just past, and after convincing you that you were indeed 'coming on' he'll send you off delighted with the ongoing service. "Same time next week?" Another lost cause addicted to another soap opera, only this time with themselves playing the main character: "And s'long as you play it like I tell it, the public's gonna love ya baby – now show us your money superstar."

Is it any coincidence that the most anxious and unhappy people are those most obsessed with the path their own life is taking, and the most relaxed and happy are those who enjoy a healthy indifference to their own fame and wealth, popularity and success?

An afternoon spent in the company of one of the world's greatest thinkers or artists will be far more beneficial than an afternoon with Dr Dosh, analysing why you were unable to connect with Chuck on an emotional level this week. I say fuck Chuck and find someone you *can* connect with instead. This needn't be so complicated.

I once went to a wedding and recognised everybody there, even though I'd never seen any of them before in my life. That occasional feeling we have of knowing someone but being unable to place them had obviously been left switched on, and there's something about Richard which does the same. He *causes* familiarity. I know nothing about him, yet I can barely remember a life without him. I felt this that first night our eyes met. All emotions feel the same to the hairs on your arm, ask the knots in your stomach whether there's a difference between love and hate, passion and fear? And anyway, he asks me stuff – no-one ever asks me stuff anymore, but that's because no-one asks anyone anything.

When did we become such good tellers and such bad listeners? When did we imagine our lives to be so worthy of all that copy? I'm pretty sure mankind isn't becoming more interesting. In fact in this golden age of IT homogeneity and push-button luxury, one might imagine the opposite to be true. Yet we've suddenly become our own PR firms. I blame the Americans, all that guff about everyone being special, there being no such thing as failure and the criminal kidnap of the word 'beautiful' for some of the ugliest chubbers ever to have walked this planet. But Richard and I are different. He seems genuinely interested in me. A more impartial observer might call it curiosity, the fascination of the zoo visitor, and I must admit I detect no fondness or altruism behind his inquisition. But for now his questions are good enough, and his jokes aren't too bad either: "Shut up Sarah" he roars (because Sarah never speaks, geddit?) and I laugh, because I'm with Richard and his Demon in a pub. I told you, I don't come out of this at all well.

But of course, most of us don't go for therapy, nor we do sign up to the open university. We pretend our unhappiness does not exist, we get drunk, we watch crap TV, we tell our friends it wasn't our fault and they tell us we're right, because that's what friends are for: "Oh thanks – it really helped to talk it through," sure needs subtitles. How about this for a translation: "Oh thanks – it was really useful to paint myself in a good light to someone who doesn't know the situation except through me." Dangerous games my friends. We describe such moments as 'good therapy', but if all they do is make us feel better about a problem which remains unchanged then they are anything but. They are tranquillisers from which we will always come down, with a bump we could have avoided.

If this sounds unsympathetic, that's because it is. Sympathy is too often the self-seeking side of empathy. It's good to imagine how people are feeling, to put ourselves in their position, but we mustn't tell them "everything will be alright" if quite clearly it won't. I know it's tempting, I know it feels good to make someone else feel good, and whose ego can honestly resist being told "you understand me so well". (tr. "you always know how to cheer me up"). But we wouldn't tell a friend their car was fine if the brakes were dodgy, or their leg was okay if it needed to be in plaster. Pain generally tells us something needs fixing, yet we ignore it so often in the mental sphere. By constantly injecting sympathy to soften the *effect* of a problem, we seem to leave its *cause* untouched, and as any addict will tell you, this will ultimately eat away at our ability to judge right from wrong.

Surely the reason we view some drugs as so dangerous to society is because the users are unaffected by the unhappiness they cause. Their empathy has been so ground down that witnessing pain in others sparks off no mental reaction, and ask any detective, a man who feels no mental pain is a very dangerous prospect indeed.

There'd be nothing wrong with killing if it touched us as much as knitting. Killing is wrong because our empathy, our mental *pain*, tells us it is when we are made aware of it. But what sort of society would we be if our only solution was to deal with the pain, the symptom, the unhappiness (say by getting drunk), rather than the cause (say by acceding to and supporting a system which seeks to prevent murder and punish murderers).

Always remember, things might have been different. Empathy may have evolved to become an innate quality of homo erectus, but lets face it, tigers aren't big on it. Those stripy psychos earn their respect from coolly-executed homicide. And in another universe we too might have become blood-thirsty murderers, with an unquenchable appetite for death but an unspeakable fear of knitting.

"Who *does* this chap think he is? First book as well – like he's lived, like he's ever left his warm writing room. Blood-thirsty murderers? Might still be for all you know, there's still plenty of time left." They say imitation is the sincerest form of flattery, but I'm even starting to sound like him now. My Richard.

In the seconds *before* cynical calculation and selfish reflection take hold, I believe the randomness and similarity of existence for one moment looms large. We imagine the suffering of others could so easily have been our own. No longer does their pain belong exclusively to them - it is merely a mask belonging to society, which they *happen* to be wearing today.

"When you hurt me it is by chance and not design that I feel the pain, you could so easily have been me, the weak one, squirming," but now I've gone too far, I know it, I step back from the bar, and await my punishment …. strangely excited. Never talk philosophy with the bereaved, they say, "or that mad bloke with the dog" they might have added. "You will be squirming book boy, if I ever hear you say that again. I know a threat when I hear one, an *offer*. I say we finish this now, outside, two chapters is plenty for someone your age. It's not like anyone asked you for any of this."

Richard the critic that time, definitely not me, although I've said before, it's getting harder to tell. Sometimes I go to the pub whether he's there or not, just like he did before he met me. And I stand there at the bar, staring out the new Monday Club, and I search out some innocent lamb from my forgotten past, someone different, just as I was back then, perhaps to cultivate into the person I've become - but there's no-one. And anyway, here comes Richard, back from the bog and it's my round – it's always my round. But at four pints an hour he assures me he's good value. This will make sense one day, you'll see.

Like the man attempting suicide and genocide we can override this empathy, but we cannot stop it, and it will always beat us to it, until we beat it to death with drugs and lies, which is of course what we always end up doing.

"Clearly you're living in a dream world," thought Richard, without words. "No-one feels society's pain, that's just talk-show trash imported from the very country towards which you once directed so much venom. Perhaps you protest too much?" I wonder how long I can take this? This is my book right, you'll all

get your chance. And although I can't promise I'll listen, I'll certainly do my best to look like I am.

But you may still argue that no natural benevolence exists, and even if it did there still need be no universal basis for morality. In fact, you say, all I've done is introduce a common sense code to cope with the expansion of our immediate family to the wider community, we've hardly joined hands across the world. And what I described as some metaphysical extension of the suffering we see in a stranger's eyes is, in fact, merely a question of logistics, of policing.

I feel I'm starting to tread on the toes of Part Two, but, for now, briefly, surely these barriers are coming down? If one day we can be Europeans first and British second, in the same way that Yorkshiremen came in time to be British first, and their county second, then is the human family that much of a dream?

But let's not hide from the heart-breaking truth, that it is *dispute* that best widens and strengthens families, for there's nothing like a common enemy to create new friends from old rivals:

Terry's talking to Gerry, they're neighbours and they're enemies, religious bigots ready to murder for the Christ they share. But it's Christmas and they're so pissed they've decided to have a blow on the pipes of peace.

"Tell you what Terry," says Gerry. "I've been thinking. Instead of fighting each other, let's be friends …."

"Most admirable dear chap," interrupts Terry. "Never thought you had it in you." (Why do we use a posh accent to tell lies? As if by speaking like someone else we absolve ourselves from blame.)

"Tell you what Terry," repeats Gerry. "I've been thinking. Instead of us fighting each other, let's be friends …. coz I don't think I can kick the shit out of the Pakis on me own."

You should've heard them laugh, Christmas cheer from ear to ear, and their kids too. Jokes are so much funnier at their age, especially when dads tell them. Some might say those little mites never had a chance, but words are such good liars.

So will a common enemy be the only way we can truly conceive of a sensible human race at all? A Martian invasion would definitely bring us humans together, forcing us to realise our similarities do in fact outweigh our differences, that our strength was in unity. But I was kind of hoping there might be something a bit more positive then a mutual loathing for green skin and big eyes to tempt us softies into a group hug. Let's face it, we've done this skin thing to death, quite literally for too many. It's so old school, so Sixties, so *dull-headed*, it must be time to move on by now?

There are many who argue that we don't need war to bring us together, for history is already coming to an end. Creeping corporatism will play swab to our bloodstained history, ushering in peace on earth through a universal love of trainers. But we still see rich countries coming together to protect their wealth, and emerging ones forming their own bonds to ensure they reap the benefits of newfound industry. Big business melts down old rings to make new ones, with those in power still no nearer to sharing it.

Oh yeah, and as if we all didn't know, Africa's dying - no-one's picking Ethiopia for their team, Sudan anyone? Er, what can they offer our new benevolent family? Nothing. The new second division offers investment opportunity. They may be poorer but they've started to earn pocket money and they're sure gonna need fags and petrol soon. We like them, we need them, they've got *potential*. But Africa just gets charity.

Forget all the school assembly moralising you've ever suffered and pretend you're reading this for the first time, for the truth cares not how often we fools speak it: "Africans are humans just like you and me; born by accident and gazing out from a mysterious soul housed somewhere near the top of a hairless upright body, like you and me; frustrated at mistakes, secretly selfish, confused about love, both fond and embarrassed of their parents, like you and me; and funnily enough would like nothing better than an evening out with their mates, just like you and me. The only difference is they're so poor that their clothes tear like spider webs, their shit runs like water and they're too weak to brush the flies from their eyes."

At every opportunity our beloved modernity urges us to set personal goals, to fight for our rights as *individuals*, and be proud of who we are, where we've come from and where we're going. And I'm sure Africa's dead chuffed for the lot of us, for if the planet was a street there's a family living at number seven in a house worse then we build for our pigs. And if the planet was a family then we've all stood by while Aunt Edna shits so much blood even the maggots have stopped bothering her withered arsehole.

We simply *have* to take them on, not with charity but with force. Volunteers in white t-shirts are not enough, and neither are school exchange schemes, no matter how well they fill the curriculum. This is about getting rid of poverty, not writing to it, filming it, visiting it. It seems our inbuilt barometer of fairness and empathy just cannot register the suffering on that continent. So let's get this dial working again. Forget all talk of the *African Tragedy*, or the *Land Without Hope*, for they're nothing but grand literary names we've come up with to stop us feeling so guilty about how little we do. Their's is no *elite* African suffering, immune to the sympathy we're more than happy to show our budgie. For in what makes humans human they're absolutely no different to us. The equality and privacy of the bubble ignores all distance, all culture.

We're all taught early on that acting fairly at a macro level, to endeavour to offset the vagaries heaped on us by circumstance, is to act as a fool, as if one does not understand the rules of the game. It seems we need bring no sympathy to our business relationships. For the free market has (in theory) been declared 'fair', and we are therefore absolved from considering what (in practice) it actually permits. And so we find the most compassionate souls happily conducting themselves in the world of money with quite the reverse disposition, maximising income and minimising expenditure with neither kindness or consideration for the harm it might cause.

And yet quite the rudest question one might ever put to such a gentle creature is one which made the faintest inquiry into this schizophrenic private passion. Am I the only one who thinks it a little weird that the village vicar can speak about the root of all evil on Sunday, while a voracious broker eagerly carves him up a job-cutting roast from the next day's stockmarket?

For we all know how the Good Book starts: man by his sin binds nature and shame together from the Beginning, and only by begging like a dog for forgiveness can he hope to escape the putrid perversion in which his earthly body is soaked.

There are times when I feel considerable bitterness towards this creed. No wonder we drink. Just face facts, face reality – there's no 'we' to come out of its shell, this is it buster, and anyway the body's not so bad. Perhaps we could all do with a bit more porn.

But Sarah won't believe this empirical lie, and not just because I came out with it. Her mother once said of her, jovially, metaphorically: "Sometimes I wonder what planet you're on." Richard too shares the joke: "Helloooo, is anybody in there," he taunts, knock-knocking at her head, without a metaphor to protect her.

"What's a metaphor?" Richard once asked me, and I was already laughing: "To met things with," I mouthed to myself, for I'd remembered the joke from the Monday Club, but he just stared right through me in disbelief. I was waiting for the punch line (which in the end was just the sort of line I got) but not for the first time did I say something to myself out loud, you'll see. Apparently he really didn't know and was genuinely interested. He was trying to make intelligent conversation and all I could do was make a crap joke.

What's happening to us? Me and Richard, Richard and me, like ships in the night. Later at home, as snot and blood fought to smother the slug swelling beneath my nose, I tried to multiply that line by 10, or was it 20 or 30 – just to get *some* idea of the horror Nathan had felt, *I* had felt, in that alleyway, the same horror I saw etched into those sunken sockets a month later. And as I dreamt up pictures in the ceiling, watching the scene from a safe distance, just as I did back then, I was ill, two racks of ribs welcoming this warm towel of slush, now seeping into the carpet where I'd collapsed. "Any other discharge?," I grinned, between wretches. "At least I don't piss myself to sleep eh Rich," I spluttered, as loud as my bloodied lips could bare. "At least my shits don't bleed eh Dickie boy?"

And I swear, I never loved him so much as I did that night.

But we were talking about Sarah weren't we? We were talking about the empirical truth she knew was a lie. Her life had no form, this body was not hers, she filled no space, spent no time, she made no decisions, felt no pain, no blame – she was a woman on a mission and once completed thy will be done, forever and ever, you know the rest. But the when and where, those co-ordinates of reality so beloved of the empiricist, was simply not important – that her will be done was everything, the one universal truth. This is why she will never forgive me. But I couldn't finish her story, even if I knew how.

Morality must be *public*: borne from the need to get on with our fellow beings. It is about interacting bodies, not minds.

But to the religious things are so very different. Morality, to them is nothing less than God's word made into human law, and applies to both public and private moments. Their dualism has forced mind and body together into one unholy union on unholy earth, and their soul, their true essence, with God on the other side. You can even be bad on your own in the Land of the Lord – in fact if you were the only being in the entire universe there would still be a fair old list of immoral acts you could get up to.

To me morality cannot exist outside a human act, acting morally simply must mean acting *towards others* in a certain way. But religion's greatest crime is to perceive an all-seeing God which has made every single moment public, for even the man alone with his thoughts must act properly before Him.

In the world of politics we would Christen such an invasion of privacy as evil, and rightly so, but we are far from consistent when it comes to religion. We happily lie in front of tanks to stop Big Brother, but when it comes to God's ubiquitous gaze we bathe in it, as if it were some protective glow borrowed from shabby sci-fi.

Quite frankly, I don't want to be watched by *anyone* – neither Unelected Dictator or Omnipotent Creator. Such an idea destroys human existence – the indescribable beauty of the private bubble.

I suspect this won't be my parting blow to religion, for there are plenty more challenges to confront along the way. But in the wake of victory, is there anything worth filching from the fallen, before we move on? Let's get back to their basics: religions create moral systems supposedly derived from an omnipotent force, which as the creator of the world gets to decide how its inhabitants should live. True happiness on earth is achieved by acting according to God's will, surely their strongest selling point.

But to an age where comfort and celebrity have become the ultimate goals, neither sickness requiring of religion, the Priest is forced to play his Ace: "Not only will acting according to God's will deliver true happiness on earth, but it will guarantee eternal happiness after death in Heaven." But what's this? That poker face has only gone and chucked in his Sick Joker as well: "For not only will acting according to God's will deliver true happiness on earth, and eternal happiness in Heaven, it will also ensure you don't spend an eternity of suffering in Hell." Wowzers. Now that's some hand.

Too many Christians just stand there telling me I need to believe in God to guarantee an eternal life with him, and challenge me to prove otherwise. And I answer: "Er hold it right there mister, which one of us has an open mind, and which one of us bases their whole view of life on the words of a shoeless son of the Creator of the Universe who talked to loads of people in the Middle East 2,000 years ago, according to a book made up of a few dozen chapters, starting with two people in a garden sniggering at each other's bits and finishing with a load of horses and chariots and fire?"

When it comes to religious belief the burden of proof surely lies with the *believers*, otherwise we could all concoct a circular-impermeable-belief-system of our own.

But if the Priest was honest, it's the Sick Joker which really defines the strength of the religious campaign, selling belief as an insurance policy: "How can you afford to risk not believing in God?," asks the Priest, but my reply is always the same: "Or any other omnipotent force at the centre of world faiths past present and future, for how can the cultural circumstances of my birth be any guide to eternal truth?" Perhaps religions should consider coming together in the most controversial merger of the lot, believe me from our distant perspective you all look and sound pretty much the same. Or at the very least you could produce an all-in-one travel card, delivering a flexibility demanded by the modern believer as he travels from Truth to Truth. But that won't happen, the Good Book will tell you: for if there's one thing worse than a non-believer, it's a believer-in-something-else.

As with all insurance policies there is a price to pay. The image of Jesus on the cross, the Saints laying down their lives for their beliefs, the celibate Priest, or the censorious attitude towards sex, drugs and sausage rolls. Christianity has a long and proud history of denial and sacrifice, stoicism providing the magic combination to unlock the gates of heaven. (I guess we can all feel a little light-headed, a little *spiritual*, when we don't eat all day).

Now is this emphasis on sacrifice an essential part of religion, or could it have been otherwise? Is there another world where each being can act purely as they please and still sail on into eternal happiness? Is there something about the conditions of human existence which have landed us poor souls with the hardest of entry exams? Of course not. In the eyes of the religious there is nothing *contingent* about the human condition. As far as they are concerned, there is only one God who made only one UNI-verse, the word itself hardly allows for much else. And in it he placed only one humanly-inhabited planet, on to which he sent down his one son to try and clear things up a bit. So if sacrifice and denial are part of religion, then they are so *essentially*.

Believers may ultimately insist that religion is actually about a personal relationship with God – but it really doesn't help that its earthly appearance, via the authors and interpreters of the Good Book, can often appear as a tangled network of prejudice and contradiction.

"If this is so then it merely reflects poorly on our language's ability to represent such matters adequately," they say. Well fine, but if that's really the case then as things stand there is little separating you from the daytime drunkard declaring from his pavement paradise that we're all made of cheese and should prepare to meet our Grater. The burden of proof is on you remember, not us.

Even prayer, that crucial vehicle of communication with God upon which the creed is based, is sold to youngsters on the benefits it can confer on others in the real world. If the Christian journey is essentially a personal one then why so often do we ask people to pray for others, with a subtext that to pray for oneself would actually be rather selfish. Oh come *on!* This is not primary school – is an eternal existence in the flames of Hell at stake here or not?

But even with such a generous reading of the gospels, at the end of the day it's your mind they're after baby. Forgive me father for I have had ungodly thoughts. It's your mind they're after. But you must never let them get in. You must keep your mind fit and healthy. Each day you must imagine the most depraved thoughts you can bare to think, just to disinfect this hallowed privacy. Morality is about public conduct, that's all. The only distinctions worth worrying about in our inner world are between good and bad imagination, daring thoughts and lazy thoughts, apathy and ecstasy, cliché and beauty.

For now, let us agree that Agent Morality has for too long been a stranger patrolling within the bubble, taking Heavenly instructions by earpiece like some two-bit security guard, checking over files to make sure no tomfoolery's taking place, his muddy footprints desecrating what was once a golden floor. He won't be receiving instructions anymore thank you very much, he works for us now.

We are the new landlord, our inner world belongs to us, and all who make their living inside must do so by a new set of rules. We're having a makeover and I'm afraid the Confessional's just got to go. There'll be no heavy hearts hiding behind heavy curtains, there'll be no space for these guilt trips. But if Nietzsche was right, and God's a gonner, then this is some slow death alright. Perhaps we're too scared to see him go, although as comfort blankets go it's pretty faultless. Even the Godless head for church after tragedy.

But I'm not pushing for a loss of innocence, quite the opposite, I want to see a *return* to innocence, the innocence of the man who's never had to face the sickening image of a man nailed to a cross. Blessed are the ignorant indeed, blessed are the free.

Part Two

Are capitalism and nationalism becoming the two most harmful ideologies in history? It certainly seems that the raw misery now caused in their name, in both the short and long-term, has far outweighed that realized by any other contenders. Yet still they remain the most pervasive, and the most in demand. So where lies this masochistic appeal, and how might their power be channelled to better ends?

Drip.. drip.. drip.. sounds like a nasty leak you've got there Raymond, you wanna get that fixed mate. Do they make snuff movies for the wireless, I wonder? Probably worth a try, technology's so cheap these days. Things have changed alright.

I'm not denying that great evil has been perpetrated in the name of other jisms, but in practice what may have began as a founding ideology has merely ended up as a shopfront to unsustainable tyranny.

Of course Marxists need only show this journey to be contingent for their dream to stay afloat, but shouldn't that tell them all they need to know about the location of their Creed? And mightn't they display a bit more curiosity as to what the rest of us are up to on 21st century mainland, rather than drifting out to sea, fighting imaginary battles with intellectual serpents. Ironically though, I see real power in the Marxist end if one realises it *is* just a dream. It can exist authentically as an ideal, a vision, and if by nature you're a dreamer, or an idealist, like those on the Left tend to be, then perhaps all might be well.

But *we* must not live in denial of reality, of the present as it is, as things have *turned out* – contingent, random, dictated as much by geographical accident and ancient power games as by some ideology borne from spurious human destiny. We must visit the theatre of dreams when it's appropriate, and that's the second half. Right now we've got real goals to score, real mouths to feed, real bellies to fill. Man cannot live on sea serpent alone, chips or no chips.

Dictators may have switched salutes down the ages, but the trembling hearts of their victims remind us their similarities will always outweigh their differences. The fear of pain will forever remain one of life's great constants - we may never find a truer bond of the human family.

Yet as dictators die, taking their crumbling empires and long-forgotten Ideals with them, capitalism and nationalism manage quietly to plod on, gaining strength with every step, breaking each finish line hand in hand, with not a competitor in sight. This victory can only be analysed if it is first *accepted*, and I'm afraid that means a lot of soul-searching for the Left. Their clichéd self-absolution, which insists that each new day Capitalism takes a further step towards its demise, must be revised. Have you seen Africa lately? Doesn't look to me like they've got that much time on their hands, are you *really* asking them to be a little more patient?

It's high time you stopped sounding so *academic*, looking as if you're actually enjoying some game of intellectual double-speak to usher the world and it's wife under your umbrella. Quite frankly, if your people are hungry and cold and get beaten up a lot, then your theory's bollocks. Ideal can only come after I eat. We must write books about the world, and stop gazing out at the world after reading books. Slip those morals into your monthly magazine and leave the lot at home, for people are being crushed beneath the March of the Market every day, and they need your help.

With some years of left-wing idealism under my belt (piece of piss when you're a student – cashless societies have an obvious appeal to the cashless) I'm fully aware that this tirade against the Left is amplified by pious reform of the worst sort, like some dreadful ex-smoker peering down his nose at yesterday's puffing soul mate. But these days I need my theories to stand out in the rain, I want them tested and I want *results*, preferably recorded in units of genuine 21ˢᵗ-century human happiness.

So back to the Revolting Twins, backed by a PR team so fantastic that they are still marketed, sold and bought as desirable goals. It is the cloak of respectability which gives these wily wizards their potency, and it is a cloak we all at times choose to wear.

But perhaps you might first consider who else has wrapped themselves up in such opulent warmth, for this is definitely hand-me-down. I see its jewel-encrusted lining has caught your eye, it's grand livery stirring up ancestral glories as if they were your own, but before you realise, your worst is indulged, and the seduction complete. Those cloaks carry messages from the dead, my friend. Check the lining, always check the lining. You'll see.

With capitalism we attack, and with nationalism we defend, aware that success in either field spells selfish progress. And it is this dual Darwinian heart, pumped by the bleeding wounds of history and blind circumstance, that makes them so difficult to resist.

We are won over by the promise of riches and the cushion of a victorious past. Anyone's will do, anything to soften those sharp edges, to allow us to think less. Pride delivered under guarantee, with no need for that tiresome effort and achievement? Of course we'll place an order – cheapskates, the lot of us.

But there is no belonging, just circumstance; there is no permanence in history, just a bloody series of death and destruction, dressed up in tatty team colours. You have been born on one side or the other – so what? It wasn't your *choice*, your *doing*. The only authentic attitude to this network of clubs is to abstain, refuse to take sides, walk away. Watch by all means, even commentate if it passes the time, but don't support and never play.

"What's that sick-note spaz on about now?," said Richard and I, Richard I, Richard the First. "Never got picked in games so he trawls out this old bollocks to justify it." Sorry, we really sound identical these days, he's completely won me over. And that's me thinking out loud, not him. But I can't seem to stop myself. I watch football and I feel like a thug and it's the most exciting thing that's happened to me in years.

I reckon I'd hit him back now, Dear Dicks, and I *know* I could definitely take sick-Nate again. I know - I should be worried, I no longer fear physical pain like I should, like I used to, and I can't remember the last time I felt the brainy version. But a man who feels no mental pain is a very dangerous prospect indeed, ask a detective. But where did the philosopher go? Where did *I* go?

In order to break the supremacy of the Right, we need to discard the worldview of the Left, the view that human history is a necessary chain of events, that tomorrow is the next page of a book already written. Capitalism may well be inherently self-destructive, but that doesn't mean the Left has got the ending right. As I said we need a new politics, or better still, a new *attitude* to politics itself. It's high time master became servant.

In a great irony, it may have been the Left which came up with that endgame nonsense, but as it fell to the floor the Right certainly filched it good and proper, declaring that the world's story, the world's history, was indeed grinding to a halt. All the characters may as well go home, they said, for there'll be no more big battles to fight. "Don't worry kids, we're almost there now. Now who's for a burger?"

The New Right is always trying to repackage a circumstantial chronology as some noble tide of history on which they, the chosen few, have set sail. But just because they're winning it doesn't mean they're not the baddies. Like the court poet called on to commemorate a victorious battle, political commentators will always feel obliged to theorise as to their country's ascendance *after* the event, even though we all know it's a simple question of geography and natural resources. How many times have these arrogant writers down the ages invested so heavily in their own era, only to see a new modernity smash it to pieces? Yet we still keep trying, still keep making the same mistake. Perhaps we just can't help ourselves.

Why can't we realise there is no story, there is no beginning, middle and end, that we're in a soap opera not a film? If we blow ourselves up in a nuclear war it doesn't mean humans were genetically disposed to embark on some Darwinian suicide mission. It was probably just a lonely scientist having a crappy old morning in his shed at the end of his garden.

This fact is not depressing, quite the opposite, it gives us our biggest hope. We *can* change things you know, whatever these *things* are they are certainly under our control, and if we've pushed them this far we can surely push them somewhere else (for I don't imagine there'll be much appetite for pushing them back again). There is no underlying force powering the direction of history, whether it be towards the utopias of the left or the right - and if a grumpy man in a shed can change the tide of history, then so can we.

Captain Starlet may see more of his cloaks worn than ever before, and I'd wear one myself if it protected me from the rule of tyranny, but things have moved on. Seems the Captain took victory in the Cold War as nothing short of an invitation to enslave children from another hemisphere to sew his trainers together. Methinks the Union of Saggy Arses has got a bit over excited. And I'm sure I never had this much stomach ache before their food came over here … so fast.

But to all of you who are still scared of the Reds under the bed, be assured they are long gone, you can come out of your bedroom now and you won't be needing that starry stripy dressing gown either. Discard your protective cloak, however comfortable it has become. In fact you must get up, we need you. For the beast that killed the cancerous cripple of the Cold has not stopped there. One might have hoped he'd have have pissed off back home to a victory parade, but it seems this soldier has gone AWOL, his blood lust not nearly satisfied. Friend has definitely turned foe and we must get to work on a new opponent, if only to Save Our Stomachs.

Let's get back to the game. As I've said before, politics properly directed is about organising societies to protect its members from physical discomfort and to guarantee a reasonable amount of time to call our own. We must be allowed the freedom to indulge our philosophical side, for only there lies true happiness.

So let's have no more talk of final solutions, because just as we aren't *essentially* political, then neither, ultimately, are our goals. We can imagine living in a world without societies, even other people, and it is this fact which makes politics contingent. But a world without us? This captive immersion in our own point of view taints even the furthest corner of the universe, each second ticks by on *our* clock. We feel we could exist without the world, but we'll never know whether the world can exist without us, and despite the obvious facts to the contrary it's a feeling we can never shirk, a bullish burden of the brain that will tease us 'til we die.

My existence buzzes in my ears like a faulty light switch – sometimes I really hate it, no wonder I drink, no wonder we all drink, no wonder we all drink so *much*. **I'm probably getting paranoid, in fact there's no probably about it, I am paranoid. I blame it on Cider with Richie, a book I'll never recommend to anyone. But something changed after that punchline, not just my feelings towards him, but his towards me.**

I was standing there one Monday/Tuesday, telling him what *I'd* **do to Nathan if I ever saw him again, and he actually told** *me* **to shut the fuck up and never to mention that night again. "You going soft on me Rich," I joked to myself, this time successfully, mercifully, in silence.**

Now I certainly wasn't banking on this, so we stood saying nothing, as we always did, but this time the silence was deafening, screaming in each ear, pealing like the death knell of lovers departing ... although I s'pose it could have been a bad batch of Suey. This is all starting to smack of fiction, me and our Rich seem to be going in different directions, someone's twisting this story and it's definitely not me.

Me? I've been abandoned in some back alley, its sodden darkness sweats panic as I lurch from one wall to the next, a desperate frantic scramble for a glimmer of light, just one tiny window that might let me read ahead, to find out what happens next, what happens next to *me*. **I never felt in control with our Rich, and I guess that was the attraction, contingency writ large, a meaningless relationship in a meaningless world. But I don't feel in control of much at all right now. In fact lately I've felt someone else might be, and it's definitely bothering him less than me. I've never seen Richard's eyes burn so bright. He's glowing, and I'm going. Enough.**

When I ask question A: "In what ways are we all the same?" I am trying to elicit a human condition, to discover the parts of our lives we have in common with others. And when I pose question B: "In what ways are we different" I'm asking in what way does my self-consciousness, itself a common human trait, separate me from others – a *me-and-you* dualism if you like.

But it seems to me that politicians and their theorists fall between the two, for when they ask question B, they are still only interested in the world referred to by question A. Such civic bullies have no time for *me-and-you* – a far more manly dualism they argue is *us-and-them*. Marxists? Employers and employees. Nationalists? Countrymen and foreigners. Capitalists? Haves and have nots. Monarchists? Royals and subjects. Racists? White and non-white.

Politics ignores and ultimately attempts to subsume the self-conscious individual. It has no time for the thoughtfully detached among us, it doesn't want to hear that the circumstances of our birth do not matter. It wants us to be proud of our gender, our race, our class and our culture.

"Forget those parts of your life you've really worked for, those parts you've created on your own," they cry. "It's that random nonsense you were born into that matters most."

Politicians are wary of the potential of the individual, and paradoxically that includes the free marketers, for the only individuality they're interested in is that which drives the self-made entrepreneur. They certainly wouldn't encourage a *genuine* free spirit, who might live life according to his own values, with an approach to cash and capital completely at odds with the one recommended by supply and demand.

We weirdoes operate in our own world, and politicians from all sides cannot abide us. Whether it be consumers or protesters, business bosses or union leaders, they're all after loyalists prepared to play a game already started, according to rules already written.

And it seems no-one hates the idea of philosophical equality, this notion of the universal loner, more than the Americans. Contrary to the heady ideals which guided their constitution, the human family is the enemy of the American dream, that starry ideology those evangelists wave like a Little Red Book as they preach the Good Ol' Way of Life, at home and abroad.

Americans as 'free people' teach us about a world split into US and them. Whether it's the Commies of yesterday, the Arabs of today or the Europeans of tomorrow, they need an enemy, they need a threat, and when one's gone they'll sure as hell hunt out another, The Dream knows no other way. Through a Mickey Mouse mask we are invited to see these poor souls as 'them', to imagine that our differences outweigh our similarities. And the only way those luckless creatures can bridge the gap is to become Americans, to join The Dream (which never forget is nothing more than a land of geological riches stolen through genocide).

But when the iron curtains are opened, when the walls come down, when the veils are lifted, surprise surprise we hear stories from real people with real lives, people with smiles, people with dreams, people with worries, people with pets, and we realise that everything we were told was nothing but a fantasy, someone else's dream, a fake dream, a phoney dream, an *American* Dream.

Then we wake up human, and losing our religion gaze up at the heavens full of life, hovering high above our barricades and our borders, a sky full of birds who've been watching all this time, and guess what, to them we really don't look that different.

It's high time you met a couple more characters, after all you've met the fathers already. They don't have big parts, thankfully, but they hang round nevertheless. Something beautiful happened that Christmas, over the divide. As drunken dads barked and burped their way through the beer test, two bright-eyed babies made the promise of a lifetime and a great friendship was born, born in prejudice, nurtured in hate and ... and what? No endings remember, no stories. Just pointless lives jazzed up with pretty lies.

But it's several years later, and while the babies' bond remained solid those festive funnymen they once called Dad have certainly gone their separate ways. Seems big business cares not for big bigotry, which I guess is a virtue of sorts, and several spins of the wheel has left one of them sacks ahead in the father's race.

Nat's now nice and Ray's real rough, that's what you might think at first glance, but looks always tell lies. We wouldn't want it any other way. We dress to counter, to cover, to mislead. "Dress for the job you want, not the one you've got," pronounces the lifestyle guru, consigning queues of designer dregs and tatty toffs to lives of denial.

And our terrible twosome are no different, but who cares. It's Christmas again, a decade down the line, and while Dad and Dad won't be drinking together (coz Terry would rather chew crushed glass then be seen drinking with the boss) their terrible teens are most definitely on the razz. Raymond can really embarrass Natasha when she's with her Girl School cronies, but when our Nat fancies a nasty night out we know where she goes ("oh ... we shouldn't laugh should we! Stop it Ray, you are awful!")

I guess we all have our alter ego, our bold collaborator, the mirror image we secretly admire, the bad angel we love to call on when no-one's looking. Ah! Satan. I wonder what she has in store for us tonight?

Raymond and Natasha, Nat and Ray, if he's her pusher then tonight she's pulled alright. She sucked as hard as a high-class hooker, but now she's begging on all fours like the dog-end she'll become, until one day, like Ray, she's shoving that shit right up her flaccid arse. I know what you're thinking: if only for once words didn't lie, if only for once I told it straight, if only for once this was just sex, drugs and purpled holes. But this is something far darker, so evil I can barely speak its name. Beware of Natasha, don't be swayed by her classy turn of phrase, that equine giggle, a baby will repeat anything you tell it, and she was Daddy's Little Girl alright.

You've met Gerald haven't you? Once business took off he reckoned he'd earned enough to buy back the name with which he was Christened, but you've seen the real Gerry, you were there that Christmas, when Dad and Dad built bridges with beer. Anyway, let's not bother ourselves too much with him, he's only got a small part (according to his missus like) and it really doesn't turn out well for the poor chap (I made sure of that, you'll see).

The best way to meet people in this book is to go for a drink, so let's pop in to the pub and check out our two lovebirds. Ray and Natasha are talking in the snug – let's listen in:

"There's no need to mix with people with different cultural backgrounds to ours. We don't live in their country, so why should they live in ours."

"Of course there isn't ... a culture is something to be proud of, to support, to be fond of, it is worth protecting and promoting – let's face it, they do it, so we'll only lose out if we don't."

"And all this nonsense about humans being part of one happy family, as if skin colour was the same as hair colour, is doomed to failure. It's just not realistic."

"Of course it isn't ... multiculturalism is an artificial theory, made up from white man's guilt at his imperial past. It is not based on observation, and there's certainly no concrete proof of success."

"After all – all the people we love share our nation – what is people's problem? But don't get me wrong – I am no racist."

"Me neither. I hate the French just as much as the Pakis."

"Oh ... we shouldn't laugh should we! Stop it Ray, you are awful!"

I guess she gave it away in the end but does it really matter who said what? Are you happy distinguishing between those two? Nat and Ray, bless 'em, their fathers would be proud to hear such pillow talk.

I have a dream, a proper dream, a day dream, not that night time nonsense: Ray's hanging by his feet, hung out to dry, a single slit scored from chest to chin, his rolling eyes barely able to focus on the crimson broth expanding in the

bottom of his beer glass. He can see it's the same colour as all the blood he's spilt down the years, those quaking souls he's been fighting for so long, and just like the repentant robber he realises in his final moments the error of his ways. But unlike the repentant robber he's isn't jammy enough to be getting crucified next to the Son of God, and he chokes to death, one drip at a time.

Incitement to racial hatred? Well if racists be a breed apart (and those boneheads do kinda look the same) one can only hope. Things have changed. Life is much more violent than it used to be – something inside has stirred and it's barking for exercise.

I saw Ray the other day, the day after the dream, in the pub, in the corner with Nat. Those two have no shame. Me and Rich just stared at them. Now I know something's changed – wasn't that long ago Rich would have given those lovebirds a piece of his mind, but I think I actually saw him smile, faintly. Might have been a bar snack grimace, but then again?

What is he getting up to these days, what's going on in his world? Surely Sarah hasn't been sorted, there's only one way their relationship is going, and it's certainly not that way. But he's definitely found some inner calm, as if something's gone to sleep. He can't have read this already, surely? Before me? (Although you've got to wonder whether he'd recognise himself anymore if he had) Perhaps he's skipped to the end, perhaps he knows what's going to happen, perhaps he knows whodunnit.

But if that's the case why is he treating *me* so strangely? I wish I knew. I need to get back on track, I definitely need to stop drinking (I now too piss myself to sleep but the surprising thing is, after the first couple of times it's really not *that* bad, we were all children once).

"A metaphor is a literary tool which a writer uses to bring clarity to a situation by likening it to another." That's about right isn't it? Long time since I did that stuff, or any stuff come to that. Those pre-Richard days, 10 BR and all that, seems like a different age, a different era. But I had my serious answer ready all the same, in case he asked again. "This time I won't laugh, I promise, me and you can talk philosophy if you want, talk anything, whatever, I don't mind." But of course he never asked again. Yeah, things have changed alright.

When I'm not daydreaming, part of me feels quite sorry for racists – especially the young ones who've been force-fed by the parents who just love to recall a more innocent era. The opinions held by these young recruits sound so forced, so *learnt*, especially when couched in the language of their forefathers, a post-war vernacular they'd surely be way too embarrassed to use on any other occasion.

Personally I've always found it quite difficult to get worked up about what differentiates me from black people, especially when I'm still not entirely sure what separates me from the trees in which I hide.

But if nothing else, such spiky sentiments must take up so much space, their crippled frames must flounder for air in a hostile oasis of reason and logic. Perhaps I'm just a bit of a wuss, but I really don't think I could bear the pain of thinking in such a barbed fashion.

Surely having to think straight must really *hurt* these people, their mind must be filled with so much violence and injury. Bloody-minded indeed. No wonder they form so

53

many groups, so many parties. No wonder they invent hand signals and dodgy logos. Loners just love to hang out together, anything so long as they're not alone.

Listen up kids, you saw what can happen to the weak-minded and I guess none of you want to meet such a drippy end. So if your parents ever start telling you which people are good and which people are bad then smile politely (but only with the mouth, *never* give them your eyes), say nothing, and walk away, quite literally in the short-term, but mentally forever. With crippled loins so riddled with disease they infect the ones they begat, the ones they "love", spreading their pustulous creed so their own weeping sores don't appear so rotten. Just bide your time, and stay cool. Keep your head clear and your guard up, they'll only get inside if you leave the door open.

In a more philosophical frame of mind what can we say about racist ideas? At our most sympathetic we might accede they reveal laziness and ignorance, the two qualities most commonly observed in the 'harmless nationalist'. So it should come as no surprise that these are the two qualities most important to the preservation of nationalism. What would become of our proud island spirit if we got up off our asses and learnt another language? ("Absolutely not – it is your national duty to sit at the back and make jokes through double French – Your Country Needs You.") But at its worst nationalism can soon become a most violent creed in whose name some of the worst atrocities known to man have been committed. And if all evil needs to thrive is for good men to do nothing then we can see how easily a lazy Nat can slip into Ray's smothering embrace.

"I can see its jewel-encrusted lining has caught your eye," he lusts, cradling her sleepy slipping head, with eyes shot to dust. "It's grand livery stirring up ancestral glories as if they were your own," he whispers. And the seduction is complete.

It may seem harmless enough at first, but gradually you'll forget those jokes were supposed to be ironic. And the worst thing is, even when you've slipped so far, it won't feel like you've moved an inch.

I'm not saying one can't be fond of certain qualities, whether it be food, music or even looks, associated with a culture or race. I'm as fond of the Brits' self-control, ironic humour and dread of physical contact as much as the next man. But there are aspects of the true Brit which I despise, like his trust in traditional sayings, his tendency to fight when pissed and his love of instant coffee. And for that matter I also think we could do with the Italians' contempt for politicians, the German's civic pride and the Frenchman's 'yeah, whatever'. It's not the *analysis* of cultural difference that makes us a bigot, any fool can see we're different. It's the automatic *allegiance* to the random teams into which we're born that turns us rotten.

Nationalism appeals to childish elements buried deep in our subconscious. Comfort in the flag and fear of foreigners are passions which can be traced back to the emotions which engulfed us as a babe in our mother's arms. So why do so many fail to grow out of it?

Perhaps if we were to deconstruct national pride with a bit more detachment, we might conclude it can best be seen as one ring of familiarity among many, found somewhere along a logically-infinite series, radiating from the core of our being to the further reaches of time and space. With such a gyroscopic model we could argue that the race ring is just beyond nationhood (although like the frustrating paths travelled by Pluto and Neptune, there are times when the two seem to swap places). And it is this proximity that tells us all we need to know about the common origins of racism and nationalism.

So tell me Natasha, just why is your ring so respectable, but Ray's so evil? And believe me I'm not justifying his, I'm attacking yours by association, Natasha. NATASHA?

"NATASHA! I'm talking to you." You know what, I think they were actually kissing, or rather she was being kissed. I knew they'd been spending too much time together, I can see it in her sleepy hollows, that poison has run too deep. I feel sick.

The nationalist ring may currently be in its heyday, standing out as the sturdiest of barriers, but this is only because it houses language, which by its debilitating effect on cross-border communication lumps we lazy bones together by default. But as I said before, a bit more diligence at school might soon see an end to that. And if this linguistic expansion simultaneously cured our tiresome weakness for nostalgia, perhaps the most crippling of all British diseases, then we all have a real opportunity to progress.

For the irony is that so long as languages are used as fences, not bridges, then the culture they seek to protect will wither and die.

Has the English language suffered from centuries of invasion, imperialism and immigration? Surely in this very multi-cultural evolution has lain its success, an apathetic acquiescence repaid with global domination.

I once new someone who used old-fashioned phrases way beyond his years, hugely inappropriate for the peers he was talking to. He told me such sayings would die out unless people kept using them – and his argument ended there. I agreed with the analysis, but not the motivation: that anything from times gone by is worth keeping purely for its antiquity.

Surely most of the time words are used to question and describe matter and movement, and such basic requirements are clearly catered for in comparable and compatible ways in languages across the world. And if, through American imperialism and the IT revolution English becomes the base language for this purely descriptive part (I've always wanted this book to date - you hear that China?) then so be it, although part of me wishes those shirkers at the back were not granted so easy a victory. And if by Darwinian process some phrases fall by the way side then *c'est la vie*, for those which remain will surely do so for a reason.

(Right now I'm imagining flights of mystical Japanese expressions flickering across our barren British landscape, and wonder what new light they might shed on this old olde world) "More words, fewer languages." New slogans for a new generation.

Returning to our concentric view of the human species, one might observe with hindsight that we always align ourselves most strongly with the last ring but one. If we were in one of two families on the planet, you can expect that even if the families were to work together, sooner or later they would divide along family lines. But if it became apparent there was another street somewhere else, which housed another two families, then old rivalries would soon disappear as together the street faced a common enemy.

History bears this out, telling us that England was deeply split along regional lines, characterised by endless in-fighting, until it was invaded. We may have been made brothers in slavery, but this was a bond brought to these shores by an enemy.

There must have been a time when races never knew of each other and so the idea of different races, of races at all, didn't exist. By the time races became globally mobile, for whatever reason, the idea of nationhood had already been up and running, fighting and killing for years. Nationhood was the most potent source of pride to the white imperialist aggressor, and the emergence of new races gave him only one thought: "How can I use these strangely-coloured creatures to better my standing in the Inter-White Challenge Cup."

Non-whites were treated as a different species, deserving of no more rights then one might accord an animal. But it was only years later, when these creatures not only overthrew their imperialist rulers but began emigrating to the lands which once held them captive, that the tabloid paranoia and bogus brotherhood we have come to associate with modern racism emerged. This is why the Far Right to this day refer to immigration as an invasion, for they've read their history books, they know all about the Roman effect.

They appeal to some phoney Celtic or Anglo-Saxon residual pride, as if it had been bubbling under the surface for two millennia. And they get away with it because history works in the olden days. Gaps in our knowledge flap like red rags to a bullish imagination, the less we know, the more fantastic our ancestors become. But of course they weren't. Life was as vivid, frustrating and meaningless as it is right here, right now. Arthur was no legend while taking a crap. Best leave history where it belongs, in the past.

Things have changed alright. My insides are slipping away. Somehow I need to get a grip, on something, on anything. So this morning I forewent the pub, pocketed a cheeky can of Suey, and caught a coach to London town. And like a tourist I stared at the sentries guarding St James' palace. But unlike a tourist I wasn't trying to make him giggle or twitch, I wasn't even trying to make him retch on the fumes leaking from my blistered throat. I simply wanted to find myself, I wanted to see for myself the face of history, my history. I wanted to face up to my past, and my Past, to stare at the centuries guarding St James Palace, standing to attention along an unbroken timeline, that noble tradition upheld whatever the weather. But however hard I tried I saw Kev/Si/Steve, who tonight will be drinking beer and arguing with his missus, who tonight will be squeezing ketchup onto his cheese toast, just the way he likes it, who tonight will look back on the past eight hours of history in the making much as the office clerk did on the other side of town. The here and now was just too strong for history, his existence forced out this sentimental essence, squeezed it to the outskirts of the moment, our glorious past was single-handedly sidelined, legs taken out by that lone lager lover, that unknown soldier. And do you know what? I couldn't have been happier for him, or me.

Describing Ancient England as a proud white country is like describing the world as a proud human planet – it's meaningless, until of course the Martians invade, and then the Arabs and Jews and skinheads and blacks can all sit around in chains, writing protest songs about a more innocent era when there were only humans around. But will I be joining hands with the brotherhood of man when the planet comes under attack? No chance. I won't share a slavery song with those misty-eyed minstrels, writing history about a world which never existed. I've always hated folk music, no matter how many different coloured folk make it up. But the real point is, I never chose to be white and I never chose to be human either. So you can all piss off, the lot of you, I'm off to talk New World business with the Martian guarding the door, see if I can talk him into abducting loads of white Americans to be sold as slaves to a now-strangely wealthy Africa. And while I'm at it I might get see if he can first spike their water supply with hallucinogens, just for a few years, just until they're weak enough to be defeated.

But I'm dreaming again. Back on Blighty no-one's about to join hands and I'm not about to benefit from the wisdom of another planet. Cheap controversy is the order of the day in this era of the talk show, this crazy age for crackpots and columnists, one which protects any old opinion with blood and bombs, yet eyes the cool indifference of the philosopher with distrust and disgust. It seems dispassionate analysis has never been so unwelcome and this leaves the racist in his element, allowed free reign to muddy the waters between race and nationality under the full protection of the law.

It's his favourite trick after all: he slips you an apparently harmless jibe about Brummies, then it's the Welsh, and then it's the French, and then it's the Turks and then it's the Pakis and then it's the darkies and before you realise it your making monkey noises with the boneheads.

The Right pretend they've laid their cards on the table, but don't let them fool you. Our Nat might be at the bar, ice and a slice, chinking glasses with the good Indian doctor, but you know who's playing pool in the back, and you know who's getting sucked tonight.

Get on all fours, sniff those grass roots at a party branch luncheon and the odour is pure dog shit. They don't talk about it because society says they can't, banned in public you see, but not behind closed doors. They still step in it, they still slide in it, they still dance in it, tongues darting as flecks of faeces spit up at their cheeks. And when the lights are down low those nigger-haters show their true colours, stripped right down to their flaccid flab they heave those anaemic bellies into a pit of shit, squirming, writhing, marinating in mess. And when every inch of skin is fully-coated the fun really starts. "Look at you Gerald, you look like a coon!" Same fucking joke every weekend. But soon enough they drag themselves to their feet, do their best to wipe themselves down, and think about getting off to bed, for it's church tomorrow and they mustn't be late.

You know I'm right, you can tell that deep down they would rather 'that lot hadn't come over'. When Hegel described the progress of a society he said there would first be a *thesis*, which would spawn an *anti-thesis*, and from the resultant conflict a *synthesis* would be born. But I say to you Gerry boy, you may have beaten Hitler but that doesn't give you licence to filch that filth.

Another problem with racism is that it is self-generating. Its victims are quick to become racist themselves, hating the colour of the aggressor instead of his views. But racism isn't proved wrong by listing the victories of black people. Like all prejudice, it is wrong because it attacks one's inside because of an outside forced upon it.

Having never been the victim of racism I would never criticise the reactions of a victim, and you've already heard from part of me which dreams of bloody retribution, one drip at a time. And I guess any appeal to logic in the brainless arena of racial conflict seems pretty naïve. So sadly I suspect racism will only die as its subject, racial distinction, withers away.

Things will change, slowly, but at least they're only going one way - the sooner we all become sort of brownish the better, which is something for which America can, at last, be genuinely proud.

So it seems cultural pride is all the more heightened when there is a perceived threat to its underlying traditions. And because proximity itself is thought to be a benign threat, the proud endlessly promote their cultural tradition, not in response, but as the very lifeblood of the tradition itself. So part of being a Yorkshireman is being pre-emptively proud of that county. It's so absurd, yet how often do we question it?

Why are French people proud to be French when we are proud to be English? We can't *both* be right. And the flags, those bloody flags, what is it with humans and their colour-coded clubs? "Liberals are Orange, Tories are blue" (Richie is Reds and so is his poo?) National pride is nothing but a childish continuum, drawn in the crayon we stole from Blue Class. At school I was house captain. Our colour was green, and we had a song too: a collision with a juggernaut couldn't erase those memories, that particular shade of green. I even had to wear a small badge in the shape of a medieval shield and I was *ten years old*! (And have I still got it? What do you think?)

And I have to admit it's we boys who love to wink-wink the most – from school to scouts to college to golf course - a kaleidoscopic history written in neckwear.

Cultural pride is a collective memory we cultivate and entrust to the next generation, who in turn must tend to it with great care before passing it on. However, it would seem that regional traditions are fading, and the smallest fading fastest. So could this mean that human beings are feeling less pride in their origins? If cultural tradition is a fire which needs stoking, then are there enough enthusiasts to keep watch?

Cornwall, arguably the most distinct region of England, is suffering a drain brain as growing numbers of youngsters look to further their prospects beyond its craggy borders, often never to return. It's beautiful landscape will always maintain a tourist industry, and tourists need a history, but only time will tell whether the indigenous culture as lived by generations will be smashed on the rocks they so adore. And if it fades there it can fade anywhere.

But what of the Cornish, witnessing their heritage disintegrate at the hands of an exodus in which they played no part? With passion going spare do they invest that latent pride in another region? Unlikely. It's not regions in general they like, just their's in particular. Do they move on to the next larger ring? The South West perhaps? Even less likely. No cohesive history, too imposed, too *political*, not really *felt* by anyone, Bristolians and Cornish alike. So perhaps they stay on the train until the next stop, England itself.

One might imagine that the increasing mobility of Britons within these shores might have served to bolster national identity. Having spent significant time living in several major cities across the country, increasing numbers see *home* as no smaller than England itself. Someone asked me where I was *from* the other day and I was left genuinely speechless. I didn't want to tell a stranger my whole life story, but I could hardly say: "Why, England of course," for neither did I want to sound like a complete arsehole. The correct response would have been to lie, but I never think of that in time.

The point is, cultural roots are becoming a question of personal choice, about the import we attach to each chapter of our life. And not only will we all use different ways of arriving at our decision, but that decision itself may change several times over the course of a lifetime. It seems we *can* choose our family after all.

As touched on before, we might read familial rings like our address, each line revealing a larger sense of belonging. There was a time when we would write our street or village in capitals (for as youngsters we *realised* how ridiculous countries were) but as we grew older our identity shifted outwards. Personally I've never lived anywhere long enough to 'cap up' the county, and have been English first and foremost for as long as I can remember. But I can still appreciate the pride of the Scouser, the Brummie, the Yorkshireman, an accent and joke-led creed (God save us all from regional humour) promoted and worn as a badge, from Thailand to Tenerife.

While it may be many years before we see it in England, there will in time emerge a group of citizens who see themselves first and foremost as Europeans. As they move houses and jobs across the far reaches of the continent their multi-lingual mind will come to view nationality as mere circumstance, an accident of birth, as relevant as Hampshire is to me. Things might be changing slowly, but thankfully they're only going one way.

However there are people who feel no pride in being British, but for a completely different reason to me – and that's because they're full of shame. Mine is a philosophical detachment, a rejection of the *idea*, I feel no shame, for shame is nothing but upside down pride, and I hate both equally. But these patronising wimps gaze back at an imperial past through dewy eyes and wail to the heavens at the trail of arrogance, death and destruction the Brits left behind as they travelled the world, forcing their eccentricities on people quite happy as they were. Of course I'm not denying this happened but they didn't do it in my name. Those men of history have no hold on me, their ghostly fingers will never get a purchase. We must take good heart. For if it's not to our credit that we're British, then be assured that neither are we to blame for our ancestors' liaison with religious genocide. For there is no 'we' - that's the point. Don't take credit for Brunel you filching freeloader. Put that flag down and build your own bridge, and *then* come back to me and talk about pride.

To wear the glories of our ancestors is to pocket cultural wealth as if it's ours to spend, to assert privilege without merit, to assume ownership without purchase, to foster pride without achievement, and to ignore the random process by which this whole mucky mess we call "me" actually came about. Stop admiring yourself you pervert. Spend what you've earned by all means, but don't put your ancestral inheritance on parade as if it were your own, for we all recognise a hand-me-down.

"Ah," you argue. "What about black pride? Are you telling me black people should not feel proud of the actions of their forefathers during the civil rights disputes of the 1960s?" I would say again that a black person has every right to feel proud in the effort *he* is making towards equal rights, but that's a pride to which humans of any race have access if they too make that effort. But he still has no right to feel singularly proud of his ancestors, for when we sit around in chains, with a Martian guarding each exit, we will tell a very different story. Martin Luther King was a human, right? Yeah, well guess what, so am I, so we can all feel proud right? Loud and proud. (Oh no! I feel another sing-along coming on).

It is a hackneyed point but a civil rights movement is only authentic in as much as it removes, not fosters, prejudice and genetic pride. When feminists argue that women are superior, or blacks argue that whites are inferior, an old argument has merely flipped sides. I guess once steeled with a successful push for equality these power-addicts fancied they'd see just how far they could go. But we can only see the truth when we let go.

We must all prove ourselves as individuals through the process of personal creation. It's our inner world that matters most, not the shell, and it's our inner world which binds us together, and yet ultimately keeps us apart, insisting on both equality and privacy. Our race, our gender, our culture, our religion, our language, our nation, our accent, our colour – all secondary, all *superfluous* detail, because we were born into it and had no part in its creation. We must stop buying glory on the cheap.

Now what's going on here? Richard walks into the pub, no joke, and *he's* got a black eye/lip/nose. "Her wonnit. Can't hit 'em back these days eh?" And that was that. What has he done to her? What possible horror has Richard inflicted upon Sarah's world to make her jump the gun like that? She's on a mission remember, she has a goal to aim for – I never imagined she'd take it early while our Rich was still lining up the wall. (Lining indeed! You'll see.) And a pretty crap shot too by the looks of it. Not only has he read the end, but perhaps he's read it to her? I see her now, tearing and screaming at each page as if her rage will rewrite the ending she craves, but like a jilted actress post-audition it's simple despair, searching that list for a name she knows isn't there.

I'd like to think I can change all this, make things better, stop drinking, start thinking, but this is fiction remember, we work out the end, flesh out some events which lead up to it, and then tell it back to front, most insignificant first. We're in Storyland now where time is in reverse – sorry Sarah but the end's already happened, it was the first bit I wrote.

Perhaps we shouldn't blame her for jumping early, but she more than anyone should know, there's no justice in this world. But something's still not right, Richard's just not the man he was. My baddie's going bad, the caricature is being fleshed out, being softened, he's almost .. well .. human and it's certainly not my doing. Could it be that Richard is now in someone else's story? Perhaps he's been offered a new role, more of a challenge – fed up of playing the villain (like a tee-total convert who got bored of the boos) he's taken on a much harder part. And he's loving it, you can tell, it's only me who's bothered by all this.

And guess what, another Monday Club seems to have started, and you just *know* who's taken Nathan's place as Chair. That's why he'll never ask me that question again because now he *knows* what a metter is for. I'd join them but I'm not sure they'd have me – I'm a bit rough round the edges these days. But if I tell you Ray and Nat *were* invited, then you get some idea how far this angel has fallen, and is falling. "Yeah … and put a cheeky in it will ya love." Me and Richard, Richard and me. We used to sound the same, but he would've never said anything that crap.

I once had a hero, a great man, a man from history, but a man just like me, or so I thought. And I used to whisper his words to myself when times were tough, when people were rough. But as I sit here pouring raw spirit down my neck that poem of once noble solitude bears down on my heart, like the sickening creep of lava on a hill village forsaken:

"I am at first affrighted and confounded with that forlorn solitude in which I am placed by my philosophy, and fancy myself some strange uncouth monster, utterly abandoned and

disconsolate. Fain would I run into the crowd for shelter and warmth. I call upon others to join me. But no one will hearken to me. Everyone keeps at a distance, and dreads that storm which beats upon me from every side."[3]

Such honesty, such bravery, if there was any justice in the world I should never be allowed to repeat such words, let alone imagine they were written for me. But Justice is gone, remember. Falling is so easy, I guess it's called free for a reason.

Jisms *need* conflict: feminism, socialism, racism, Catholicism, republicanism require a struggle to survive. They live and breathe the battle, quite literally, for without it they would suffer the fate of the plucky Cyanists of fifth century Finland, who so successfully won equality for people with blue eyes that no-one's heard of them since. All disciples of Jism say they want equality but deep down they want to get even, (no matter that in reality the victims of such revenge are rarely the original agitators - for we're in the Land of Theories remember, where reality's never meant so little).

And it's not only the jisms of the weak and the afflicted which need to fight. A champion boxer with no opponent attracts no crowd, no following, however impressive his stats are. Flag-waving triumphalism also needs the battle. It can never allow us to consider whether we may be more than an ability or propensity to box, whether we might in fact be better off without the fight at all. We must box without thinking - now and forever a national fighter.

British hooligans may pretend to hate German hooligans but quite the opposite is true – they love them, they need them, their paranoid longing to interact with their own kind must be satisfied with real people, fighting people, far far away from those weak minds back home, tutting their way through a TV dinner. The enemy of the British nationalist is not the French nationalist or the Pakistani nationalist. His enemy is the man who is indifferent to national heritage, feels neither pride nor shame in history and holds no special fondness for the country and culture into which he was born.

But regardless of this rather academic analysis, nationalism always makes the blood boil, whether you love it or hate it. And if we want to make significant inroads on passions so engrained we must look beyond cute philosophical equations. If we are indeed a noble savage then it is the latter which houses our national pride. That it dons the tawdry robes of nobility is a wily paradox we have already touched upon. But lets not lose sight of the brutal savagery which powers our national pride, from the blood-stained swords of history to the beer-bellied bile of the soccer terrace. It appeals to the animal, the romantic, the heart not the head. No wonder they drink so much: "Blotto the braino, for today our fists will be talking."

But are we a nation of nationalists or a bunch of humans prone to nationalism? I'm certainly not the noun, but I'd be lying if I said I'd never felt the adjective. I've never believed English people better than other nations, apart from the Americans of course, but I *have* loved my Englishness at times, and have loved it in others. The cynicism, the indifference, the silent dignity when times are bad, the silent dignity when times are great. I think we Brits could lay claim to being the most human of humans, our main characteristics an exaggeration of those parts of the human condition we share *least* with animals. A love of games with obscure rules, a love of sports you can play in a collared

---

[3] Treatise of Human Nature, David Hume, 1740

shirt, preferably sitting down, preferably with a fag, a mysterious fondness for camp behaviour, a love of pet dogs and underdogs, an intolerance of children and a suspicion of the successful. These are counter-intuitive qualities indeed, Mother Nature turned splendidly on her head.

And don't you get tired of that eternal moan of the British millionaire: "We should be more like America where people like me are praised, not criticised." Rather, you mean we should make the UK a more tax-friendly place for the rich and give them benefits beyond that which their wealth already provides. And tell me Gerry boy, just how did you grow those shiny piles on which you perch so gracefully? "Why, by paying my fellow countrymen as little as they were possibly prepared to accept and then, now here's the clever bit, come the weekend I sell the products of their labour back to them for as much as they are possibly prepared to pay." And you want us to be grateful?

There isn't a millionaire alive whose success pays no heed to luck and circumstance - in a private moment they'd admit it themselves. Out of the millions who tried for millions, they got lucky. Don't flatter yourself Gerry. People will always spend their money on something. They're not impressed, they're just bored. And anyway if you think America is so great then you know what you can do. We simply don't want to be like them – you must have realised that by now. See, I told you I can cheer on England, I told you I've felt it.

Any critique of nationalism must account for its near global appeal, and as good empiricists we must first consider the evidence that's right in front of our eyes. I guess it's confession time.

While I do not cheer on the English hooligans, I genuinely cheer on the football team, and could never cheer on any other, whatever the weather. I feel pure pleasure when we score in the World Cup, and quite literally jump for joy on a frightening scale seemingly reserved just for such occasions, shoulder to shoulder with my fellow countrymen. And yes, in those few seconds there is a feeling of brotherhood, a brotherhood which reaches out to the players on the pitch and the terraces cheering them on. I need not question the authenticity of this feeling, for it is involuntary, unstoppable, from the heart. The beast can only obey the rules of the jungle, moral codes of conduct are powerless in such an environment. And when we score there is little to distinguish me from the bootboys prowling those foreign banks, the terrace terrorist my newfound brother is about to become. The arms raised, the cheers, the chanting even – in those moments nothing could tear us apart. But wherever there is Pride you can be sure that Shame is never far behind. And when my brother starts fighting I imagine they're my boots crashing down on that poor head, those longing eyes desperate for him, for me to stop. We may be separated by hundreds of miles but tonight, like some creeping oil slick, our blood seems thick enough to poison those far off shores. Perhaps I should give it up, perhaps such passion is, on reflection, a bad thing, a net loss. It's not like we ever win anything.

No more talk for now, let's (for the last time) raise a glass to our friends, our family, and our countrymen. For we will not meet again in this uniform, it's time for a costume change and our new garb might pit us against each other. For we know what really groups us together, and keeps us apart. This talk of cultural pride only serves to keep our eyes off the ball – and don't those in control know just that. Remember, it's in their interests to foster national pride, not ours. We have dillied and dallied long enough in the land called Nostalgia, we need no more folk songs, and I'm full to bursting with regional pastries. At the end of the day all this talk of familial rings has only served to demonstrate the fluidity of regional identity. It's time to say good night and rest our beery head, for we have a long day ahead of us.

It may appear, at first glance, that there are contradictions at being both nationalist and capitalist. One might argue the former relies on promoting our selfish side, encouraging us to sell ourselves as the most deserving in a society defined by competition and stratified according to accumulation of profit. While nationalism, on the other hand, appeals to a sense of identity and belonging, a pride in the community into which we were born, and an animosity towards those careless enough to have been born beyond our shores.

But clearly both exist side by side, on the right at least, and just how this paradox persists is key to the prevalence and perseverance of our class-ridden society. Consider this:

Capitalism (rich people) + nationalism (looking after your own) = the class system (rich people looking after their own).

The class system and the upper classes are synonymous, believe me this shite wasn't demanded from the bottom upwards. Despite the best attempts of the ruling elite to convince us otherwise there is no backward band of smelly serfs desperate for a select group of rulers to defer to. Given a blank canvas this is not what they would have drawn up, it's a romantic myth which the powerful minority invented, imposed and maintained.

As the divine power of the monarchy and the church waned, then those in power needed another system to hide behind. No more was England some arbitrary lump of Northern Geology to be protected from invading hordes, populated by a disparate band of peasants with little more than a tax-raising war-mongering autocrat to provide the most tenuous and remote cohesion. National unity may once have been expressed and proclaimed through military victory (or defeat?) but England had to become a positive *pre-emptive* organic unity, a noble idea, a metaphorical gladiator on the world stage, with brains at the top and brawn underneath, each part essential to the healthy working of the whole, and so the class system was born.

Take equal measures of business, land and ancestry, mix well, season with manners, accents and a pinch of schooling and there you have it – delish. By the way, if you can't get hold of the real ancestry then any old supermarket bollocks will do, for since time immemorial patronage has sought out fashion and circumstance far more readily than character and desert. "But don't examine that family line too closely son, that big old painting is all you need to know about your great grandfather. He had his ways, and we should be grateful he did. They didn't have a word for it in those days. So sip that bubbly and think on, for there's pain behind this sham." It's their boil in the bag remember, sold back to us as healthy produce plucked fresh this morning from nature's very own garden.

So what heartbreaking irony that the class system is now most transparently alive and kicking not at the top where it was cooked up, but at the bottom where it's gulped down wholesale. Don't forget, the upper class will always do their business behind closed doors and deny any system exists, but our housing estates tell you they're lying, where thousands exist without ever having considered what ambition might mean – fighting a life they should be living.

Overuse of the phrase "old boys' network" may have stripped it of its potency, but eavesdrop on a conversation at a garden party in the summer shires and you'll hear the truth behind the cliche. Recall if you will our Gerald at bath time, or the bedroom antics of dear great grandfather Tom. It's always been about power, wealth and superiority - taste and decency were always a smoke screen. And if all it takes to maintain power is to discard such frippery and don a baseball cap for the cameras, then of course they will. Let's face it, they've probably been dying to go to the footie anyway.

As things once stood, huge swathes of innocent people were born into a life sentence, 60 years hard labour with little more than subsistence pay to keep hunger at bay. No-one expected any more until the arrival of the Greek God Demos, a Mediterranean import to cherish indeed. And if each human could threaten equal power at the ballot box, then they would surely vote to change the system. Inevitably the movement for equality of income gathered pace, and suddenly the Captain was about to meet his maker. Quick-thinking was required, but like all wheeler dealers Cap'n Class was born with a blag in his mouth, and in the nick of time blurted out the biggest of the lot – *Let's play Equality of Opportunity - Come On Down!*

It's a Victorian evening, boasting a fog of the sort Richard's great-ancestor Harry shuffled through many generations ago. A night of dark streets and darker doorways, each cradling a creature to revile, a little creature to resist. Still, I guess they didn't have a word for it in those days.

But his luck was about to change, for burning at the heart of this maze, this muck, this hideout for the defiled and the dead, appeared a spectacle to put a fire in anyone's belly.

"Roll up! Roll up!" hollers the Captain, to the shuffling serfdom below, his barrelled chest silhouetted against the gleaming lobby of his new-look Empire. "Do you really want the same as everyone else? You're worth more than that me old mucker. Do the maths, there's ten times more of us than them, how much more do you reckon you'd get by the time it's all shared out? I've got a better offer – don't get rid of the system, just get rid of the people. Come an' 'ave a look around, things have changed, and with a bit of elbow grease so could you." And with sickening ease he lured them into a tour of his new show home, a complimentary top hat for each and every sucker as they clambered up the Stairway to Heaven, as paperweight as the Promised Land they would never reach.

"Leave those flat caps at the door, that's it, you won't be needing those where you're going," beamed the Captain, not quite believing how well this was all going. And whaddya know, as soon as they had arrived our party guests found themselves shuffling back into that fog again, into the back streets they would never leave. But still, their luck was about to change, that's what the Captain said. That paper-thin freebie may have long since torn and blown away, but their dreams were now full of gold.

However, if any had bothered to turn back they night have seen their honourable host in a quite different light, a much softer light, a much *older* light,

his barrelled chest trembling with laughter, silhouetted in an upstairs window of the old-look Empire he can once again call home: "Phew! That was close."

That those in ultimate power are middle or upper class is not in dispute. It is a fact borne out from simple observation at our country's courts and parliaments.

But something has definitely changed over recent years. The cake is still made and bought and eaten, but it sure tastes different. Crafty craftsmen those master bakers, they may have no taste to be affected ("pearls on, collars up, *timeless* darling, don't you think?"), but they're sure aware that the rest of us are obsessed with it.

Fashion fancies the High Street far more than the Boutique – I'm sorry, but it's true. Such brightly-coloured disposables once separated the muckers from the suckers, but now it's the other way round. The poor have always been obsessed with clothes. Once it was other people's, but now it's their own. But today's muckers are just too posh for fashion, don't you see? They don't want to mix with you, they hate you, they'll do anything to keep their distance, and if that means cords and quiffs then so be it.

But now we're back in the kitchen with the master baker, who must concoct a new style of cake, one which meets the modern taste. And the modern taste tastes of cash. So lets be a bit more generous with the business, perhaps go a little easier on the heritage (too gamey for the modern pallet) and we can probably forget about the land altogether. Seems they'll take anyone these days as long as they've got the cash and the desire to learn the lingo - even pop stars. Remember, it's always been about power, not etiquette; behind closed doors only the poor care about manners.

The fact that citizens can change classes quicker than before speaks volumes about the system's new fluidity, but predicts nothing of its demise, quite the opposite. We should always ask *how* the system survives, not *whether* it will. Our Captain took plenty on the door that night, proud to represent his country he still displays the caps he won, stacked to the ceiling like the dusty skulls of genocide.

People may be able to buy their way into the system like never before, but it's still the old system they are buying into. Why do you think Gerry sent Natasha to private school? It's because he wanted her to become rich *and* posh, hoping that he too may change class vicariously through his Little Girl. On a scale never witnessed before hordes of winning suckers are sneaking into that once-forbidden kitchen to season themselves and most importantly their offspring, with accents, etiquette and schooling. Since it was put up for sale it seems posh has never been so popular.

But don't believe you're getting away with anything, don't fancy yourself some top-class sneak stealing into their Promised Land. They're letting you in because they need your money stupid. They're no different from you and they've known this for years, but faced with such cap-doffing reverence what did you expect them to do? Blow their own scam? The most upper mucker of the lot ultimately traces his lineage back to the grunting caveman – we all do.

The system may pass on superiority by birth, but the class system wasn't here before humans. Someone had to claim superiority at one stage, someone had to stake their clam, and you can bet it wasn't won via a hard-fought victory on the croquet lawn.

Let's look back at a time when Gerald was Gerry, and Gerry was nervous, for this was his first appointment with Bred for Bread & Sons, an impressive outfit who'd promised him "A *Class* Act That Won't Be Beaten On Price" and a cash-back guarantee yet to be matched by downmarket rivals Posh for Dosh.com.

"Ah Gerald. Come in sir, do sit yourself down. Can I get you some tea? Earl Grey, no milk, you say? Very good, glad to see you've had a look at the leaflet we sent you. Now let's get to the point. Contrary to popular belief we can get you right where you want to be. Whether a fruitful spell of medieval homicide kickstarted your noble lineage, or an inside tip on the stock market seven centuries down the line, it matters not a jot to us at Bred for Bread. The important thing is you've arrived now, you can relax. I've read through your details and I must say it all looks rather straight forward. So long as you're willing to invest in a couple of generations of private schooling, you'll be surprised at the fruit that family tree of yours may soon bear.

"And if you promise me you'll put the hours in on that funny accent of yours, and be extra vigilant in the friends you choose for dear Natty then in 50 years time I'm confident no-one will know the difference." *("Least of all you, because you'll be dead," he whispered, daring himself to say it louder each day, knowing full well that by now his clients were so hopeless with joy they were completely deaf to the world of reason)* "And on behalf of B&B might I be the first to say welcome. *Next!*"

This stuff was always taught, it's just that now it can be bought. But don't believe the hype, it's only a recipe. If they can teach their own kids they can teach yours too, for a price. A posh baby locked in an attic is hardly going to develop a love of polo - the only thing hereditary about those freaky deaks is a tendency to sleep with their cousins.

Take a look at our leaders, those with real power, look at what they do, see how they speak – and ask whether they've signed up yet. Even if they haven't they will one day, when they retire. They all do. The relaxation of patronage has not made the Lords more common, it's just made the common more posh. The muckers should welcome such liberalisation, for never has a title been so desirable, and never has the establishment seemed so cool.

"Roll up Roll up," hollers the Captain, 200 years old and never looking better. "If a popstar can become a Sir then Knighthoods can't be all that bad." He's bought the lot of us, at rock bottom price too.

The connection between the powerful jobs and the pool of muckers is clearly complex. And the fact that new muckers are constantly being recruited muddies those waters still further. But the extent to which they enjoy a smoother route to positions of power, courtesy of the friendly faces already in place, is the extent to which the class system survives and thrives. Muckers' children (Muckies? Muckettes?) are encouraged to aspire to such jobs, they are told they are their's for the taking. There's a sense of ownership over such careers and the life paths which take them there.

But I fear expectation is a potion fed to some but denied others. The world's best teacher can do little with a child given neither the encouragement to listen or the confidence to respond. I'm blaming no-one here, just observing facts, describing how things are. The muckers wine and dine, while the suckers whine and die.

But I warn you – damned statistics will not be my 'facts' – that's the politician's standard of proof to which I will never stoop. My proof is observation: I believe in the class system like I believe in the Bunsen burner, for I have seen it with my own eyes. That old bugger is back again, its new buds are about to flower, nourished afresh by a tangle of roots now thriving in the gap we've allowed to grow between our best and worst schools – again.

I have seen the muckers and suckers play out their little scenes, although never sent a script those suckers are always desperately adlibbing, hence the stammer, the nervousness. They imagine they are expected to act a certain way, but they only know the films, the pastiche, and so they perform for the bemused crowd, like seals at a circus. Muckers have always seen suckers in this voyeuristic way. You can see it in the magistrate's uncomprehending gaze, the frowning smirk of that former headteacher considering yet more schoolyard misdemeanour. That years down the line he's now faced with some rotting smackhead who knocked a pensioner out cold for loose change matters not, in his mind the quivering creature is just as wretched, his excuses just as dismal. But drugs are not the only poison which renders the accused speechless. There is a real language problem here and no-one's going to translate, for that would spoil their day at the circus.

"Work can be such a bore," broods trainee toff Nat to herself, stealing a glance at the defendant with no defence. Daddy was so keen, but after six months she was really starting to question whether this law thing was really her cuppa. "Let's hurry up and get this pour sausage processed one way or the other. Who cares, least of all him. He'll never stop stealing - he'd tell you as much if you only bothered to ask."

But another ten minutes tick by, then twenty, and still no end in sight. Just posturing, postulating, postponing. "Work can be such a bore," broods our Nat, half an hour later, stealing another glance at next year's corpse in last year's clothes, now muttering some tune to himself, swaying gently with boredom, and malnutrition. "*Please* fall," begs Nat from behind her serious-me spectacles. "Please fall, just for me." Bless her. The country's finest. She's turning into a lovely a girl that one.

Go see for yourself if you don't believe me. We must be analysts remember, not theorists, and I've seen it with my own eyes: never does the class system scream so loudly as it does in the town court. You may sit uncomfortably with such an archaic assertion, but this is only because our vocabulary has been scrubbed clean with *Corporo!*, a catastrophic bleaching agent which has destroyed all but the blandest lexicon, ensuring the most uncomfortable truths remain hidden forever. (And what irony that this politically-correct vocabulary engineered by the Left has actually served to blunten its own tools – for if we can't even describe the poor, the ignorant, the hopeless, how can we ever begin to help them?)

But I say again, go sit in the public gallery, and watch. See the truth, *feel* the truth. It's there in the haughty laughter of the young muckers, solicitors dreaming of their Crown Court destiny, chortling through each and every adjournment about holidays, cars, dinner parties – the gorge between them and their client forged years before they began to tread the family path.

But it's also in the eyes of the defendant, his heartbreaking gaze flicks desperately from solicitor to magistrate to clerk to press to police, to anyone at all, for any hint of recognition. "I'm not asking you to shake my hand, but why are you looking right through me as if I'm not here," he wonders, without words, the way most of us do.

He's looking at ten people packing salaries he couldn't dream of, yet clearly they are all here because of him. But if they are here for him, then why do they leave him standing there, swaying, silent, puzzled, lonely. "Ten proud muckers standing proud and tall," he mutters to himself. "And if one proud mucker would accidentally fall….." Ten proud muckers earning, laughing, insisting at huge huge length, all over a few seconds of random narcotic madness some days before. "Why are you all taking this so seriously," he thinks. "You all know I'm going to do it again. I'd tell you as much if you only bothered to ask."

Richard smiled at me from the dock. I was there, you see, in the early days, as yet another pour soul fell foul of Prince Charming of the Highway. And I'd have given him a character reference too, and who better? He's my character after all … or at least he was. So court ban now over, is Richard back behind the wheel again? Of course not, not the *new* Richard, chairman of the bored, head of the dead. He doesn't drink and drive anymore, he drinks and *rides*! He cycles to the pub, blusters in about six/seven/eight, the redness slipped from his nose to his cheeks. What is *happening* to that man? It'll be knitwear next I swear. What happened to the good old days?

I miss the court, I miss the law, I'd break it myself if I wasn't so pissed all the time. But there'd be no-one in the public gallery looking out for me would there? No me back then to save me right now. No-one cares about me anymore. And do you know what the saddest thing is? That was no self-indulgent aside, no pathetic expression of grief, it was a plain good old-fashioned fact. Ask any of the gang and after a moment's reflection they'd chorus: "You know what – you're right. No-one *does* care about you." I may as well be dead.

The law cares not who it punishes, but how it punishes. The law needs defendants like an engine needs fuel. It needs them to justify its existence, the law needs breakers, it would be lost without them. But once the juice has been collected, once Saturday night's skagheads have been pressganged into Monday's morning matinee, its existence, its actions, its purpose is revealed. The Bentley is slipped into automatic and the show is on the road.

B ut enough about the reality, what about the theory – when and where did all this law business start?

If we took a simplified view of law-making from its birth to the present day we might detect a certain shift in emphasis. While laws may have begun as an expression of God's will, in time they became a pragmatic means of controlling society. But this view is indeed too simplified if you are to welcome this shift in direction as a signpost pointing to Utopia. We are philosophers remember, and must always consider similarities first, differences later. And the similarity is that in both instances there is a ruling power which has an idea what shape society should be and is willing to make laws to achieve those ends. The crucial similarity between the church and the state is their craving for power, a historic and bitter rivalry spilling lakes of blood.

After defeating the monarchy and the church the good citizens of Britain might have imagined heaven on earth was but a few doors down. But it wasn't long before the people's parliament became anything but, a new ruler possessed by an all too familiar thirst.

What we need, what the people need, is protection from the *idea* of a ruling power. We need a genuine alternative to the mindless merry-go-round parliamentary democracy has become, an endless fruitless endeavour to replace bad rulers with good, only to discover they weren't actually that good after all (for we all know what power, and absolute power, does, *always*).

Authentic law-making should only serve to protect our freedom, enabling a fluctuating dynamic society which proportionately reflects the hopes and dreams of its members at any one time. Politics must protect our houses, but we must never let him peak inside. For not only is it none of his business, but in that moment of espionage he's no longer on the look out on our behalf. We owe this slave nothing, and must chastise him every time he makes to turn inwards.

But I'm reading ahead again, I'm as bad as Richard for that. Let's first take a good old look at the influence religion and its morality has had on our law making and law makers.

As democratic secular management began to take over from religion as the driving force behind law making, the church found itself skidding towards a sticky paradox and fast. In the good old days there had been no problem declaring it immoral to break the law, because morality and legality were as one - God spoke through his King and everyone knew where they stood.

But once the people's parliament took control it was the people who spoke and they did so through a new king. God was nowhere to be seen and the church was facing a serious haemorrhage of power. It could no longer pit itself against the new lawmakers, that much it knew, but it somehow had to retain some influence, and so the idea that breaking the law (regardless of who actually made it) was wrong came to light, a Godly halfway house which remains to this day.

But now the church is on the ropes we've got a real chance for that knockout punch. We should obviously tell our children they'll be *punished* if they break the law, but we must resist telling them it's *wrong* to do so, as we might tell them it's wrong to cheat or be nasty to their friends.

The law should be so flimsy yet it remains so strong, and does so through fear. But it's not the grown-up fear of the jackboot we suffer most, for there'd be no shame in that. The fear we feel is more akin to a playground panic, the sort which once overcame us when we knew we'd broken something, when we'd done something naughty. To this day the sight of a police car evokes such childhood dread and I hate that about them. But I guess I hate it even more about me.

Ask Richard or Sarah or me for that matter, whether the law is morally acceptable and you might face the paradox with renewed intensity. When Richard declared "you can't hit 'em back" he never actually said he didn't. And when you look at Sarah's mission, writ large in her unflinching stare, no mark in sight, the worst crime of all certainly doesn't seem so bad. And what about me? Pouring acid down my neck like there's no tomorrow (and the rate I'm going there might not be) in public, in a bar – Suey Cider is killing me softly with her warm embrace and the law won't lift a finger to stop her.

The law is no guide to morality when left in the hands of the powerful. They're the last people we should look to. We must shape the law, or it will shape us. New slogans for a new generation. But let me just remind you, there are no laws in the bubble my friend. I'm dying to get there by the way, aren't you? All this politics is giving me a right headache..

...and me a hangover, don't mind if I sleep through the next bit do you? It's not like anyone would notice my absence. Things are getting ridiculous, Sarah has joined the new Monday Club – she doesn't say anything, and never seems to listen. She just sits there and stares, lips made up like an Amsterdam transvestite, a moat of blood protecting the darkness which never speaks. Just what is her game? Do you know what the Monday Club is? I've been so rude. But I won't tell you just yet, I won't talk about how I met Nathan and the boys, you'll find out in time. Our time line is back to front remember, the first will be last, and anyway I never planned any of this.

Religious law tells us how we should live now societies have grown up. It is religious theory as it applies to modern societies. Religious salvation on the other hand is secured through a one-to-one relationship with God. That's why we have the story of the repentant robber nicking a last-minute cheap flight to heaven.

So why is it that so much of Christian teaching is about how humans should be towards each other while on earth, when the story of the robber shows us that salvation is about private repentance, not public action? Surely this sort of relationship does not need societies in which to exist – in fact it might be argued they somewhat cloud the issue.

According to the Good Book it seems it's better to murder and be sorry than never to have murdered at all, for the first man can repent and believe and slip right on through, while the second man can only look back on a life of being a nice chap. He never sinned so bad that he felt the need to repent. He never fell so low that he was forced to gaze to the heavens. And for this he's got as much chance of getting past Peter as me. And as he realises his name's not down, and peers through the pearly gates at the cheering failures who can't believe they blagged it on a wing and a prayer, he might well wonder what sort of paradise rewards the weak and desperate, the servile and the spawny.

Seems to me Religion's gone a bit red top, always looking for that front page splash, scouring the courts, the prisons, the alleyways, for the lowest of the low, the ultimate challenge, the ultimate story. But if we're all God's children then why concentrate so much on the wretched? Surely Mr Average deserves equal time. Still, whose ego can genuinely resist being told: "You saved my life. I was lost but now I'm found." I guess you just don't get that quality of cliché from the successful, the educated, they're nowhere near as much fun.

When it comes to the law religion cannot have it both ways. And if salvation's not possible through good acts then have the decency to retire to your private prayers and let the rest of us get on with making the law. I know we don't live in a religious state any more and you may think I'm making too big a thing of our churchy past, but I'm convinced it's vital we consider the origins of our legislature.

For we Brits have dared no revolution, we knock-kneed new boys have never chopped our Masters heads off and taken the reins. And such a wretched respect (of which we're bizarrely so proud) has left plenty of medieval stains on the rulebook.

One can no doubt argue that many religious laws make a lot of sense, but the church is guilty of some pretty hefty plagiarism if it's seriously claiming Moses was the first person to suggest that murdering your neighbour isn't actually such a nice thing to do. Do you really believe that until he got his tool out (told you I was proud to be English), poised to carve God's wisdom in stone, father was busy hacking son's head off just to test how sharp his knife was? (Although hang on a minute. Wasn't it down to one of God's mind games that a doting dad nearly did just that?)

If I had to market a religion which required belief in some pretty rich metaphysical conundrums about eternity, salvation, the trinity and original sin, then I too would dilute the mix with a few old gems about wives and goats and getting drunk. After all nothing makes sense like common sense. Yet they will never admit to having done this. All has come from God they insist, and his sauce will not separate, under any heat of scrutiny.

If we analyse Christian-based law then it tends to forbid those acts which go against God's will. So the wrongness of murder was stolen from the common sense of the common man and repackaged: "We're not interested in some circular silent pact between citizens to forbid that which if permitted would lead to the dissolution of the society which protects them," declares the Priest to the man stained with his own son's blood. "Your little misdemeanour is now forbidden for a new reason under a new law.

"And what's more," he whispers, with a tiny wink to the murderer, "for someone in your position I think you're going to find the conditions rather more favourable. For murder is an act of destruction against one of God's creations, and a pretty serious indication that you dear chap really need to buck your ideas up regarding the nature of the world and the person who created it and so forth. Here's a Bible for starters." But he's not even finished yet.

"Funny thing is," he adds with a chuckle, "for you there's plenty of time left to repent eh? Which is more than can be said for that poor mite you killed, who can only be judged on the life you cut so short. I know, I know - it's a funny old world alright."

But the link between the Law and the Lord needn't be revealed through such mockery, it's there for all to see. The evolution of legislation regarding homosexuality is a classic example of a law which sat happily outside the pragmatic concerns of maintaining peace, security and freedom, yet remained in all its glorious bigotry on the statute books.

One day we will all be made to feel very old by some incredulous chap who, pointing at our sickly frame clothed in its nursing home rug, whispers to his husband: "He can actually remember when it was *illegal* you know."

Restrictions on Sunday trading and drinking are the same. If I need a day off the booze **(and that fact is clearly not in question)** then that's a matter between me, my liver and my doctor - and I'll take it when I choose, right? **And it just so happens that Sunday is not a good day for me. All that free time, it's a day just asking for trouble. It's as much as I can do to wait until midday – wouldn't want to miss the Sunday/Monday/Tuesday club now would I? Not that they'll ever ask me to join, not that I'd ever know what to say if they did. Such coyness never used to matter in the good ol' days - when you're clever, a quiet demeanour can appear**

intriguing. But when you're a pointless pisshead no-one wants to hear your silence.

Still I guess some people alive now can remember when women weren't allowed to vote, which might suggest things are only going one way, the right way. But some parts of the world are going in completely the opposite direction, and theoretically that could happen here too. Laws don't change on their own, as if possessed by a sell-by date beyond which they simply fall off the rulebook. It is we who must ensure they keep pace with the hopes and dreams of those who must abide by them. Yet time after time, as if we took Moses too literally, we allow the worst to weigh us down like the heaviest stone, one which requires an army of selfless volunteers to sacrifice their time, energy, and even their lives, to drag it into the present day.

As secularism takes hold in western societies it might be tempting to sit back, put our feet up, and watch with a smug grin as one by one our archaic religious laws are repealed. But we must ask ourselves, what do we have left in this golden age? Law-making left to politicians with no guiding light beyond the desire to be re-elected every five years? Remember, power cares not whose robes it wears.

We may hope that through the process of parliamentary democracy whoever's in charge will do that which most people want. But we do not choose laws, we elect parties and politicians, our choice narrowed to two or three 'sets' of policies. What benefit is there ever, other than frugality or laziness, in choosing a set meal? Without fail it always tastes much worse.

I'm pissed now, I'm always pissed, but I've just had a thought (without words of course, why translate when no-one's listening). We might choose our politicians but we don't choose the political system. This duelling dualism inherited from history is barely comfortable with one new midget in the ring, although as long as he plays ref in the middle it appears the little tike can be tolerated. But the thing is, I've just been informed by Suey, who's surprisingly good with figures, that 15 is the smallest number of parties required to allow everyone to vote feeling a satisfactory degree of choice and representation. I fully intend to vote every election, I really do, but every time it's the same faces, the same faeces, and so I soil my ballot paper and Parliament's tedious tug-of-war remains in power.

Are we really happy being governed by the least shit? Have we lost all hope for anything better? I have. And actually it doesn't feel that bad.

Not only do these people come into power with a manifesto, they are not beholden to it once elected. What we need is some written guarantee which defines the proper role of Government.

But this will be no dictator's Little Red Book, quite the opposite. In it we will set out with complete clarity not only what a Government *cannot* do *to* us, but consequently what it *must* do *for* us. The means by which each party sets out to achieve this one agreed end ('to provide, protect and promote the means and space for each individual to create and pursue their private dreams') should throw up enough variety to hold some sort of election, and who knows maybe create some genuine interest, although I wouldn't hold your breath.

We must rid Government of all ambition and idealism, for their bloody pasts stain the whole political spectrum. What we need are experts in efficiency and management.

In an ideal world we would first want our physical life protected and promoted, through the Government's main responsibilities: the police, the economy, the health service, the transport system etcetera. And when that's done we would want them to do what they can for our private mental space, without ever, of course, suggesting what it might contain.

This mental element is more minor, for it actually belongs to us, but there is still plenty the Government can do, say, by providing an education which equips each individual with the three Rs, and instils a fizzing confidence in their own powers of innovation and creation. We want every child to leave school full to bursting with arrogance, with an unshaken belief in their own ability, just to give them a fighting start once they're set upon by we grisly grown-ups, shot through with a bitter worldly wisdom (which is nothing but a mask for failed ambition).

But we are not living in an ideal world, and the power we give Governments to *protect* our freedom will inevitably, if left unchecked be used to *restrict* it. Somehow we need to police the police.

Before we go on we need to look a little deeper at the thorny issue of freedom. It is a word used by politicians of all colours which in itself indicates its potency. But such malleability rings warning bells in the philosopher's head. We want meaning to stop spinning and be still, so we can all look at the same thing.

Put simply, there is positive and negative freedom. Positive freedom is the freedom to choose one's own actions, and includes what we might call the 'philosophical' freedoms (i.e. the freedom to speak, the freedom to associate etcetera). The opposite to this sort of freedom is control, here seen as a *bad* thing. Negative freedom is found along the winding mountain road with no barrier, the freedom of the poisonous snake cast into a playground full of children, a state of anarchy where our fellow man can cause us harm with no fear of punishment. The opposite to this sort of freedom is again control, but here seen as a *good* thing.

But there is a way of pleasing both camps, a way of bringing Law and Freedom together, rather than pitting them against one another.

Remember the mantra: "Do not do unto others that which you would not have them do unto you." Well in this lies the key to our beautiful reconciliation: "A man is free to do anything he wants, so long as in doing so he does not restrict the ability of his fellow man to do anything he wants, so long as in doing so *he* doesn't …..etcetera"

I call this circularity the Law of Freedom.

I charge my Government with the right to restrict my freedom whenever I'm trying to restrict someone else's. In exchange for walking around free *from* attack, I accept that I am not free *to* attack. So there is a pay off, there has to be. After all no-one wants anarchy - it's so noisy, so inefficient, so time consuming, and it smells just awful.

So it seems we must do our duty after all, but don't be afraid, for its to the society we desire, driven by logic, and logic alone.

Nathan expected this freedom and in return he restricted his own, that is to say he never put up a fight – I saw, I watched remember. Would I really do Nathan meself if I saw him again? Probably not, in fact definitely not – I know because I *have* seen him again. For guess who …. Now look here, don't give me that knowing sigh. I feel you all know what I'm going to say before I've said it, are you ALL reading ahead? Going on without me? I know I'm slower than I

used to be, and perhaps I don't walk as straight as I should, but time was when my word, my words, counted for something round here.

But I guess all I can do is keep dragging myself along fiction's unswerving tunnel to that paleness at the end, (oh *The End*! I can't wait and it's still not half time).

So, for the record: guess who's become the latest member of the neo-Mondays, and you've got to admire Richard for this one, his character's really fleshing out, moving on. You've guessed it, our Nathan. He sits there laughing and joking alongside the nameless face who nearly killed him, just like Sarah in many ways. Like some modern magus Richard surrounds himself with his victims, to share the very philosophy that brought them to their dying knees. Perhaps I too should go pray to Demon Dickie, for in many ways he's killed me too. I'm so drunk, and I'm not sure I can see a way back from this.

If the aim of politics is to provide and protect space for the individual, the biggest threats to this space are anarchy (not enough government) and dictatorship (too much government). So while we need some government to keep anarchy at bay, what will save us from too much government, what will save us from dictatorship?

After all it's not just each other we need protecting from. As deep thinkers we need certain philosophical freedoms to be protected: freedom to speak, to argue, to assemble, to associate, to criticise, to protest, to read, to write, to research, to publish, to communicate, to speak what's on our mind. It's our world, not theirs. We pay them remember, so they should be working for us.

Somehow we need to *guarantee* this relationship, this right to create our own society, and this is where a written constitution is vital in protecting the private freedoms which Government, any Government, all Government, is prone to restrict as it gives in to its own unquenchable thirst for power.

While Government laws stipulate what we *cannot* do, a constitution will protect those things we must always be allowed *to* do, regardless of the Government in power, like those rights enshrined in the American constitution. But while the Founding Fathers might have banged on about birth rights, we must not make the same mistake. It seems irrational sentimentality is a disease which infected that land from day one: "Geee … won't ya look at him? He's got his mama's eyes but they're definitely his papa's rights." It's when we get so lazy that rights are most open to abuse.

Rights are sold to the Left as a way of protecting the vulnerable worker, but history shows us they have in fact been far more effective to the Right. Look at America, the very founder of human rights, and ask yourself which ones it protects most vigorously. The Left right to a fair wage, food and freedom from exploitation, or the Right right to property and guns. We in the West may appear to bemoan the working conditions of the child in the Far East, but we wouldn't dare enforce his Left rights, for then we wouldn't be able to afford as much lovely property to protect with our Right rights.

So while protecting much that is good, the American constitution can be no blueprint for ours. The right to bear arms and the right to property are surely matters for the Government in its capacity as physical welfare officer. Their inclusion in the American constitution reflects the free-market spirit of that nation and its origins, as its forefathers murdered and pillaged their way across the Native American's homeland.

But I wouldn't want our constitution to remind us of any part of our history. We're looking for something more timeless, more optimistic.

But genocide aside, America was borne from an admirable mistrust in Government following its eventual victory over the imperialist Brits. Genuinely, I'm jealous. For all their faults, those early settlers recognised that Governments cannot help become players when they should be referees. They cannot help themselves legislating for morality and the mind, and no-one ruins their game like the tricksy philosopher, all skill and no position, given a free role in the middle to show off his detached cynicism, maddening level-headedness and damn compulsive truth-telling.

History shows that Governments have always sent out their dirtiest midfield generals to take out these free-thinkers: "In fact take 'im out in the first ten just to be safe." You may dismiss this as paranoia, but if there are hidden powers then I'm sure they've realised that conspiracy *theories* have a habit of remaining just that, they know such fantastical speculation always shields the guilty.

We voluntarily give the Government power to uphold the Law of Freedom but we know it will soon become bored as bodyguard. This is no wild accusation, it is based on observation which rings true from the very grass roots of politics to the heads of state, an observation of the sort of people that enter this game. The numbers who crave power and influence on both sides of the House far outweigh those who simply want to make the world a better place.

Perhaps in Ancient Greece at the time of the Philosopher Kings there existed some genuine altruism, but these days we are resigned to politics being submerged in personality, ego and power. If this were not true then people would not fight for their political careers, form secret allegiances, stab colleagues in the back, market themselves, employ campaigning tactics, campaigning teams, campaigning *experts*. If making the world a better place was all that mattered then surely they would be indifferent as to whether it was they or someone else who carried out that role.

But when a party gets into power, how much of the delight is borne from the opportunity to make the country better, and how much comes from having just won a contest, having just defeated the opposition? There would be no winning in my political dream world, just a constant stream of faceless experts doing their civic duty, for the anonymous love of the country and its people.

But enter the House and it's a different story. Victory and defeat are all that matter along those braying banks of pot-bellies, it's written all over their quivering smiles, the pink-cheeked prefects who never grew up, smirking and smarming across that petty divide.

When politicians admit ambition to become Prime Minister it is the rise up the ranks, the journey to power that so fixates them, not leading their country to greater glory. It's the adventure they crave, not the destination, for there's only one direction to go once one's reached the top.

This is why we need protection from Government, because it's a tank manned by a vociferous bloodthirsty army, bent on war, on victory, on destruction - the seating arrangement in the House expects and demands nothing less. Every argument, every vote, is there to be won or lost. And if a particular policy furthers their personal and ideological advance, then of course they won't care about the victims in the real world.

So long as they reach that magic 43 per cent at the ballot box then we lab test piglets can go to hell.

All Government cares about is winning the next election, and recent history has shown that a weak opposition is far more effective at achieving this then its own policies ever could be. "Don't bother yourself with the common man," goes Whitehall's brief to the new recruits. "The real battle's to be won right here."

But we shouldn't be surprised, all governments are logically peopled by winners, its the process which creates the beast. Our leaders were taught to treat politics as a game, a contest to be won, from the very start. Before they even set foot on the ladder they'd already seen off a handful of opponents. They had to win a nomination in their own party, they had to win their seat from their political opponents, then they had to win arguments in the House to impress their leadership. Each victory can only make that taste for blood stronger, a craving no doubt cultivated on those kiddy killing fields at school and university.

Is it any wonder these muckers rule our lives with such detachment? By the time they reach real power they've long become hardened by battle, by death. No chess player mourns the loss of a piece, all that matters is the result. Nothing personal, just a game.

But as things stand there is no check on parliament, its politicians and their police. We can't relax, tomorrow's another day.

So here we at last, face to face with Captain Starlet, matted robe stinking stiff with dirty dollars, jackboots jam-sticky with the blood of all nations, fat-fucker fists knuckled shut, ever-ready for war, for conquest, for victory. He may have fooled us all as a preppy in a bow-tie, but Cap'n Class has grown up now alright. Still, you've gotta laugh. It's not like we put up much of a fight.

While untrammelled capitalism has huge failings and its omnipresence must be rolled back at its frontiers, I could no more imagine a society without money, private property, supply and demand or business enterprise, than I could one without sex, drugs and sausage rolls. And who'd want to live without these things? Heaven can wait, and that goes for Christians *and* Communists.

However, although I'm no political idealist it doesn't mean the only good market is one without regulation. What I like about the idea of a market place is that theoretically the consumer's freedom of choice should push quality and value up, and profit margins down.

But this mechanism can only work when a greater political system carries out its constitutional duty to fight for and maintain a market which operates on a level playing field with a healthy number of players. For it is not the theory of supply and demand which keeps people poor, it is its abuse in the hands of ancient power games began centuries before the idea of a free market was ever suggested. The hysteria with which corporations dismiss any attempt to get the roller out reveals the modern market to be as fixed and phoney as anything dreamt up during the Soviet experiment.

And that its main players fight Government intervention at every opportunity tells us all we need to know about the shady origins of their market position (conveniently shrouded in the lawless mists of history) and more tellingly their fear of a fair fight.

For if everyone played by the rules then why are some accountants and solicitors more in demand than others?

Historical elites have never gone away, they've just changed clothes. There have always been two ways of making sure people buy your biscuits rather than those sold by Mr Singh next door. One is to make yours better value through hard work and enterprise, and the other is to get Daddy to bump off Mr Singh. It seems nothing kills off honest enterprise like a powerful giant, whether he be head of a left-wing Dictatorship or a right-wing Corporation. Raw power cares not for the labels we give it. The modern market might be a new battleground, but it's the same old games of power, pride and prejudice being fought out, and the government as arbiter has never been so weak. But this is a battleground worth fighting for. For it is not only our sense of fair play that's cheered up by a level playing field - efficiency, value and innovation may also start to smile.

One of the many failings of modern capitalism is its failure to appreciate that the value of a dollar is relative, and changes every time it changes hands. My $100 wage packet is more valuable to me than to my millionaire employer, but when he lays me off then he gets the $100, not me, and it's relative value, it's real value, is all but lost. The aggregate value of money, and as a result the sum of human happiness, is kept as low as possible by modern capitalism, which prefers to concentrate most money in the hands of a few. Surely the link between money and happiness is strongest amongst the poor not the rich, you get much more 'good' for your money if it's spent on poor people. Poor people care far more about money than the rich, given the chance they would look after it so much better.

A group of millionaires could get together and transform the lives of a whole African village, for ever, and not even notice the difference. Why don't we think this is weird? And why don't we think it's even weirder that each day they choose not to? It really is bad economics.

It seems the majority of people in the world are doing worse under the current system of untrammelled profit-maximisation than they would do under almost any alternative, even one devised by children, or monkeys.

Don't let them kid you that capitalism is an adequate end, for it's not an end at all. It's a means, a method, a system, and must be judged alongside any other in terms of happiness production. Soviet-style communism clearly ballsed up in that department but in the current game of global roulette we have a five billion in six billion chance of eating that bullet. Now that's shit odds by anyone's standards.

But the alternative is still tricky. As I said before, we've lived with money too long now to throw it all away. Perhaps we better talk hard cash. To my mind it's ridiculous to talk of wasting cash when it's *natural* resources which are genuinely under threat. For short of actually setting those dirty dollars alight, all we really do when we spend spend spend is give them to someone else, a game of pass the parcel where the music never stops. And to judge something a waste of money purely by analysing its benefit to the spender reveals a deeply misguided view of the potential of capitalism. Theoretically if my 'spent' money is now in the hands of someone who has the power to use it for the good of society in a way I could not (and yes I do mean in the commercial world as well) then the product I received in exchange is a bonus isn't it? Double-plus-good. Similarly if my purchase gives money to an organisation which only does bad then that knock-on effect must also be taken into account when I calculate the net benefit accrued from the item bought.

But throughout history we have maintained this childlike idea of wasting cash, by spending it in a way which doesn't benefit us as much as it might, regardless of any good it might do the trader. Such waste (when what they really mean is such poor market knowledge) has even come to be seen as immoral. If spending is the devil's work than it's clear what lives on the moral flipside, after all everyone knows that Jesus saves. But if there's anyway way of wasting money, or at least freezing its value, its potential, the happiness it can bring, then surely it's saving. It seems for some party poopers the music has indeed stopped.

Money which could be whizzing around the economy, being put to good use by a countless succession of owners, instead gathers mould under the mattress, or feeds the groaning gut of yet another 'friendly' bank, the schizoid smile of that High Street cashier belying that bare-knuckled bruiser's real job, as global loan shark sent out to knee-cap those already crippled by interest rates they could never afford in the first place.

I actually think cash can make you genuinely happy if used well. But it never will if it is viewed as an end, instead of a means. To my mind the worthy Protestant pensioner with her pot of gold under the bed has more in common with the mindless millionaire than she would like to believe, for those blind fools both see the accumulation of money as an end in itself. "You can't take it with you me love." Some clichés are just perfect aren't they? For how can money be an end? It is completely worthless until it is spent, until it is wasted, until it is gone. It has no value as cash – you can't eat it or drink it or build with it. Spend it, get rid of it – then you'll be truly rich, but still not necessarily happy. Sorry mate but this isn't the Bible, there is no moral symmetry in the real world, goodies won't always win and the baddies certainly don't tend to lose.

Take me and Richard (haha! Don't start me). Now in what way is our reversal of fortunes, connected with moral performance? I still can't figure it. You know what I think. Not only is someone else writing Richard but someone else is writing *me*! I've never felt less in control and for some reason I'm convinced that Sarah's involved. And just what the hell are those two lovebirds doing down the pub every week? She's even started talking! Now that would never have happened in my day I can tell you that. I think she read ahead, saw the ending I failed to write for her and got in someone else, someone who could put her mission back on track. And as she was paying she thought she'd get me back good and proper as well – I told you she never forgave me – and so here I slump, some country fete fart-arse, face-down in a barrel of apples, bobbing away with my fizzy new friend. Whatever.

The point is, money is *not* the point. Neither having money or spending money guarantee anything. Sit back now and think of those moments in your life which you can truly say have been your happiest. **(Are you taking the piss Sick Note?)** There is no need to sell yourself by your choice – this is a private exercise to be carried out within the confines of your bubble **(and believe me, we will be going their soon – bloody politics, no wonder we drink)**. Now being no mind-reader I would guess that love, friendship, family, football, personal achievement will be common themes running through your top ten moments. **(Now I *know* you're taking the piss)** It sounds a cliché but money and wealth are never really key agents in our happiest days. Even the success of our own business may be more about personal achievement, reaching a goal we set ourselves, the same pride we might feel after finishing a marathon, or a jigsaw.

Poverty obviously causes genuine unhappiness but once a certain level of comfort is guaranteed we are bound, at least once, to peer above the mists and see for ourselves that the most important things in life are far harder to achieve. Clearly such an exercise is just too terrifying for most people, so they duck back under the weather and carry on earning, desperately raising their personal comfort requirement to justify working all hours of the day, anything to avoid thinking, anything to avoid thinking of *that*, the horror in the skies that will haunt that poor soul forever.

For no matter what the adverts tell us, we cannot jump outside the bubble and become as one with that BMW, and neither can we bring it inside. Politics and business are trapped in the outside world and therefore can never lead to true long-term happiness. Put these henchman to work, to guarantee and protect a basic standard of physical life, but recognise when it's time to stand alone with that man in the mirror, when it's time to start asking the big questions.

But such soul searching is not for the first half. Right now we're just trying to reach the clouds, and that means creating, promoting and protecting a system which attacks poverty like we once attacked smallpox. Our cars might run quieter than ever but our beggars haven't changed in centuries. Poor people look so *historical*, they reflect badly on all of us. Why aren't we more ashamed?

One of the most cunning and successful qualities of capitalism, one which it's counterparts across the ideological spectrum must view with great envy, is its ability to define us all. As we spend we consume and we become a consumer, and that applies to the beggars the borrowers, the socialists and the Christians. It is this normalisation of the variety of human life which makes us feel so hopeless. It's so easy to believe the lies it tells us, that everything has a value, a cost, and none more so than time and space, the very pillars of reality itself. Is nothing sacred?

So instead of seeing the world and its people as rightly split into two, with those on one side who have enough time and space to consider the big questions, and those on the other side who don't, we take hold of some ropey rope ladder thrown down by Captain Starlet, each tiny increment, each tiny rung beckoning us higher, further, gnawing away at every spare second with its miserable pay rises and measly status symbols.

And that's why we don't give the beggar our money, because in the grand scheme of things we're all fighting to keep moving, we're all poor in relation to someone else. Captain Starlet is here to save us, to throw us a line, but as we take it we let him make us *all* needy. For once you buy into the capitalist dream then it does become all-consuming, and you will indeed be at its beck and call.

You need this today, but you won't tomorrow, because you'll need something newer, better. Consumer culture puts our life on hold until we die, never quite giving us enough to be satisfied, enough to move on. The dreams we're offered are never quite matched by the reality we buy, but rather than question the dream we always blame ourselves, we always blame our purchasing decision. Money can only buy frustration, each purchase designed to leave us wanting more. For the dealers know all too well that the point when you're satisfied is the point when your purse snaps shut. We call them possessions but they are in fact *possessors*. We like to think we own them, but they own us. They haunt us when we're not with them, they keep us awake at night - they're not worried about us, but we're sure worried about them.

Satisfaction maybe a corner stone of happiness but it's the enemy of capitalism. Satisfied people do not spend money. Satisfied people do not care for the new, the latest. Satisfied people do not consume.

Freedom, we are told, is no longer the ultimate human goal, that universal aspiration which has united the great struggles of human history against evil. "No, sorry me love, freedom's been moved next to the pasta." After all the struggle for freedom has already been won, and how can we tell? Because whaddya know? Two different companies, perhaps even three, are now offering us cheap spaghetti.

Now this poppycock would be all well and good if no-one was poor, shopping can be fun, or so they say tell me (personally I find nothing induces in me a wide-eyed frenzy of violence quite like a Saturday spent in the mall.) But remember how the system keeps the value of each dollar low by putting as many as possible in the hands of the rich. So just think what that tenner means to that beggar, and just think what it means to you. If he was starving and you were full, I'm sure you'd give him your cake. But when it comes to money I guess we're all penny-pinching piss flaps, who'll scrabble in the mud today for a coin we won't remember spending tomorrow.

What a muddy mess! First the saver gets it and then the spender. And I promise I will show you a way out of this paradoxical dead end, but for now let's continue our look at the suffocating expansion of consumerism, and wonder as we go whether we might imagine some new space for a new authentic consumer.

American political theorists rejoiced in the victory of the Western World at the end of the 20th century, which had now apparently become nothing less than a blueprint for human happiness. No more philosophy, no more history, no more ideology – apparently the burger boys had cracked it. While world events of the last ten years have effortlessly revealed the deep deficiencies in this anti-ideology, I believe it was clear on publication that the argument was at best circular, but in truth completely hollow.

Predictions about the end of history will only come true if we let them, their powers of persuasion are designed to make such prophecies self-fulfilling. These theorists were no dispassionate commentators, they were merely prescribing what must happen if their homeland was to achieve global dominance. One might argue they're giving the game away, for now we know what not to do, how not to see the world.

If we concede that "we can't beat 'em so we may as well join 'em" then of course the world will go their way. But that's not taking part in the political exercise, it's abandoning it, and the beggar too, his medieval grimace telling us all we need to know about our beloved progress. When I think of consumers I don't see empowered individuals making crucial life-affirming choices, moulding out a future full of meaning and beauty. I see shopping mall smackheads, grinning dribblers standing to attention in queues, transported from dealer to dealer in elevators and escalators. I see shabby shite sold as aspiration, blood, sweat and tears from an Indian factory boy barely left to dry.

We suckers are still doffing our caps, maybe not to the mucker's face, but certainly to his cut-price dream. I told you they had to be craftier these days. "Why bother creating beauty," they taunt us. "Why bother being a real player, when you can just buy their clothes and pretend?"

It's such a sham. The only thing that's *not* been stitched up is the clothes we buy off them, for the muckers need our dreams to fall apart at the seams just the same, every year in fact, every season.

There will always be a number one. No matter how many singles are bought, someone will have sold the most. All we can do is choose the best available, not the best possible because this is *never* made – Quality, like his brothers Satisfaction and Value, makes absolutely no financial sense, it's lost on us suckers who will only throw it away next year. We are obsessed with choice, but the greater the competition, the greater the need for advertising, and this endless need to boost marketing budgets can only see quality suffer. So instead we are sold ideas and lifestyles because they've run out of money to spend on the actual product, which has never felt so shabby.

All that matters is making something that will *sell*, winning the consumer choice, and as with politics it's just a game, a game that's won far quicker through defeating the opposition than by looking at those awkward issues of quality and value. Look at the food in our supermarkets. Dogs may have eaten better meat 50 years ago but that won't stop we worshippers filling our trolleys every Sunday morning. When did we become so hooked on bargains, on saving, on keeping our precious money? When did we turn our backs on butchers, bakers and candlestick makers? When did we change the meaning of good value to low cost?

There was a time when you couldn't buy poor quality goods because no-one knew how to make them. No siree, shabby shite is our very own invention, a homage to the modern world of which we can all be proud. But remember the western world is the aristocracy of the planet, this is no average existence. Chance of birth has given us one of the best deals going, and it's still this bad.

Still, you know what they say: "Never fear, China's here', and it's got five to one on those Burger Boys. Who knows, perhaps philosophy and the family *will* make a comeback, that would be nice. Perhaps we're at the *start* of an era, not the end – sorry boys but those corn dogs never tasted of longevity to me.

I've hit rock bottom. I've always had these rages you see, in my head, joy-riding monologues screaming out everything they pass as they race round the tangled road network my brain has become, no time for breathing, reflecting, indicating, braking.

But last night was different … if ever I needed proof that the dualism between our inner and outer world was never metaphysical, if for one night I ever really wondered just what the fuck a meta was *really* phor, it was last night alright. For before I could even get to the end of my private party piece I was being lifted armpits first out of my stool, dragged across the bar and discarded into the night. I know you've guessed this one, but everyone had heard everything, every word. And this was no mysterious transfer of thought through the power of telepathy, it was an altogether less mysterious process via the power of shouting. I had apparently stood on my stool like the pub drunk and let them all have it. I caught Richard's eye on my way out, and I tell you, if looks could kill. He thinks I'm scum now, they all do, you do too, I know. It's not even half time and I've no idea what the score is. Mind you I could do with a rest, a lie down, that's obviously what the landlord thought as my head hit the pavement with no witnesses to count me out.

I can see the fur rising along the back of those corporate cats, but if burger bars can persuade us to by their pet food, then why must I keep quiet about philosophy? And art? And beauty? Seems to me if people try and persuade you to choose a lifestyle which can be quantified in cash then that's fine – it's advertising, it's an essential part of free-market choice. But if people try to persuade you to choose a lifestyle which is free – then they are commies, loonies, enemies of freedom (i.e. enemies of money). Capitalists are terrified of philosophy – because cash is not changing hands and that's just not cricket. I'm sure the church should consider offering religion on a monthly subscription, or even charge an admission fee. People feel so more comfortable paying for something, so less suspicious. "Best if everything goes through the books, me love, 'bove board y'see."

And don't even mention those people who dare to 'make their own'. It seems the greatest suspicion of all is reserved for those beardy-weirdies: "You make your *own* sandwiches for work? What are you - some sort of kiddy fiddler? Why don't you join in? Just what is *wrong* with you?"

I'm not saying the good life is lived in wooded communes away from normal society, and I hope I've already made my feelings clear on the political limitations of the acoustic guitar, but at its most intense we will certainly have no company and no audience, you'll see. But for now I'm merely asking you to consider what a rough deal we're dealt by consumerism. The relationship is abusive, commerce will always sell us short, stitch us up, so the only way to play it is to be abusive back, and then walk off to our own world, the real world.

You'll never guess where I woke up after my unforgettable dabble with the pub-rage I could never remember? Richard's sofa of course. He never forgets a mate that one. And other things have changed. I also talked to Sarah and she doesn't hate me either, well certainly not as much. We did a deal, see, and now me and her are cool, perhaps there isn't another author, another book after all – as theories go I can see now that it was a little far-fetched.

Anyway things are looking up – my pants are clean, they're almost dry, and I'm actually looking forward to the second half, apparently things will get better, a lot better. Still a few minutes to go in this one though, play to the whistle and all that.

We're coming to the end of the first half now, the interval is fast approaching, and I feel I should make amends. If you think I have been suspiciously hard on socialism then you may be right, perhaps I have indeed protested too much. I guess I'd always considered myself left wing, but since writing this book, since realising that a philosophical account of the world pisses on anything politics has to offer, my disillusionment has at times turned rather bitter. I fear the abandonment of that which once raised so much passion has in turn inflamed my criticism.

Perhaps my philosophy really shouldn't stick the knife in so hard, for while it does so the incessant March of the Market continues. As the world speeds into the mists of the technological age and beyond, a stifling lack of confidence hangs in the cold wet air. Terror descends as we powerless paupers scamper nowhere fast, sandwiched by a shameful past and a fearsome future. And we're right to be scared. If the growth of right wing economics continues unchecked then its main players will soon be more powerful than any Government, for they're already more powerful than most. *Then* we'll start to see what a super power without democratic mandate is really capable of. You thought the Soviet Union was bad? You ain't seen nothing yet.

Something needs to be done, before we forget how *radical* these marching henchmen really are, how idealistic are their beliefs, how passionate is their desire for dominance. There's nothing natural or universal about Indian child slaves sewing our trainers together.

Left-wing politics, or rather a left-wing approach to economics, must somehow be liberated from the heavy hearts and heavy industry of last century – it must be rescued from the history books and stripped of its yawnsome vocabulary.

Ah! The fresh faced rallying youth, screaming left-wing truths from the swaying folds of a huge red flag, such heart-racing imagery, I love it, or rather I loved it. I'd understand anyone who joined the Communist Party for aesthetic reasons, really I would. But you could also argue the Nazis scrubbed up okay. Leather boots *and* a tash? Concentrated camp indeed.

Socialism must be seen as a direction not a destination, a means not an end, we must be *socialist*, not socialists. We must become actors, not members, card carriers are so easy for the enemy to spot. But socialism as a movement, an attitude, can only be a force for good considering the state we're in now. At its best it is a drive for fairness, compensating for historical injustice through the redistribution of corporate wealth, providing genuine opportunities to improve one's situation with a free state education, and constructing a universal safety net to catch those whose honest endeavours fail.

But at its worse it removes incentives to work hard, and encourages people to do the minimum. At its worse its messages of equality regard humans as essentially the same, with the same needs, wants and desires. At its worse it demotes and dismisses all that is not work-related, like art, privacy and adventure. And at its very worse it ignores freedom of thought, freedom of disassociation and democracy itself, treating those who disagree with its tenets as at best misunderstood, and at worse mentally ill.

But I will show you dear reader that despite the hopeless failure of socialist states in the last century, we have all taken a left turn, and there are not many who would want to turn back. If socialism is a cure for the worst maladies of a cash-based society, then we can see that it is a medicine we have swallowed many times, and continue to do so. Perhaps we shouldn't be so hard on ourselves.

Let me take you back to the time of the workhouse, and the town factory, to a time when huge families lived in one room, to a time when sickeningly rich factory owners held violent sway over the impoverished masses, to a time of no progressive tax, no free education, no free health service, when a working class person would have found it easier to marry a Martian than someone from a different class, when women regardless of intelligence or ability were rearranged into teenage wives and raped until they died, when pregnancy out of wedlock resulted in shame and homelessness, to a time when there were no human rights, no right to protest, no freedom of speech, to a time when religious freedom would have been seen as evil, and punished under the cruellest laws of blasphemy, to a time when only the rich were allowed to vote, when only the rich were allowed to rule, and the very idea of democracy would have been laughable, even to those who might have benefited.

Meet Harry. We'd go for a drink but he's got neither money or time, he's normal remember. So we'll just have to knock on his door. "Now then Harry," I venture, hand over mouth as he opens the cover to his cesspit. "We've very little time to waste," I continue, with no little haste, for I swear I'd puke over his squirming litter of runts if I was actually to set foot in that place. "Won't be long," he assures his wart-whiskered wife.

(But in fact dear Harry you're going to be away for 200 years which is quite some time to be popping out. But she'll never know – for it's time to board my time-traveller, it's time to follow the Red Brick Road.)

I show him our schools, our hospitals, I show him the average man, I show him parliament and I show him the police, and I show him peace on our streets (my friend, you have no idea quite what a bunch of old hippies we've become over the last two centuries). I show him money, I show him the workplace, I show him leisure time, and I show him our courts (funny, that's one place he didn't seem that surprised by, that and the railway tunnel for the homeless).

I tell him about progressive income tax and state benefits, I tell him about the minimum wage, and what that can buy you, I tell him about rights to free education and free health care and let me tell you our Harry is in tears. He is trembling, he tells me, with happiness at what is to come, but I can see in his eyes he also trembles with fury at what he must return to.

Poor Harold, I'm sure he doesn't believe half of it. But then I tell him about equality for women, cripples, homosexuals and blacks, and he shoots me a fearsome look I'm convinced I've seen somewhere before. If I don't take him back now I swear he'll start to recoil, and even start sticking up for the heap of shit he calls home. And there's another reason I want to take him home, why I want to be rid of this human turd. As I wave goodbye at his sewer door a huge feeling of emotion wells up inside. Don't worry I'm not going soft on you, for this is no compassion, just raw regret, for I should have shoved that sniffling buffoon and his fated sperm out of our time machine when I had the chance. But then I guess we'd have had no Ratty either....

But anyway, Richard is still my friend! Oh happy happy days. I know – big turnaround, and while I was at Chez Ils I sure found out a few things, a few home truths about their home. The crying is *unbearable* at that place, I'll tell you more later, there's no time now. But believe me I'm going to break this fiction thing, I'm going to take control, I'm going to give Sarah back her mission, we've discussed everything. So if you see a spring in my step when I take to the field for the crucial second period you'll know why – I'm back alright.

But taking a long view of history is not the only way to see left-wing sentiment alive and kicking. Communism is alive and well among communities of friends all over the world, who give without receipt, who come together for nothing other than mutual earthly happiness, who crave laughter and warmth, a genuine space in which to be themselves, a place which cares not for profit, status or image. So I won't hear anymore about the death of socialism, not while you're giving your mates interest-free unconditional loans and free advice for no other reason than an improvement in their lives is a good thing *in-itself*, as you might see an improvement in your own.

Right-wingers might argue that friendships are essentially selfish bonds, underscored by an unspoken understanding, and our favours are nothing more than insurance payments for when we might need help ourselves, but this clearly isn't true. It may be at the start, when we're trying to suss each other out, but once both sides are happy then the favours become natural, emotional, automatic. And how we cherish and parade these unions, as arm in arm we glide gracefully above a street strewn with dirty dollars.

So just what is preventing this precious system from being enlarged, or at the very least analysed, admired, aimed for? Why are we *expected* to shaft every stranger we meet? If the circumstances of your own existence is random, then its random squared for your set of friends. Which table at which class at which school, the clubs you chose, the college you chose, the jobs you chose and those that chose you. You might like these people, I'm sure you love them, but they're not *actually* special, they're only special to you.

The tiniest change in the path you took as a youngster would have separated you guys forever, I'm sorry but deep down you know this to be true. And if you can treat this random rabble of misfits with such selfless devotion, then why are you so wary of those you just happen not to have come across? We all know a stranger is just a friend we haven't met.

We insist on absolute fairness and equality in our daily life with the people closest to us, yet scoff at such benchmarks for the financial world. Even the armed robber, arguably the most unfair of all businessmen, would object if his best mate, not him, were executed as punishment for his deeds. We all immediately recognise unfairness on a micro level, and will turn blood-boilingly indignant on any number of occasions: witness the violent reaction from a long queue when someone saunters to the front, imagine the gut-wrenching anger we feel when after a long and intricate board game we realise the winner had been cheating all along.

Yet when we proud guardians of such selfless justice are questioned about the fact our wages are as low as possible, the fruits of our labour priced as high as possible, and the difference is split between our double-barrelled boss, his lazy son and a faceless horde of shareholders, the response is always the same. A raise of the eyebrow, barely a shrug. "C'est la vie," we say, dismissing the system as nothing more than an itch, as we dribble with glassy-eyed reverence at the latest Royal Wedding. How can this be? Why does unfairness on a national scale not extract the same venom we discharge in our everyday lives? Short changed in the corner shop? "Just you try it sunshine." Short changed for a lifetime in the workplace. "Oh go on then you little tike – you talked me into it."

Now before I admitted that I could not imagine a society without money or commercial choice, and we should be rewarded for effort and enterprise. If someone has a dream and is prepared to work all hours of the day to make it come true then he should be rewarded for this. But what about aptitude – how should this be dealt with?

We know the man who works more hours should get paid more, but should the man who is more productive or more beneficial to society get paid more *per hour*? Should there be differentials in wage *rates* as well as income, just because we are simply born with an aptitude for the better job? Well, yes. Not because that's inherently fair but considering how used to inequality we've become, I can't imagine any other system that could realistically *work*.

If we need an expert job doing then we have to be prepared to pay that expert enough for them to think it's worth the effort. But the fact remains that those with aptitude must realise their privileged position, and must be prepared to pay for it. No tax system should take all extra income, for we couch potatoes need motivation like we need salt and butter, but tax has got to be seen as payment, not punishment. Instead of moaning "the more I get paid the more I get taxed", we must turn the phrase around, for surely the more we get taxed, the more we're getting paid, right?

Be proud of the contribution you are making to your society. It is you who are paying for the nurses, teachers, firemen and doctors, that noble band of public workers who have opted out of the money game to face life's bigger challenges.

Does anything make the blood boil quite so much as the millionaire pop star who looks for financial holes, for *weaknesses*, in the system, in the society which gave him so much, finally turning his back on his country, his fans, because taxes are lower off shore? *Who do you think made you rich you fucking cunt?* Who do you think paid through the nose for that modish over-priced vacuity you dare to call art? It's the business, the *system*, that lined your pockets, not your paltry talent. People will buy any old toss if it's marketed right, you more than anyone must realise that. Some poor bastard's saving someone's life right now for a pay packet that would shame your cleaner, and you plagiarised a couple of corny anthems. Yet you still claim you *deserve* the tenner he coughed up for that work of genius, that somehow it's *rightfully* yours? You're a lottery winner mate, nothing more. Right face, right time. If you're gonna leave then fuck off by all means, but not before you've given us our money back.

Sorry about that, but the public purse simply must get bigger, much much bigger, and that's easier done by those with plenty of low-value dollars spilling out of their designer pants than by those whose pennies are worth so much more. To abuse the vocational motivation for society's most challenging jobs with low wages is a shameful reflection on all of us, it is capitalism at its most ruthless, most heartless, and it poisons our society from top to bottom. We must all do much better, and that includes you Gerald. Gerald?

Can you hear me Gerald? Can you hear me over the bleep of your artificial heart? Poor Junior here has worked round the clock to save your life, to patch up your pathetic injuries after that gin-soaked skid in a ditch, earning less this month than you did this morning from the shares you sold in that trainer company.

Gerald? Can you hear me? Are you going to tell that loop-hole magician you call an accountant he's no longer wanted, are you going to promise to pay Junior properly, or shall I pull that tube out right now? Junior won't – he's committed, he's one of the good guys, the sort of person you secretly mock on a bath night. He has a vision of what a human should do for the society that protects him, he's giving what he can and he'd sure love to take what he needs, but he can't. Because someone's had their sticky fingers in the till, someone's been siphoning off his fair share, off shore somewhere I think. So instead he takes what he's given, which isn't even close to what he needs. The deal is falling down at one end Gerry boy. Someone's not paying up, and I think we all know who that is.

Am I arguing these people should be named and shamed in their local neighbourhood, their pictures posted on tree trunks next to the kiddy fiddlers? Well let's see. Let's listen in on Pete the Perv as he negotiates with the law makers.

PP: "We all know I like young children, the younger the better, and if you make it illegal to fiddle with the middle then the very young are gonna get it, for if I'm going down anyway then I may as well go down in style, right? (I hope you're following this – I really don't want to see him again). So let's compromise, you make it legal to fiddle with the middle, and I'll leave the little ones alone."

Now what do you think Mr Law Maker's response should be? Of course – we all know.

LM: "No compromise Mr Perv. It is your duty not to fiddle as it's wrong, immoral, damaging. This situation is not about you after all, it's about us. Your picture stays up on the tree."

So what might this charming little scene teach us?

Let's listen in on another conversation with the law makers, let's see how Gerald gets on, fresh out of hospital, back on his feet, ("oooh they were fantastic darling, you should have seen him, and a coloured too, absolutely marvellous to me he was.")

G: "We all know I don't like paying taxes, who does, but if you put the higher bracket up 20 per cent then you're going to lose the lot I'm afraid. (I hope you're following this – I really don't want to see him again). So let's compromise, you make it 40 per cent maximum rate and I'll promise to be a good boy and pay up properly. Otherwise someone else will get it, all of it."

Now what do you think Mr Law Maker's response should be? Of course – we all know.

LM: "No compromise Gerald. It is your duty not to fiddle with the system as it's wrong, immoral, damaging. This situation is not about you after all, it's about us. Your picture stays up on the tree."

It was me who did him in the end you know – not like you think, I'm no housing estate vigilante hunting out the nearest paediatrician, but you can't deny it was me in the end. I just didn't know it would be that way.

And finally, before we leave the political world for good, before we come in from the cold and enter the inner world, might I share a final thought, an idea that, God forbid, *might actually work.*

If the law of supply and demand genuinely policed our free market, like the vendors tell us it does, then surely we'd get we want, and logically always would do, right? But clearly we haven't, not in this weird weird world where high quality has become a marketing gimmick, our children's food is made from hosed-down carcases and our hi-tech home entertainment is snapped together by child slaves.

Remember my promise to face the consumer paradox, to see if there might be a third way which avoids both mindless saving and mindless spending. Well put simply, the answer is to spend wisely, and to do that we need help, some expert direction, so my humble idea is this: let's expand and universalise the system of quality marks which already operates in many markets and then give consumers the choice. Then we *will* truly get what we have asked for. In maters of politics, description is better than prescription, it's always better to reward good practice than punish bad.

So while we may never kill the capitalist machine, or may never want to, we can create a force of our own, which will push in the opposite direction. After all it's not money we hate – it's what's done with it. No-one wants to live in some cash-free six-string commune overseen by Big Brother and Nanny State, we humans are just too individual, too private, too grouchy, for that. But these Communist Theme Parks don't have the monopoly on economic justice and market fairness, anymore than big religions have a monopoly on being nice to our neighbours. So here goes:

I imagine a world where graded quality marks appear on everything we buy. Producers will be marked on a range of non-profit-making qualities (i.e. standard of ingredients, treatment of employees at both ends of the pay scale, level of eco-damage/repair in the production process, community projects supported etcetera).

It will then be up to the producer to apply for this standard, a process they will pay for themselves. The application will be assessed by a non-profit making democratic Ango (for there must be nothing queasy this time) which Government is bound by law not only to fund but also to stay well away from. Remember, we will have a constitution by then where we can put useful stuff like this.

There might be some sort of election process to this wonderful protectorate, where leading figures in society would campaign for our vote, treating temporary membership of this elite force for fairness as one of the highest civic achievements society can bestow.

It will become a matter of public knowledge (again by Law) when an organisation applies for its grading, and a matter of public knowledge as to what mark it achieves and why. We do it to our poor schools and hospitals for God's sake, we're forever beating up on the public sector, yet we ignore those who most deserve such scrutiny.

I imagine it being a matter of great national interest when a new set of standards are calculated and announced for another sector of the economy, as little by little the whole market place is covered (or not) in these little stars, finally providing an effective practical anti-capitalist badge to wear with pride - perhaps we just needed to ditch the sickle after all. And imagine the shame if a company was found to have gone back on its promises, for any company who earns the stars must also pay for us to confirm their ongoing legitimacy through regular inspection, and be prepared to lose them.

But listen guys, this is not more red tape to trip you up. This is about making life better for everyone. Imagine the pride as you score top marks on live TV – imagine the marketing opportunities. Increasing sales just got easier didn't it, by increasing quality and treating your workers better – now surely that wasn't so hard.

And it wouldn't just be fast food, American clothes and electrical appliances that would be assessed, although somehow I imagine they'll be first in the firing line. There's also those mainstays of consumer nightmares – plumbers, builders, estate agents, holiday companies. And how would you know whether a certain firm has their stars or not? Simple, each household would be delivered a big Directory of Quality Marks along with their phone book.

But the real genius is that there is absolutely no obligation for any company to apply for these stars, *it's up to them*. They can always take the chance no-one cares about fair pay, animal cruelty and the environment. I know this isn't a new idea, and many industries already have award systems, but I think they are weakened and ultimately ignored in their mismatched multiplicity.

Knowledge is the greatest weapon against profit-maximisation, it's time us consumers were given true power, properly-organised power.

And who knows, things might start to taste better, people might start to get paid more and things might not fall apart after a year. Or things might stay the same and the socialist cause will be dead forever, and rightly so. For if we knew every dirty trick played by the corporate giants, and *still* bought their stuff, then we have truly been supplied the society we demanded, and deserve.

Perhaps this fiction thing will turn out okay. I've a lot of ground to make up I know, sorry for getting so pissed so soon. Guess I was just a bit nervous at meeting you. We've already come half way and I feel we've barely spoke. But things will be different now, I promise. Time at last for those oranges.

Interval

Sarah and I have done a deal. I told her I could sort it. So would you if you'd been there, if you'd had to lie there with me at the break of day, listening to that bird wailing. And as each tear dropped like acid into the gash tattooed across my face I realised I had to take action. So I lied as I lied, some lie-in that was. So Sarah and I have done a deal. I told her I could sort it. Do I feel bad? Not really, certainly not any worse, apparently they're not doing relegation this year so I've been given a reprimand, a sabbatical. I feel no rules now, a ten-nil loss is a ten-nil victory. It's not the winning that matters, it's the finishing. So Sarah and I have done a deal. I've issued her a licence to kill and we're a team now. I guess we all need at least one friend. Do I feel bad? Not really, certainly not any worse.

My framework of human existence, as one made up of an inside and outside world, may sound like a classic dualism stolen from the traditions of philosophy, yet I cannot stress enough that the distinction is *metaphorical*, not metaphysical.

Dualist philosophies of old largely followed the same structure: there is an ideal realm of perfect essences which while logically beyond the reach of our senses, somehow still manages to drive the physical world we experience. And I'll not deny the sentient limits of human observation, but just because our fading eyesight can't see a particle and our failing science can't see the farticle lurking in its shadow, it doesn't follow that there's an angel hiding behind both.

I too believe there is a reality which escapes the observations of science, but it has nothing to do with Our Father *or* Our Farticles. The true essence of reality, the aimless agent which infuses this whole universe, *inside and out*, is sheer naked existence, indifferent to the judgement of man, the utilitarian labels of his language and the pompous measurements of his science.

Yet we suckling weaklings are so desperate to believe there was some Parental Benevolence which gave birth to our existence, that we live the lie anyway. We imagine spirits and souls, but they're nothing but the ghosts of our imagination, set free to flicker over an indifferent landscape. Like the man with no friends we send ourselves birthday cards and feign surprise and delight when they arrive.

Time is a succession of unique moments, space is a mass of meaningless matter, and only the courageous can face up to this world as it really is. Ultimately we are all alone, abandoned in the here and now, with no language to express its sickening depths, no words, no numbers, no science. In this sense genuine Understanding will remain forever private, much more akin to a feeling, a *nausea*.

We invented language, it is our baby, our blanket, and it sure makes us feel confident doesn't it? But the real world to which it refers, well that was here when we arrived and will still be here when we're long gone. We might care, but *it* certainly doesn't.

I hope Sarah realises things could all change, but I doubt it. She's a lost cause that one, living proof if ever we needed it that existence does cause essence. There she was, back in the 50s/60s/70s with Stan and Jan the Man, whoever ... and things were fine, just fine. She never bothered reality and it never bothered her, like the rest of her clan she clothed herself in humanity and just got on with life. Keep your head down, keep talking, and before you know it your dead, after all what else is there?

But it all changed that night, *Oh What A Night!* The night of which so little is remembered and even less is spoken. For now there is nothing, no thing, to speak of. She took it bad, our Sarah, what mamma puss wouldn't, but I mean real bad. The hands on her clock literally stopped, jammed high above her head in fright, marking for eternity the time when time called it a day. Time can be no healer without its healing hands, and our Sarah has been sick ever since.

She knows the empirical lie, these silent carriers of the darkest secrets, they all do, mouths sewn shut by those nights they can't remember, or can never forget. I used to think the Confessional was a microphone for the Drama Kings and Queens, and to many it might be, the one stage on which talking about themselves was encouraged, indulged even. But when I met Sarah I saw how dark a secret could become, I saw the time-bending space-munching weight of that black hole, born during the night of which nothing is said, and I realised that some people do have secrets, real secrets.

Not the petty confessions we set free to wriggle beneath the surface of our moistened eyes, desperate they be fished out like a cracker joke at Christmas and read aloud to a sympathetic jury. I'm talking proper dark secrets, those kept by the abusers and the abused. These people know the empiricist is a liar, they know that some things never change, that there are God-awful lands which time has genuinely forgot. They know that the early Christians were right (before it all went weekly) and there is actually a horror bigger than us all, a creator of sorts directing our every movement, driving our pathetic existence through the murky shallows of time and space.

But of course it is no lie, Sarah and Richard should read more philosophy, and they're not the only ones. The created cannot turn on their creator, that's just for sci-fi movies.

What was born from one night can be no bigger than one night, a pointless snapshot of care-free existence. We all look for meaning in a meaningless world, and none more than the givers and getters. They cannot help but ask why, but as any death camp guard will tell you, there is none. When the clock stops, could be it just needs a new battery, when the music stops perhaps the plug has been pulled out. Reality isn't affected by complicated lives; we may care, but it *certainly* doesn't.

Is someone who lies to themselves still a liar? Probably. So do I feel bad telling Sarah, the biggest liar of the lot, that I could sort it? No, not yet. If the truth doesn't matter then why should lies? They're only words, and are far happier fibbing, you'll see.

I believe that language itself lies at the source of our misunderstanding of essences and ideas, a language which has allowed the growth of science and religion, both of whom rely on a notion of achievable truth, and are eternally damned because of it.

The scientist and the religious believer are often bedfellows in my world – my world of noble cynicism, desperate humility and pointless change. For the extent to which they both believe that immutable truths can be exposed and expressed by humans, is the extent to which they are cuddling up my friend. But I for one will not enter their smutty boudoir. Life's too short - I want to be out in the fresh air, looking learning thinking. You know where you are with movement, with verbs, ask the terrorist, he'll tell you.

Whoever contrasted science with religion failed to see how much each borrows from the other. They failed to see the pragmatism which underscores a successful religion, the

MESSAGES FROM THE DEAD

leap of faith which precedes scientific discovery, and the irrational belief they share that humans are somehow operating at the centre of the universe.

Some of you might detect a hint of postmodernism in my outlook, and it is indeed true that I believe science performs at its best when it is aimed away from objective truth, but that doesn't mean the only remaining target is power. When did genuine happiness and comfort become so unfashionable? Power is so dull, so *vulgar*, its disciples take life far too seriously. All that effort, all those words, all those suits, and for what? Gerry on the bleep, that's what.

Take Americans on the other hand, with their gridiron streets and gridiron sport, their gridiron teeth and gridiron talk – always trying to force the beauty of real life into the crude constructs of geometry. Their scientists would have us believe they're deconstructing the mysteries of the mind, but to me they're mimicking the machines the rest of us treat as servants. If man and computer are enjoying a meeting of minds in that land then it's clear to me who's moved most to clinch the deal.

But one man's exploration is another man's decimation, and like their ancestors they cast aside that which they cannot explain, dropping Might is Right from a very great height on a reality they rarely consult. Lest we forget, it was they who wiped out the race which understood best of all man's place in nature, it was they who deformed generations of farmers now and forever with their sprays of war, and it was they who killed 200,000 with two bombs. Force has a way of becoming Truth. What irony, for it seems those God-fearing burger boys may be the biggest postmodernists of the lot.

Let's take a closer look at the two great truth-seekers allowed to roam that land, science and religion, these man-made monstrosities who now seem to be taking it in turns to turn on us, their Creator. If the philosopher's job is to compare and contrast, then lets see which hymn sheets this terrible twosome might both be singing from. And ultimately if I can strip them naked and dress them in something far more suitable, then my job, for this part, will be done.

For a start - miracles happen all the time. All we really need to declare an event a miracle is for it to be beyond our scientific understanding, and it remains so until scientific knowledge has in some way caught up with it. Rainbows, lightning, thunder, volcanoes – we're all born into a spectacular physical world which, if we were to step back for one minute, we might admit is in large part counter-intuitive, if not utterly miraculous.

If you want to see a real life magic trick, film an apple rotting to nothing over a few days and speed the footage up when you watch it back. The Greeks said the Gods did it, and we've replaced the Gods with equations, but the rainbow remains. We allow poets and scientists all manner of metaphor to describe the physical world, yet are quick to scoff at the Ancients for ascribing thunder to the Gods. But go and stand out in a storm, a proper storm, and tell me which description leaves you most satisfied, which description best accounts for the terrifying enormity of that explosion above your head. Science may explain things, but it can't explain them away.

As a child, as soon as we wonder at the impossibility of life we are immediately put *right*, the beauty is explained to us in terms of cause and effect and the magic, which we are told is *wrong*, is gone. But if the world's miracles are merely the contents of the scientists' in-tray, then perhaps we are all the poorer for our relentless attempts to empty it. Take a break white-coat man, or at least think about something useful, hungry babies cry whether time bends or not.

If science is to be given public support then it must do its public duty, and it will be all the richer for doing so. This is superform.

By furthering scientific discovery purely for the pleasure of humans – whether it be the solar car or the healthy fag – they will better realise the essential humanity behind scientific knowledge.

That science so often looks to the stars reflects poorly on our relationship with the subject and its practitioners, but ultimately it is our science to do with what we will. A new breed of scientist must emerge, one who sets human happiness as the ultimate goal, the ultimate truth, the ultimate test of a successful experiment.

There is much talk in modern science about coherent final solutions. Not only, we are invited to believe, is there one defining principle powering nature and science, but when we discover it, it will indeed be something beautiful to behold.

Sarah is a great believer in coherent final solutions – but she's no Nazi, she really only has one in mind. And of course we've done a deal, let's not forget. Yeah whatever, in my book deals aren't worth the words that speak them, and this *is* my book by the way. I'm taking back control.

Because quite frankly I've had it up to here with this lot. Imagine it, first outing in the realm of fiction, first go at a story, and who turns up for the audition? I had no idea did I? Sure, I was expecting a challenge, but I didn't count on a mutiny. I guess you need a reputation to attract the biggest names. So is this the deal? Is this the band of pirates who couldn't cut it anywhere else?

There's clearly been interest in Richard, and I take credit for that. He should remember me if he makes it big (What's that you say? You're *missing* him! Well go fuck yourself. I told you, I'm taking control again. Read some other story if you want to catch up with dear old Dickie – and personally I reckon it's cruel to feed other people's pets.) But for now it's just me and Sarah. We done a deal, a done deal indeed. Richard can wait (okay .. if I'm honest I don't know where he is, I just hope he'll turn up for the end).

But Sarah cannot and will not have her way. There will be no happy ending for us, or me or her or anyone else, in fact the rate this is all going I wouldn't be surprised if there wasn't an ending as such at all. Don't get worried, this will *finish*. You can feel between your fingers how long there is to go. Just under half, so don't panic, don't put me down, don't drop me, not you as well. (Has Richard dumped me? You know I think he has. Is there any greater shame? Who knows, since me and Suey met I seem to have misplaced all mine. They say pride comes before a fall, but they don't tell you how sharpish it leaves before you're even up again.) I've had it up to here with this lot. There will be no Final Solution for our Sarah, no perfect moment, no destination reached, giving meaning to her journey, essence to her sorry existence. Sooner I get shut of this lot the better I reckon.

In this way science and religion are coming together – haven't you noticed how these enemies of auld are starting to talk and look the same? Two sides of the same misspent coin. They both pedal eternal truths about the universe, they both trumpet the existence of some beautiful indestructible timeless constancy behind our ever-changing physical world, and they are both convinced humans will somehow recognise it when they see it.

But beware my friends, for this is a dangerous union which each partner would wish to propagate for their own devious and political ends. We must steel ourselves with deep scepticism whenever we come across this terrible twosome.

For ailing failing religion would love to bring science on board - what a PR coup that would be, dismissing in an instant those recurring charges of being detached from common sense. And science too could use a softer sheen. Its sterile image sure needs a makeover and it would love to embrace or our intuitive obsessions with life after death and a world by design.

But as any German will tell you, there's only one way the old Grand Unified Theory is heading, and that's towards the Grandest Of The Theories, why that can only mean one thing. Good God! They haven't even tried to hide it. We simply must let go of the idea of a knowable truth, a privileged discourse. Scientists are making the religious assumption about simplicity and design, and setting it as their goal. But to assume that a final answer will be expressible in the infant tongue of dear old blighty – well, it's just too ga-ga for words, which I guess is why they carry on as they do, because words are all those white coat dummies *can* do.

They are looking for constants in a world of fluctuation, trying for closure in a world that's open, and they will find their constants, and no doubt they will find their closure, but like a leaf left to flutter among the winds of a wasted sky, their words, their equations, will float forever.

Do you think Smorkrons care what temperature water freezes at for us lolly-lovers? Our zeros are human, our axes are arbitrary and our language is only understood on planet earth, where infinity in fact means really big, never the jaw-dropping horror of the endless, coz that's a circle and our plus-one counting system cannot deal with the bends.

Surely mathematics itself is just another type of evolving language, borne from the benefits of grading and signposting multiplicity, operated in abstract to create patterns and connections in its own virtual world which help us understand *better* those which might appear in the external world.

My scepticism towards objective truth is that our ability to find it is thrice hamstrung: our senses and our machines can only detect what they have evolved (or are designed) to detect, our language intuitively labels the new with the old, and our inability to opt out of the journey of existence loads each observation with a temporal and spatial subjectivity it can never escape. But so long as there's time to spend and space to fill there's always work for the scientist.

Just because A smashing into B has caused C since records began, we have no way of knowing what will happen in the future. For all we know A and B only cause C when D equals one, and it just so happens that D has equalled one ever since scientific records began and so has lain undetected as an invisible constant (for surely detection requires change). But soon D will equal two, and A and B will no longer cause C. But as D was previously the great undetected cause, it will for a while seem as if nothing short of a miracle has occurred, Hail the New King. But soon we will discover it's not Our Saviour after all, the beauty will be explained to us in terms of scientific cause and effect and the magic will be gone, the miracle dead. Meanwhile the old ABC science will seem rather naïve, although in time the new ABCD will itself discover an E and so on, and you just know it won't end with Z, not least because reality isn't written in our alphabet.

By the process of deduction we can posit an unthinkable future. Hundreds of years ago we believed all sorts of things with a great certainty about the shape of the earth, gravity, time and space, which have now been shown to be questionable, if not wrong. If, back then, we were told all that we know now, we would imagine the future as one peopled by some superhuman race which had entered a whole new era of understanding about reality, with unfathomable wisdom and insight, turning all knowledge on its head.

Just think of what has been discovered in the last 50 years – do you really think the next 500 will be a fallow period? Ever since we fumbling featherless fraudsters decided to stand up it has been our recurring folly to believe our current era to be in some way defining, a turning point in history.

We did it after da Vinci, we did it after Newton, we did it after Einstein and we're doing it again now, (although if this be a spur to greater knowledge then is it a delusion that *should* be propagated?).

However, when you really consider the size of the universe, and the proportion of which we fully admit to being utterly incognisant, our belief in human science begins to exhibit a level of absurdity we may once have reserved for the religious believer, one based more on faith than fact. It's so local, so *parochial*, as laughable as the radical British students of the seventies with their policies on nuclear proliferation.

But in a less critical mood I do love us humans, I love our optimism, our unshakeable belief that we've almost cracked it, that despite what those nitpicking philosophers say, we all know that deep down there isn't *really* any significant difference between what we reckon is out there, and what actually *is* out there, as if the mysteries of the universe were just round the corner.

So scientists, do not despair (not that you will, for I know full well that if there's one merry bunch you won't take any nonsense from it's we philosophers) for there is always value in searching. It is *because* we can never turn our digital sieve into a perfect pan that there will always be room for improvement, progress. And if you're tired of chasing unachievable goals then my branch of science is always open if you fancy popping in. And with happiness as the simple end, goals can be achieved every single day.

But back to the point of this chapter, to tackle the dualists' world of essence and ideals. It is my contention that all ideas of essence persist in language, which was born as, and grew up to become, an excellent tool to support the emerging dominance of the human species. And as the threat to our safety decreased our language grew to describe every aspect of our waking and sleeping life. Idle minds will dream.

But perhaps there was no fundamental shift, perhaps language has always preferred the universal to the particular, the timeless to the here and now. We came up with the word 'tree' because we needed to refer to those greeny-brown sprouty things before us, which all seemed to share important qualities. The noun didn't evolve from the singular to the plural, from tree to trees, it did quite the opposite. What is a noun if not the family name for the many individual examples of it. Only when numerous enough can those objects earn their badge. If Mr Caveman suddenly saw the last ever lesser-spotted weaverdaub scuttle across his vision it is unlikely that poor creature would have ever been so baptised.

Of course, trees also had certain properties, which it was useful for us as survivalists to recognise. They are made of wood, and wood burns, wood floats, wood is strong, etcetera. The fact that the line of definition between a tree and other plants could be blurred, and there were yet more subsets within the family of trees, was not so important. It was useful to us to have the word tree so we created it – that's all. No groundbreaking insight into the inner workings of the natural world – just survival. I guess there's little use getting bogged down in detail with a sabre-tooth snapping at your arse.

And if you were shipwrecked on a desert island and some strange purple root seemed to be the only edible plant around, are you really telling me you would wait until you had a decent handle on the ecosystem of your hostile home, and the proper place this delicious lifesaver held in it, before giving it a name? Of course you wouldn't. You'd Christen it *thankfuck* and get it down your neck. If it works most of the time then what are we waiting for? Hunger, death? I'm sure a pretty sophisticated science of utility was up and running long before the white-coats smeared Latin over everything.

Our gyroscopic defining process put down a mark each time it delivered us the precision we *required*. We didn't need the words ash and oak and maple when we were building a fire (now look here! If some burn better than others than I'm sorry – but you know the point I'm making. You know my feelings on research) so we stuck with wood. But when it came to building weapons then the difference mattered, so we put down another marker.

When he was running away from a killer beast then I guess Mr Caveman wasn't overly concerned about what it tasted like, let alone its migratory habits or the way it brought up its children. But once we had mastered our enemy, and started putting him on our dining table, then such things *may* have become interesting.

The point is, words are only interested in trees in general and the qualities they share, in fact they would rather this actual tree I'm sitting in right here, right now, didn't actually exist at all. For each new day, each new existent, is like a potential landmine, waiting to explode across its splendid world of steadfast rules and perfect ideas.

Ratty sits in a tree, gazing down on a field of poppies. It's cold and it's started to snow. Two snowflakes settle on his arm, just for a moment, and then they are gone. If he had thought to look down he would have seen they were actually identical, but he didn't and those icy twins just melted away, lost forever in time, seen by no one. I guess we're all lost in our thoughts and theories – we can never see the wood for the trees, the ultimate similarity staring us right in the eyes.

There is not a language alive that could match the uniqueness of this tree. How could there be and who could understand it? For language must ignore distinguishing details, it baptises individual objects according to what they have in common with others - language knows all too well that similarities are most important.

Think of ourselves. At best we get some literary 'name' chosen from a list, which is then added to another denoting our family, or we turn to the world of maths for a national insurance number. Language really skirts round the issue of the particular, if it had feet then I reckon it would be really shuffling them right now.

In fact the progress of man might be described in terms of this desire to master, to simplify, to categorise (and to ignore) the reality with which it is faced. We name and shame this hostile planet, we dress everything we find in our own clothes, I think we're all a bit scared. But something far worse than paranoia is going on here, something new is being born, a ghost is emerging from the shadows.

For once we stared at these trees long enough then an 'idea' of a tree formed in our head, a mental image created from the qualities each individual tree shared. And once we gave it a name not only could we imagine it, but we could talk about it as well.

There now existed a *mental* tree, somehow separate from the physical trees from whence it was born, and also strangely *resistant* to the dangers faced by its real-life parents. Agent Orange may wipe a farmer's field clean from the earth, but his crop will remain so long as there's a poisoned soul to remember it.

And these ideas are powerful – they affect our observations, providing a seamless predictability and continuity to each new day. That tree I've never seen before doesn't scare clever old me, for my wonderful ideas and the names I gave them have seen all God's trees. "There's nothing new under the sun" we chant to ourselves, hoping that if we pray loudly enough it might just come true. But I've told you before, words can't tell the truth. They always lie.

"They say everyone has one in them. But perhaps not all stories should be told. The crying hasn't stopped, it never will. Oh sure, our Sarah has a book in her, and that's where it's staying." Remember that? Well, it turns out I was half right. After a few hours/days/weeks in that place she started to trust me for some reason (although I guess we all look our best stood next to her Dickie), apparently she considered I was ready to hear the Truth (when will she realise that it's talk like that that makes her so damn easy to lie to), she insisted she was now ready to tell me *just everything* (she didn't of course, but her sort always spout superlatives like the world's gonna end); about Richard, about Justice, about how that night became her Year Zero, (hey, what can I say, man, she's a Cold Warchild).

And she told me how she had come to realise that the chronology of events and facts and details which make up daily life in space-time is in fact a pointless distraction, a smokescreen for the reality that lies beneath. Obviously she didn't say any of that but I was finding it real hard to listen, and real easy to speak for her. Anyway I could see what she was getting at in her pleading needy eyes, her sort are so easy to spot. She told me about the crying but she also told me about The Crying at which point I seriously started to lose interest, one philosopher is plenty enough for this story, and Richard's already taken that role. I listened, or rather I heard, and it's some book I can tell you. You must hear it some time, but not from me, I won't even tell my own story, let alone anyone else's.

But she was honest, I'll give her that, she believed in what she said, and I guess that's all we can ever mean by truth these days. I listened, I really did, and do you know what? I really missed him. As she bared her soul I could barely wait to escape. I'd definitely been there long enough. Bloody truth-tellers, bloody confessors, when did people become so obsessed with themselves? Shit happens, so flush it away. I really must find Richard, if only to clash diaries, to arrange

some time and space for the last scene, if only to go to the pub. No wonder I drink, I just hope Richard still does.

It is science's need for a language expressed in a pre-ordained structure that falsifies its endeavours from the start. And the expanse of its vocabulary can only confirm the minutiae of its endeavours, not their profundity. Such a mathematical use of language will always leave the most important depths of experience untouched and that clumsy clot will always be refused entry to these hallowed depths, because of his own insistence on public universality.

The universal is as shallow as it is broad, but like the spire of a forgotten church peeking above the surface of a dehydrating lake, the real action, the unspeakable nameless wonder, the terror of the here and now, bubbles beneath.

The arts on the other hand can easily slip through this man-made mesh, diving to the depths, disturbing those parts of us which remain unsullied by our constant jabbering. The meaning of art lies in the very moment of experience – a unique dialogue between artist and audience, never to be recorded, never to be repeated, gloriously lost in time, until the next time. Poetry too performs in this moment - the familiar is flipped on its head, turning household names like secret keys, unlocking the unspeakable within. And as ancient passions are aroused we are invited to delve further, to throw light on the darkest corners of human existence, far beyond the shallow reach of tedious description.

But only if we choose – good art is a dialogue remember. As a monologue it is mere aesthetic, rhyming couplets, where so many of us are too eager to rest, perched on the harbour's edge, bathed in the glow of a watercolour sunset, blissfully dangling a rod castrated of line and bait. The interval may not be the proper place for such talk but I'm conscious this performance is becoming too serious, and I so wanted to give you a small taster of what's to come.

I've often considered a bowl of pasta to be a most intelligent creature - when you're hungry at the start of a meal, it feeds you, and just when your full and want some real taste it begins to deliver that too. The food makes the decision, while we sit back and enjoy. The English roast on the other hand can be so dumb, offering the eater such a plethora of choices, so much freedom, that the experience can become quite overwhelming. This book has always been a performance of two halves, and we must sit through both. Patience my friend, for there will be sauce.

For now, let's agree that science cannot use language in the poetical fashion so described, for it is rightly scared of such moments of inescapable privacy, of such *clarity*. The individual is his enemy and the sooner that hippy mess can be hidden beneath those uniform lab whites the better. The language of science must never spark off an individual reaction in those who read it, that's the last thing it must do. There can be no dialogue, no unique moments lost in time, quite the opposite. It's theories must transcend time, they must strive for religious perfection, now and forever more, Amen.

We worshippers in white robes must sing from the same hymn sheet, my e must equal your mc squared, just like my *idea* of a tree equals *your* idea of a tree. Set free in a virtual world of abstraction maths can achieve the predictability, the perfection it craves. Don't you see? It's a self-fulfilling prophecy. We built an island and like a man with no mates hid some treasure, only to dig it up the next day.

Even the relationship between objects and nouns is saturated with humans and our language. The real world is made up of objects yes, but that's because we see it that way. A race of senseless ghosts who could only see heat would not assume the physical world was made of such distinctive parts. Our objects are actually collections of tiny particles, forms of constant change, growth and decay, possessing a vulnerability not found in the badge we stick on them.

Yes, the lethargy of this movement gives language the chance to take a firm enough grip to operate effectively, easily enough for us to tell each other about objects in the world we experience in a way which essentially *works*, but there's no congruity of type.

Philosophically the idea and its form, or rather the form and its idea, couldn't be further apart.

Language forces us to talk backwards. We ask ourselves, what are the qualities of a tree, as if this were a scientific inquiry. But the truth is it is a linguistic one, for this is *our* label, about which natures cares not a jot. We may inject man-made gunk behind the prehistoric reality into which we were born to make it look younger, prettier, less scary, but in the end such plastic surgery only fools us if we let it, so we fools do just that. It is testament only to the *success* of language that we have somehow come to revere the monster we created, willingly believing the lies we taught it to tell us.

However counter-intuitive, nouns are in fact moments in time, a label we give to certain recurring patterns of matter *when* that arrangement so occurs. We pin 'tree' on all those greeny-brown sprouty things while their trunk is stuck in the ground and their leaves bursting out the top. But once we've chopped them into matches and discarded them into the ocean, it's old name is never spoken again. The same physical matter exists, but in time its arrangement has changed and the noun, the word, returns once more to its virtual home, the world of ideas.

"Does that throne exist?" we mock, to the Philosopher King trying to enjoy a drink on his own. A tired man who with tireless dignity replies: "Chop off one leg – still a throne? – chop off another – how about now? – a throne with no legs at all? – well we're approaching a wider definition now, a piece of wood again, firewood perhaps – set fire to it, don't be scared – I believe it's started to char, but I reckon it's still wood – ah, but now it's burning, soon it will be a pile of ash – and what's this, the wind's started to pick up, taking with it our precious mound of black dirt which has now all but disappeared. My throne, my wood, my ash - mere signposts marking the passage of time until our disintegrating union of molecules went their separate ways, from regal splendour to cool thin air. Magic!"

If nothing moved, if nothing changed, if there were no events to mark the passage of time, then the physical world would be as one and there would be no need to identify or differentiate between its parts, because it wouldn't have any. It's one of life's many paradoxes, but it is endless fluctuation itself which gave birth to our myriad of nouns, which in turn can do nothing but strive to hover steadily above these shifting sands.

Sarah, are you listening? No object is free from change, no 'thing' is free from change, therefore nothing is free from change. Objects *are* change, if there was no change there'd be no objects. There would be merely *some thing*. Are you following me Sarah? So if your meaning to life, your mission, is similarly liberated from change then it too is no thing, or nothing. Your life means nothing, your life is nothing, you would almost argue that yourself if it wasn't for the fact you

wanted to ... well, let's not be rude eh? But sometimes I think I'd prefer you as a homicidal maniac than some poetic rationalist whose life's work lies outside the petty morals of dear old blighty. And to be honest when it comes to a motive, courts are always going to look kinder on passion than metaphysics.

But being the timeless tortured soul you've become you'd probably never even considered such empirical filth as cause and effect, action and outcome, guilt and jail. And would I bail you out? I think you know the answer to that already. And anyway it's not going to happen, not if I have anything to do with it, not if I get to Richard first. There's nothing for it, I'm going to have to go back to the pub, back to the Monday club.

So it seems the world of nouns is no map of constancy, but quite the opposite. It is a constantly changing record of movement, like the stockmarket ranking, a way of keeping track of the temporal, the temporary. All companies have names, sure, but at the end of the day they're just a bunch of performing shares, which grow or decrease in number and value, become powerful, remain mediocre or wither to nothing.

Now I'm not denying there are distinct families within the world of beasts, Darwin realised that the fittest will survive and reproduce, and the weakest will die. But if we take a longer view of the evolution of each animal over the years, we might see more similarities than our naming system might suggest. Eyes, mouth, legs, hair, offspring, pain. You either accept that all life started from the same chemical reaction, and the subsequent variety of life forms merely reflects the variety of environments each successful survivor came to call home - or you believe God designed each one separately. It's up to you.

And this process of evolution might just give us a clue to the driving force behind our obsessive desire to calculate and categorise, our nerdy will-to-*spot* which Nietzsche somehow overlooked. While the tomes of modern science might provide enough data to keep a white coat quiet if he were reborn a hundred times, you can be sure his ancestors were no mindless twitchers.

Like all language, the sciences grew out of human evolution, human survival and human need. Ultimately it is the pain we feel which makes matter matter, and the minutiae of modernity would not have thrived without it. We cannot help but label and measure the world through human eyes according to human needs. Beyond this subjective sentient view of the world there would be no difference between life and death, healthy and sick, bright and dull, light and dark. Without us it's just a swirling mass of meaningless matter, the darkest secret from which we all hide, existence itself.

But never fear, for who's that galloping over the hill to save us from such cold truths? Why, it's those Three Amigos again: life preservation, pain avoidance and species empathy. Our thoughts, words, our language, it's gloriously saturated in them – and not even the inane lexicon of technology is safe. In reality, a car cares not how well it works – it's as happy breaking down as cruising at top speed – it's as happy screeching as humming. It is only we who see the unity. That is to say, happiness, efficiency and value live in us, not the machine. When a car works well, we mean it works well for us. Yet when we lend it to a friend we're so careful to advise: "She likes it when you put your foot down" or "she grumbles a bit in third", as if we were doling out instructions to a babysitter.

An obvious point you might say (hey, I got a million of 'em) humans use metaphors all the time, as a way of bringing technical statements alive. But the problem is – when it comes to science we forget we are using metaphors, and we continue to see the non-sentient natural world as either healthy or sick, alive or dead, good or bad, happy or sad - as if the physical world had a purpose, a destination, as if things *feel* better in-themselves when arranged one way rather than another.

And all this when we know damn well the sun's gonna burn us up right and proper one day, and this beautiful green eco-friendly nature will come a cropper how ever well we take care of it. And when it does our precious earth will scorch and smoke with neither reason or ceremony, and all will be extinct, including us, thank God.

Now obviously we know that if we look after trees then they will look after us, that they make the atmosphere healthier for humans, that they house animals we like to look at, that they look pretty and are fun to sit in – but let's not slip into some hippy veneration, for over there squats Smother Earth, the one metaphor that outgrew us all, where all philosophy is suffocated by her stinking suckling embrace.

Why do we insist on seeing nature as green? It's pathetic. Real nature is black and red, death and disease, rock and rape, fire and fury, it's chemicals and poison, it's genocide grey, it's cancer dry, its hostile, it's anti-human, it burns us, it suffocates us, it drowns us.

Yet we poor lawn-lovers insist on smothering our tiny square of planet like a house seller paints over mould, and if our offering doesn't take to this hostile crust we feed it with white-coat sludge until it becomes some sort of supergrass that won't let go. And then we lie on our all-weather carpet, suck up our homicidal sun and declare ourselves *at one with nature!* Still, you've gotta laugh.

I realised this some days/weeks/months back, perched on a bench in what I consider the only Field of Gold worthy of the name, the Beer Garden. (My! Haven't your Whiskies come up well this year?) This is *my* Eden, the true home of original sin, where grass is for smoking and Buds for drinking. The occasion was of course the neo-Monday Club (clearly *they* don't call it that, only Nathan and I ever knew that name and I guess his memory chucked it out with all the other facts he forgot on *his* special night, his fifteen minutes up that very special alleyway.)

That the neo-Mondays chose to meet al fresco made me a little less nervous about joining their charming Senate. People are far more communal when exposed to the heavens. But as I surveyed the gathered assembly, called by Caesar Rich, as I gazed at Richard, and Sarah, at Nathan and Ratty and Demon, at Natasha and Ray, it came home to me just how far I had fallen. There's no question, I wasn't running this thing anymore, they'd let that damn mutt speak before me. This was not my cast, my production, even Sarah stares right through me in public – no doubt conspiratorially, as part of her cunning plan, but you've got to suspect she'd do that anyway.

Nathan didn't even register me, Richard felt sorry for me, with the sort of smile one reserves for five-year-olds who've just dropped their ice cream, and Ratty, well he was clearly too infatuated with our chairman to care, and becoming more so with each meeting. Don't the chattering classes just *love* working folk these days, with their boobs and beer, their fags and footie. Richard

had become Ratty's forbidden fruit alright, and at four pints an hour I'm sure he considered him worth every drop. And you just know that Sarah and Ratty were inseparable, those oblivious in-laws twirling ever closer on philosophy's dance floor which by all accounts should make for a very exciting last scene, depending who writes it of course.

B ut there is more to language than silly old nouns, it's time to tidy away those bright-coloured building blocks and get back to work.

Philosophically we are all islands, we were born that way and Star Trek pending we'll die that way. So please stop lighting those damn fires, don't waste time spelling out your fears in the sand, capitals 10ft high for a passing what? Face facts, this is a metaphorical island and I'm telling you there ain't no metaphorical planes gonna fly past.

Language – while appearing to have built bridges – has in fact done the opposite. Language and the society which polices it has destroyed all transport links, securing our island status for ever more. For while our outer self may appear to thrive in the city language has built, our inner self is trapped indoors.

Remember though, there is no essential difference between these two, it is only language and the limits of science which keep them apart. For there are indeed times when our inside fancies a day trip, but once committed to such a rare foray into the forbidden realm it soon panics, and blindly gulping for air is quickly lost. It cries out and everyone hears, but no-one ever dares listen, so embarrassed and breathless it stumbles home again, to comfort, to privacy.

Dear reader you may have wondered why up until now I have not talked of friendship. You may have cast me as some condescending loner who places little importance on such bonds, but I can assure you quite the opposite is true. In certain privileged company our inner selves can thrive, can venture in tandem into the city and have a riot. With a carefully chosen partner we can use and abuse their shiny city bars and drink 'em dry.

But on his own, 'im indoors is just too weak and the Public Police just too strong, too impatient, too suspicious. They are not interested in means, only ends, they care not *why*, just *what*. And so we give in and give 'em *what* for, while our *why* cowers in the corner, ignored and alone. And let's face facts, they asked for it, demanded it in fact, for is there anything considered quite so rude in polite society as honesty. You'd be better off shitting in your soup.

No wonder we drink our inner selves to sleep. We talked ourselves into this mess but there's no way we can talk ourselves out of it – not now. Never again will we find a new way to communicate. Given infinite time we might, but we haven't got that have we? As a species we're about middle aged and there ain't a damn thing we can do about it. Only children can learn languages, we all know what adults are like. Let's just face facts for once, humans and language are the same package, and when that big hot landlord finally calls time you can bet we'll still be jabbering our socks off at the bar, pissed again.

Language by its nature needs to generalise, it needs to give many 'things' the same name, it can work no other way. But we hide, or rather are hidden, behind this imprecision, this ambiguity. We can be nothing else. We describe our feelings with the same words everyone else uses, sloppy seconds every time. We even choose words according to the listener. We talk so much to divulge so little. Like a pool of phoneys we pack the shallow end and splash like learners, but our feet in truth never leave the bottom.

But the here and now is forever avoided, in fact we are glad to let it allude us, because talking is so much easier than thinking.

This is why drugs can leave us speechless, because the prodigal present fills our mind with such spectacular force that the pleasant pastures of the past are squeezed out, and along with it the reference points we need for talking, for splashing, for flapping.

Freed from our desperate duty to fill the air with words, the skies are left to clear and the stars begin to shine.

And aren't you abstainers so scared? You dismiss as shallow that which actually fills you with deep fear, the deep end, those dark bottomless waters we buccaneers have dared to tread. Perhaps we do ourselves no PR favours, our moments together just too immense for Grandma Grammar back on blighty. But don't be fooled by our anodyne lexicon. I have a message for you Absters out there, sharing a glass and a gossip in those shiny city bars. Do you *really* think our brain has been pulverised into a gibbering pulp, do you *really* think we inhabit a simple childlike world, where everything actually *is* 'wow' and 'man' and 'cool'. Forget the talk, check the walk. Look at the *way* we are with our friends. Don't destroy what you've never had, don't spoil our fun, believe me we never even *think* about yours. Think twice old man, because your soft-hooded offspring have ventured to parts of the mind you couldn't even dream of. I'm not saying it's all about stamps on passports – but haven't you even been tempted? He may be treading water, but that's because he's in the deep end chicken shit. Now where are *you*?

Language is all about the past and the future, stretched over time like chewing gum from the heel of our shoe, leaving us no words to express the intensity of the present - and so the moments are gone, forever. Just as well I say. That way there's no memory, no record and no evidence, your honour. We are all naked in the present, naked and nauseas. With no armoury of labels from the past we feel terrified to venture into the future. Like children afraid of the dark we tell ourselves there's nothing new under the sun.

We cannot tell what will happen in the world from the words we use to describe it, for they are always *after* the event, always at odds with the here and now, struggling to keep pace. Our puny predictions are nothing but shaky pencil lines drawn into a non-existent future, extended from an even shakier understanding of the secret momentums of the past. But we weak minds are left with little choice, for without language we are all eyes, and soul and heart - and our world is turned inside out for all to see – a shivering quivering existence with no name to its name. Without our script (come *on* - we've all got a book of tricks up our sleeve to operate in a whole raft of scenarios, we all repeat ourselves, after all, practice makes perfect right?) we are stuck fast, stranded in the spotlight of the present. So instead we anchor ourselves in the glorious mists of history, and strapped to the elastic linguistic launch ourselves into some fickle future full of false promise, safe in the knowledge that we bungee jerks can be jerked back to safety whenever we chose.

This is bad faith my friend, but thankfully the condition is not terminal. In the final chapters I will hope to show that what defines human existence is actually private wordless consciousness. But for now consider that if we really thought in language how would we describe the brain activity of the caveman? And how come there are times, usually the most important times of our lives, when we feel it difficult to put our feelings into words? For in those instances we are never stuck for the right thought, quite the opposite for it is the very wordless thought in our brain that as the source of our frustration becomes so dominant. And why, at those times when conversation with someone is at its most intense, when we are trying to express those ideas most important and personal to us, is our language littered with such desperate hopeful scrambling pleas as: "Do you know what I mean?", "do you know what I am trying to say?", "Oh dear, I'm not sure this is making much sense".

Sarah on the other hand is being *very* clear these days. "I'm a killer," she told me the other day. Why do people *insist* on confiding in me? They think I'm good at keeping secrets, but the truth is, I'm just bad at remembering them, because really, I'm not interested. But you try telling Sarah the Confessor this, for she is being *very* clear these days. "I'm a killer," she told me the other day.

Now on any other occasion, from any other person, that would clearly have been something of a showstopper. But I guess knowing what happened that night, and knowing Sarah's increasing obsession with the world according to Ratticus (has *she* found out what Ratty must never know? – wouldn't surprise me, people like her are forever banging on about the lack of a father figure) it didn't come as much of a surprise. "Yeah yeah, whatever … you're a killer I'm a killer, Richard's a killer … say it loud, say it proud."

For in her world truth needs no facts, knowledge needs no evidence, essence needs no existence. Still, it's all therapy for our Sarah. She's really found the plot that one, living this story like it was her own, flying fist-first towards our done deal, stitched up to the neck in one of Ratman's crusading cast offs. And do you know what? Killer Woman is really starting to piss me off. All mouth and no trousers, all means and no end, a killer who sits, spits and shits like a killer, but still without a kill to her name.

I guess we all treat words as capes. I even played that overlooked anti-hero *The Pointless Pisshead* myself for a while, but such Capes of Good Hope always become Capes of Bad Faith, *always*. I guess I should have read between the tatty Ratty lining, I should have known he would be no seamstress, of course, seems obvious now, the seamless wouldn't do seams. Oh dear, I'm not sure this is making much sense … Trouble is, I can't promise it ever will. Given infinite time it might, but I haven't got that have I? I'm middle aged now, you can feel in your fingers how long I've got to go, and when that big hot landlord finally calls time you can bet I'll still be jabbering my socks off at the bar, pissed again.

I see language, especially when written, as a score of music which for the purposes of recording familiar tunes is ideal, with no significant loss of meaning in translation. But when we have composed something truly wondrous – we may find there is no notation at our disposal to convey sufficiently the defining character, the driving force, behind it. And we can hardly invent our own notation any more than we can invent our own words, for who would understand them? So we do the best we can.

Try playing jazz which has been transcribed onto a classical score, and you'll understand. The notes are all there, and in the right order, but they couldn't sound more different from the original, like a father singing his son's favourite music. For this sweet young melody has been plucked from its maternal goo and hung out to dry on some foreign stave – surprise, surprise, it withers and dies.

Why must we have words for everything? Why do we insist on reducing this beautiful terrifying existence into key combos on a typewriter? For there are essential elements to jazz which cannot be expressed on a stave, and its heart is absent unless the motivation behind its melodies and harmonies is played, is *felt*. And when you've got it you'll know. That's all. It seems good music has a 'story' behind it, a fiction which binds the notes together. And to play it we must first get to *know* it - first impressions are nearly always wrong.

So is the real music of Beethoven music lost to time, all that remains a sorry stack of notes scribbled on a stave? To some purists it may well be, but clearly the genius lives on, and this metaphor is stretching so thin it's about ready to split – well almost. For as a knowledge of the composer's intention is priceless when it comes to performing their music, so too is knowledge of the writer or speaker when trying to understand what they say.

And how few words do we need with great friends – and what delight when together we make the most sophisticated mental link with such a cool paucity of effort. It may piss everyone else off but we all love the knowing look from the one we know so well. Such privileged unions intoxicate us all. When we declare horror at mind-reading, it is the invasion of privacy by a *foreign* body we fear, not the phenomenon itself. For when our best friend "can tell just what we're thinking" we couldn't be happier.

But our best friend is not always there, our best moments are lost with them, and it's back to Jabberland. The reason we are so fluent in everyday life, and the thought-to-word process is not apparent, is because we do and say the same things every day. Instead of representing our thoughts, words start talking to themselves, taking on a life of their own, forever circling the ground like a class of skydivers who've finally learnt to fly. So practised is our art, so compartmentalised our life, that we glide effortlessly from one language game to the next without the merest flicker of activity in our brain. How many times have you held a conversation with someone while actually thinking about something completely different? Well guess what - they're doing the same! Hilarious or what!

There are some however who appear very fluent with language, who make us mere mortals sound as if our native tongue was actually our second, or third, who can – seemingly without pause – argue in and out and around the most abstract of discussions, skipping along the avenues of pure wisdom, plucking sweet metaphors like fresh blossom as they go, our plodding parlance forever one step behind this merry dance. Yeah, well, bollocks to 'em.

Sophistry is a skill to be learnt, like juggling, and we all know how boring that gets after a while, even with four balls. And it is a skill commonly acquired by the least sincere people. If, for just one moment, you can avert your gaze from their handiwork and let it fall at their dancing feet, you might actually spot some well-worn trainers treading some well-worn tracks. Bag ladies in make-up, dear Ratty, bag ladies in make-up.

Such routines are often performed within friendly waters, with at least a couple of familiar faces planted in the audience. But when the conversation sails slowly beyond their tiny horizon that feigned look of boredom barely disguises their growing fear, for very soon they will be out of their depth and you just know those shallow-end shamsters haven't bothered learning how to swim.

When it comes to dialogue the swiftness of response correlates inversely with its value, unless of course one is trying to be funny when the exact opposite is true. So treat these speed demons as such entertainment, unlike their plodding counterparts at the opposite end of the spectrum, who take long pauses, gaze into the distance like some Master of all Knowledge and then deliver, in precise terms, the biggest crock of clichés you've ever heard. These people should be treated with the ammonia they deserve, if it's gonna be faux then the least you can do is make it fun, and fast.

Talking about clichéd sophistry, I guess you'd better know about that meeting of the Neo-Mondays. Where was I, oh yes: "That the neo-Mondays chose to meet al fresco made me even more nervous about joining their charming Senate. But as I surveyed the gathered assembly, called by Caesar Rich it came home to me just how far I had fallen.....'

Six of the worst that lot, their faith smells real bad, they're truly rotting to the core. There's our Ratty: so eloquent, so sure of himself (if only he knew), his fervent spiralling monologue (for dialogue needs appreciation of discovery through reciprocation, experiment, superform, for which our Rats cares not) encircles the group like some eruption of the Unholy Spirit, St Elmo's fire alighting on the furrowed brow of each yielding disciple.

There's Nathan: a true paranoid freakster, all accident and emergency, his good hand grasping at each word of wisdom, as if it might be the last he'll ever hear. He's also joined the Sunday Club now, for he knows all about the fragility of a life lived for time and space, his bad hand tells him each day how bad people can be, that the plug can be pulled on the music at any time, he's fought for his life remember, he's fought for his own one-man country. From now on he'll take any word, anything, anyone he can get. Life's too short to be fussy, and not believing is too damn risky, right?

Then there's Ray and Natasha: inseparable in word and life, Ray still firing each spoonful of irony from below, as Natasha sucks obediently from above, and the group chooses to see nothing ("oh *really* Ray, you shouldn't" – and she's right Dr Drippy, really you shouldn't ... you fixed that yet?) But I don't want to talk about them anymore, in this politically-incorrect world they're enjoying a comeback and I will not be any part of it.

Of course there's the star of the show, our very own Sarah. Nodding in solemn silence, like a suicide bomber taking instruction, a story waiting to end, a killer waiting to kill, she's read ahead and she thinks she's seen it all before, but if she has then I don't know what she's reading, I'm pretty sure it's nothing to do with me.

And then there's Richard. It was the first time I'd seen him in ages ('my, haven't you grown') and I'm pleased to say my initial fears were rather unfounded. For he hasn't grown, none of them have, I shrank, I fell, that's all. And so out there in the sunshine me and my roasting neck felt we had got

something of our old life back, not meaning, certainly not purpose, but at least a couple of dates in the diary, a couple of walk-on parts. I never wanted for much more before and I'm happy with that now, basically I'm happy to see Richard again. By any standards he's as bad as bad can be, but I can only report what I feel, and I'm telling you, it's good to see him again.

"Bloody birds drive you to it don't they – you can't hit 'em back though'. No you're right Rich, *I* can't, but *you* can, you're different to us. As far as he's aware no-one has repealed the laws of the jungle, the only thing that's changed is these days you can't leave your mark, ain't that right dad? "Yeah .. I'm proud of you son. A bit sloppy with the hand thing, but that alley was dark and you were right pissed. Yeah .. I'm proud of you son."

So not a lot has changed. There I was, the silent partner in Neo Mondays plc, just as always. Have I told you about the Monday Club, I mean the original Monday Club? Well I will, but not now. I want to leave something half decent to the end.

And what about Emma, the observant among you may ask? Well, to cut a short story shorter, Emma's dead. Hit and run. From the director's point of view that hit and run hit me real hard. I had big plans for Emma, I thought she could become a real girl's girl, the coolest chick, a true champion – and that strange bond with Sarah? But she turned on me when I got drunk for a couple of days/weeks/months and you know the rest. And now she's dead.

That's life for you, the biggest killer of the lot. Oh and in case you're wondering Ratty doesn't know any of this. He hasn't seen her since that cold lunch in Camilles, but he's living off the memories as if she's dead anyway, so what's the difference? She wouldn't like him now, she certainly wouldn't like his new mates. Perhaps it's best he doesn't know?

I'm really nervous now – there's so much more to come and I'm just not sure I've got the bottle for this thrill-seeker, this story with no end is starting to resemble the life of the immortal Superhero, doomed for eternity to leap from tragedy to victory to tragedy, with no pattern, and no reason. For surely reason is The End of all stories, the why behind the what, the end of the means, the killer revealed. But back on Dear Old Blighty there's only quarter of an inch to go. Go on mate. Feel the Finish on that. True craftsmanship that is. Never forget, existence precedes essence and stories can't be bigger than the books which carry them. *Now* do you feel this truth, literally, at your fingertips?

If I have a theory on language at all, then you might have gathered it's rather dismissive to say the least. But we can't surround ourselves with privileged unions and knowing glances – if only because their beauty would dwindle with repetition. We must have a public life, superform demands we do our bit, and I am well aware that I have not provided a positive theory of language to equip us for this tour of duty. But if I am to do so then I'm afraid we will need to talk about the thorny subject of meaning.

Potentially this branch of philosophy has the ability to blow minds and comes to many, as it did to me, as an utter revelation. But I move hesitantly, for all too often (and I blame the practitioners here, not their subject) it can descend into the sort of circular pomposity which most characterises and demeans philosophy in the eyes of the unsaved, and very nearly threatened the very existence of the discipline itself for much of the last century. So might you bear in mind I'm doing this more out of modish obligation than any genuine desire, for apparently all philosophers need a philosophy of meaning these days. The problem is, I suspect mine's not very good.

Philosophy was considered by an increasing number of philosophers in the early 20th century to be about language.

Therefore any pretensions to metaphysical analysis must be postponed until, firstly, a proper investigation into language and the meaning of words was carried out. The meaning of a word, they said, must be eternally shackled to the observable world, else we be in danger of entertaining all manner of woolly-minded lily-livered post-modern hogwash. And so it wasn't long before the stern-faced Language Lobby called poor old philosophy to its study and executed a swift caning, declaring in one fell swoop its hopes of gazing out into the blue yonder to be utterly misplaced.

Language was not the carrier of some deeper message, they insisted, it was the message itself, nothing more, nothing less. The philosophical enterprise as was practised by the Greeks and all who followed was fatally flawed, an unachievable project hilariously doomed by the only means in which it could be expressed.

I guess these people didn't get out much, and like the burger boys across the pond, it might just have been that their view of life *could* be completely expressed in words. If you talk like a computer, and so do your friends, and you spend all day and night staring at one, then is it any wonder you start to think like one? And it must be very easy to believe life is about philosophy and philosophy is about language if you're cooped up inside those dreaming spires all day long. But being a man of the world, well at least the world beyond south east England, I cannot hold with this view.

Consider our muddled panic as we are forced to think on our feet. We may choose what to say first for any number of reasons, whether through tact or tactics, nerve or nerves. But such a sophisticated strategy could only be possible with a multi-layered understanding of our particular situation and a simultaneous appreciation of the outcomes it might throw up. Does the Language Lobby *really* believe this is all *written down* somewhere in our brain?

Surely our minds could not work at the speed they did if each train of thought was structurally as plodding as a grammatical sentence. And my thoughts certainly do not share the linear composition such utterances cannot escape. We only come to talk about 'trains of thought' and 'mental links' because like everything else on our man-made timeline they can be clocked chronologically according to the second they occurred. But we will misunderstand the true nature of our multi-dimensional mindscape if we derive any hierarchy or import from the order of this list.

Time may be good for archiving, and is perfectly happy to offer a label when none others are forthcoming, but it is a primitive way of presenting ideas. Like a book and its chapters, one's thoughts are far better expressed through category, rather than chronology.

Not for the first time we humans thought backwards, imagining language to be the arbiter of our dreams, rather than its servant. That this error is repeated to this day by both the most romantic of rationalists and the sternest of linguists tells us all we need to know about the folly of extremity, the secret love affair of science and religion, and *finally* the unspeakable truth of a middle way.

Let's move on. The question historically placed at the centre of philosophical discussions about meaning was this: "Do *words* have meaning, or is it *people* who mean things when they use them?"

But to my mind such raw binary is unnecessary. Clearly words have meaning at a level of basic language, and we may gaze at these incubations through the protective glass of a dictionary. But it is the combination of these basic words which gives sentences meaning. To find out the meaning of a sentence we need an understanding of grammar, and sentence construction, and such skills we will hardly gain from a dictionary. What we now need is formal schooling.

And finally, there is a third level, where *people* mean things, using certain sentences in a certain way. These skills we can hardly improve with either a dictionary, or formal schooling. What we need is plenty of *practice* and public exposure. Consider a musician's journey from novice to expert: first he learns about the theory of notes, then he is taught how to play them, and then through practice he learns how to add expression and meaning, to *interpret* the dots on the page, to consider *why*, not merely *what*.

However, the Language Lobby believed that for the purposes of academia we must stop at the second stage. Contextual excess should be discouraged, they said, for it only reveals sloppy thinking in the speaker. "If you can't write it in Latin then it doesn't make sense," they declare, gridiron lives shoehorned into gridiron theories.

But subsequent theories, of which mine is one, recognised that meaning is essentially found in *use*. It is speakers who bring words to life, not dictionaries or grammar lessons. Of course we need schooling when we're young, but ultimately language must be spoken, music must be played, otherwise it's just black marks on a page, rules to a game no-one's playing. Only by being there *at the time*, the there-and-then if you like, can we gain access to the all important third layer, to know what a *person* meant.

Hidden jokes, coded reference, facial expression, emphasis, sarcasm, knowing looks, cliché, metaphor, humour, shared history. We all carry an armoury of sophisticated tools to carve out the most important thoughts which can rarely be transcribed onto paper without a substantial loss of meaning. For by the time our beautiful words have suffered that deathly descent from mouth to page, from spoken to written, they are all but dead. Wings clipped their ancient bones lie scattered across a classroom floor.

Clearly a lot of language, the sciences in particular, needs to make heavy use of the first two layers, but I am convinced the deepest meanings *need* context, they must be released from the general, the universal, they must be allowed to fly with the wind.

But let's not get too carried away, for if religious hogwash is the sole outcome of such liberty then I'd rather we had stayed in the classroom. I've mentioned before that it is the generalising nature of language which has somehow tempted us big 'eads into believing we have elucidated some idea *behind* the object we refer to, turning what should have been an empirical afterthought into some phoney exercise in pure reason.

Surely the clue is in the question – what is an idea? Why, it is nothing but an *ideal*. It is an abstraction from the temporary world we see around us, and abstracts are derivative, not productive, and their existence as contingent as the data which gave birth to them. But boy did those idealists get carried away, for once they had posited a world of ideas, or ideals, they still wanted more. What troubled them most was that they still had a multitude, they may have chopped up the horror of the meaningless reality into nice compartments, but these compartments were now growing in number, and fast.

Clearly something, someone, needed to take control. These ideals needed more, the children needed a Father (you know where this is going), an essence of essences, the most ideal ideal - or God to give him his other name. And there you have it, the Double Derivative who's come to save us all. "Does God exist?" "Well of course he does," they cry. "For look - *there he is*! Smiling right out at us from the middle of the question."

We must reject such nonsense. There is more to life than sitting around clicking our heels, waiting for a God *we* created. Religion sells us so short, it tells us we're crap when we're not. We're so much better than that. We must create a New World of Ideas, a world of glorious afterthoughts flexible enough to ebb and flow with the tide.

As we sail into new and unchartered waters, we must be Masters of Reinvention, ready with open arms to accept each new dawn. But never again must we allow ourselves to imagine this world was created for us, about us, somehow with us in mind.

We may and must care, but it *never* will.

But that doesn't mean we can now dream of an escape flight to heaven. Just because the universe is an oasis of belligerent indifference, it doesn't follow that it's opposite lies just round the corner. Such childish craving for symmetry is just a waste product of the Notty world of mathematics. And anyway just what is wrong with time and space? Personally I really like it, I don't see it as imperfect, I don't need to imagine there's something behind it all, some faceless nameless goo. I ain't going down on my knees in that. Is it just me or do all descriptions of heaven make it sound like some sort of milk pudding? I think it's about time we all grew up. I want to fill up on main course, I want to crunch and chew, I want heat and spice and blood and guts, I want a life that makes my mouth water and eyes stream, I want fusion, daring, experiment and excitement, not some sickly-sweet muck made to a recipe passed down the generations.

But it's not just religion which has warped our understanding of truth almost beyond recognition. Science too has started dressing in those arrogant robes. With religion in retreat it has merely become usurper. Instead of chopping up that throne for firewood, he's sat down and decided to make himself comfortable. From white robe to white coat, from pulpit to laboratory, these idealists, these blind-faith believers still don't get it.

We can look at the world through man-made glasses, else day to day life would be impossible, but we must always take them off as dusk falls, before we get too used to them. For we cannot risk the new, the here and now, passing us by. We must stop pouring real life through the filter of history, we must reject this cowardly reliance on wisdom, which as Antoine realised is nothing but old knowledge, treating the present as part of the past, each second as one more tiny revelation of some predestined reality, on which only the elderly hold a true perspective. Bloody bedwetters are terrified that in a few years' time we'll all be enjoying the party without them, witnessing new phenomenon they could never have dreamt of, and it seems that's just too much for them to handle. But we must do an about turn. We must start rewriting the past in terms of what we've learnt today, ask Newton, he'll tell you, that's if he's not still sulking.

The truth is nothing has stood the test of time. We must let go of anything sold to us as timeless, for at its core it's phoney. How can we ever hope to discover something that happens 'all the time' when we haven't *had* 'all the time'. "Have you been blind all your life?" we ask the blind man. "Not yet," he quips. Don't you see, there's so much more time to come, and none of us will get to see more than the tiniest fraction of it. Why is this such a bad thing?

As a species we may be middle aged, but we terminal schoolboys sure have a lot of growing up to do. For while we *young* bedwetters are still saluting flags and beating each other up in gangs, we haven't really left the playground. Just think what life could be like if we ever started to get educated, if we ever started listening in class, rather than dropping stink bombs everywhere.

The phrase "written in stone" serves as a wonderful metaphor for our Ideas, our Theories, our Science, our Rules, our Morals and our Religion. For stone may last thousands of years, passed from generation to generation, but at the back of our minds we all know that little by little it is crumbling to dust, and with it the mantras it bears. We must indeed look for sturdy Ideas, and those with the strength of stone we may come to call Theories.

But we must never forget who we are digging for. No more toiling for God on the never never, for we are the Masters now and must demand our reward before we die. We must stop unearthing truths from some curious Unearth we don't really understand, our pockets must be emptied of such Fools Gold. We must start taking pride in our real work. Human Truths, Noble Truths which like us must one day be prepared to die.

Nevertheless, misguided though it may be, idealism has thrown up a vital distinction which has come to play a huge part in the study of philosophy, and is indispensable to all its disciples to this very day.

If philosophy is seen as the analysis and subsequent ranking of similarities and differences between two or more phenomena – then in fact we should be quite grateful to dear old Plato. While we may scorn his idea of a world of perfect entities, we cannot afford to discard the tools he used to carve out his Utopia.

In our world existence may precede essence, but we too have a world of essences to build, just fashioned from the stuff of every day life, that's all. We are returning the prodigal language to its rightful parent, kicking out the imposter in time to reinstate *Mother* Earth. We will be guided by her and her alone, our temples will be built from her finest stone and there'll be no more shadowy talk of a distant Truth behind reality.

I used the upper case Truth as a perfect example of the mess we need to untangle. Christians often 'cap up' anything thought to have come directly from God: The Truth, The Book, His Love. That school hymn book must be a grammatical minefield to the young scholar. Christians here appear to be contrasting the upper case Truth as somehow possessing a higher status than our worldly lower case truth. But in Soviet Russia they too had two words for truth – the common usage and the official Truth as espoused by the Government: "We have no unemployment", "everyone is happy" etcetera. (Although on second thoughts, perhaps the comparison reveals more than it confuses?)

Anyway, the distinction between upper and lower case as far as we are concerned goes like this: the lower case tag is the Platonic idea, the upper case version its delegate back on planet earth. Gandhi summed up the distinction when he said: "I would become a christian if it weren't for the Christians." Gandhi almost seems to be confirming Sartre's mantra in a different way - I would be a christian (essence) if it weren't for all the Christians (existents or existence). Or rather, I would follow the theory (as laid out in the Bible) if it weren't for the practice (as it is observed in reality by Christians). Gandhi saw

Christianity as some sort of social club, highly selective in both membership and interpretation of its handbook. It had, to him, become yet another way for Westerners to indulge their passion for order and hierarchy, which on a dark night could all too quickly turn to exclusion and persecution.

We have other phrases which illustrate the distinction. "But they look great on paper" bemoans the football fan, despairing at the disparity between his team of stars and the performance before his eyes. And the sport itself can offer fresh guidance: What exactly do we mean, for instance, when we say we like football? Do we like the idea of *football* where teams of eleven players try to kick a ball into their opponent's goal, or do we like *Football* as it has come to be played, with all its tactics and pettiness, its greed and glory.

What about families? Is a dad the man who brought you up, the man you call 'dad', or is your dad your biological father? And in this case which is upper and which is lower? It's no use asking Richard, he never knew the man he called dad, the man he called "pleasestop" wasn't his real dad, whatever that means. But you might want to ask Rats, he knows the difference, and he looks at Rich still knows nothing.

What about politics? Is communism the theory that each of us should give what we can and take what we need – or some sort of mean experience of all Communist governments which have ever existed in history? And what do people really mean when they say communism cannot work? To which definition are they referring? Are they attacking the theory or the history, the essence or the existence? And what about capitalism? Is it the theory that goods will find their best value for the customer through the operation of a marketplace which rewards hard work and enterprise, or is it the soul-destroying globalism carried out by a handful of supra-governmental corporate giants who care as little for a fair price as they do for fair play.

Gunmen may get shot but ideas will never die. Think of the elusive al-Qaida, for it's not just those mountain caves which hides them so well. They can never be obliterated because the name applies to an act, not a person. Osama bin Laden is calling on anyone who agrees with his views on America to *act* against them in the *name* of al-Qaida. There might even be weekenders or holiday terrorists who fit in a bit of al-Qaida *action* only to return home undetected, with no badge, no card, no uniform. It's this very ideal-driven fluidity which gives the movement its strength. They realise all too well that groups group, members meet and organisations organise, making them so easy to spot and so easy to attack. But movements *move,* for they can do nothing else.

What the Americans fail to understand is that you can bomb cities and citizens, but you can never kill an idea, which will only become stronger and stronger the more it is attacked. But I ask them: "If a dual air assault on one of your cities can inspire a flag-waving resurgence in national pride and the American dream, then don't you imagine this rule applies to the cities *you're* bombing too?"

If I was in charge of recruitment for a terrorist organisation then the first thing I'd do is secretly murder half of its leaders and claim it was the opposition, for such acts earn an exponential return in public sympathy and support. For every terrorist killed today, three more will replace them tomorrow – I know brains aren't really an American thing but the maths surely isn't that hard. Al-Qaida can probably mark the current resurgence in its popularity from when the Americans started trying to kill its leader. They couldn't have dreamed the Americans would be so kind – a decades-long recruitment slump turned round within months, and without any effort on their part.

Do you notice how things are turning around, in preparation for the Romantic finale? It wasn't long ago I seemed to be criticising the 'idea' we have of a general perfect immutable tree, when we should be keeping our eyes on the actual trees themselves (for you just know it's us they're chatting about when our curtains are drawn). But now, I seem to be praising the 'idea' for its very resistance, and I guess I am, but only as an effective tool, a means not an end. For surely the success of idealism as a force for Power tells us all we need to know about its unsuitability as a force for Truth. As a means it sure works, but as an end it will remain as elusive as the pot of gold at the end of a rainbow (and don't its leaders know just that).

I guess when we say existence precedes essence we are merely switching rank on philosophy's two great leaders. There's been no execution, no victory, just promotion for one and demotion for the other. I'm not denying we need ideas or theories, quite the opposite, we need more ideas, or at least more half-decent ones. But they must be born from human need, propagated through efficacy and be ready to adapt or die in an instant.

All modern philosophers need a theory of meaning and that was mine. The trouble is I don't think it is very good. Like all modern philosophers I get tongue-tied, nervous, paranoid, despairing at the futility of any words I might speak. And when something truly important happens I stand there like a rabbit in a headlight, naked, shivering, my silent scream lost to a hostile night.

It was a nasty accident. All accidents are. Man-made nastiness at its nastiest. Never does essence leave existence so fast as it does from a car after an accident. The adman's ideal, that smooth lifestyle we bought, simply scarpers at the moment of impact. It is the first to hit and run, abandoning us to our broken glass and broken bones, twisted legs and twisted metal.

That's how Ratty saw it. That's how Ratty saw it as her blurred face screamed out at him from that front page, the family snap smile of the girl he knew so well, the friend he lost over a chilly lunch in Bouville. The girl he would never see again, with the face that would never leave his head, locked in that final second of realisation, a snuff movie's final scene illuminated for eternity by the director's speeding lights. And as the credits role Ratty looks for names, for clues. Not for meaning. Not anymore. Just revenge. For that car was not the only existence to lose its essence, not the only world to lose its meaning. "If there is a God then how come there is so much suffering in the world?" The old ones are the best, those anonymous clichés truly stand the test of time. But Ratty had seen no new light, quite the opposite. Never talk philosophy with the bereaved, it's the last thing they want to here. For their's is a world without explanation. When you lose your religion it's not because you're looking for another.

And so that was that – the end of an era – the end of Emma, the end of Dear Old Ratty, and the end of the second Monday Club, when I haven't really told you about the first. And what about Rats? Well we'll be hearing more from him. Sarah may have despaired at the loss of an ally, but in another way their lives are now closer then she could ever imagine. On that night of freezing fog, when screams were lost to a hostile darkness, Emma wasn't the only victim. On that

night in the freezing fog another murder was committed, another death which no-one witnessed. Nature has truly triumphed over nurture, it found its beating heart and sliced it open, the beasts have been set free, the Rats are on the loose, one hunting the killer, one waiting for the kill. Sarah may have despaired at the loss of an ally, but their lives are now closer then she could ever imagine.

I have already talked of our inner and outer world as if they were no more complex than a common sense definition. Perhaps I have become so used to seeing each moment in terms of one or other of these worlds that I have become rather lazy with my descriptions. But on reflection the common sense, or rather commonly held, view of reality may be rather different to mine.

The pervasive account of human reality, as we progress beyond the age of the religious is one dictated by science. Obviously religions are as strong as ever in terms of their influence on world affairs, but by and large they have become a cultural right to protect, a symbol of survival against oppression, no longer a philosophy to look to for answers. Think of Northern Ireland – surely for the vast majority being Protestant or Catholic is an ethnic-geographical belonging, their spiritual journey with the Lord long since abandoned in a roadside ditch, kneecaps blown out from behind.

Yes, God is dead alright and we scientists have killed him, replacing His Children with an army of robots along the way. We may be amazingly complex, say the killers, still possessing of many qualities as yet unexplained, but ultimately we are mechanical, *explicable*. And while illness and drugs can cause our senses to play tricks on us, by and large what *looks* like is there, actually *is* there. The only truth that matters is derived from, and corroborated by, our senses and their machines. And if some philosopher argues otherwise then this merely illustrates their ability to twist language to tell lies about reality, while remaining conveniently consistent with themselves (the very view held by the vast majority of non-believers, who with great camp and spectacle delight in posing such questions as "What is reality?" to lampoon and demean we disciplines).

But I ask you to bear with me, to journey by my side into the depths. Any of you who thought that what is out there is out there for all to see, read on, for mysterious shadows are thrown long and dark into this universe of ours, and they may just have been ours in the making.

Did I tell you I write most of my stuff on the move, and then transcribe it when I get home? No? Well I'll get round to it I'm sure, very proud of my method you see, I find screens so uninspiring. Anyway, I found this menu/train ticket/beer mat the other day with the following scrawled upon it. I wasn't planning on telling you, seeing as me and Sarah get on so well now, but it seems to fit okay here, so what the hell, waste not, want not:

'We all know blind people have better hearing, but what of voluntary disability? Our Sarah hasn't uttered a word since I've known her. Is this how she knows so much, by saying so little? Has she installed some extra perception in that space vacated by her tongue? She's a good listener our Sarah, and she's on a mission remember. Like a good detective she knows all information may be vital, however insignificant.'

So much has changed, so much speculation dashed on our rocky ride. Seems our path just gets narrower and narrower, narrowing to a point they say, although having never seen the point myself I think they'll be lucky.

Our Sarah has uttered a few words since, but I still wouldn't say she had the chattiest box in town. This Cold War vet's stole her 1,000-yard stare straight from her husband, her intended, and he stole it from his time in the army (of *course* he wasn't! But it amuses me to hear him say it, he is a trained killer of sorts after all: "Passed first time didn't I? Barely 17".)

It's funny the things that are making me laugh these days, perhaps this isn't such a tragedy after all: "Shut *up* Sarah." That one cracks me up, you should hear Richard tell it. But for now Sarah is shut up to all. One way traffic on the information highway – she's a good listener alright and I've heard that some people feel it's good to talk. Not me though. This may be turning into a comic-tragedy but I still wouldn't put it on the stage. Would you? Worse still the radio. No-one *says* anything! I've landed a tangled bunch of total freaksters and they hardly speak a word.

But whether they like it or not this tale is coming to a head, so if they've got anything to say then perhaps now's the time. As the path narrows, as we draw to a close I suspect we're all gonna become a bit more solid, more tangible. Unlikely to end as an action movie, I grant you, but certainly a lot less French.

Let's first ask a basic question: What evidence do we have that our senses and the machines that ape them are all that is required to deliver to us a complete picture of reality?

We know the world looks a certain way for we have eyes. We know it makes a sound for we have ears. And we know it smells, tastes and feels because we have a nose, tongue and fingers. But what if reality had other qualities, beyond detection by the famous five?

Are scientists seriously arguing that because they cannot imagine a sixth quality, detectable by a sixth sense, there cannot be one? We fivers can tell a born-blind four-score how things *look*, and the concept would be truly beyond their imagination, yet we still insist the buck stops with us fivers. It's so presumptuous, so complacent - cocksure campers, laughing, drinking, sinking towards oblivion, as if we were God's gift to the universe, just because we've never met a sixer to show us how dumb *we* are. If the human species was blind then would there be such a concept? Surely blindness is derived from an understanding of what it is to see, from an understanding that things *look* a certain way. So in what other ways might we all be blind? In what other ways may we be sensory deficient? Don't you *see*? Our experience and understanding of the world is essentially human, inescapably human, and is thus so limited.

However such philosophy, like anything half decent it seems, is counter intuitive. For life cares as much about philosophical tidiness as reality does about the way we describe it. It is when our theories on life, the universe and everything conveniently serve to paper over the cracks in our inner world, that we should be real suspicious.

We should be trying to break out of this shell, to cure that 'I' infection (and we wouldn't want to step on psychology's toes after all). Despite the ceaseless bleating of our ego, the universe was here long before us and it'll still be here when the sun takes us with it, the human story written off as a cocky aside in a timeless epic.

But while good philosophy should not hide from the truth, that's not to say it shouldn't also be useful. While it may reject plastic psycho-surgery, it has achieved nothing if it fails to quench our thirst for meaning, promoting human happiness, human freedom and human creation along the way with a bit of luck. A poppy-gazing philosophy which continually disparages common sense while offering nothing in its place, is only doing part of the job, and the easiest part at that. While philosophy is no besponged trainer scurrying onto the pitch at the slightest sight of injury, it doesn't mean he should be banished to the commentary box, for this is a sentence he's often been only too happy to serve – philosophers suffer from bad faith too you know.

Have you read any philosophy by the way? Most of it bears a stronger resemblance to a poorly-translated car manual. No wonder people scoff, no wonder people laugh at us. My question for such philosophers is this: Have you ever considered that if something's hard to understand then perhaps it's bollocks? Doesn't the history of academia tell us that complexity is the *enemy* of insight? However much you disguise your circular arguments in that tortuous prose, philosophy simply isn't rocket science.

So if there's any role for philosophy in our soccer metaphor then it should be as manager – a plain-speaking chap who'll do everything possible to guide you to success, but will never do it for you and certainly won't tell you you're having a good game when you're not.

But let's stick with our intuition for a minute. For all this talk about senses, at the end of the day it certainly doesn't *feel* like we're driving a car decked out with dials on a dashboard. We may at the back of our mind, somewhere behind the spare mattress, accept that a different number of senses might deliver us a greater or lesser version of reality, but Human 5.0 is the version we're stuck with.

We can chant "existence precedes essence" until we're blue in the face, but our beautiful mind sure makes it feel as if it's all the other way round. While we are all too aware that this life, this body, is a contingent phenomenon (for our parents may never have met) the resultant combination of mind and senses seems totally smooth, seamless, underpinning, *overriding*, as if we do in fact possess an essence which preceded this earthly existence, regardless of the unthinkable antics of our mother and father.

We cannot escape the feeling that somehow we were *meant to be*, an existing soul just waiting for a body in which to drive round a patiently waiting universe. We can even imagine 'we' could have been 'someone else', as if there were a mysterious floating 'I', somehow separate from its body and the circumstances and events to which it was so randomly, *so unfairly*, assigned. It seems that me, as the driver, could not have been any other way. I may not have chosen the car but I was always going to be in the race. And this ridiculous notion that the car gave birth to the driver, who is no more a necessary part of the vehicle than the gears or the engine, and no more attached, is just too frightful for words.

Well to you lot maybe, but for me the story ends when the book finishes. When the flag comes down there'll be no writer revealed, no victorious driver clambering out into the spray of champagne to take his plaudits, searching for a new car and a new race. No siree, me and this coughing contraption are going off the cliff together, it can be no other way.

Let's step back a bit. Say there are two ways of thinking: with a heart which feels and a mind which calculates. We can call on either depending on the occasion: love, laughter and beauty on one side; maths, money and survival on the other, and wouldn't life be all the poorer in the absence of either?

Mostly each side is happy to let the other play its role, and we all admire the balanced creature who can make us laugh one day and rescue us from a sticky situation the next. Yet when it comes to the biggest questions of the lot, the questions posed by philosophy, we turn schizoid, each side shouting to be heard above the other: "Of course there's a God – there has to be." "Of course there's not – that's ridiculous." "OF COURSE IT'S NOT ALL OVER WHEN WE DIE". "OF COURSE IT IS – THAT'S RIDICULOUS." And so on, and so on.

But while our heart is indispensable when it comes to the finer things in life, it is wholly unsuitable to consider what might happen beyond it. Belief in God is based on a desperate heartfelt longing for life to mean something, for little old us to matter in some way, to actually have another chance, because quite frankly this life is not all that was promised in that romantic trash *Blighty: A Visitor's Guide*. And if the world's not prepared to indulge our self pity then we'll create a heaven that is. This is bad faith and it's really not good enough. It stinks of ego, it stinks of nostalgia and ultimately it stinks of weakness.

I say again, it is the paradox of being human: "Why does the world intuitively seem to be a way we know deep down it just cannot be?" Evolution and survival that's why, our self-awareness, our idea of personality, and ultimately our idea of a spiritual soul are - just like our language - there to keep us alive. It's about food not truth, for nature in her prudence has decided that being metaphysically misguided is a fair price to pay for a full belly. Our arrogance protects us in more ways than we can imagine, but we are fools if we believe the lies it tells us.

When Sartre declared that existence precedes essence I suspect there was more than a touch of scorn in his voice, snuffing out the Romantic's candle as he yanked on the electric cord of reality. You can have your essence, he might have scoffed, but know it for the cheap trick it is. (So it's better to wander aimlessly in parks and drink coffee with those you hate? "C'est la vie mon ami, c'est la vie.")

But when Hume said reason is the slave of passion he was only making a point about our overriding humanity, a question of marital hierarchy. I don't imagine he was endorsing wholesale domestic abuse. We must somehow find a way of putting the tiresome facts of the matter to one side, for our consciousness comes across as pure essence and this is the metaphysical ailment we must address, not ignore.

A new King may have taken the reigns, but mine is a sympathetic Court and I will not banish the deposed. I will not sacrifice my soul for anyone, never to the church but certainly not at the shrine of some metal-headed mechanic, such thinking is so last century darling. This soul is mine to keep and do with what I will. It has a life with me now, and like a proper peerage will die with me too. And do you know what? We're much closer then we ever were before. For this is no distant cousin, separated by Priest at birth, kept incubated in the wings to take the wheel when I've kicked the mortal coil.

Love the cliché and the cliché will love you – turn your back and one deathly shove will show you whose shoulders you've been standing on all along – love the cliché, not for the sake of culture, dummy, but for the knowledge, the *knowledge*.

No – this little beauty is inside me, not metaphorically, not metaphysically, but quite literally. I never did like his religious phase: so distant, so worthy, so dull. But now we're mates, and neither philosopher, politician or Priest can ever tear us apart. Keep your thieving mitts off, for it's me and him now, 'til death do us kill.

Emma knew she had no soul, she knew she had no soul as those headlights turned the corner, fixing her to the sodden concrete like ancient gum, she saw she had no soul in the eyes of her killer, two dark pools staring right through her empty body, with no intention of smiling, flinching ... braking.

Far be it from me to diss the deceased, but I disagree with our Emma. I'm certainly no rationalist angel, some milk pudding cherub, but I'm no robot either. I'm not playing either of their games, I'm in the middle, and guess what? We all are. You see Emma, you did have a soul, ironically far more than most. As if there weren't enough paradoxes in the world, but it seems to me that those who believe least in an after life are those creatures with the biggest hearts, the biggest souls, the brightest fires inside. They guzzle down life's every moment like there's no tomorrow, for they know that one day there won't be. Project after project, success after success. They won't tell you, you must go to them, for they're only doing it for themselves. They realise life's too short to sell their soul, marketing oneself is so time consuming, so *life* consuming, and there's nothing like the realisation that *this is all there is* to make you stop selling, stop talking, to get off your arse and start thinking.

But those who live life as a story, those who wear their hearts on their sleeve, those who feel a great purpose and meaning to their existence - these are the true lightweights. As thin as the pages of the novel they stole their ideas from.

These drama kings and queens use sheer volume of words to fill out their shabby form, the stench rising from such raw self-obsession fills the air, fills the room, fills the conversation. Scared of life, scared of death, they affect to avoid both by, quite literally, 'creating a scene', inhaling audience adoration like bubbling crack from a teaspoon.

But Emma's soul shone brighter than any sun, so bright that had there been any witnesses on that night of freezing fog they might have imagined that something had remained, some shimmer in the air, some recognition, some record. Such strength, such nobility, such humanity *must* persist, every particle of her body screamed it. But if there were any witnesses they would have seen Emma's nothing race across the fields into the night, into nothing - that's all folks.

Rats is making progress by the way, he wants revenge, I've told you that, he needs to find the killer, that's newish, and so who does he turn to? Well this is new. The same person I did when I wanted to "get something sorted', the only person apart from me in this sorry tale with no mission, no meaning, no baggage. Our Richard of course.

And Richard made that promise, he promised the father he'll never call dad that he'd ask around, he'd find the man who killed his best friend. And you know what? He did, he found him ten seconds later, alone in the pub toilet of all places, gazing back at him from behind the cracked surface, two dark pools staring right through his empty body, with no intention of smiling, flinching ... braking. So now you know. But do you know what else? Richard did something he hadn't done for months. Cried? Hugged? Laughed? No, don't be daft, he wet himself. He stood there in the place of piss and pissed his pants, for a whole minute, two starless nights fixing him to the sodden concrete like ancient gum.

Now all of a sudden Richard needs me. Whaddya know. Seems even our Rich is finally finding this all a bit rich. I knew things would change again, they had to. It's a story after all. My story.

It is we who must make our matter matter, for in reality it matters as much as the pebbles we discard into the sea. This Dear Me we cling to is nothing more than a vague and selective awareness of ideas haphazardly saved to memory, felt in an elusive misty self-consciousness, itself a mere bi-product of evolutionary supremacy. It's nothing but pride which smoothes over the cracks, cherrypicks patterns in the chaos, perceives substance in the ephemera. Persistence of person is nothing but persistence of body, its celebrated personality as fearsome as a fairy tale.

But if reality offers no meaning then we may end up looking to the fairies after all. Ultimately we too must live the lie, but we will do so knowingly. For this journey is an attempt to create meaning in a meaningless world, to replace that which the sceptic rightly destroyed. The search for, and creation of, beauty may need us to suspend reality. It may not be pretty but that's the way it is.

Perhaps it would be better if God was still alive you might think, that way we wouldn't need to fill the void. If that's what you easy-lifers want then fine, but until now we've explored a mere fraction of our inner world and you're turning back already? Now I see more clearly than ever, religion gives souls to the empty, to those who have no interest in searching, no interest in finding their own food. So they check in to the nearest spiritual soup kitchen for a freebie, to get their fill of pre-packaged pre-congested baby muck. Me? I prefer a curry, and I prefer to make it myself. So if you're listening Mr Priest, I'll get back to you when I've had a proper look round - until then I'm real busy, and real hungry.

But assuming we've all lost our religion, let's play the believers at their own game. Instead of treating ourselves as the eternal outsider, looking in on a world we can never feel part of, let's mould this world around our own existence. After all, this existential clay is here for all to play with and it's pretty good stuff - its limits are our limits – its metaphysics pure metaphor. Remember, we're just trying to get through this shit without losing our marbles - that's all.

"You think the world revolves around you Johnson" - a common accusation levelled at me by a succession of teachers treated with yet another display of pre-pubescent conceit. I was awesome back then, you should have seen me. And that attitude is still there. I may not perform in public anymore but boy do I ferment in silence, in private. On my own I'm stronger than ever. I don't need a God, *really* I don't. I'd apply for the job myself if it came with a secretary to answer all those prayers. And I suggest you try it too, just once. Imagine yourself as the ultimate density, a beautiful black hole to which all matter and movement, each thought and every experience is drawn. Can you feel it? That's the beauty of the bubble my friend.

When new science talks about the subjectivity of observation it provides a useful warning about the controlling tendencies of our consciousness. Consider the classic quantum physics conundrum: "Does a falling tree make a noise if there's no-one there to hear it?"

The answer is of course 'No'. A tree only makes a noise to *us,* otherwise it's just meaningless movement of matter. Of course particles move in waves regardless, but we only baptise them as sound as we *feel* them. We say we hear a noise like a receiver receiving an object, but in reality it is *we* who *make* the noise.

I met a sixer the other day and I told him about heaven and he could barely stop laughing. Apparently in his world there are no souls, such an idea simply hasn't arisen in their greater understanding of the universe. In return for the joke he told me about the sixth quality of the universe. But don't get excited, in the end I couldn't be bothered to listen.

I woke up the other day just furious with the world, genuinely incapable of seeing the disinterested universe beyond my angry observation of it. After a strong cup of coffee however, this gloomy outlook soon began to clear. A common enough experience perhaps, but for some reason it hit me with frightening force. I realised with a fresh clarity that such attitudes are no more mine, no more *part of me*, than the hangover I had just seen off with a shot of caffeine. I realised that the brain, as carrier of consciousness, gives all its contents a sheen, a beastly common denominator we might like to pretend is not there.

Have you ever felt that for all intents and purposes you may as well be walking round a film set, when all the world's shapes and colours suddenly appear as make-up, its noises as sound effects, a human blanket we've draped over grim grey existence?

You think you're reading a book but something's not quite right. Suddenly it's just a video clip playing before your eyes, cleverly backed up with a sensation in your hands. With a daffy shake of the head you think to yourself how the book feels, how reality feels, but at the back of your mind you know full well the book feels nothing, that it is you who's doing the feeling. But thank goodness for words, the book's full of them after all, the perfect escape from the here and now, from your ten little slugs and their clammy clasp.

"It's smooth," you whisper, hoping to talk your way out of the rising nightmare. But fear wells up in your heart, and you're struck dumb in this eternal moment, unable to tell whether it's the book or your fraudulent fingers who's doing all the work. "Go on touch it – someone – anyone - please."

You're trembling now, literally reaching out, desperate to be set free from the endless now, this unique encounter with naked reality. But in the nick of time, as your last marble makes to roll off the end of the world, someone else does touch it, and with no little prompting agree that it does in fact feel "smooth".

"I thought so too," you cry, shaking now amid joyous tears. "Because now we've shared the same word, so it must have been that damn book all along, not we, not me. What mischief!" As you dry your eyes you allow yourself a nervous chuckle at your moment of madness, and pretend to carry on reading – but the terror hasn't left, not completely. It's visited once and it never forgets a face. And as you giggle in the light the dark serpent called existence recoils to plan its next attack, relishing fresh conspiracy with a body you may never quite trust again.

By extracting what all human observations have in common we might hope to eliminate those parts peculiar to each observer and come up with a common reality, the true observed. But to be totally sure we would need to compare human observation with Martian observation, and again proceed to eliminate that which differed. But hang on a minute, there's always the possibility that humans and Martians are in fact distant relations (although you just know they never mention this at parties), savvy solarsystemites bearing yet another peculiar family trait, another limiting layer. And so the search goes on.

We must tread carefully here as I am certainly not positing some mysterious Kantian noumena operating behind the spatio-temporal physical world we see, some gooey realm of God and Good. As philosophers Ratty and Emma would have done better to consider the similarities in their analysis, rather than the conclusions which split them apart. For there is indeed a world which lies beyond us, but it's a wordless horror we four-eyed fools like to keep at arm's length, a position taken and maintained through our *own* volition, not God's.

But nothing will stop the scientist and his camera filming this facade, rushing back to his laboratory with hope in his heart, a sobbing lover piecing together the holiday of a lifetime from a hotel floor scattered with skies and smiles.

The world keeps turning baby, and it couldn't give a flying fanny that you describe it in terms which conveniently match the very senses with which you were born, (well whaddya know, now that is *uncanny* isn't it?) Deep down you know those jolly colours and stinky smells are nothing but nursery school gunk, splattered over the terror you pretend to ignore. I think it's time we grew up.

B ut it's not just our senses which get in the way of accurate observation, our precious personality rarely fails to keep its nose out.

There's a song I recall from Sunday School which endeavoured to explain the infinite size of God's love, which looking back was no mean feat to a gaggle of five-year-olds. But anyway its chorus went: "So high, you can't get over it, so low, you can't get under it, so wide you can't get round it…" There are also clichés about "not being able to see the wood for the trees" and phrases from psychology about "being too close to the problem" and "needing fresh perspective".

All these are trying to tell us the same thing: that there is an inverse correlation between accuracy of judgment and our proximity to the object of that judgment. We may yearn to witness without opinion, but this pointless point of view keeps having its way.

But the more involved we become with any object or project, the harder it is to apprehend its proper place in the scheme of things. We export its personal importance to the object itself, even though it remains totally unaffected by the regard in which we hold it. That road meant nothing until it became part of my route to work, and when they dug it up they may as well have turned the drill on me.

We are forever endowing each part of our life with a significance and merit it rarely deserves. Best film? Best composer? Best friend? We even protect our most obscure favourites, frightened that each new fan might dilute a part of us. We really must stop claiming ownership of things which don't belong to us. Beethoven might be *your* favourite but you're really not *his*, and that's not just because he's dead.

But it doesn't stop there. Even those parts of our life which seem to choose us, like culture, family, job even, are soon injected with a pride we should be reserving for our own achievements. I think disciples of all disciplines are susceptible to this criticism, whether they be Christians, economists, scientists, philosophers, historians, geologists, psychologists or artists.

The temptation to confuse our own subjective fascination (moulded in no small part by the contingencies of our upbringing) with its object in the real world is almost always too hard to resist: Christians see God as the creator of, and key to, all life. All their tenets can be traced back to this belief in Him, and all other forms of life must be seen in this overriding context (very strange!). Economists see financial transactions and the study of cash flow as the key to life, humans having evolved to become consumers primarily, interested only in making life as comfortable and pleasurable as possible (bloody Americans!). Scientists believe the meaning of life lies no deeper than an understanding of the mechanics of the physical world, and all other disciplines must be seen in their context (must get out more!). Historians see history as a series of repeating chapters, at any given moment we are at the pinnacle of huge human story and we need look no further than the previous chapters to find out where we are and where we are going (yawn!). Geologists see the mineral in us, human beings being a mere blip in the progress of the planets, and the truest perspective is to see our evolution as nothing more significant than that of a piece of stone. (Hurrah for them! What a bizarre and beautiful union I now feel with these lovers of hard rock). Psychologists think reality is all in the mind, and it is to our conscious and subconscious and unconscious existence that we must turn to unravel the mysteries of life. (Perhaps they're right – who cares, no research remember!) And artists see the pursuit of man-made beauty as the only possible meaning to life, all other pursuits being there ultimately to serve that purpose (*Nice!*).

So you see, the narrative you favour depends where you place dear old Mr Human in the scheme of things, and that is the story you will tell, believing all others to be misguided to a greater or lesser degree. But at the end of the day, it's Mr Human that matters. I'm not arguing that the pursuit of one excludes any belief in the others, or even that we must choose one and one only, I'm merely inviting you to stop hugging your particular tree for one moment, to take a step back, a few seconds out, and appreciate the forest of human thought. To gain some deeper, more distant perspective, to confront that I infection, we somehow need to treat them as different perspectives on the same reality, a circle of sunglasses linked by a chain with no command.

And what of philosophy you ask? Now I truly believe that philosophy can be seen as this very exercise in stepping back. Philosophy endeavours to spot similarities where others see differences, and through the use of metaphor provide a fresh perspective on a problem to which one may have become too close.

"Now just a cotton pickin' minute," I hear you cry. "That sounds to me like the rantings of a true believer. Turns out he's just the same as us. Grab him someone. *Get him.*" Perhaps so, although quite frankly this is my book, my stage.

I challenge any one of you to successfully plant philosophy as a tree alongside others, if only because philosophers are also interested in the philosophy of music, the philosophy of religion, the philosophy of science, the philosophy of business etcetera – voluntary derivatives revealing an altruism which is, dare I suggest, rarely reciprocated. And anyway, when was being a little absent-minded such a heinous crime? Don't you see? Continued ridicule only serves to strengthen our resolve, our belief that we *do* in fact stand apart from such crowded competition. If you have forbade us from trading on your market floor then we are all the healthier for it.

Mind you, I hate reading other people's philosophy, or other people's books fullstop. It's like creeping through a minefield. Society's obsession with plagiarism and proof is beginning to weigh heavily on my shoulders, and I hate it all the more for that. If I arrive at the same idea as someone else, and we have both arrived there from first principles, then to my mind I have as much right to write it as they do, whatever year they were born in. Academia may provide a good launch pad, but if you were to attempt a project like this then my advice is to break free as soon as possible. Be inspired by the thoughts of others by all means, but stumble away as soon as those spindly legs can stand. I love Sartre for what it means to me, not him.

But I can see you are tired of my defensive tirade, and you want more – so here's my Ace. Okay, I don't see philosophy as a narrative alongside others, but many philosophers have done, and for now I'm willing to admit that I too may be hugging my own tree a bit too tightly. After all philosophy is about life, life is not about philosophy.

So here's a solution from which all us hippies can benefit – one that will unite us all with a common aim. Instead of chasing various Truths, whether it be profit maximisation, a Grand Unified theory, or God's forgiveness – let's all aim for the same one, human happiness. My particular philosophy already does, where are the rest of you?

Which means even though your tools are ultimately the wrong shape, you scientists must keep chipping away. Just because ultimate truth is beyond your reach it doesn't mean it's time to hang up that white coat. If I've been too hard then I'm sorry, really, but just put that damn thing back on what ever you do. Don't attempt to replace one ultimate truth with another because we all know what priestly nonsense is hiding in the wings - I've been trying to split you lovebirds up. As an act of goodwill I'll stand by you for a while, for I'd rather be chipping away at the frontier than wallowing at the back, eyes closed in prayer.

Cheer up chap, my anti-truth isn't anti-science, and I think I can speak for everyone when I say we're all dead grateful for those cars and computers. The reassessment of Newtonian physics in the new light of Einstein didn't make you disconsolate did it? Quite the opposite if I remember rightly. But surely such a seismic shift illustrated the very nature of science, and its need for constant inquiry, constant discovery. So don't think true, don't even think right – just think best and think happy.

Newton wasn't completely wrong, he just wasn't completely right, no-one ever is. But let's face it, he was more right than most. Sub-particulate reality might be playing up a bit but such disobedience doesn't disguise the brilliance of good old Isaac. It just gave him a new, and I believe more noble, status, for now he's suddenly become part of the adventure. He may have fallen from heaven but in science's voyage of discovery he's definitely secured a place in the captain's cabin. I just wish he'd realised that at the time. It was a theory of genius proportion and the best around for a long time, but Einstein's was better and those of modern scientists are better still. And Einstein couldn't have done his bit without Newton. He admitted himself he was standing on the shoulders of giants.

As science attempts to calculate the perfect third, Newton may have found 0.3, and Einstein might have improved it further by adding 0.03 to make it 0.33. And we can add more, and get closer and closer, but we are logically barred from ever reaching our destination. Because if that three was genuinely recurring, science would have to comprehend infinity, which is just about the foulest language one can utter in a room full of white coats.

And what about the lack of pattern in pi? So typical of us big 'eads to see a mysterious beauty in the hole left wanting by our maths. The only reality we can ever know is human reality, and us digimen can only keep adding those threes. But however small we make those pixels, we'll never make them disappear.

So if all we have as a human viewer is a human view, then what does that say about what is being viewed. What is reality in totality, and what parts of it might forever be beyond comprehension? It is not a question we can answer, clearly, but what proof have we that the answer is nothing? As an outsider it seems the further we venture out into the universe, both metaphorically and literally, the more we realise we do not know. A new discovery is becoming something of a double-edged sword, as it always brings with it ten more questions without answers. The more we discover, the more there seems left to discover. At this exponential rate we'll end up knowing next to nothing!

Those Ancients had it so easy – the earth was flat, Egypt covered most of it and the whole thing was balanced on the shoulders of elephants. Sorted. But now as we wander round our new quantum age we are confused and lost, perhaps even a little lonely, baffled with wonder but faced with so many shadows, so many holes, our scientific map struggling to cover the tiniest percentage of what we are now forced to admit is out there: an unexpected wobble on a monitor, a minute tremor caused by a new existent, which only by chance shares a detectable quality with something back on blighty. We have light detectors and lie detectors because we know all about light and lies. But how can we build sensors for our Smorkron detector when we don't even know what a Smorkron is?

So it appears all we can ever hope for is the accuracy afforded by a digital camera. Easily enough to fool our own senses but deep down we know full well its just a load of pixels chosen from a finite list of pretty colours. Think of the impact the movies and the news can have on us. It's proof we say, it's fact, we can see it with our own eyes. But we know it's only 50 frames a second, and guess what? A Smorkron stands up smug and drops his trousers between each frame. He does it for a laugh, wouldn't you? But if we can create digital images with a complexity far deeper then the best eyesight can detect, then so too can we build a science whose statements ring just as true. And here lies the danger. For how much more shocked will we be on that day the earth quakes, and our indestructible palace is reduced to a pile of bricks.

But science progresses you say? Yes – of course. The smile on the face of a cured cancer patient tells us that. A million Bernsteins slave away for years with nothing new to say, until an Einstein comes along, steps back, thinks outside the box, and shows them a new light, or rather finds one more switch for one tiny room in one house in one street, city, country, planet.

Crunch the last trillion years into one second on a watch, a watch which reads exactly 4.20am. When the second hand has done a full lap, a larger cycle called the minute hand clicks on one and some huge reality 60 times bigger than our universe shuffles along a mere tick. Other beings with another science have moved on a mere trillion of their years, just think how long they've got to go before anything really changes to their way of thinking.

But meanwhile back on Blighty it's biblical mayhem. The era of 4.20am is over, and all the physical conditions which allowed those 60 trillion years to resemble constancy have completely changed. Gravity has turned upside down, energy transfer rendered unrecognisable. Heat. Light. Cold. They will never act the same way again (or if they do it won't be for another 12 hours on the watch, for I fear circles are somehow the answer to the impossibility of infinity.)

In other words, what if we've missed the point? What if we've made a big mistake? Not in our investigations but in the larger conclusions we've drawn? What if we've been a little hasty, a little presumptuous, a little arrogant? What if we spivvy little Blighters have mistaken temporary re-occurrence for timeless constancy?

I'm sitting in a tree gazing down on a field of poppies, the wind's blowing and I'm drawing conclusions, making assumptions about that swirling sea of petals, even though I know each head is ultimately reliant on what lies beneath, a stalk I'll never see.

Rats sits in a tree gazing down on a field of poppies, the wind's blowing and he's drawing conclusions, making assumptions about that giveaway gash, those tyre tracks ripping through the Red Sea like a Chelsea smile, a bonehead's double-blader that will never heal. He's at the scene of the murder, apparently Richard told him exactly where to go, (what *is* he up to? And why am I always the last to know?)

But perhaps he just wants this to end too, to finish, perhaps we're all getting a bit tired now. Some people fight because they want to be fought, some people shoot because they want to be shot, you'll see. Perhaps blood is thicker than Cider, perhaps this son is being swayed by his true father, the father he never had, the father he'll never call dad. Rats would have left his mark, but not in that way, he would have loved his Rodney.

It could have all been so different, perhaps we shouldn't be so hard on poor Rich. He's even let Rats look after Demon now, no doubt some wordless apology for the crime he won't admit, but believe me, to break that bestial bond is some gesture indeed. He also tells me that Nathan's been acting a bit strange recently, he's caught our Nate staring right at him, not through him, but right at him. If our personality is nothing but a collection of memories then it seems our Nathan might just be getting his back. I really need to be there for Richard now, soon there'll be three after him and that's just too much for any one to handle. I never wanted to write this book, this fiction, building up like some screaming crescendo. But I will not let them have a finale, I will not let them get their big ends away, believe it or not this was supposed to be good clean family fun.

Seems we're nothing more than second hand truth dealers, hopelessly stuck to an insignificant cog in a bigger machine we'll never see, never understand and certainly never control. Round and round on the sloppy seconds of life. We're rubbish! We can't even drive round space yet, not really, not very well. And do you know how big space is? I've already made my feelings clear on research, but you're quite welcome to look it up yourself. Massive isn't the word apparently. Yet a trip to the moon, which in terms of the universe is effectively *touching* earth, still breaks the bank and sends its pilots to a spectacular grave.

My cat sighed like a human this morning, or so it seemed. The tenor of the sound, the high-pitched wheeze, just like me. We spend so much time with each other, with one species, that we fail to see what's staring us in the face. Seems we're nearer those elephants than the finish line my friend, and the more we try to pull away, the easier it becomes for those party animals to close the gap, having a lot more fun along the way.

But as I said before, like an all-night garage my science is open 24-7, and I'm just waiting to put in an order for healthy fags and solar cars as soon as you're ready.

So if everything about being human conspires against nearly all his endeavours then is the situation hopeless? It can be for life *is* short, or rather it will be unless we slow it down. Left to its own devices it'll be – what – four chapters tops? One child, two adults and an OAP please, no return – a right dysfunctional family of a life. Not enough, not nearly enough. I don't want to go all Shakespeare on you but we mustn't play these different roles. Hard-working disciples will always die in misery, deathbeds can have a habit of shrinking that passion of a lifetime into an embarrassing obsession.

These four chapters, these seven ages must be rolled into one. Buy their suits by all means but don't get too snug. Ill-fitting they must be, and cheap too, because to wear that uniform with pride is to buy into their lie, and the only lies we should live by are those we tell ourselves. And rip that suit off whenever you get the chance, change back into your own skin, the skin that has evolved around you, felt its way around every nook and cranny. Slip back into your time, and skip out of theirs. If you let him Father Time will do nothing but mark the hours until you die, life is the greatest killer going remember.

We must use our time wisely by ignoring the perverted clutches of that abusive guardian – he's not your real dad, those bedtime hugs, those night time kisses, you must know what's really going on. "Bad dreams" he whispers in your ear as you drift off - you'll see, but by then it might be too late. Best not risk it, best come with me. For we must journey as one along our endless pointless story, we must ride the Circle Line, cruise the Orbital. (Perhaps those Londoners have had the answer all along, no wonder they still go clubbing in their forties.)

We shouldn't be embarrassed when we feel the same inside as we did when we were 45, 35, 25, 15. This is not kiddy fiddling you know, you can't be done for loving yourself. Think back to when you were 20, and stared at those besuited 30-year-olds walking around in the midweek sun, confidently grabbing half an hour for lunch, munching on something vaguely European for all like they owned the world on which they walked. And you thought, sausage roll in one hand, fag in the other: "Not me, not ever." Well, I don't have to tell you what happened. We don't get older, the world just gets younger. That mad bad mental case that so enjoyed publicising his anti-life, who so hated society that he made a point of mixing with it at every opportunity, shoving his stinking protest in its face, is still lurking around inside. He may have swapped ideas for knowledge, passion for precision, but the buzz of existence hasn't got any less freaky.

So a message to you young folk: flick back that multi-coloured fringe and stop telling me your fucking opinions for just one second - they're nothing but mental freebies after all. Look a little closer and consider just how well-fitted is that suited and booted at which you scoff, especially compared to your designer scruff? Your judgement is so shallow, your opinions so *ineffective*. Don't you see? We wear a suit to earn cash, because cash helps us reach our dreams, that's all. Anyone can dress like a clown when no-one cares what you wear.

But the saddest thing is they're probably right to scoff. So many of us live our lives inside out, so scared of society's gaze we even dress our insides in a suit. Before long we start to think like we speak, and our life goes in reverse. The stars still come out, but when once we gazed in wonder, we now draw the curtains shut.

But it's time to rip them open again. Come on mums and dads, stop making fools of yourselves, tearing towards some non-existent finish line like an embarrassment at your son's sports day. There is real work to be done – proper work. We are about to be driven by our dreams and you must start talking to that teenager inside again. All this talk about truth has been hard on all of us, but it had to be said, else the next bit wouldn't make sense. But at last it's time for a bit of Romance, it's time to save our soul. It's time to go inside.

Part Three

Trusting that morality, politics and science have done their job, let's now enter the space they have kept us free, to consider just what separates each of us from the world we experience. Not the political *us-and-them* this time, but the philosophical *me-and-you*.

But remember, if this inner world ever starts to sound like a religious soul then discard the thought as a hangover from our pubescent heritage, that moody medieval phase so full of paranoia and superstition, when we painted our walls black and imagined ourselves possessed of some ghastly spirit, or spectre.

How wonderful to have been born before religion, a privileged position we poor souls will never understand. I'm sure pre-religious man was far more enlightened than we could ever be, with such a clearer and *cleaner* view of the human spirit, of this inner world and its earthly potential, way before it was contaminated by sin and guilt. But perhaps when religion has withered away, this once lethal practice will one day be recalled, with humour, perhaps even some nostalgia, as a charming chapter in human history, similar to the Greeks' belief in Gods plural.

The plain truth is we only fancy ourselves able to conceive of the religious soul by borrowing from the hazardous process of negation and then succumbing to the all-too-common pitfall of thinking like we speak. *Not* rightly belongs to the virtual world of logic, the abstract man-made realm of mathematics, and when prefixed to a noun should dissolve the resultant compound into just such ephemera, a name that's lost its face.

But we romantic fools never listened in maths. For when the Priest declares: "God is not of this earth" he couldn't actually be nearer the truth. He thinks he's said something meaningful about the glory of God, whose unquestioned existence lies beyond our blighted tawdry home, but all I hear is a definition of a word. Swap 'is' for 'means' and me and the Priest are getting on fine. For that's just what God is, the opposite of physical reality, the opposite of earth and its things, not earth, not things, or (as we say for short) nothing. Yet the Priest continues to peddle the imaginary as real, and the real as worthless, a paradoxical creed served up way before we're old enough to question - our mind's tiny feet bound at birth.

To me however, reality sure *seems* pretty sturdy. I actually quite like it, and it certainly seems to fill the time, and space. Why did we ever believe there was something more? (Although, rather confusingly, there is more, but it's found in a place which somehow is neither beyond reality nor really quite part of it either). I talk about my inner world purely because it feels like I have one worth talking about. But this is not a fact arrived at philosophically, for I feel no essence, no ideal, that's just words talking nonsense. All I know is that part of my existence feels a bit different, strangely subject to the outside world, but also strangely not, sometimes controlled strongly by my will, but sometimes barely more than reaction, feeling, sensation even.

Remember the way words come about? Well the soul is no different, for I have seen or felt this strange something enough times to give it a name, as I would a tree, a bird or a face. I could use another word, but I'm saying it was ours in the first place, before *they* stole it, almost scaring it to death in the process. So yes, we have a soul, because that's the word we've given to this seeming seamlessness of inner experience.

Self-consciousness is indeed a sophisticated awareness, knowledge even, of our own existence, but our over-protective language seems to have ushered it away from the common horde of other stuff we know. We spotted a common denominator to our brain activity and for some reason proceeded to extract it from time itself, treating it as some great mysterious force operating behind our chain of thoughts.

But back on Dear old Blighty we know that an elephant can have a certain simple thought today, and a different one tomorrow, just like us. The same elephant using the same brain. The only difference is that we have a memory which has remembered a familiarity of feeling to each thought, has felt a common 'thinker', and the elephant hasn't. But is there any *real* difference dumbo?

We call a house *our home* because it feels like the one we had dinner in yesterday, we recognise a *persisting idea* and it makes sense to give it a name. But that doesn't mean this home can now go to heaven! The idea came *second*, not first. And if the home can't survive the bombs which flatten our house, then how come we get to keep our soul once the firing squad lets fly? I can't see our soul as anything other than the *familiar feeling* of thinking from the same geographical point of view, located somewhere in the same head on the same body. Why isn't that enough? It seems *we've* got the problem, *we're* the ones doing the drinking - monkeys are fine.

How did we abandon ourselves into this endless cycle of guilt-ridden decision-making, when all we really want to do is climb trees and eat bananas? Those funky gibbons have it so easy. Things were great back then. Why on earth did we come down to earth? Now that's what I call a Fall, much worse then a schoolboy snigger at each other's bits. I bet those monkeys stare at us in disbelief, with our clothes and cash and endless endless chatter. Yet another distant cousin who'd never admit as much at a party. They're laughing at us you know, I'm convinced of it.

But back to the human soul and the metaphysical muddle from which we're trying to escape. Plato conceived of the dualistic notion that objects in the physical world are illusory, the mere transitory appearance of a deeper world of perfect ideas. As a model for philosophical discussion Platonic dualism has become indispensable, with its formal descendants, necessity and contingency, clearly surviving and thriving to this day. But to me it's all very confusing how one can actually believe it. It resembles a fairy tale, it sounds so *made-up*.

I fear it has less to do with understanding and more to do with providing hope in an apparently hopeless situation. Seems to me the hopeless gave birth to Hope and the Godless gave birth to God. We're all looking for meaning in a meaningless world, but that requires courage, not sacrifice; facts, not faith; and honesty, not forgiveness.

Let's consider this new inner world, now stripped of it's religious coating. What can we say about this mysterious persistency, this elusive "I" of which we talk so much, yet understand so little?

There seems to be a certain subjectivity which somehow makes choices about how its bodily home interacts with a world outside. Our brain activity is clearly influenced by this world, but we would like to think that in the large part, the way we react is somehow *under our control*, a control which bears a semblance of constancy, characterising (and giving character to) our chains of thought.

We may have been born into this life without consultation, but now we're here it seems to bear certain responsibilities we cannot escape. Like it or not it we seem not only required to act, but also duty bound to account for these actions. There is a meaningful 'us' to which the world happens, and none of us can be indifferent.

"Does life have a meaning - if so what is it?", "Will any part of us survive physical death – if so, how could it still *feel* like us?"

Such weighty matters will torment us into unhappiness unless they are properly considered, although I'll promise no answers to questions which don't make sense - we may have been burdened with a *desire* for meaning, but if wishes were always granted then I guess we'd also be flying by now. But neither must we ignore these questions, as we might drape a towel over a television set. We must face them full on, before that white noise in the extremities of our consciousness begins to gnaw away at any chance of real happiness.

After pages of putting the religious to task I think it's time to take on 21st-century robot man, that thoughtless word-processor who traded in an inquiring mind for a brand new car.

Now God's not looking I understand that you wanted to let yourself go a bit, but this is now your *only* life, your one chance, and if you're aiming no higher than synthetic luxury at home or on the road then you're nothing but a clean-shaven monkey with nuts for brains. When did comfort become so desirable? When did thoughts become such a burden? For we have indeed become highly-skilled at hiding this inner world, we have become junkies of the meaningless, thoughtless consumers of Information and Sensation, it seems we would rather talk and watch and eat and drink and smoke and choke and lie and die – in fact anything to avoid thinking.

We hide from ourselves, and where do we hide? In the outside world of all places. We are desperate to be like the humans we see around us, to feel inside as they appear on the outside. Bad faith in a nutshell - and we've all got it real bad.

I had a feeling it would come out like this, I had a feeling it would be all narrative and no action. Perhaps next time I'll give it a proper go – make the characters fit the story line, bog them down in detail and dialogue, rather then giving those scamps such a free reign. And perhaps next time I won't feature in it so strongly – because some of this has hurt, being on the outside looking in, not really knowing what any of them were really intending, misinterpreting actions as decisions.

I'm writing ends but I'm ignorant of the means. I feel like a reporter who's been sent out of a court case while everyone else hears the best bits. There are contributory factors of which I know nothing, 'goings-on' behind the scenes, behind *my* scenes, and the worse thing is dear reader I'll never know, and therefore neither, I'm sorry to report, will you.

I can only say what I see, you may have to fill in some of the gaps yourself. At least Richard is back on the team, we need a captain to guide us through the last bit. I wouldn't say we've spotted land yet, but we will soon.

I've started drinking again by the way, not a lot, but not a little either. Just like before really, but this time with no script, no character, no means and no essence, to egg me on. I decided to put my will to sleep as one might a rabid dog, and now fancy myself pure reaction. And do you know what? It's far easier than you'd imagine. All that guff about personality and accountability, it's just a society thing you know.

You can act weirdly if you want, we all can, and while it may seem a little strange at first you'll soon get used to it, and so too will everyone else. But I'm

not even doing things for no reason, for I'm not actually doing anything. I'm just gonna sit on this stool and wait for it all to finish, and if it doesn't resolve itself neatly then so what. I've no childish craving for symmetry. I'm indifferent now, good ending, bad ending, no ending, whatever. My office is at the end of the bar and I'll answer any questions, for Richard should have plenty of those. And so too do Ratty and Nate, for each other that is, not me obviously.

Those two are talking a lot now, they're colluding like a couple of blockbusting heroes reading through someone else's script, some transatlantic trite peppered with 'getting even' and 'payback time'. I'd never have put such trash in their mouths, especially not in dear Ratty's. I'm sure I even saw them lo-five under the table the other day. Will they ever realise, I wonder, that they could kill two Dickie Birds with one stone?

I've started drinking again, not a lot, and not a little either. But this time I ain't no drunk, I ain't playing no bar-room soak. I'm just having a few Sueys. I'm not suggesting being an alcoholic is always a role we chose to play, but it certainly was for me. And do you know what? For the first time in this sorry tale I'm actually feeling okay with things, okay about myself.

Whether that's because I'm on the up while Richard is sliding fast, or whether it's because I've let go of the reins, decided to take each moment as it comes, like a relapsed addict living life one drink at a time. Yes ... perhaps next time I won't feature so strongly.

The incongruity of a life lived with a future once imagined lurks at the heart of the human condition. We fictionalise the lives of others, and even our own, we give them a sheen never felt when we arrive, and so are eternally at odds with ourselves. Yet it never stops us daydreaming....

I'm at work and I'm dreaming of getting home and having a glass of wine. The dream feels good, I can almost see myself looking out over the back garden, framed by the back door, silhouetted against the kitchen light, night falling somewhere behind the shadows. But when I get there, when I arrive, it's somehow just me again, the same me that was sitting in the office. And the wine, the garden, the kitchen, they're all so immediate, all so similar, all made of *stuff*, this existence, *my* existence. The wine is nice, for sure, but the dream is nowhere to be seen. It's always me, why is it *always* me? I feel as if there's been a bomb scare and my dreams have been evacuated onto the streets. I feel empty, I feel sick, I feel nausea.

But the next day, when the terror has left, when the emergency's gone, the dream, which has now of course turned into a memory, can move back in again. Feeling much better I even venture to tell a colleague what I did last night, how I came home from work, and enjoyed a glass of wine, overlooking the garden, silhouetted against the kitchen light and the dream comes back to life. And they too can share it, and imagine my life to glide along with such sophisticated elegance, true literary substance. How they now envy this life I live. The moment itself however is dead and forgotten, buried deep in a present since past, replaced by a memory which never actually happened. We dream of what's to come, we even dream of what's gone, but we never live it, ever. But as I say, the wine was nice.

Even though we instinctively judge others from the outside in, we know deep down that this is a way they can never see themselves. Given a moment to reflect we might realise that each one of them is also looking out on the world from their own mysterious cockpit, head full of their own strange collection of air-heavy pictures they too call thoughts. We know it yet we deny it every time. We are forever judging people in ways we hate being judged ourselves, forever judging the *outcomes* of their actions from the safety of our own world, a world where *intention* matters far more.

Consider one bridge across one motorway on one Saturday morning. The number of cars travelling beneath will be remarkably similar to last Saturday, and next week we expect a similar density again. But there must be a hundred reasons behind every hundred journeys, each one utterly unconnected with the next. And regular travellers aside there'll be another hundred next week.

One's off to a family funeral and another is anticipating today's footie match, one's testing out a new car and another's returning from her first night of adultery.

Rats sits on a bridge gazing down on six streams of metal, the wind's blowing and he's drawing conclusions, his son's dog at his side, taking the place of the son he's never known. He wants revenge, and revenge is about to get out of hand. For proper stories exist in the imagination where there are no rules, neither beyond reality, nor really part of it either, a place where power and potential have no limits.

But the Dark Destroyer and his faithful sidekick, gazing down from the bridge in a parallel world, see nothing but boring bit parts playing their drive-on role to predictable perfection in this Saturday morning matinee. Yawn, yawn, yawn.

Ratty raises quivering fist to mouth, fingers locked solid from neglect. Like an ever-failing attempt at suicide, he sucks at the tiniest sparks at the end of his oily smoke. Proper stories exist in the imagination where there are no rules, no science, no language.

"Let's have some fun," he smirks. "Let's remind these lemmings just how random life can be." And with one imperceptible flick of the eye he brings their wayward souls crashing together in a twisted heap of white hot rod.

A splinter of ash drops from bloodied lips, he wouldn't have known, he wouldn't have seen it fall, he wouldn't have seen that little firecracker glow afresh on the breeze, fluttering earthwards to be caught in the nick of time by the face of a speeding adulteress, that sought-after soft top that once sought the Heavens' gaze, now sealing her fate in Hell.

At once this unconnected cast of strangers are transformed into "Saturday Morning M-way Crash Horror", blood brothers united in pain, and fear, of what comes next. Them being there on that fateful day, under that bridge on that motorway was purely a means to an end. But a hundred miscellaneous tasks shared an identical contingent quality for one moment only. A proximity orchestrated by naked ridiculous chance.

Most of these poor souls probably weren't even thinking of the motorway, or even of driving. The here and now, each unique passing moment, was the last thing on their mind. But that cheeky devil twitched his eyelid and their existence was suddenly defined by means, not ends. The contingent became defining, and from then on *necessary*. Day to day existence is always there, the one underlying essence behind all our thoughts and actions, behind all our lies and lives, and that dark serpent will always strike when we least expect it.

And as the stench of death and diesel rose towards the bridge, an old man and his dog stumbled away into the distance, seen by no-one. "I should care," thinks Ratty, shutting out the wails for help, the screams for survival. "This really should bother me." But he thinks nothing more, and will tell not a soul. Random proximity, that's all it was, them being there in that deathpit, him sitting there in the viewing gallery, pointless parallel lives he will never bring together with a story, with a lie.

So he left in the chill of the concrete breeze, fizzing around his ears like flies over a dying Aunt. He stared in his shell, imagining himself the last person alive, oblivious to suffering, detached from the sensations his extremities relayed. Boy was he cold.

"Hope, Emma's okay," Ratty tried, out loud. But he couldn't cry anymore, not one tear. Emma was dead and now Rats knew that death was the end. He stumbled off in silence, the steely silence we wear like armour, the soulless resilience we all draw upon when something has been lost, forever. There's no drama left in this queen. The queen is dead. I guess we're all victims now, all waiting for this to finish.

Many times we fail to achieve our goals and in such instances our ends are lost in the means - with no delivery we are caught short, frozen spastics pregnant with failure. Our foolish attempts to woo an intended lover will, if they fail, leave us looking like a fool. But if they succeed then no-one remembers the fool - the action is justified by the outcome, the means by the ends.

The cheat who never returned home from her first night of adultery is forever a dead driver, her tragic innocence locked in time, her night of deception kept private for eternity, hidden away in that six-speed cemetery.

And the writer with no publishing deal is nothing but a hopeless dreamer, and all the more a fool for those years of scribbling effort gone to waste. But if he is a success then he becomes his dream, those noble years of hard graft clearly worth it. "We always knew you had it in you," his loved ones chorus, the outcome now stretching back in time to the first chapters of the biography to come, rewriting a childhood resplendent with fresh significance, but one which never really happened that way, however things happened to turn out.

This labelling of people according to actions, as if they are essentially actors, is to propagate the world of bad faith. Surely we're more similar to those people with common ends, surely *why* we're doing something is more important than *what* we're doing.

We predict the future from the outcomes of the past, and such naivety, such past imperfect, will always predict a future imperfect. We can never know how profound is our analysis of history, how many honourable or murderous motives have been lost to chance, to circumstance, to ineptitude. We say the current President has a one in four chance of being assassinated because a quarter of his predecessors met such an end. Now are you telling me that if we then discover that 200 years ago some president we previously thought had died in his sleep was actually poisoned then the assassination odds of our current president have just shortened?

Apparently the number of suicide bombers in Thailand is on the increase, while the number in Palestine has remained constant, which I'm sure makes those Israelis feel a lot safer, now their problem has proportionately decreased.

Surely the man who shoots a president dead over the Vietnam war has more in common with the bad-shot protestor who narrowly missed the day before, than the moonshine madman who poisoned a president over a game of Black-Eyed Bob two centuries earlier.

Statistically this morning's robber will have contributed to his town's worsening reputation for street crime, but in truth he's a smackhead, and if burglary, fraud or sucking cocks on camera would have fed his habit today then you can be sure he'd have been as happy doing these instead.

Surely the man who writes for fame has more in common with the page three girl than the man who writes for personal fulfilment, and the man who would kill for love more in common with the man who would die for love than the man who would kill for cash.

But the problem is made no easier by those people who willingly live in bad faith, who live the lie, who indeed become nothing but their actions. It is a great irony that our job, which should be the most transparent passionless means to an end, so often takes us over. So easily we *become* bank clerks, managers, journalists; at work, at home, on holiday. We hide behind our actions, we invite people to judge us from the outside, indeed we attempt to live life from the outside, in private and in public.

More of that later. For now I am keen to elicit the silent inside we cannot ignore, however often we ignore it in others. I'm talking about the hoper, the dreamer, the paranoid schemer. I am talking about those parts of us which are forever separate from every other human. That part of us which, as Sartre will say, is condemned to be free, like a poisonous snake set loose in a playground of children.

This thinking thing, whatever its nature, is definitely located in the head alright and it's as light as air, a ghost doomed to haunt the same room, perhaps more location than extension. But just because it may be some*where* rather than something, it still needs explaining.

To walk round declaring there to be no soul leaves one of the most important human drives unexplained. This feeling of having a soul, a feeling we just can't shake off, is fuelled by our endless reflection on ourselves as a choosing agent. Not only do we choose, but somehow we *feel* the chooser, and cannot help but reflect on the fact that we might have chosen otherwise.

Yet if we were to take a moment to analyse our consciousness, we might in fact come to the conclusion that our brain is far more *reactive* then we might like to admit. Perhaps in the main it *responds* to our senses, but does so with such inconceivable rapidity that sooner or later a pattern emerges amid the chaos and we baptise it a *thought*, which sooner or later becomes a *decision*.

Nonetheless, we are invited by all aspects of society to see this endless choosing as nothing short of the operation of a noble *free will*, even if in reality, modern life has reduced this ancient secret to little more than an exercise in commerce, exploiting a burden we are condemned to bear.

Perhaps it's time to step back, and consider whether this mysterious little tool with which we carve out our precious personality is really all it's cracked up to be.

When playing chess how happy do we genuinely feel on the cusp of victory, our destiny firmly in our hands? In this moment of ultimate freedom, why does anxiety rise from the deep? And this feeling is made all the worse as we glance enviously at the steely determination in the eyes of our opponent, now called upon to battle for his life, his glorious moment of truth.

For we never come out fighting as strong as when we're in a corner, because our resolve is not so preoccupied with the need to choose. Regardless of the outcome, we fancy we can really put ourselves to the test here, carry out some high-quality personal research, make some long-term gains. But when we're winning we're abandoned in the game, stuck in the short-term, duty-bound to deliver the killer blow, to finally skin that rabbit. Now that's the trickiest position of the lot, and thankless too. We can't learn anything positive when success is expected and all else failure. Winning is so often a no-win situation.

Please don't take this metaphor literally, for I've no desire to lose games, quite the opposite. In fact, I say be competitive when it *does* matter. What do you think games are for?

And while we're on the subject, do you know when the best time to offer a double in backgammon is? Ratty showed me this in the pub yesterday/ today/ tomorrow (what's that you say? "Oh, you're just making stuff up now." Well just what do you think fiction is?) So where was I? Ratty showed me this in the pub .. er .. oh go on then, yesterday, if you insist, and seemed to take great delight as he exposed my romantic side only then to stick the knife in good and proper (I told you, there's nothing like the moral rage of a former believer).

Anyway, the best time to offer a double is when your opponent has just come back from the edge of defeat and is *approaching* parity. For he is filled with the pattern of the past and desperate to see out the rest of the game, to see if he can complete this act of heroism, as if the game had already been written, as if his succession of sixes contained some inertia, obediently taking their place in this amazing winning streak, as if the here and now was somehow in the middle of time, as if the dice were fighting *with* him.

Ratty showed me, without words, like they all do these days, that we are wrong to see our life in such a romantic literary way, as part of a story already written. Of course he won, not every time, but just enough to show me that every second is the first second of any empty future, and only fools think otherwise.

But we are so foolish, and never more so than when we win against the odds, for it's then we start believing that our glory belonged to us, nothing less than an historic revelation of the timeless hero we always were. Bad faith may not get any badder. The team who wins the cup will always look anywhere but the structure of the competition to explain their glory, the cocksucker who makes it to Number One will always dedicate her success to talent, hard work and inner belief, even the lottery winner will punctuate his acceptance speech with "blessed fortune", "destiny" and "fate". All these histrionics: when we all know a cup will be awarded every year, however crap the teams are, a Number One will be announced each week, however shite the songs are, and the lottery will crown its Chosen One on a suspiciously regular basis, because that's just what it's designed to do.

Winning is so often about quantity not quality, being better than the rest but rarely ever the best possible. But the worst thing is, we blur the line between our calculated victory-producing systems and the worthwhile goals we can achieve in real life. We are invited to imagine that the artificial waves we create for our petty contests are actually out there to ride in the real world. You may call it confidence, even harmless optimism, but I say it's wholesale denial which holds this fiction together. Competitions are designed to produce Winners, but rarely winners.

For in all that really matters we can all be losers, it's quite possible no cups will be handed out this year, not unless we work harder, aim much higher and stop wasting time comparing ourselves with others. Use competition to pass the time by all means, as fitness training, to test yourself, to improve yourself, but never forget that the only combatant worth taking on is the fool you were yesterday, a lifelong opponent who may always win in the end, but that doesn't mean you should give up fighting.

What I'm trying to stress is that in real life it's far more important for our will to be *strong*, rather than free. And this strength will be nurtured on *our* terms, not other people's, one concerned far more with achieving, than winning. When we tell our children not to worry about being unpopular we are not celebrating their weakness. We just want them to realise that it's better they foster a strong will to reach goals in their own games, rather than learn short-term tricks to score in someone else's. Because if their opponent's a heap of shit then they're only one better than that. I want to learn and I want to get better, but that means better than I was yesterday, not better than you are today. I've got my own standards to maintain.

I find the synthetic importance of real-life choices so tiresome, the do-or-die binary of the unknown, the forked path leading to street-cred or no-cred. Our noble will has been stripped naked, reduced to some feeble free choice left to flap about in the wind, and with it the tedious obligation to choose *well*, to compete, to succeed, to win. Our noble will has been hijacked and humiliated by corporate modernity, banishing it to the *public* arena, where it is reared and seduced in the tawdry stadia administered by the free market, where pointless competition spawns pointless variety, an infinite number of *choices* to make, that's if you're not fussy about quality of course. But our will in its purest form *is* about quality, not quantity, and that means giving it the time and space to pursue excellence.

The beauty of a project is that the big decisions, the *quality* decisions, are made largely at the start, the high standards set from the beginning, a pact between you and yourself, and believe me there's no harsher judge. And there's no use using learning any shortcuts either, for as player and opponent you're both cheat and victim.

While I could not have anticipated what this book would become, or who its stars would be, it has in large part been an exercise in necessity. I've filled in holes, put in link roads and bridges, built extensions on parts which appeared too cute, too presumptuous. Far more than I could ever have imagined the day to day work has been largely a matter of maintenance and fine-tuning. And in that sense strength, discipline and standards have always been greater issues than freedom and choice.

Yeah right, it's all very well for you to say, but that's not how it's turned out for me, when your cast, that bunch of cast-offs, started getting a little big for their boots. Nathan's started looking at *me* strangely now, but I'm not worried. He'll remember Richard before he remembers me, and I only held a watch your

honour. Nathan's looking at everyone strangely these days, everyone in the pub anyway. I think he's narrowed his search down to this watering hole, and now, like some Victorian sleuth, is eliminating us one by one. But if he thinks he's gonna get some whodunnit ending, with all his suspects dressed in tuxedoes for the grand finale, then he's even more foolish than he lets on. If Sarah's not getting hers then he's certainly not getting his. I'm sorry, I'm sure it's real inconvenient and all, but there's been plenty worse crimes among our number for me to worry about those floppy little fingers.

If it's not what you've got, but what you do with it, then clearly strength of will is more desirable than freedom of choice, for a strong will surely cuts down on the need to keep choosing. The more disciplined we become in learning from the outcomes of past decisions, the fewer choices we will have to make in the future. Isn't it in fact a lack of knowledge which calls on us to make a choice, its opposite a confident *decision*. I've never enjoyed placing trust in some ephemeral *intuition* – for it's nothing but a guess in a dress, and quite frankly I'd rather have a map.

Have you ever wondered why people toss a coin to make key decisions, and why they do so in public? Quite apart from the fact they clearly haven't done their homework, there's another far more important reason. It's because society holds us accountable and judges our characters by the choices we make, and for some this is too much. So they let it be known they have let Mr Chance decide, because then he's to blame if things go wrong.

Choice can indeed be a burden and a heavy one at that, and on occasion it has rooted me to the floor, quite literally, staring at the wall, with no reason to choose, no reason to move.

Antoine is the image put forward by the most pessimistic reading of this philosophy. Also faced with an infinite number of choices of equal value (in his case zero) he does nothing, or rather he means nothing. He fancies himself as pure unadulterated existence, and freed from purpose wanders aimlessly around Bouville.

But we must learn to take life in the outside world of less control much less seriously. We must face up to our freedom, laugh at it almost, place it in its proper context, for such short-term anxiety rarely finds its match further down the line. This is another reason why we need large projects: to keep us occupied, to fill our existence, to give us something meaningful to do.

But don't worry, this isn't bad faith in brighter clothes for we are fully aware what we're doing. The Creator is one role we must all play, a job we can and must allow to take us over, at work, at home, and abroad. God's job is one we must all apply for.

This mysterious choosing cavern is also the realm of beauty and we will be searching for it soon, but we speculators must do our research before the final push, for Fool's Gold is everywhere and we must know our nuggets.

All I am trying to do is make sense of this world before me, and I travel light, bearing no reasoned or reasonable expectations. This journey is one of wide-eyed innocence, an investigation penned on blank pages. I will not make the Platonic blunder, I will see no meaning behind my desire, no reason behind my ideas, and I will never trust intuition over knowledge. All explanations are possible until proved otherwise. So when I say we are unable to escape our consciousness that is an assertion borne from observation, and an historical one at that.

If one day we can read other people's thoughts, then so be it, and in my world of zero research the idea doesn't actually seem that far fetched (they're only electrical pulses after all, aren't they?) The prospect appals me, for my dualism and this bloody book would be lost to antiquity for ever, but I must grudgingly accept that privacy is not an essential quality of consciousness.

A life without privacy of thought would be sheer hell. It's not what I'm thinking that worries me, it's what I've done, the memories. I've started drinking again, properly, seriously, with commitment. It's Richard's fault, he's drinking more than ever. He's started staring back at Nate now, he's even the first to stare sometimes – what *is* he up to?

Why doesn't he just break his other wrist if that's his game? Reverse psychology? Our Richard? I suppose he may have started reading a bit when he went Absent Without Lines, without *my* lines, but it still seems unlikely. Perhaps he thinks Nate would never suspect the biggest nutter in the pub. Perhaps he reckons that since Nate became a tash-twiddling sleuth he's looking for a twist, the unexpected, the clever (as if!)

Perhaps that Nate's not so bad, good value as they say, good entertainment, at least one of us is getting into it. Not me though – I'll just watch, you know where my office is. The door's always open. I've started drinking again, properly, seriously, with commitment, my Suey demands nothing less.

But mind-reading is not progress! And to the white coat who makes it possible we cry: "Our jail still stands but its walls are now made of glass. We may be prisoners, but allow us our dignity."

So would I give up the privacy of my own thoughts for the ability to read other people's? – No way. Left exposed my consciousness would soon melt into a paranoid pulp under the scorching heat of the public gaze. My mind is an arena of pure experiment, a Victorian circus ring to which all freaks are invited. Some of the world's greatest evils play ball in my backyard and I need, in fact I demand, this freedom. And this is one freedom that actually is worth fighting for.

From a desperately young age we are taught to seek happiness in the outside world, lead to believe that popularity and acceptance are prizes, not burdens. And before we know it our public life has become our true essence, and our private world dismissed as irrelevant, self-indulgent, perhaps not a little perverse. And Dr Public is all too ready to dispense his miracle remedy should we develop a nasty rash of Narcissism: "Act according to the judgement of others thrice a day - it'll clear up in no time."

But this medicine leaves us so vulnerable, stripped of our natural anti-bodies we become hooked on prescription hugs, like the humanists in Nausea, convinced that society and human interaction describe the limits of truth and meaning. As Antoine realises in his defining conversation with the Autodidact "humanists love humanity but they hate humans".[4] Or in other words, they love the communal ideal which humans have created, their society and their relationships, but on his own each individual is hateful, a pathetic self-obsessed paranoid freak saved only by the bigger idea, his

---

[4] Nausea, Jean-Paul Sartre, 1938

membership of humanity. So they live life back to front, desperate to come out of their shell their flailing tentacles search out any other life, any other blood but their own.

I'm not arguing that we must stay wrapped in our own self-obsessed world, but if someone's about to shoot me I'd much rather feel silent and secure in my bullet-proof vest than be obliged to talk them round, or even shoot them first.

This might suggest those who say the least know the most, that outspoken criticism is often an act of defence, that aggression hides the flimsiest of beliefs. We might suspect that a man's propensity to shoot reveals a paranoid fear of being shot. Pre-emptive defence as the burger boys call it. But is this true? Perhaps they shoot because they want to be shot. Perhaps they suck because they want to be sucked. Perhaps they judge because they *want* to be judged. Because in their world to be exposed is to be made whole: "I'm an arsehole you say? Why fancy that, silly old me is actually a big old arsehole! You don't know how happy you've made me."

Gerald's day will come, when his bullets don't hurt, when his tentacles don't stick, when he will have one life left unconsidered, one life left to judge. By accident he sees it one day in the mirror and with terror bulging from ever particle his dried up suckers unfurl one last time, and in the heroic throes of death curl back on themselves to face one final prey.

On his stinking deathbed he recognises the neglected grotesque creature inside - locked away to fester and ferment for so long it's blind and bent double - but its heart beats, and its beating real loud now. And so the door is opened, years too late, and this bloodless being inches into the searing light. A brittle outstretched arm reaches for the bullet proof vest it should have worn all those years back, but it's crippled frame cannot support such a weight. Our Gerald has seen the future, his pitiful white eyes reel in their sockets, desperately seeking a mercy killer. This isn't pretty, one bullet is all it needs, and I knew I'd get him in the end. But I didn't think it'd be like this.

Meanwhile we've all started drinking more now, we've all gone prime time, seven nights a week. No-one wants to miss any scenes, a walk-on role would be fine, they're volunteering for it these days, Rat and Nate, Ray and Nat, even Sarah's nodding more, or am I imagining that? She's got plenty to say that one, but she knows this is not her part, not yet. She's convinced there's a sixth quality to the universe, a sixth part to the story, a supersub to snatch the glory in the dying seconds. And who knows, there might be? We did a deal after all.

Things are really cooking now, there's even talk of a second series which means we can't really wrap it up the way she'd like – anyway that's what I'm telling her from now on. With no heaven or hell I guess one lie's as good as the next. Second series indeed! Not me mate, not with this lot.

None of us sit together anymore. There's Rat and Nate and a dog called Demon, there's Ray and dog-end Nat, and there's me, Rich and nodding sodding Sarah – *shut up*! Our Ratty's cheeks are as red as ever - seems every time he looks over at us his colour becomes more intense. Richard on the other hand is not looking good, each stare draws more and more colour from his heroin chic, father unwittingly sucking on his very own bloodline, killing the son that never called him dad.

I don't think Richard's gonna last the distance you know. But he must, he's the one person for whom I *have* guaranteed an ending, it's gonna be great, and Nate might just get his surprise, not one to call his own of course, but a twist he could certainly twiddle his tash over. I have guaranteed an ending for Richard, I told him I'd already written it. I guess I've lied to everyone now, but hey, we all need a friend, and I'll think of something. I'll nick a late one in injury time if I have to, I always do, I'm confident.

But let's not dwell on lives lived *in extremis*, whether they be directed by, or indifferent to, the judgemental gaze of others. For the most part we can feel both, one day craving our own company while seeking that of others the next, and journey quite happily between these two worlds so long as it is we alone who draw up the schedule. But it is on those occasions when our hands are ripped from the controls, when our desire for privacy is not granted, that the walking contradiction underscoring this once-merry dualism is revealed.

When Sartre said: "L'enfer c'est les autres" (hell is other people)[5], he was talking of the look and judgement we can feel when in another's company. To his reckoning, when someone enters a room we cease to be the unique centre of a world and are suddenly an object in another's. An identity is forced upon us, one not of our choosing, and beyond our control. Like an endless game of charades that little devil begins guessing at a personality we can never reveal.

This may sound like the bleating of a paranoid philosopher but anyone who has seen a video of themselves taken unawares will understand the hell to which this poor lamb refers. For most of us will positively *hate* the recording – for we are *so* much more darling: "Who is that twitching stuttering fool, and with such a poor sense of timing! Where's the richness, the substance, the sheer life force which has seen me through all these years? This pathetic device has recreated nothing but a half-breed mimic. I guess it looks like me, a *bit*, but the mannerisms are all wrong. I'm much smoother, much more *effective*. Get me my agent, I want out."

But when our friend sees themselves and cries: "That's nothing like me!" – how often do we agree? We are more likely to consider their's a rather vain exaggeration, the outburst of a true Drama Queen. Technical limitations aside, the representation in fact seems rather accurate, similarities at least outweighing differences. When we see our friend on film it's essentially the same person we spend our time with. But when we see ourselves on film, we see the person our friends spend *their* time with, and they are a stranger, a stranger our friends may know and like far more than we do.

So we have a choice: we can either face up to this reality, settle into the cockpit and try to fly this jet with confidence, or we can want out. We can see this incongruity between our private life and public appearance as an inescapable quality of human existence (as things currently stand) or we can see discord, like a freaked-out Frenchman whose world falls apart with a knock at the door.

I guess for some the shock, the gap, is just too much. After suffering that video nasty they decide they want a match, they need congruity, or at the very least some *vague* resemblance. And now they've realised their public face ain't going nowhere they move

---

[5] No Exit, Jean-Paul Sartre, 1944

outside to meet him, throwing themselves and their belongings out onto the street, a voluntary eviction for all to see.

Suddenly they welcome the camera, the mirror, the attention, in fact they start to *crave* its gaze on what has become their true self. Life alone with their thoughts becomes a pointless waste of time, self-indulgent, selfish even. In fact they never are alone – they watch TV, they talk on the phone, they sleep, they plan the next day of public life, and boy do they talk: "Simply *never* stop talking, that's the rule darling, simply *never*." If you secretly filmed these people at home alone they would be models of perfection, it would be like watching a play, for they have forgotten how not to act – they no longer need a public, for their life *is* public, even in private, always and everywhere. The sudden appearance of another human at the doorway would usher no transformation in their lives, for these 24-hour party people the room's always full, there's always an audience.

But we *must* welcome the gap, the mismatch - the deeper the gorge the better I reckon. Suddenly I love my self, my view of the world – being me is no longer pointless, quite the opposite. This world is suddenly soaked, saturated in me, and it feels wonderful. It has lost its public facade, each part which falls under my gaze is mine and mine alone. The world may be turning beneath my feet but I'm going nowhere, enthroned at its centre, King of the Universe. My eyes devour its pathetic scenery, my point of view breathes life into everything it considers, every thought, every opinion. It seems I too am looking for a match, but there'll be no eviction tonight. My tentacles are strong. Beware all who cross me.

I believe in the primacy of the inner world because I feel it all day every day. I live inside my head because I have no other home. Ask yourself: if you had the choice between your immediate painless death or the immediate painless death of all humanity which would you choose? (Don't fret too long about an answer, for the journey your thoughts took is far more important than their destination.)

I cannot imagine a world without me because everything I imagine has me running through it. Every thought is my thought, this world is nothing more than my world. As Descartes realised, start with what you know. Beware of conclusions drawn from philosophy, for philosophy should be drawn from conclusions and conclusions should be drawn from life. Just you and yourself, sitting at a table, perhaps even in a tree, bashing out a big one.

Consider again a game of charades. In your head you have the answer and you've taken to the floor, smoothly, fluently, professionally conducting your limbs in time with the unspoken truth inside your head. "They must be able to get it by now," you're thinking, "it's *so* easy." But to the clueless audience, that desperate random flapping could represent any host of answers, those flailing outsides could be the result of any number of insides.

The connection between intention and outcome, truth and performance, may seem necessary one way, but that's because we're on the inside. The other way it's all contingent, and if people do imagine some substance behind it, some essence behind this existence, then the number of guesses barked at you in an average game reveals how likely they are to be getting right.

But in the end we must celebrate this privacy, the knowledge that no-one can ever know us like we do. We must live *with* this reality. Personally I like to emphasise the chasm, inviting people I care little for to draw the most bizarre and inaccurate conclusions about me (without lies of course - that's the rule which makes the game). The closest they could ever get to the truth is essentially made from different stuff anyway, so I figure one little fib's as good as the next.

I've tried on different personas like some try on fashion – Christian, Pagan, Socialist, Fascist, Town Boy, Country Girl, Common as muck, Posh as fuck, the Nutter, the Fighter, the Reader, the Writer, whoever, whatever. I've never declared myself to be any, but it's fun watching imaginations work overtime and my points total rising ever skywards, a game of charades where the guesser is always, Gawd bless 'em: "Absolutely spot on again! May I just say you are *seriously* good at this."

I feel the gunk they inject behind my mannerisms, I see these impressions turn to knowledge, and I get quite excited. I don't feel bad, really I don't. After all, I'm not the one jumping to conclusions. I'm not the one who's over-estimated their ability to judge character (for we all imagine ourselves so good at this don't we, we all reckon our judgement to be the most sophisticated going).

Silence it seems (and, okay, the odd twitch of the eyebrow) can ferment the most extraordinary ideas in others. You should have seen me and Gerald, boy did he go for it. I was his proudest convert, the original Tory boy, and then I shot him.

Richard's looking pretty bad now. He's stopped staring Nathan out, which would be a good thing if it weren't for the fact he's just stopped staring. Richard sure needs focus, not in any American sense you understand, the plain old visual variety would suit him just fine right now. Faced with a pub full of victims bent on revenge it's no wonder he doesn't know where to look.

Sarah knows what to do though, like a good wife she knows how to handle a drunk husband, she gets in Suey after Suey spiked with a double trouble in each. Fattening him up for the kill no doubt, yeah right … guess it's more than silence that makes her dumb. Perhaps I shouldn't be so hard. A little gratitude mightn't go amiss considering the effort they're putting in.

So it seems Nate's not the only one getting into this, perhaps they've saved their energy for the final stretch. And me? Well I told you, my office is always open, but I've quit. My part was rubbish anyway, some typecast pisshead, mere caricature, totally bereft of soul, substance, essence. This director's fleeting experiment in front of the camera is over. Still, you can't blame me for having a go.

Let's consider again Sartre's 'moment' when an 'other' shatters our self-conscious existence. He would have you believe he is eliciting a metaphysics, a philosophy, from a real-life situation, and what indeed could be more admirable?

But when I read it I see philosophy as his slave, drama his clay, and his director's chair nothing short of a throne from which he surveys his hopeless hapless courtesans. Reason is truly the slave of his passion; but unfortunately, it seems, so are we.

To my mind the more *dramatic* the example, the less plausible the resultant philosophy. Basing a quasi-metaphysics on what amounts to a moment of paperweight insecurity may appeal to our modern neurosis, but ultimately it amounts to a modish sideline in our timeless quest. Sartre insists on wringing philosophical truth from such episodes, he is obsessed with meetings, 'scenes' with 'others'. In Nausea, even Antoine's ultimate rejection of other people amounts to something of an obsession *with* them. The more he disregards them, the more his life is somehow about them.

I too want to create a philosophy from the ordinary experience of life, but hopefully my examples and conclusions are much more familiar, and the philosophy far less *stretched* as a result. There may be a tradition of using bleak drama to express existentialism, but this needn't be so. I'm not denying Sartre's characters their moment of hell when someone enters the room, but I don't believe he reveals anything *universal* in this scene, for I could imagine being quite indifferent to a new arrival.

We'd be packing the corridors of every nuthouse in the land if our world kept melting under the gaze of others. Any also I say, so what? These relationships may serve well as the cornerstones of a psychology, but surely not a philosophy. We must be about bigger things than this, for our journey is essentially a solitary one.

I want to give more credence to the strength of the human mind and to people's feelings of individuality – a more optimistic account of the human condition than is displayed by Sartre and his army of paranoid androids.

A rejection of Rationalism must not become a rejection of the human spirit. While many people do feel the objectification of the other's stare, some don't. Of such people it is said "they live in a world of their own'. But perhaps this condescending accusation is actually a philosophical truth they'd do better not to ignore. I smell fear in that sneer, fear and envy.

Is this all finishing a bit too quickly? Feel it in your fingers, it's definitely got thinner since last time you, checked and none of us are getting any younger. Mind you, I don't think Richard can get any whiter, too much even for our Ray. There's a point when Aryan becomes Alien, and I think Richard's just about on the turn. Bless him.

Don't be afraid of this inner world – people may judge, but that's because of the way *they* are. Perhaps you girls are right, a mirror might just be that essential item after all, not to gaze upon ourselves, but as a weapon to point at others. Don't rise to it, don't sell your self short, they haven't got nearly enough for a good deal.

Just for today, just for me, just stop – stop living and start thinking, stop acting and start dreaming. Not necessarily mine or Sartre's gory imaginings, although the exercise will indeed do you good, but just revel in your inside, explore your bubble, and get to know the only 'soul' you're ever going to have, before it's too late. This dear old chap dies with you remember, so don't see it for the first time with only a few seconds to go – the parable of Gerald showed us that.

If I'm arguing that we must "spend more time with our inner self" then are the Americans right after all? No siree. For their's is no *philosophical* self respect, but merely another technique to achieve success in society, alongside upturned palms and a positive dental outlook. "Love yourself and others will love you too," they say, because it's the second part they're after – for those cocksuckers self-love is just a measly means to a measly end.

This self, our only chance at having a real soul, is here and now, and each day spent away from it is another bad day at the office. When we are teenagers it is so bright, so sharp, that insular idealism, those golden years, when all is possible, before the real world's deathly scythe first reaps then destroys its precious harvest.

But it now seems some young people want to turn the clocks back to the time of their ancestors. Teenagehood may have been born in the 20th century but it's sure dying in the 21st. War and want may have thrust our grandpas into manhood as soon as puberty kicked in – but these days it seems our kids are signing up for the same, and what's *their* excuse? They're storing facts where outrageous theories should live, treating their beautiful brilliant superbrain as a two-bit database. They're cultivating the mature indifference of the grown-up and they're dead before they've left home. When did irrational idealism get replaced with rational consumerism? Where dreams once raged a frost has taken hold, as cold and conditioned as the air in their brand new car.

I guess they get everyone in the end. We're all called into the real world by a bitter band of adults already marooned in a sea of regret and denial, waiting to drown another young soul: "Yours is not to reason why, just sit back, relax, let it whither and die."

Like most metaphysical mistakes, the extrapolation of a doer, a thinker, a feeler, is egged on by our language.

We insist on prefixing action with an actor, but when the sun shines, water spills and shit stinks, we assume no mover with a motive, least of all one that can go to heaven - it's just the way we talk. All that ties our actions together is the persistence of a physical casing, deteriorating daily under the relentless strain of life, until one day it withers and dies. Oh to live without a liver.

That we have a memory is useful, but so do animals to a lesser degree, and they more so than the man who loses all of his. But too much troubled water has passed, too many things have changed. I feel we're just too self obsessed at the end of the day. We have exaggerated the distance between us and the animal kingdom and projected it towards the heavens, as if our very ability to talk up that stairway gives us authorisation to walk up it too.

Not only might we humans never have existed, but given that they did we might not have developed a self-consciousness, but given that we did we might not have developed such a fantastic memory. Three contingencies precede this essence of ours, see it always as such.

As Sartre said, existence precedes essence. Perhaps we should carry this one line of poetry with us at all times, to remind ourselves when we get carried away with the sanctity of our soul that happiness must always triumph over Truth, and earth over Heaven.

We should search for meaning because we have an inner world prone to guilt, denial and horror unless so occupied. See it then as a way of life, an antidote even, to the angst our contingent circumstantial intelligence will spawn – tigers don't need it, and lucky them. But please don't talk of survival beyond this world of time and space, beyond Dear Old Blighty, because your words have absolutely no idea what they're saying.

But Sarah won't swallow this empirical pill, she knows there's life after death although I've a feeling she doesn't mean her own. Nathan too knows there's life after death, he was born again in A&E, discharged with a new memory and a new identity, which is not so bad for a health service already under strain, and then he was born again again at the Sunday Club, bless him. But something is stirring from above the grave, the First Coming is tapping the Second on the shoulder. I hope this all comes together at once. Ratty now knows there's no life after death, he drowned that little cutie in a pool of Emma's blood - like me he now believes the empirical lie.

Talking of Emma, do you think *she* believes in life after death? Well if you see her you'll just have to ask her that yourself. Sorry did we forget someone? Oh yeah, Supertramp propped up in the corner, he's never thought about it, obviously, but show him a mirror, then ask him, and he might well think there was. Because I've seen corpses with more life, and he's still drinking. Second thoughts, don't do that, it was a mirror which did him in the first place remember. He looks bad enough, there's no need to make him sit in his own mess again.

Gradually throughout his weeks in Bouville Antoine slides towards transparency, as his existence becomes saturated in his own nausea. He realises that all essence, all solidity of meaning, is nothing but a man-made illusion, borne from fear, fermented by language, and maintained by the wise (a term of abuse in his world).

The universe, so it transpires, is little more than a seething mass of carefree existents, at best habitual, yet ultimately indifferent, lawless, hostile. As he feels his own existence merge with that of the tree, when their similarities seriously begin to outweigh their differences, his persisting selfhood, the 'I', the essence that pretends to precede his existence, slowly melts away. The movement of his arm seems as significant as the movement of a branch, and he no longer feels the actor behind the act. With Sartre, never does life seem so lifeless, and the lifeless so full of life. His imagery is among the finest poetry I've read – giving deep character to what can, at times, be the most counter-intuitive and frustrating of philosophies.

It's only 2pm and it's dark already. Under the glow of the café light Antoine considers: "I possess nothing but my body; a man on his own, with nothing but his body, can't stop memories; they pass through him. I shouldn't complain: all I have ever wanted is to be free."[6] Later on his spirits are lifted and he takes a walk along the seafront, and with devastating impact, declares: "I wander along at random, calm and empty, under this wasted sky." [7]

(When I first read this line I was literally stopped in my tracks, unable to read on, unable to move, to think straight. It's a revelation from which I hope never to recover.)

The next Saturday he feels this weightlessness again, at the town museum: "I hadn't any right to exist. I had appeared by chance, I existed like a stone, a plant, a microbe. My life grew in a haphazard way and in all directions. Sometimes it sent me vague signals; at other times I could feel nothing but an inconsequential buzzing."[8]

The existentialist vision in one. It is existence which defines us, as it does the mud on which we tread, and to live as something of greater consequence is as misguided as it is unavoidable.

One final visit to Antoine for now, to see how the existentialist revelation can turn into nausea. He's been sitting still in his room, doing nothing for an hour, becoming increasingly anxious about the big questions, and hoping for some light relief.

"If only I could stop thinking, that would be an improvement. Thoughts are the dullest things on earth....The body lives all by itself once it is started, but when it comes

---

[6] Nausea, Jean-Paul Sartre, 1938
[7] Nausea, Jean-Paul Sartre, 1938
[8] Nausea, Jean-Paul Sartre, 1938

to thought it is I who continue it. I exist by what I think. If I exist it is because I hate existing. It is I who pull myself from the nothingness to which I aspire."[9]

According to Sartre we might imagine we come up with thoughts, but in truth, it is the thoughts which have come up with us. Mental activities flicker upstream like a herd of salmon, leaping darting, making splashes, making waves, until suddenly we spot two plotting the same path, and suddenly we have an idea, we remember it, we take a mental photo .. and sure enough it happens again .. we have another idea which we join to the first one to make a bigger one ...or we don't, we just sit and stare, gazing at heavenly space for divine inspiration as the torrents of the real world race round our feet.

Now clearly our man wants out, closure, not to die but not to live either. Things are getting desperate. Forced to think, forced to create an 'I' which can never properly exist, unlike the hands in which he holds his shaking head.

Right now Richard would love to escape his body, he would love to get inside someone else's head - not out of any fascination, but just to hide. Right now he would love to believe in a transportable soul, he would love to believe he could dump his car in a field and escape into the freezing fog. But he knew he was trapped for good in this soaken broken crock of shit, and that suited just about everyone but him.

They say time doesn't move in a straight line - not these days anyway. So, in a non-research sort of way, if it can bend then might it actually be travelling around the outside of a circle? Fancy that? Suey and Richard: ice skaters stuck in an endless finale, faster and faster they spin, same places, same faces, same faeces, same closing moments of a life repeated for eternity. Suey and Richard, like trainer and knacker, just a ropey old rope between them. Gallop for your life dear Dicks, you'll only get to the same place faster, the same places, same faces, same faeces, the closing moments of a life repeated for eternity. He knew he was trapped for good inside this soaken broken crock of shit, and that suited just about everyone but him. Haven't we been here before? Of course we have, get 'em in Rich its your round again, fizzy-fresh, sung in ... er, a round. Altogether now: "Ere's a rhyme I once was told, to 'elp me in me drinkin'. Start the next 'fore last is done, there'll be no room for thinkin'." Haven't we been here before? Of course we have, gallop for your life Dear Reader, you'll just get to the same page faster. He knew once and for all he was trapped for good inside this soaken broken crock of shit, lah-di-lah-di-dah.

For he was attached to that body, and right now that body was attached to the pub, which sucked him in and eight hours later spat him out, drenched, only to be swallowed whole again the next day. Like a vomiting fly preparing his next meal, this cycle of regurgitation kept our Richard well within the sights of the three musketeers - it really couldn't be easier for them – surely the question now is who and when, for I'm sure past talking about the whether.

How much more can one man take? Just how soggy can one soak get? And how ironic, how disappointing for our terrible trio, if Suey gets their first, the fourth man, the outside bet.

---

[9] Nausea, Jean-Paul Sartre, 1938

They say time doesn't move in a straight line - not these days anyway. So if it can bend might it actually be travelling around the edge of a circle, fancy that? It couldn't be easier for them. So I guess it's a race now, there is a finishing line, a time limit, after all, this is definitely all gonna end one way or another. I know who my money's on. What about you?

Antoine may be sitting with his head in his hands but to me he's seen the light. Nausea is only a temporary symptom of human existence, not human existence itself. It is an absence, an extreme mental hunger following an enema of the mind. I too have felt this wave of realisation, but if there's nausea then it's more like the gut wrench of being lugged to the starting summit of a fun fair ride, or waiting for a party pill to kick in.

It may be the final insult to religion to steal this idea of revelation, that intimate realisation beyond all language, beyond all doubt, that God does exist and can in fact save us from eternal damnation. But what made my 'moment', my revelation, all the better was that I was actually sitting in a café drinking coffee when it happened. At first I suspected this existentialist nausea was nothing but a caffeine overdose, a mere symptom of an Englishman being a bit too French.

But the feeling was unmistakeable. Suddenly I felt the huge weight of the world existing beneath the patter of our tiny feet, which left nothing but the faintest of impressions, paw prints on sand which will blow away forever come the pointless dawn of a new day. I saw all human life, its colours, its smells, its sounds, as mere make-up; its science and knowledge as mere ripples fading out to nought across the surface of a vast ocean. And I saw the human race as simple children, desperately trying to conjure up life on a blank-faced balloon, with nothing but a magic marker and felt for eyes.

And I too lost what identity I had, I knew I was sitting down but I no longer knew whether I could feel the cup in my fingers, or my fingers on the cup, but either way we were suddenly, somehow, in this together. I almost said hello.

Like a child's finger dangling in the ocean I began to realise the futility of making any impression on a world which would keep turning whether I played or watched. I left my coffee a changed man, a happy man, a man full of the most profound truth, more profound than any scientific discovery. For I had touched beauty, I had lived the unique moment, tasted the here and now – I had existed in a world with no names or labels, meaning or personality. Just me, that coffee and a 30-minute lunch break I'll never forget.

And that's my testament to the philosophy which has enthralled and nearly suffocated me ever since I first came across it. However my frustration with existentialism, apart from having a totally crap name, is that it almost disappears when discussed, guaranteeing both its obscurity and omnipotence. It is so hard to explain because we are at our *least* existential when thinking and talking about philosophy. The soul, this makeshift essence, never burns so bright as when we are thinking about thinking, thinking about our *selves*.

However I prefer to think the reason Mr Ex appears to self destruct in conversation, is that this great man with the silly name is turning his back in disgust, morally affronted by the lies I'm peddling about him. If we must insist on talking about him then he much prefers a good story to some academic analysis, although ultimately it's when we're not talking that existentialism makes so much sense, it's when we're simply existing that it really takes grip.

There was a time, way back in the heady days of the Monday Club (yeah, yeah – I'll get round to it) that I would be invited to dinner parties (can you imagine?!) and the conversation would eventually come round to what we all *did for a living* (I'm kidding no-one, that's where it started, middled and ended) and in time I would be required to take my turn in this tedium: "You're writing a book? How wonderful – what's it about?" (Isn't that enough? *Must* you pry further?) "It's about what I reckon," I proffer, with an apologetic smile, hoping that would be an end to it all, hoping yet another one of my prize tumbleweeds might drink dry any excitement the moment may have contained.

But at a parallel party I fix my host right in the eye and let her have it: "It's about weak-stomached limp-wristed paranoid fuckwits just like you, it's about the death of God the death of Me and the death of Truth, it's about chattering Charlies bathing in shit, it's about pointless revenge and dripping execution, it's about lying and crying and dregs and drugs, it's about the end of life as you know it, although never having made it past the first profanity you'll probably never find out."

"Why - that's unspeakable," she cries, but it's too late, for I'm already standing on my chair, turning slowly. I'm pulling down my trousers, my pants, and … well you know the rest, this is only our first course after all. Unspeakable indeed, the truth always is, I guess she'll never know just how true that was.

But while such supersonic scenes explode in every direction from each and every second, I inevitably tread the path marked 'caution': "It's about what I reckon," I proffer, with an apologetic smile, hoping that would be an end to it all, hoping yet another one of my prize tumbleweeds might drink dry any excitement the moment may have contained. And of course it does, and we return quietly to our soup.

Real life should leave no tracks, no marks, not even words – it's those dinner guests in desperate denial who insist on scratching slogans into the crust of a hostile planet, Cold War cosmonauts launching flags at a space they'll never conquer. At best we're all camping out on the surface for a few years, lighting poisonous fires, eating badly-cooked burgers, making far too much noise and barely burying our litter before that festival sun sets for the very last time. Singing, sinking, desperate and drunk, we die.

Just maybe those travellers have it right after all. Just maybe hygiene *isn't* everything, I certainly don't see them working 40 hours a week. Think how much we pay for our brick tents, our four-ring gas stoves, our tiny shaven fields. The sheer relentless weight of existence thunders down on our deep-pile conservatories every second of every day. We must learn to love it more, dear reader. We need to get outside and get soaked now and then.

But nausea is not the only alternative to denial, and while we must get outside and drench ourselves under a wasted sky, it doesn't mean that once the explosive impact of this revelation wears off that we'll be left with nothing. Because if that *was* the case then I'd probably go for a bit of glorious denial myself, although I'm not sure Uncle Grumpy would approve of such vulgarity.

Sartre insists "man is condemned to be free" and in this magic one-liner not only describes us as essentially free creatures, but suggests this freedom might be a burden, a tiresome duty to make choices and be accountable for them, a life sentence we could possibly have done without. We might consider fighting this affliction by doing something for absolutely no reason, but then there's always the danger of becoming one of those "I'm-flippin'-bonkers-me" creatures who get up to all manner of crazy antics "just for the sheer hell of it".

There is an alternative to being a bit wacky, because if there *is* no meaning in the world then surely it is a blank canvas upon which we can paint our own. However we must not consult the Encyclopaedias of Importance, those Catalogues of Convention with which a million lemmings run their race, treating life as something to be lived *up* to, a challenge already set by rules of success drawn up by their ancestors. Fame, family, fortune – marks, get set, go!

But if it doesn't actually matter what we do then we can do anything, and that includes pretending that some things do matter even when we know deep down they don't. Surely it's only bad faith to *believe* the meaningless to have meaning. Surely there's nothing wrong with *acting* as if it does. What other option do we have?

We can't spend our lives in cafes, head bowed over yet another cup of revelatory coffee. Even Uncle Grump feels the need at the end of Nausea to provide some sort of solution for poor Antoine. Hardly a happy ending but definitely an un-unhappy one, (and believe me, you take what you're given and be grateful with that cheeky chapsteur). There's a vague allusion to art and creation as a way to escape the temporal birth-life-death cycle, although thankfully it is suitably half-baked, for Nausea, to my mind, is about questions, not answers.

So with a cheery heart lets join the race, if only to see other people's faces as we whizz past, and then veer off at a comic tangent yards before the finish line. And race past them we will, for I fancy the importance of being earnest weighs heaviest on their shoulders.

Lighten up, *light* up, let's have a laugh. If I must be conjoined to a body and lug around a package of memories like a passport to my existence in this world, then I'll do it, but don't expect too much maintenance. I really can't take your health warnings that seriously. I feel fortunate to have been given a car, but I'm far more interested in the driver and the destination than the contents of its bonnet.

But never forget, this watcher of the roads needs a private life too. At home he must be enthroned, a fiery will set free in a land of limitless imagination. It's got to be better than treating our inside world as a waiting room, a sterile holding house in which we sit and worry about the latest damage to the engine.

Consider the saying: "When you're on your deathbed, what do you want to look back on?" As a guiding light it may be horribly flawed, but for some reason I still find it strangely compelling. I'm not saying our life's work should be directed to form some sort of satisfactory novel, upon which we can gaze back, chapter and verse, and take our plaudits, for life is certainly not about creating happy endings, or even happy memories. What the deathbed scenario does give us is a warning from the future. It's not about our dying days to come – it's an attempt to shed light on days lived here and now.

Clearly it doesn't matter two arses what we're thinking on our deathbed. Personally I hope to be pumped so full of Class As that I'll be strolling down somewhere rather more exciting than Memory Lane. But if you imagine the scene, and your heart is breaking for a life left unfulfilled, then isn't it time you did something about it now? If you've packed your inner world to the ceiling with files upon files on the kids, the job, the mortgage then you are indeed the author of *My Own Downfall*, and what a dull novel that'll be.

Creating meaning, controlling meaning is all very well. To make things matter is fine, but we must not let things matter to us, *at* us. Success, wealth and popularity are merely new Gods to worship if the relationship is still one of subservence. Remember Gerald. Spot the signs. Are you a Gerry Junior? A Gerald-in-waiting? Are you wrapped up in *their* lives, do you live your life from the outside, craving approval like a junkie craves drugs and death? I see a paunch has appeared – you're looking quite jowelly these days my friend. They're the chops of the dying dead you know. Are you sure you can't spare a tiny morsel for the chap inside? This heartbreaker may just be your lifesaver.

Consider another saying: "Better to have loved and lost than never to have loved at all." Now that's more like it, a real contender for best damn cliché of the lot I reckon. There will be risk and there will be failure, but there must never be compromise, this little chap doesn't do deals. You either want to save your life or you don't. We must sail close to the edge because the middle is where it's worst. Beware that channel of calm, for time sails superfast for the supercautious. Instead we must seek out those craggy margins, ride those whirlpools, bank on the banks. You get the message sailor, for it's high time we cast these metaphors adrift into the setting sun.

The whole population is slipping towards an existential abyss and they don't even know it. "God is dead – and we have killed him," declared Nietzsche, but that was bloody *years* ago. We must write new slogans for a new generation.

I urge you to consider that it is the man-made environment, ruled by those great Class Acts - speed and ease - that has allowed our creative fires to burn dead. In fact in many tragic cases they were never lit in the first place for I guess some schools just don't want to get their hands too hot (and how you secretly hated we bright sparks, so confident, so happy, so *dangerous*, so *disruptive*.)

Consumerism is not a new way forward, because it's no way forward at all, it's just nihilism in big trainers, it's a *dead* end – the End of History, the graveyard of meaning and beauty, the place where cheap dreams can be pedalled in the place where our own have died.

I for one am getting to quite like history, especially when put up against a corporate future already starting to taste pretty dull. And I actually think there's plenty for us human's to be chuffed about, as we made our journey from cave to rave. But on the whole, as a species we've barely got to Chapter Three, barely half way there. Lets not throw it all away for a free portion of fries.

We must not let ourselves be drip fed on low culture, for that salty façade hides toxins of deadly force. It's time to rip those tubes off, we're checking ourselves out, through the hospital window if need be. And don't turn back, for this world's salty enough. **And anyway, it's only bleeding Gerald. I couldn't do it in the end you know, those weeping eyes drew the last drop of mercy from my hardened soul, so I shot him in the leg instead.**

In the old days they used to amuse themselves, so they say. But now? Just rotting couch potatoes stuck in TV-land, a viewing gallery for the have-nots. Why is an absence of unhappiness now deemed good enough? We must have a bit more self-respect, we must stop being so lazy, so crap, we must stop equating the good life with doing nothing. Doing nothing makes me so tense, I'm never so unchilled as when I'm supposed to be "chilling out". I guess this is why I've become an insomniac, for sleep is nothing but recurring death, my bed nothing but a coffin.

This cannot go on, it's really not good enough - did you know you're actually dribbling? Wipe your face fatso, I'll make a hero of you yet. Together we can paint the world some beautiful colours and we'll be hunting out that paint real soon, Part Four's not far off now.

U pbeat as ever, Sartre contends that "consciousness, by the pure nihilating movement of reflection, makes itself personal".[10]

Egged on by a mammoth memory our consciousness becomes aware of a commonality, a familiarity, an *inside,* and is fatally reborn as *self-consciousness*, a queasy Cartesian realm of thoughts about thoughts, a self-fulfilling prophecy borne from reflection, cast adrift in a sea of unyielding freedom, with neither boundaries or rules.

So when we talk of freedom, or a free will, we are really talking of the *knowledge* we are free, a status to which we are condemned by a stupidly large intelligence. Now we can either treat this new mental space as a playground for the imagination, or see it as a terrifying burden, preferring instead to lock the school gates and send everyone home.

We might consider Sartre's idea of bad faith to help us separate the two ways our self-consciousness can go:

"According to Sartre, bad faith involves the deliberate creation in myself of the appearance of a belief which I in fact know to be false. In bad faith we exploit the ambiguities between *pour-soi* (the inner world, *for-itself*), and *en-soi* (the outside world, *in-itself*) to avoid facing up to painful facts about ourselves."[11]

While Sartre may not contend that the worlds pour-soi and en-soi are *metaphysically* separate, he insists the distinction strikes at the heart of human existence, and bemoans our endeavours to blur the line between the two: the inner world of belief and imagination, and the outside world of facts and events.

In bad faith we turn our imagination on ourselves, to soften life's hard edges. We create a personality and then live like the character we've created as if he were here along, we see pattern and purpose in a world of indifference, imagining life as a journey along a road stretching out far behind and far ahead of us. In bad faith we live and tell as if we were characters in a story, one in which events happen for a reason, almost *because* of us, and we imagine that reason and the character we play both ultimately to be born of some greater purpose, the very answer to the question "why are we here?"

The military man who scowls at a world of indiscipline, the wine lover searching for his evening dream, the wife awaiting her daily slap from the cruel hand of fate, the self-made millionaire damned to impress the ghosts which haunt his privacy, the killer who's never killed, the actress who lurches from romantic drama to frantic crisis, the backgammon player in the heroic throes of a comeback, the father without a son, the working class hero who won't see the love of his life behind the breeding he was reared to despise.

---

[10] Being and Nothingness, Jean-Paul Sartre, 1943
[11] The Oxford Companion to Philosophy, Ed. Ted Honderich, 1995

Such characters can be used to describe our actions, after the event as it were, yet like guests at a dinner-party game we're all too happy to choose first and live later, becoming one who lives in scenes, reads from scripts.

Now ours is a traditional tale of revenge, set in a modern world with no justice, no forgiveness and no cheeks to turn. The revenge that stews in the depths, in Ratty, in Nate, in Sarah (in Emma? Ask her yourself) is no mere reaction to events, like a pain that will one day wear off. This feeling has become an idea, a mission, egged on by each other's furtive glances and secretive whispers our killers without a kill are imagining some glorious future, a spectacular climax when justice (wherever she is) will indeed be done.

But consider this you lot: would your idea of revenge have reached such a convoluted intensity, and have come to involve such dramatic scheming, such longevity, such a past, such a *future*, if it weren't for the word and the literature that has clung to it down the years? As author you may well blame me for that, but I'm trying to step back from that role now.

It strikes me that a caveman might well have punched the neighbour who cheats with his wife, but without words, without stories, without ever having seen *Ugga and Me - a Tale of Love, Betrayal and Bitter Vengeance*, how much further would it have gone? We are invited to live life as a story by stories themselves, we are invited to see the gap between real-life and fiction as something of a failure on *our* part. But in truth it is fiction that should be doing most to clinch the deal.

But I do not share the conviction with which Sartre describes and dismisses those living such lives. The wine lover standing in the doorway of his kitchen may realise the difference between the stories he tells (to himself and others) and the life he leads, but he won't necessarily feel nauseas, not if the wine's good enough. I fancy he might instead gaze at the stars and simply dismiss the disparity. "C'est la vie", he mutters to the here and now, and good for him, a philosopher at his finest. And this fine chap by no means represents the cornerstone of my hesitancy, for there are far worse cases of bad faith for which I have a similar sympathy, empathy, *envy* even.

In yet another café sequence our Antoine notices how a group of card players in the far corner are transformed by the divine intervention of the jukebox. From where he is sitting, the melody somehow flourishes *behind* the music box transcending its scratchy vinyl, its speakers' crackle and indeed the drinkers themselves, injecting fresh meaning into each card they play.

They say the dull-headed always turn to music in their lowest moments, seeking out a sympathetic soul to smother their rejection in melodious melancholy, a comfort blanket to cover the naked shame of failure. So what might you expect some forgotten freakydeak like Richard to choose from our jukebox (possibly the most exclusive in the country, for to this day I've heard it sing no more than ten tunes).

Love Don't Live Here Anymore? **Nah, not our Rich, for that would presume a time when he did in fact play landlord to such sentiment.** *Two Out Of Three Aint Bad?* **Yeah right. What's that Rich? The number of people staring at you right now with little else but homicide on the brain.** *We Don't Need Another Hero?* **And what might this be? A warning to Nate, to Ratty, are you sure that's wise? Coz in pub parlance I'm sure we'd all fancy our chances right now.**

Okay, I'll put you out of your misery, as a free invitation to gawk at his. Richard's choice was *Hi-Ho Silver Lining,* always was, always will be, its nightly recurrence daring anyone to suggest an alternative, as if now there need be no other music. *The* song has been written, what's your problem?

The wedding night classic he's never danced to, because no-one's ever beckoned him over, to join that bouncing steaming inner circle, brave bedraggled beer monsters bonding in sweat, how our Richard would love to jump arm in arm with them, just once, just for one night. But he's never been asked.

Don't feel sorry for him. Think back to school: people were rarely left out as a random act of cruelty, there was a reason back then and there's a fair few now. It's all Richard's fault of course. He never realised the playground games should have stopped, he never heard the whistle, so he's still flushing heads and punching girls, and we're still sitting as far from him as possible, the censure of those long-lost lunch breaks travelling in time with old Stinky Bones. So please don't feel sorry for him.

It's 20 years later and we well-adjusted souls, on the other hand, are nothing like Richard. We've successfully taken flight from those nicknames, those playground games. We busy bees could never find the time to hate as much as we did back then, for we have become mature grown-ups, sure in our life, sure in our friends, sure in ourselves.

(Oh yeah, *sure,* for in fact our cock is so *less* sure, our gangs so less obvious, less public. We become so less daring over our friends, so less honest, so less *choosy.* Truth is we paranoid weaklings simply can't *afford* to hate as much as we did back then. For as that final fifth year fag hit the deck the geeky world of grown ups brutally flipped the tables, casting us into a world of wankers, a world where money, success, and responsibility determined rank, a land which welcomed the bullied who now excelled, all too ready to put us to work, all too ready to wreak 50 years of bloodsucking revenge for those five paltry years of hell.)

And not for the first time am I wondering whether Richard is in fact the only one living authentically here. Perhaps he sees his isolation and the life which secures it as an exalting glow, born by the Chosen One, a hero amongst men who carries with great dignity the inevitable solitude such elevation brings, a position to which he is, voluntarily, gallantly, condemned.

Or then again perhaps not. This is Richard we're talking about, a soaken broken crock of shit who'd dissolve into a puddle of tears at the merest hint of recognition from any of us. But what do I care? I'm still not sitting with old Stinky Bones.

The card-playing scenario is used as a metaphor for the way humans imagine essence behind existence - we presume design, we love to dream, we crave perfection, and we sentimental broken old soaks are desperate to see it in the world whenever we can. And what better than music to oil the cogs of our imagination, giving life a sheen we just love to mistake for something deeper.

The card game to Antoine suddenly had a purpose, a direction. The soundtrack lifted the whole room from the indifferent sneer of reality. The players were suddenly battling

Gods, each card delivered like the swipe of a hero's sword, each line, each verse, each chorus cajoling these gladiators towards a spectacular climax.

But Antoine reminds us that the scene could be destroyed in a second, simply by removing the plug, the perfect moment lost forever, reminding us that existence is a *necessary* quality of meaning, yet meaning is only a *contingent* quality of existence. We sure need the world but it will *never* need us.

Existence gave birth to essence and can destroy it without ceremony, for a jukebox is as happy gathering dust with its plug pulled out, an artist's tube of paint is as happy daubing race hate on a wall and a hand of cards is as happy offering Nine High as a Royal Flush. It is we who bring meaning, it is we who care.

But instead of living with this reality, loving the disparity, the mismatch, nausea takes grip. Our anti-hero realises that all life is made from one chaotic blob, existence is the only true essence, the one quality of reality which renders us all from the same stuff.

But what is Sartre really saying? That Antoine in that moment of depressing realisation became superior to those deluded card players, no doubt oblivious to the metaphysical transformation engineered by the grumpy loner staring at them from the opposite corner. Because right now I'm wondering just what is so wrong with a life of endless drinking and card-playing? Suddenly it's hard to see. In the realm of the imagination what *really* separates delusion from creation? Antoine might imagine those cards players would love to cry, in unison: "WE KNOW, BUT WHAT ELSE CAN WE DO?" but perhaps they would really love to scream: "WE KNOW, AND IT'S GREAT."

Perhaps we look for fiction because we enjoy living that way, it's fun, it's exciting. I'm seriously starting to lose faith now, or perhaps that should be gain faith, bad faith, good faith, whatever's going. For perhaps it is we the philosophers, the analysts, who are actually life's victims, and those oh-so-deluded card players actually its victors. Perhaps they are playing life at its own game, laughing at its indifference, living the lie, riding the fun fair they've built on top. And perhaps that snake Sartre is trying to lure us all into his playground of pure freedom, a lonely hell he himself feels powerless to escape.

But it's not such wine-induced episodes that Sartre is really attacking. It's not the improvised scenes we live that immerses us good and proper in bad faith. His most scathing attack is reserved for the stories we tell about ourselves, the way we submerge the endless present by fictionalising both our past and our future.

Over to Antoine again: "For the common place to become an adventure you must start recounting it. A man is a teller of tales. He lives life as if he were recounting it. But you have to choose – to live or recount. There are no beginnings. Just endless addition. When you are living nothing happens. Events take place one way and we recount them the opposite way. We appear to begin at the beginning but we in fact begin at the end. The hero lives only those moments which heralded adventure. I wanted my life to follow like a life remembered – you might as well try to catch time by its tail."[12]

Not for first time am I left speechless by the analysis, but cold by the conclusion. When Antoine declares that we must live or tell I couldn't disagree more. Surely the incongruity between the way we live and the way we tell describes the human condition in a nutshell. It is nature's paradox against which any alternative must strain.

[12] Nausea, Jean-Paul Sartre, 1938

I think it might actually be time for some analytical philosophy. A simple deconstruction of Antoine's dilemma might leave us with four options:

(a) To take life as it comes but recount it as a story
(b) To take life as it comes and endeavour to recount it that way
(c) To live life as a story and recount it as a story
(d) To live life as a story, but recount it as if we weren't

I believe Mr A is man in his natural paradoxical state. Unlike Antoine I do not believe he must choose, he must merely learn to live with the incongruity, and deal with the frustration when the future he arrives at is never like the one he imagined.

Mr B is of course Antoine himself. So disillusioned is he with the lifestyles he imagines being acted out before him that he has decided that not only should he take life as it comes, but this professional loner should endeavour to grasp this indifference whenever he is called upon to speak, which not surprisingly is very rarely.

Mr C is the man most despised by our Antoine, lying diagonally opposite him on our grid, the man who not only tells stories about his life, but lives it that way too. The man who has failed to see the script as a description. The man who takes the revenge sought by his paperback princes.

And then of course there is Mr D, a contrived and contradictory combination at first glance, the odd fourth man seemingly brought in to make up the numbers, to fill the gap in our logic puzzle, or is he?

Given the three characters just described we couldn't be blamed for seeking another, so let's have a closer look at the quiet chap in the corner, and see if we can't flesh him out a bit. To live life as a story, but tell it the opposite way? This sounds more like an act of defiance against life itself, a two-fingered snub to the paradox into which we're born. But this cheeky chap might just be the man who can save us all. Perhaps the song is wrong, and we *do* in fact need another hero.

Perhaps we can revive or even create a new authentic idealisation of the human condition. Perhaps superform itself will create a new breed of superheroes, perhaps it *must*. In this Age of the Cynic we are all too embarrassed of hierarchy, excellence, true heroism. It seems all our efforts are channelled towards trivialising the ancient, domesticating the great. We are sceptical of the hero because he seems to have found a meaning to life of near-literary substance, one realised and executed without us: "Why won't he do what *we're* doing?", demand the amassed A-Team, torch lights in one hand, scythes in the other. "Just what is he thinking that we're not? What does he *know* that we don't? Come on everyone - get him!"

Mind you the B-Brigade aren't much better, captained by Antoine, the leader with no pack and nowhere to take them. He too dismisses the hero, describing him as yet another carrier of bad faith. He may be a good enough silent partner in the cafe, someone to share his cynicism about the card players in the corner, but the thing is he's never there, he always seems to have *something else to do*.

And what about Mr C? This drama queen on the other hand has nothing but admiration for the new silent saviour on the scene, for they both live life as a story, or that's how he tells it anyway. But the hero's silence speaks volumes about the gorge that separates them, about Mr C's need to be thought of by others as a hero, and Mr D's happiness just to be one. "It's always the quiet ones," we say.

So it seems we can be indifferent in public yet real-life adventurers in private, we must burn like the brightest fires, guzzling down life's every moment like there's no tomorrow, we must ride the waves of beauty and fiction till we are fit to burst, but can never ever tell it that way. Modest office clerks by day, yet superheroes by night?

Now hang on a minute? ... But like the man behind the thick glasses there is an element of reluctance underscoring this hero's life. Our anti-hero is not anti heroes, he's still a type of hero, just a hero doomed to fight, for his mind knows no other way. So let's have some respect for this committed thinker, this relentless dreamer, and if he writes a few stories to ease life along a bit then don't be too harsh. It's probably only therapy, give him a break eh?

I believe our weak minds are prone to search for pre-defined roles. We are fearful of Antoine's total freedom, supposing it to crumble into mindless drifting or mind-bending worry before long. We see this freedom as the freedom of the unemployed actor, with nothing to do all day but stare at his walls. But as we reject such liberty we must never forget that the roles we play must be chosen in the cool light of day, they are not precious and they are certainly not ours, they're just a way of keeping us out of parks and cafes.

This is why the final chapter is so important, for I know only too well that we are born hungry for meaning in a barren world which will feed us nothing. Sure we must ditch those projects which choose us, from the shell-suits of birth to the career-driven clichés of adulthood, but we must quickly take one on of our own making, else nausea will take grip – for what price freedom, what price infinite choice, if we have no reason to choose?

I guess we are all guilty of self-deception to differing degrees – and I warn you now, the search for beauty will entail a hefty dose of imaginative re-invention to maintain momentum. Take what I'm doing now for instance. Here I am sitting at a desk writing this book. To do this successfully, to even have the chance of completing it, I have, to some extent, to *be* a writer. Now surely this involves a certain amount of invention, of bad faith. I act like a writer, I think like a writer, I shit and spit like a writer, I even walk and talk like a writer. I know that in reality writers are people who write books which are published and read by thousands, and clearly I am not one of those. But how far would I have gone if I kept reminding myself I'm only a journalist. If we're only as good as our last then how would we ever get started? By living the dream, of course, for with nothing solid on the shelf, dreams are all we have.

And believe me, these dreams can become quite intoxicating. I've imagined so much fame and fortune that no reality could possibly deliver, I know that. But there's more that's kept me warm throughout these years of pregnancy. For there is part of me, right now, who imagines existence is tainted by all who live in it, a tawdry association alongside which my current world of dreams shines even brighter.

Let's recall the wisdom of Gandhi for a moment. What is a writer? Is he one who lives and thinks and writes like a writer, or someone who gets books published in his name? Clearly the impetus of the writer is one day to become a Writer, to progress from moth to butterfly. But the unpublished writer is in many ways morally clean, he can do no better, he is perfect, whereas the Published Writer joins a disparate band of folk, from favourites to failures to freeloading fakirs, one which no doubt contains his idols, but will also house some of his bitterest enemies, some of whom were never writers, not proper writers like he was.

We will come across a variety of shamsters in the next part, the Artists who've never ever considered what art is, and simply never will. But for now I'm holding onto this beautiful pre-world, where all is possible. I wonder whether painters too look back fondly on their days as a penniless wannabe, a leaking studio bursting with ideas, stacked to the ceiling with paintings no-one ever saw – days of hopes and dreams, days before the tiresome circuit of exhibitions, price lists and wine receptions, licking arses they'd rather kick into traffic.

Right now it seems as if the transition is actually from butterfly to moth, regress not progress, from the freedom to fly to the expectation to be sturdy, reliable, colourless. I act like a writer, although I know I am not, and if that's bad faith then please sir, can I have some more? It is this Superhero transformation in these few short hours each day that has given the project its heartbreaking excitement. The avoidance of bad faith would have meant hours of research in the real world, into the likelihood of first books being published, the demand for certain types of book, its competition in the marketplace, the gathering of contacts, networking – what a tedious robotic and unbeautiful approach, a sure-fire way to snub out the brightest creative spark. We need to clear space, not fill it up. My advice is: crack open a red and *start*. Trust me, no-one's looking.

But such dewy-eyed nostalgia doesn't mean all bad faith is forgivable, for at its worst it can infect our philosophy, our psychology, in fact every inch of our outlook. And that worst case is the promotion of our self-consciousness to a soul, treating product as producer, our son as Our Father.

Belief in eternal life is the ultimate denial, the ultimate pretence, the ultimate act of bad faith. A card player may allow himself to be carried away on the notes of a tune, but that doesn't mean he'll be in church the next day, and good for him, for it turns out religious faith is just about the baddest faith of the lot.

The very prospect of eternal existence fills me with absolute horror, whether in heaven, hell or anywhere else. Surely this is the worst of all God's jokes: not satisfied with creating and bringing us into a world of suffering, he conceives of an eternal realm of unimaginable pain beyond it, into which most of us will be damned. If we created such conditions for any beast we'd be strung up before the authorities – and quite rightly so.

We're swift to attack battery farming, the imprisonment of animals in cramped dark cages, where they will feel little but pain in their short life before they are killed for profit. But at least profit is *some* sort of motive, at least we can *explain* why we do this to them. Remember that image Mr Priest, as you shuffle along your kneeling flock, bequeathing that paper grain of comfort to each bobbing head come Sunday morning. But even if God *did* stand up there in the dock and prove beyond any doubt that He created the world, I reckon this juror would still vote 'guilty'. He might have forgiven me, but I certainly haven't forgiven Him. Given the same blank canvas I just *wouldn't* have done it this way. Perhaps I'm just a nicer bloke.

Enough religious ranting. After my three score and ten I'm sure I'd have had quite enough of being me thank you very much, and certainly wouldn't thank anyone who condemned me to more. Life can be genuinely great if you don't take it too seriously, but when our time comes let's not drag this shaggy dog tale out any further.

But don't imagine indifference is inspiring this Cavalier, for right now I certainly don't feel life is trivial. My being simply doesn't feel like nothingness. To my mind bad faith is far more about what one believes, not what one does. Quite frankly this is my party and I'm gonna be the life *and* the soul. What's in a name?

I know I said my door was always open, but I certainly wasn't prepared for Ratty's little surprise. Do you know whose picture he carries in his wallet, next to our Emma's of course? Yes you've guessed it, Rodney.

Right now my Shakey's as shaky as me, but what was that about names and roses? *He* **knew the world cares not for the labels we stick on it, anymore than babies care for the names we baptise them. Our Rats still can't see it, he can't see the family eyes, yellowed with time, reddened in space. But as I gazed at Ratty's long lost, the sepia son which never called him dad, and then looked up at the Broken Soldier in the corner, tears of hopeless hilarity abseiling his pitted skull, fighting for a country no-one flies to, I realised there can be no story here. There would be no father and son reunion in my little tale, my book will certainly not end with that Revelation. If we'd be nothing without our memories than what really connects Dying Dicks to that dog-eared image Ratty holds so tight to his chest? I look at Rich and I look at Ratty and I decide he must never know, I decide in this Age of Cynicism that we can all know too much, and in fact probably do.**

The idea that man knows just too much finds romantic life with Rousseau. He insisted: "Man is born free, and everywhere he is in chains"[13], and then went on to imagine some idealistic natural existence, where simple folk idled their days away drinking wine in the sun. Freedom wasn't an issue – there was no obligation to believe – no eternal heart-breaking choices to be made. Such ties are of our own making. But whatever the origins of this malaise, Sartre insists that the modern human condition demands projects. We must create meaning in our life before this sickness envelopes us like some Dickensian terror-smog.

Sartre contends that we act authentically, in good faith, when we choose our own project, and act in bad faith when we let a preconceived project choose us. But he also says we become nauseas when we have no project at all, when the sheer magnitude of our duty to choose and to be accountable for that choice roots us to the spot, rendering us little more than the tree in which we hide.

It seems we now have two types of projects – good and bad:

For those who once pursued the latter, nausea as the feeling of coming 'off project' is both a necessary and noble condition. That cold turkey is definitely worth eating. Religious Rita who in a moment of revelation realises that God's existence relies utterly on her belief in Him will no doubt feel very sick for a while, empty and alone like a child mourning the death of a Nanny. But remember, never talk philosophy with the bereaved. What they need best is time, and perhaps some decent whiskey. So I suggest

---

[13] The Social Contract, Jean-Jacques Rousseau, 1762

you give them just that and leave them alone with their grief, not least because someone's walking the other way who needs your attention far more urgently.

Arty Arthur who's spent a frustrating decade scribbling away at the book of a lifetime, and one day completely loses faith in the project, will also become nauseas. But he's the one in real trouble. I would urge caution here, I really would. Encourage a life of meaningless anarchy, sell him the pursuit of physical pleasure, perhaps he just needs a break. No-one said it was going to be easy. Keep buying him drinks, keep him sick if that's what it takes, but never leave his side.

As Rita approaches from the other side our Art must think hard about the direction he's travelling. Do not cross the Great Divide old boy, and definitely don't look them in the eye, for once they've spotted a weak target those Priestly Syrens will rush en masse to the riverbank, waving, beckoning, poised for the snatch: "Looking for meaning?," they sing, as pink lips pout through porn star beards. "Feeling unfulfilled by the pursuit of earthly pleasures?" Be afraid Arty, it's your mind they're after, and you must resist.

I'm surprised our Nate hasn't tried to recruit Tricky Dicky to the Sunday Club yet. Drunks are one of the Bible's most regular characters after all. Getting pissed definitely has a fair claim for being the second oldest profession, and surely if anyone was looking for a way out (or would if he could see straight) it's our Rich.

But by the look in his eyes I'm pretty sure DC Nate has returned to the scene of the crime and found the rest of his personality, and somehow I don't think he's gonna turn the other cheek. The question now is how the bookies will react, could there be a new favourite? I know who my money's on.

I have sympathy, I really do. There have been times when I could not wait for the day when this particular project was over, so I too could take a break from my own journey. We must never forget how contingent such a noble life is, how circumstantial, how bloody *hard* at times. Human existence and all that it contains could have been otherwise, it might never have happened – and this includes the search for beauty itself. The world doesn't need our projects, *we* do!

Our journey was borne from contingency and in that sense its design exists by pure chance. And so as it pays no heed to perfection it is not, therefore, self-contradictory every time it becomes difficult to tread. If there is suffering then that's because - not being God – we are powerless to prevent it. We may not be designed to undertake such a project – but the glimpses of beauty will be enough to keep us going. So don't give up and don't be afraid of taking a break. Cards and wine are so much better when earned by hard work.

Believe it or not Stinky Bones has taught me a new game. Of course it's a tactic stolen right from the attention-seeking child but this little dribbler needs company real bad, my company it seems, anything to keep his mind off the circle of vultures. So it seems we've left the Monday Club and joined the Tuesday Whist Drive.

And guess what? We only play in a pair against Ray and Natasha! I should really take a closer look at the company I keep. But I'm moving on soon. Didn't I tell you? Sorry, but surely you weren't *really* expecting more? When I said the ending wouldn't resolve matters I wasn't eyeing up some lucrative sequel. It's just because I'm lazy, and I also enjoy annoying Sarah, so please don't mistake any of this for a cliff hanger. I'm happy to share a couple more scenes with these

soaken brokes, these broken soaks. But let's face it, this is likely to be Rich's last, I can't see him making any more, unless someone's sick enough to attempt *The Early Years* of course.

And without our lead man we're all gonna struggle, without our shared suffering there's no other reason for we glorious victims to be sitting here, pissing our lives up the pub wall.

So believe it or not Richard has taught me a card game. "It's not what you've got, it's the way that you play it," he proclaimed as he dealt, as if that was the only rule we needed to know. First full sentence I've heard him say in weeks, surely this old dog isn't fighting back? Perhaps they've all got wind that there's only one more episode after this, perhaps they're all putting themselves in the shop window.

And the incredible thing is, he's absolutely right: "It's not what you've got, it's the way that you play it." Like most games, hands are dealt, cards are played, suits are followed, tricks are won. But cash changes hands in a most peculiar way.

For each player predicts how well they are going to do and when the game's finished they are rewarded or punished according to the accuracy of that prediction. A game where not only is the punter obliged to bet on his horse, and his horse alone, but is then given limited power to make that forecast come true. What a meritocracy! Such equality of opportunity! What a true republic! Where a pauperly three, four, two eights and a nine can triumph over the aristocratic kings and queens. "It's not what you've got, it's the way that you play it." Quite Richard, quite. The only rule we ever need to know. Surely that old dog isn't fighting back?

So as we approach the end of this chapter my compassion for the common man is gathering pace. While I appreciate Sartre's idea of people living in bad faith, I fear it is almost completely unavoidable, especially if the alternative is to grow into a tree. We all did enough of that in drama lessons.

I want to emphasis that the alternative to bad faith need not be no faith, for there is a realm of good faith, good projects, where we can suspend our disbelief, let our imaginations run riot, and live our dreams, even though we know them to be false. And if the line between good and bad faith occasionally becomes blurred then so be it, we're only doing our best. So I've decided that from now on I'm a writer. And whether this is a role which begins in bad faith I care not. One day the dream may become reality but right now this is my story, and I'm sticking to it.

I believe, like the religious man believes in God, that there is no higher existence than the creation of beauty, and no greater tool to help us achieve it than the imagination. Beauty does indeed lie in our dreams – but perhaps those dreams lie far closer to the interface between our two worlds then we realise.

I've always been a dreamer, although much more at home in the daytime than the night, for my imagination is sure afraid of the dark. Much of what you have and will read was borne from daydreams, it's how I live, how I think, if dreams were really all we had then I'd be a healthy boy. And ask any daydreamer why he does so and he would tell you, if bound to honesty, that the pleasure is as genuine as any other. Those are real hairs standing on end, my friend, and those are real tears of laughter, and not an onion in sight. But our head is indeed stuck in the clouds if we treat our daydream as nothing more than a sneaky spliff to soften life's sharp edges. We must use our imagination to enhance our experience of the world, not hide from it.

To realise our dreams, to achieve our goals, to put our imagination to good use, a certain amount of reinvention must take place, in fact we might see reinvention itself as a lifestyle, a succession of reincarnations within one lifetime.

I'm not talking about the various suits I tried on earlier, posh as fuck, common as muck – they're just a bit of fun – but there is an underlying principle: that persistence of personality is a lie we tell ourselves in bad faith, that the roles we play only choose us if we let them, and true happiness is only achievable when we turn our back on the comfy pigeon hole carved out by circumstance. But it's not about fighting the status quo, for society needs protesters as much as it needs defenders, two sides playing the same game. We must simply look the other way, we must ignore that playground spat and grow up a bit.

It's time for some good religion: The beauty of Buddhism lies in its account of the illusion of the human soul. Firstly we must realise that there would be no concept of a personal identity without our memory. And if memory can be broken, distorted and eventually wither away, then what of us, the 'I', that once seamless actor held responsible and accountable year after year for his conduct, his attitude, his actions?

A severe accident can wipe the data from our brain, but it will soon fill up again. We may have lost our pre-accident memories but we haven't lost the *ability* to remember. And in time a new identity will be born, a new post-accident self. So what? Soon after the accident we might well try to remember our prehistoric past, but twenty years on we may well be rather happy with this post-war soldier. Twenty years is a long time after all, and would we really want to give more credence to a forgotten childhood than a living adulthood?

I see my identity as a graph, with a line climbing up to the present day. Clearly there is some persistence from moment to moment. I might say I am 99 per cent of the person I was last month, 90 per cent of the person I was last year, 80 per cent of the person I was five years ago and so on and so on. But we cannot carry our whole life in our head, giving equal weight to every second since we were born.

Rather, our identity becomes like a cloak flowing behind us, from shoulder to floor, allowing yesteryear's life-consuming dreads to flutter away on the winds of time. Some traits may have persisted over the years but by dropping some, keeping others and acquiring new ones, we are in effect controlling and recreating ourselves.

If people are unhappy with a personality trait which has dogged them all their lives then nine times out of ten it's because they are either too lazy, too stupid or too frightened to change it. Elements of our personality may be connected with our genes but at the end of the day no court in the land will forgive domestic abuse in the man with his "father's temper". As I said - I think it's time we all grew up.

But many people still hold a most perverse pride in their consistency, gripping hold of their memories like family trinkets. They delight in beginning sentences with: "Well – I've always thought …"; "The thing I've always said …"; "You'll never see me …"

I treat such prefixes as a health warning against what I'm about to hear. But people wear such opinions like medals, or even worse, hereditary heirlooms, to be passed on in tact from generation to generation: "Congratulations dear boy, on holding this opinion for fifty years, and what's that you say? It's the same view your father had and his father had before him. You must be very proud."

Opinions have a sell by date you know – if you'd ever stood next to Gerald you'd know they go off after a while. But unfortunately society gives us no encouragement to make such changes, holding predictability and consistency in high esteem. Although of course the one glorious exception to this rule is those sentences which start "I've always wanted to …", heartbreaking signposts to our dreams, dreams we've usually given up on years ago, not because of aptitude but pure resignation, accepting the lies we're told about people having their place, *fitting in,* as if the universe had fashioned a we-we hole just waiting to be filled.

For the truth is, there is no logical barrier to wholesale transformation, only a moral one if we let society's dullards have their wicked way. Identity is a moveable feast and if we so wish we can make that change to something new, even something we've seen in someone else and fancy trying out for a while.

An admired life can be replicated and in time become part of one's fabric, after all it was never *their's* anyway. You can't patent an attitude and neither can they. Personality is only a way of life, an *arrangement* as ephemeral as the faces we spot in the clouds. But we need not restrict ourselves to other people. We can construct a personality from any number of sources: read books, watch films, write your own, for not only have you plenty of time to choose but so long as you never forget that persistence is a weakness you can always change your mind. And if you're worrying that you're only a replica of the real deal then forget it - you're already as real as them, because they're forever as fake as you.

I don't know what films Richard's been watching but he came to the pub in a waistcoat the other day, along with a pair of dark glasses and a peaked cap that cast a dark shadow over his all-new poker face. He's had some personality surgery alright – sits, spits and shits like a card player apparently. And I must say, he's looking all the better for it. Trouble is I suspect that in his mind I'm part of this new him, part of this recovery, and this just cannot be, waistcoat or not.

I told you Dickhead, I'll answer your questions, and I'll even play your stupid game (I never win by the way, and as a matter of fact I've gone right off it) but that's the only game I'm playing. Sorry Richard but me and you are history, literally. Read back for yourself, you'll see, this one's always been a game of two halves.

Sartre says "self-consciousness is actually made up of a set of commitments and aspirations that give a projective unity to our acts of consciousness"[14], and hey presto a person is formed. The maths says we must wait some time before we are say 50 per cent different from how we are now, but soon the outlook will become familiar, second nature, first nature. If it's never too late to learn a new instrument then its never too late to learn a new personality.

When Menuhin declared genius was 90 per cent hard work he was also revealing the huge potential we have for achievement, lifestyle change, the creation of beauty. We describe certain artists as 'a natural', as if their craftsmanship and technique was born into the tips of their fingers (as if their pianos grew from the ground like trees?). But we

---

[14] The Oxford Companion to Philosophy, Ed. Ted Honderich, 1995

know the hard work that has gone on behind the scenes, and what is practise if not disciplined repetition until the unfamiliar becomes familiar? I know there are varying degrees of aptitude which are to some extent fixed, but never forget it is in the artist's self-promoting interest to sell his talent as a God-given gift. The last thing he wants is everyone having a go - but we all can, and in fact we all must. With patience we too can place the familiar in a different category, declaring ourselves to be naturally gifted that way.

It is this endless striving for essence, to escape the contingency into which we were born which defines *the* human paradox, and tells us why the search for beauty through creation is its best antidote.

By practising we are aiming to overcome our clumsiness towards the outside world, we are trying to bridge the distance between us and objects, between the inside and the outside. We are trying to make them behave as do our own limbs, servants to our will, to our essence. And when we have acquired the knack, it will feel as if we were born with this talent, as if the ability to read and write and ride bikes and tie shoelaces were all tricks transcribed in our DNA.

The act of creation gains its potency from being under the sole control of the creator. I've never liked (Ha! Caught out by my own words!) people helping me, unless under my control. If I want to be better at something then I will tell them how they should teach me. But more often than not I will through trial and error and practise and repetition learn a new skill completely on my own.

Because that's where the beauty lies, not solely in the product but in the act of creation too. If I write a song, and a 'musician' comes along and insists on improving it then they may as well strangle it to death. It was beautiful because it was mine. If I had wanted to listen to *good* music I would have put on Beethoven, dumbo. It's not about you, it's not even about the song, it's about *me*.

I believe a lifestyle change can also be seen as a talent to be acquired, practised, a beautiful creation to be realised. Because not only will it reveal the philosophical impermanence of our identity, and the complete fallacy of the religious soul, but as a project of creation it will use up huge amounts of imagination and be relatively easy to maintain complete control over.

We must discard the circumstantial baggage of birth, second-hand is so often second-rate, and create something new, something we can really call our own, a new life for our inner world through the search for and creation of new beauty in the outside. And you will find that these two worlds will eventually become as one, time spent on your outside project will also be time spent with your inside, double plus good, pure Superform.

And finally, if you are worried about the judgement of your genes, then shrink back inside yourself – take a moment to realise your separateness. You may scoff at this Starship Enterprise view of the human condition, with you the captain plotting a course of action through the cosmos according to data received via a myriad of sensors. But sit still and imagine yourself that way and you'll see it's actually not as weird in reality as it sounds in words.

The fact we rarely feel this way is testament to our mind's ability to blur the distinction for the means of social survival. And those without this ability we call mad - those who live inside the bubble, those who can't carry life's loads as one. But how

MESSAGES FROM THE DEAD

strange that we are happy to overlook a man's artistic ineptitude so long as they tell a good story down the pub. Yet someone with a wealth of inner riches, who might happen to stutter socially, is rejected at the drop of a hat. Always jabber skills to the front, and the rest mere afterthought.

Society it seems has developed a life of its own. It may be wholly man-made and could clearly not exist if all of us were dead, but like the internet it has started to resemble an immortal living organism, which can never be switched off. It has us by the short and curlies – with its high standards of behaviour, etiquette and cool – cramming rules and regs into spaces which should be left clear for creation.

We are like cathedrals packed to the ceiling with office files, so high that light no longer pierces this hallowed space. We are taught from an early age to defile this beautiful arena, to treat it as a store room at best, for useless information about achieving *success*. And before we know it our creative lifeblood is tapped at source, diluted by society's need for order and replication, and sold back to us like wraps of contaminated smack to be digested without engagement: "Be a good boy now, we'll do the creating – you just make sure you keep buying the stuff you like best." But their silent guide always reminds them: "Give them anything they want, but *never* let them know how beautiful they are." But it's time to fight back. We are approaching the last stretch. Good luck.

Ever since Year Zero Richard's head has played host to a ranting nightly confessional: "So sorry – I didn't mean ... I can't remember – Just... - I was dr.. – I'm sorry – but the crying – she wouldn't .. – I mean, didn't you ... - I couldn't... - I shouldn't ..."

But just recently he's started hearing it in the daytime as well, in the pub. A mental monologue, without time for breath or reflection. However yesterday was different. I blame myself really, I had apparently arranged to play cards the week before but it had slipped my mind. Of course I still went to the pub, but not in time for the big deal, or so it seems, for by the time I arrived the Dickster was already involved in some pretty heavy petting with Suey, and I certainly wasn't about to play gooseberry. To be honest, the idea of a regular date of any sort with Richard now makes me feel quite sick, even if it *is* proving to be good therapy for him.

I suppose I should blame myself really, but if a weekly game of cards with a couple of Nazis is all that lies between you and wholesale ruin Nappy Boy, then unreliable friends are the least of your problems. Face it baby face, it was going to happen some time, it was always on the cards, the truth will out as they say. So as I was saying, ever since *that* night Richard has played host to a ranting confessional. But just recently he's started hearing it in the day as well, and in the evening, in the pub, when he's truly alone. A mental monologue, without time for breath or reflection. But yesterday was different.

If he ever needed proof that the dualism between the inner and outer world was definitely *not* metaphysical (Richard thinks a lot about this stuff, without words, like we all do), if just once he ever wondered what a meta was *really* phor, it was last night alright. For before he could even get to the end of his silent tirade he was being lifted armpits first out of his stool, dragged across the bar and discarded into the night.

You've guessed it, the whole pub had been treated to Richard's private performance, and I don't think I've ever seen a man fall so far. And I don't think I had ever seen Sarah look so angry. "It's not supposed to be like this, you *idiot*," she hissed, as she felt Suey break free and bear down on the winning post, beyond her tight-reined tutelage. For this was supposed to be no-one's story but hers, this was no public show.

But now the court had heard the evidence, straight from the defendant's mouth, and the world had its motive, *her* motive. The question now is how the bookies will react, could there be a new favourite? It's time for the end to begin. I know who my money's on.

Part Four

So this is it. I guess we're here. The last stretch. No doubt you imagine I have offered nothing but fleeting and unsubstantiated rhetoric about the search for meaning and the creation of beauty. At times I have been filled with real dread, that I might never progress beyond such ephemera, all preparation no delivery, rumour and gossip from a land to which I could never take you.

Like all philosophers I must answer *the* big question: "What is the meaning of life". And I am well aware that if I cannot give it some weight, some density, then all that has gone before will be devalued. But that's not to say that if this next bit fails then you, dear reader, will fall right back to square one. You wouldn't have come this far had you not agreed, when required, to put in a bit of effort yourself.

I guess there may just be time for me to blag it – to tell you that it's for each individual to discover their own meaning to life, and in many ways that's true. But of course there's Richard and Sarah, and I should at least see them through to the end. I owe them that much.

Before we go on I must make clear that this last part is no quick fix. I have no desire to add to the growing library of self-improvement guides floating across the Atlantic, their soggy logic disintegrating into a tide of pointless pulp, sweeping across defenceless shores, clogging up streams of thought which once sparkled clear. Like the Red Indian to a bottle of whiskey, we have no immunity, we don't share their history of psychobabble, and they know that all too well, leaving us hopelessly addicted to their raps of speed and ease.

But this was never meant to be easy. We can assume no beauty at the heart of this world, as if the universe will one day accord with the simple symmetries of human maths. Such naïve optimism is Enlightenment claptrap repackaged by modern science. We can never speak reality's language, only our own. My metaphysic is borne from personal experience, my meaning to life is evident from clear calm observation.

And we must journey there. It is a summit, a destination, more than mere location. Sure, you could helicopter yourself to the top (for what else is a self-help manual?) but believe me the view won't be nearly as good, for there'll be no path to gaze back on, no *context*.

If these are among the first sentences you've read then I must submit my disclaimer now, for as you stumble on you will feel increasingly cold and alone in a foreign land. And as you overhear voices approaching from below, and turn your envious gaze on the emerging party of tired joyous faces, you'll realise the truth of that bit you never read, about what the journey brings to the destination, the observer to the observed.

I did so want to build a solid foundation to this creative finale, but looking back, I fear I may not have done enough. Perhaps I have been too harsh on politics. Perhaps I haven't explained adequately it's vital role in creating and policing the space in which beauty needs to grow.

We must make space for the best things in life, but I never wanted a total clear out. If I've ever given the impression that our freedom from the shackles of tradition should be nihilistically abused, like some jacked up junkie joyriding his way through a night of destruction, then I'm sorry. Although there is part of me that identifies with that young scamp, not because that's my idea of a good night out, but because like Antoine I crave disorder in the lives of others, just to pierce their conceit, just to rattle that confidence in those hand-me-down clip-on philosophies, to force them just once to stop living and start thinking.

But I'm not holding my breath. We must leave now, and be warned, each and every step we take will strain against the corporate grain, whose shining lights will burn all the brighter as we make to turn away. But remember, they frame nothing but bay window whores and you know how those lovelies look close up. The world will hate what we are doing, there's so little money in creativity and self-belief.

Society's henchmen, its self-appointed guardians, will try and attack our new way of life, for they like a fight, they love a putrid protester - they keep an eye on him that way. Or worse still if they can't beat us they will secretly join us. A covert operation gently nudging at those elusive commercial boundaries until we find ourselves wandering around *their* world again, like designer drop-outs paying through the ringed nose for yet another sham of a summer festival, easy to enter but near impossible to leave.

But what they cannot stand is being ignored, feeling as though they are somehow out of the circle, that there is a meaningful life operating beyond their borders, beyond their markets. So don't get caught in the search lights, don't look back, there's enough salt in this world remember, keep moving with me.

So what now? What did our gathered throng make of Richard's little outburst? Well, apart from the fact they probably heard one word in four, that noisy night was never mentioned again, not to his face anyway.

Seems we're all so hard to impress these days, all so hard to shock. When did we all become so cynical, when did we feel we've seen it all before? Perhaps I set a precedent with my Suey sermon, and Richard's was hardly going to top that. Perhaps they all knew what was coming anyway. I didn't tell them, but I've already voiced my suspicions that I'm not the only writer around here. This should bother me I know, my pride should be hurt. But I just don't have any, really I don't. Look at them, look at this twisted bunch of wrecks. Could *you* feel proud of them?

But perhaps I misread Sarah's stony silence, I saw indifference when I should have recognised plain old disgust, good old-fashioned family shame. Because like it or not, that spit-soaked pile o' piss in the corner is her husband, her man, and I guess we're all judged by the company we keep.

Anyway, this is my story, my soapy fiction, where everyone goes to one pub, no-one calls the police, and justice is administered locally, as it should be (and there's only one chap in this sorry tale capable of doing that). So that noisy night was never mentioned again, not to his face anyway.

Before we go any further we need to rescue the whole concept of work. No longer shall it be something to be done grudgingly, for someone else, the smallest effort for the most cash. For when we work for ourselves, towards the creation of beauty, we can discard all money worries, because they're taken care of by the day job. And whatsmore, there are no set hours, the food's as nice as you make it and you get to choose exactly what you do each day.

Let's not defile our real work, our real life, with their puny pieces of silver. Indeed – do 'their' work grudgingly, bleed 'em dry if you can. Shift up a gear into capitalist overdrive while you're there, money's pretty useful after all. By all means charge top whack for your brain and brawn, but never *ever* show them your heart. Oh, and don't do too many hours either, for we will need plenty of time.

We cannot compare the rewards in our world with the superficial wages paid in their's. Compare them instead with the benefit from doing nothing outside the nine to five, nothing but recovering in time for the next shift, which is of course all they want you to do.

The devil's trident scythes our precious day into three (eight hours sleep, eight hours work, eight hours rest), squeezing out any time for any real work. They steal our spare time and sell it back to us as 'leisure', 'relaxation', 'getting away from it'. (Two weeks at a time mind, wouldn't want you getting used to it). "Why not take the chance to put your feet up," they suggest to our face, ("because when they're down they belong to us", they whisper in our ear.)

Take a break? Take a break from what exactly? All time must be sold to the world of commerce and all 'time off', must be 'spent' relaxing, winding down, even preparing for the next day! Five days out of seven, with one week off in 12 for good behaviour, and that's even before we're lured into that extra special place, where we're to push ourselves even harder in search of *promotion* ("Why of *course* you can have a new title - especially if it'll stop you banging on about that pay rise".)

So here's the deal, a new day has dawned but this time it's been split into four: Firstly, and most important, we have our time, our work, our personal and private search for beauty. Secondly we have our new leisure, where we let our mind run down after a day at *our* office, a time of joyous self-indulgence and inspiration, not desperate mindless recovery. Thirdly we have sleep, and finally, we have *their* work, that tawdry obligation to make ourselves some money.

But don't worry too much about fitting it all in, for you will find the lines between the first two will begin to blur as superform gets a grip. I've written some of my best philosophy when supposedly 'taking a break', a bottle of red can really oil those cogs, especially when the pressure's off. And you'll also find you may want to talk about this new work down the pub (for let's face it, we talk enough crap about the *other* work). Don't you see how the hierarchy has changed? Don't fit your life around them, fit them in around you. You are your own unlimited company now – both worker and boss. It's finally time to work as a team, the Marxist divide breached once and for all in the realm it could never survive.

Creating beauty isn't moonlighting, the day job is, and you'll be getting away with it every day. And there's nothing the taxman can do because we are living beyond his petty world of petty cash. I've considered myself self-employed ever since I started this book – and when I need a break I don my stupid uniform (carefully positioned *just* out of fashion if at all possible) put my feet up, and get down to their dirty business. I guess it's a matter of perspective.

So to all you squillions out there who work just to pay the bills, and do not enjoy one minute of it, I have no intention of leaving you behind. Quite the opposite in fact, if anything this book is for you.

We can't all do jobs which are rewarding in themselves, in fact which of us do? And I for one have no intention of telling you to do a good job for personal pride alone, for you simply don't owe them that. Believe me your Protestant parents were wrong, you should *not* do your best at all times because in corporate capitalism extra effort rewards everyone *but* you, and they must be made to pay for this system. You must know when to hold back, don't let them use you, be proud, be strong, be lazy.

But that doesn't mean there aren't ways we can use 'their' workplace to our advantage, to help us along our journey. Jobs take up too much time for us not to consider how we might put those hours to better use. For one of the most delicious ironies I've discovered is their work can actually create the perfect conditions for you to further your own, and I'm not just talking about nicking stationery.

You will find as you pursue your particular project that there are some parts which become immensely difficult, problems which you push to the back of the mind, and which then begin to drag on your creative flights of fancy. I suggest you jot them down in a secret notebook and take them to work the next day. Believe me, superform operates in the most unlikely places and will find you completely charged with unexpected inspiration and motivation during the frantic scribble of an office lunch break. For come that one hour of freedom in the middle of a day of drudge, last night's stubborn muddle will become today's most welcome distraction. And just imagine, some *real* excitement in your working week. No-one need ever know, it'll be like taking your favourite pet to work, one that can really power those mean mean cogs of Greenwich Office Time. You'll be home before you know it.

But back at home, in our own office or workshop, we will take time to do things properly. There's no need to rush because we've taken Father Time's stopwatch and shoved it up his arse. "Least-outlay-for-the-most-return" may hold sway in *their* world, driving both the capitalist boss *and* his unionised workers, but we must turn that shared mantra on its head when it comes to ours, for there'll be no-one around to pick up the pieces left by shoddy work, and there'll be nothing gained from stringing it out.

And thanks to the ever-present rewards of superform, you'll find your attitude to other parts of your life will improve once you've embarked on this personal journey. Good quality workmanship will become a question of pride, to be applied to the simplest most mundane jobs. I might be a bit slower but I can suddenly be much more bothered to do stuff in a way I never could before. Energy-sapping problems are suddenly revealed as a clear succession of challenges before my X-ray eyes, to be solved with perfection and balance. Success without mess. New slogans for a new generation.

The search for beauty has not been conceived in the clouds by some high-minded rationalist. Maybe it's a space and time filler after all, but there are places in our brain of which we know very little.

And there are times in our brain of which we know very little, times past, events recorded, deeds done. How else would you explain that couple in the corner? No-father and no-son clinking glasses as if they've known each other all their life (and in the world of words that's probably very true). I never thought he had it in him but it seems our Rich gave Suey the elbow as he hit a sodden pavement on a noisy night. "Given 'er up mate, thinking of taking a bit easy," he explained to me the other day, bottle of House in one hand, tumblers in the other. "Proper way to drink the vino this is." Yeah yeah Dickhead, whatever.

Someone's got to call time soon. They're all at it by the way. Face down in the Red Sea as if it was about to dry up. Just what *is* it about Dirty Dick? That trend setter, that Daddy Baddy, surrounded by his bruised and abused, the family that

can't live with him, can't live without him. I've even had a couple of cog oilers meself. I told you before, I'll copy anyone, I'm not proud.

There are times in our brain of which we know very little, times past, events recorded, deeds done. How else would you explain that couple in the corner? Rats is making progress by the way, he wanted revenge, he needed to find the killer, and so who did he turn to? I reckon he's twigged, he must have done, after all there aren't that many people in this sorry tale, and what fiction can resist a bit of dramatic incest?

We may have limited time, but when you embark on your search for beauty it will seem as if you have unlimited space, thanks largely to a habitual timidity when faced with the virgin territory in our own head. But as you become more adept at this inner space travel, you may find your desire to find meaning begins to fade. Perhaps this journey is about replacing the big question, rather than answering it. And perhaps philosophy is about a life we can never crack, for we sure wouldn't need it if we could answer its questions!

All this talk of antidotes and trips through space is making our journey sound more like a drug now, and I would indeed urge you to get hooked, even if the first hit makes your mind puke. Like some fairground disclaimer, I feel I should warn that: "Sudden attention to one's true self may cause nausea in some." We may never like our shell, but we must grow to love what's inside.

However, we must set limits to this Narcissistic honeymoon period. We must never forget the rule of superform, work for it and it will work for you. Remember, there are many clothes to wear, many ways of life to try out. We must give each project enough time to grow and bear fruit, but once tasted we should always have an eye on the next season, the next harvest.

I wonder what our Sarah will do when her deed is done? To be is to do, to do is to be. They mean the same don't they? When she's done, when there's no more do to do, will she, I wonder, be like a bee, one sting per life, one bang your dead, meaning served, goal reached. She hopes so, she thinks she's all being, no doing, just waiting. Reality's second hand doesn't tick her life away. I wonder, what will become of our Sarah when she willingly offers up her heart to be ripped out and consumed by the claws her ending will never have? What will become of our Sarah when her pathetic life sails past that aching climax she will never reach, when her beloved essence is jacked off by the grip of reality and revealed to all as transparency itself, mere salt, mere seasoning. New outfit perhaps? New life on the Med? Remember, there are many clothes to wear in this soapiest of operas, and she's barely troubled the costume department so far.

What does a woman on a mission do in a retirement she will never enjoy? Will she have to believe the empirical lie after all. God knows she's swallowed enough pills in her pathetic life for one more not to matter, however bitter. I wonder what our Sarah would do if her deed was done? I guess none of us are getting any younger. No wonder we drink.

Time is not on our side, only space is. Just for once these two bedfellows are separated for our inner world is so vast that we will all die having seen far less than half. But let's not get too down.

There might be time for boredom in the hi-tech future of thought travel, memory transfer and personality banks, but life is not about philosophy, philosophy is about life, and that means this life, right here, right now. So don't get too proud. It's not really your space as such, it's just that as things stand it can't be accessed by anyone but you, so take advantage while you can. Right now you're the only one with keys to a vast mansion. You have the place to yourself, yet still you only pop in to pick up the post – just what are you scared of? I think it's time you threw a party.

Space is indeed the last frontier – but it's our mental space that lies undiscovered, not that boring blackness surrounding the stars. Three dimensions are so limiting, so yesterday darling. Time on the other hand is not so sneaky. Baby, child, teenager – young man, middle man, old man, dead. Seven chapters, The End. It's all so familiar, so *vulgar*. We must never join this procession, we must never feel as if we're living a story already written.

We all know how it feels to be starting a book, and how it feels to be finishing it, but we rarely know when we've passed from one phase to the other, until it's too late. In the world of literature this clearly matters not, starting and finishing a book are very pleasurable experiences. But that's because we're looking forward to starting a new one, or even re-reading the one we're finishing. Life on the other hand offers no such luxury.

Somehow we've got to stop reality's second hand ticking our life away, and that of course lies in the search for beauty and the process of creation. If we all took on such projects, baby, adult and elderly could take on whole new meanings. We might see pensioners shot through with pubescent intrigue at the prospect of getting to know the works of a new film director, teenagers full of nerves as someone hears their finished symphony for the first time. Come dream with me, things won't get better on their own.

But I'm not suggesting you get your paintbrush out straight away and stroke your way to eternal bliss, for we must never forget the reality of the human condition. Nature has designed us to walk and talk and sit and shit and blag and shag, that's about it. So don't expect anything vaguely worthwhile to be easy.

And if nature wasn't bad enough, nothing in the *modern world* will point you in the right direction either, for it seems the first barrier to creative activity is found in the first word, not the second.

The short history of the internet has soon revealed the ascendancy of quantity over quality in this Golden Era of information, this Golden Era for fools.

For the information age read the spoon-fed age - lethargic licence for a new generation to spend their lives in front of screens. Whether it be work, television, games, work, computers, work, the internet, shopping, work. Take an alien eye's view, step back a while, like soma-junkies we're hooked up to every waking moment. If computer and man are enjoying a meeting of minds on this planet, it's clear who's moving most to clinch the deal.

We don't trust the real world anymore, not unless it has been filmed. But these screens only *represent*, the colour's so poor, the depth barely there, what damage might these pixels be doing to our aesthetic juices? I looked at a flower the other day, real close, and it was almost too much. A delicious vulnerability we'd never tolerate in modern manufacturing, a faint yet complex scent barely detectable above the stench of deodorant, an unfathomable richness of colour we could never be offered by a DIY mixing machine.

Humans used to be able to take this stuff, but I'm not sure we can anymore. Nature is just too damn big and impressive, too *emotional*. It cannot be controlled, cannot be tailored to our workspace. We used to love that about it – but now we're just scared: "Shut the curtains and put that damn light on – that's better – the sun's so *bright* these days don't you think?"

Perhaps that's why we English are so confident, so arrogant. Perhaps that's why we thought we could conquer the world, the universe, because if you live in a green and pleasant land then the natural world must seem very timid. But you can't blame people in America or India or Italy for being religious – look at their mountains, look at their earthquakes, look at their *rain*.

I'm never more reminded of the impotence of man and his machines, his thoughts and his theories, as when I'm at the foot of a mountain, a proper mountain, not those crappy English hillocks, those mini middle-class titties. Mountains are infinitely heavy, proper *human* infinity which really only means "absolutely loads", not that hippy shit about fractals.

When I see a mountain I see a landlord and I feel like a tenant, a noisy badly-behaved one at that, the sort they just know will try to do a runner. But I guess we've only have been renting a matter of months to their way of thinking, they'll probably write us off as a bad lot ("win some lose some, still, their pets seemed nice") and I love them all the more for that.

So lets crack this cookie while we've got our boots on. Outbrains amigos, it's time to go outside, out *there*, for I would suggest nothing more, to start off our creative journey, than a walk. After all it's one thing most of us are pretty okay at.

Walking has become an integral part of my life - a beautiful fusion of the inner and outer realm, an activity which rarely if ever falls foul of bad faith (for it's always as good and often far better than you imagine beforehand) and, if I'm honest, it's a great way to shore up this flagging journey metaphor while I'm at it.

At its best one is simultaneously lost in one's own thoughts and someone else's woods. But, I beg you, do it alone, for a walk's not really a walk unless it lasts at least an hour – and are you sure you can talk for that long? Even if you can, are you sure you would want to? Silence among two is deafening, you won't be able to hear yourself think. I'm sorry, with company you simply won't feel the benefit.

There is a self-indulgence at the heart of the creative process which is absolutely vital. You must make and take time to think only about yourself. You've only got yourself to blame if you don't - you think anyone else is going to encourage such decadence?

We can only ban the public by removing ourselves from it. Scared? Embarrassed? I'm sure you'll feel a little of both. Your feet may still be pounding this planet, but in terms of function, outcome, goal, you'll actually be leaving the world for a while, for when you're finished it will have no record of what you've done. Having changed nothing you will have left no trace. Nothing bought, nothing sold ... but everything ventured, everything gained. So take the leap, this first activity, this first hurdle, this first step on the search for beauty. An episode of pure unadulterated you, your inner world made manifest in time and space – oh, and watch for the cows.

Ah! You're back. How was it? Do you feel guilty? Do you feel you've kind of cheated on everyone? Well good! Fuck 'em. And I wager that having abstracted yourself from the outside world for a couple of hours you're now feeling weirdly energised, self-confident, untouchable. Conspiratorial with your new secret friend, that silent noble self. Master of Your Universe, Master of *The* Universe.

Shall I let you into another secret? Such directed physical activity will become a close friend, providing invaluable respite from the creative process, those times when for now you just can't go on, but you're still not ready to go to the pub. Two hours of writing, two hours of walking, two hours of writing – this has described many a productive day for me, superform revealed under a useful sky. Although when fully submerged such a strict timetable makes little sense, for I've found that nothing bends time like creation.

We must not ruin our new life by squeezing it into their nine to five. If people are going to have a problem with the demotion of the 'working' day then surely that's just what it is – *their* problem. I can't help the fact they've allowed Big Business to bash their brains into the shape of a tiny cog. But although I won't blame them for creating that world, they must take full responsibility for living it.

This is no call to revolution - it's only you I want to change. For society can be nothing more than the people in it, and if enough of us walk away then it will have no choice but to follow. But if you're stuck on the status quo, if you've already spent what they paid you for your soul, then do me the courtesy of averting your judgemental eyes. Perhaps guide them earthwards instead, for you'll need to see where you're going as you shuffle towards that grave.

As I was saying, there is a realm of joyous routines which while requiring minimal creative thought certainly provide fertile ground for its regeneration and application. And indeed there will be times when beauty itself must be built brick by brick. But beware, for in doing so you may not find favour with another group of people, those who would cast themselves as the polar opposite to the aforementioned feet-shufflers, but who are to my mind just as ineffective. It seems a new-world suspicion of routine is emerging, as if doing the same thing every day is somehow boring, unimaginative, tantamount to settling down, settling for second best. Far better they say to live for each second, make decisions on the spur of the moment, and to turn away from pattern and predictability at all costs.

I couldn't disagree more. When I criticised the sleep-work-TV treadmill is was for its content, not the form. For in their desperation not to put down roots, these mystical tourists actually betray a *fear* of beauty, a fear of the project and a fear of being judged, which is of course a fear of failure. So they truss up their shallow life in 'adventures' and 'stories' and 'excitement'. They're happy to step onto the first rung of any number of ladders, and list them all by name. But suggest they dare lift their other foot towards a *second* rung and watch as this global hobbyist is demolished by vertigo.

"Oh you must meet him – such an incredible life – you should hear the things he's done, the places he's seen." And I'm sitting here thinking: "Yeah whatever – and I can't wait to hear his philosophy on it all, really I can't." But in a certain way that's true – because evenings in a pub are thankfully devoured by such people, their endless tale-telling, those lovely lists, leaving me ample time alone with my thoughts. Honestly, I really am grateful.

So here it is then. This is how it all started, the beginning in the end like a proper little novelist, turning the Good Book on its head, with Revelation at the start and Creation at the end. For we are surely finishing this thing now, that's how it feels to me anyway - you, me, Richard, Sarah, the whole bloody lot of us

are definitely finishing something. Maybe not The End but definitely An End. I can feel it in my fingers, and so can you, I know. And you know what? I might just pull off a final scene. But don't expert fireworks or a gripping climax, believe me there'll be nothing sensual when us lot come together. Simultaneous ejection more like, someone must call time soon.

So here it is then, this is how it all started. I met Richard in the pub, in his pub, and we got drinking by accident (clearly a very nasty one). The accident happened one Monday/Tuesday/Wednesday (don't bog me down in detail - if I'm making this up then what, pray, are you going to check these fickle facts against? You should count yourself lucky I gave them all names.)

But it wasn't the weekend, that much I know. It had to have that secret formula reserved for the midweek, that forbidden zone home to the best nights of the year. In the newspaper business they call it 'off-diary', the days we never plan and never forget. And here's the math: rich energy residue from surviving *their* work + low expectation + being naughty on a school night = front page splash. Unbeatable combination, the weekend's got no chance quite frankly. Like Advent's 25th window, Saturday stares out at us from the calendar – and just like that Christmas child we demand fun and excitement in an unmeetable measure. And to make matters worse Father Time's fiddling fingers give that wheel of misfortune an extra fast spin, and with disbelief burning in our hearts we are sent flying from the merry-go-round towards the Sunday Club where all life dies. Still, you've gotta laugh.

Anyway, whatever day it was I'd got the date wrong for our hilariously named Monday Club, coz guess what? It wasn't even held on a Monday! Okay, some details at last. The Monday Club was a gathering of people who talked about 'issues' – political, philosophical, even sporting when they over-lapped with the first two. Leftfield perhaps, left midfield certainly not.

But that didn't stop me trying: "The England team's perennial problem on the left a metaphor for socialism's decline? Are you quite *sure*?" enquired those suspicious spoilsports, treading water way out of their depth, those superior intellects who have never run, never competed, and so have never *felt* the importance of fairness and team spirit. "Of course I'm not sure," I'd think to myself, playground passions flooding back on this forbidden school night. "Like that flimsy sick note that once begged your pardon I made the whole thing up."

I wasn't (and didn't) like them. But for some reason this team with no spirit liked me, or rather liked me being there, staring from the kitchen cupboard like the ageing sage they never really cooked with. Beyond our boundary they'd have never given me a second look, but inside this boozer, Richard's boozer, so carefully chosen as club HQ to satisfy that middle class craving for filthy floors and filthy jokes, I existed for them. It's funny though, they never really existed for me. For a hundred smackers I honestly couldn't tell you their names, and I really can't be arsed to make any more up. Looking back those times seem so unreal, so unRichard.

If you ever want to feel the intensity of the here and now, the meaningless mass of existence we choose to ignore, then spend a wordless three hours with our Rich at the bar. He knew how powerless language was when up against genuine silence, the deathly hush of existence we can never escape. *He* knew we can never really talk our way out of this hole. And do you know what? He loved it, and given all this time, so did I. Together we became the strong silent type. Words are so cowardly after all, talk is so cheap. And like blood red lipstick slapped on a corpse we fool no-one, least of all ourselves.

But where was I? Oh yeah, I'd got the wrong day for the Monday Club. Apparently the week before (for clearly the joke hadn't gone nearly far enough) it was decided that the next meeting would indeed be held on a Monday. But of course as I never listened to what anyone said (for it had become very difficult to hear anything over the stream of abuse my mind discharged in the other direction) I never knew.

Those arseholes – they fancied themselves as some sort of Dead Poet's Society, which as a description of the society was more than half true. I only went for the free beer anyway: playing the penniless pen-pusher soon becoming a real talent of mine. But anyway, those dead poets *should* have paid me to be there, and at two pints an hour I reckon I was pretty cheap.

So that's how it happened. Me and Rich, Richard and me. As you know our eyes met ages before and hit it off immediately, but it wasn't until much later that the rest of me felt brave enough to follow: "Stood you up have they," he challenged, this allusion to courtship instantly filling my cheeks with blood. I told you it was weird.

And so I got up, and to this day I don't know why, I walked over to the stool next to him and sat down. And that was precisely where I spent the next two hours in deafening awesome silence, drinking, thinking, living. Some things just have to be described from the outside – not everything has an explanation. Some actions are as shallow as the movement that carries them. So I got up, and to this day I don't know why.

Superform shows us that repetition and practice are a necessary part of the creative process, which itself is a necessary part of giving our life meaning. So don't worry yourself about routine, Time itself ensures each moment is unique.

Think how different, how rich, how enlightening the second read of a favourite novel can be, perhaps more rewarding than the first. Same words, different time. It seems we quite happily get drunk on the same drink in the same pub on the same day with the same friends for a lifetime – yet are quick to sneer at our neighbour who dares to go on holiday to the same French village each year.

But surely they are going there because it just gets better – do you really think they'd still be going otherwise? Perhaps they don't want to waste that richness of experience built up over the years, perhaps they've climbed this ladder too high to consider jumping off, perhaps they don't want to start again. "Never give up on a good thing," as the song tells us. Try new things by all means but make extra space for them, or at least wait for something else to have genuinely run its course.

People who flit from one place to another, one set of friends to another, one job to another, are often the very people for whom life becomes very easily boring (and that's certainly the effect they have on mine). Why can't they see what's staring them in the face? *Everything's* boring at the start, learning's *never* been fun, ask any schoolchild. Projects need to be worked at. The best stocks won't pay dividend immediately, but if you're only ever going to invest short-term, then short-term gains are all you're ever going to earn.

Much better to embark on a six-year adventure writing a book, then a six-week adventure conquering a mountain (what a laughable way to describe such scrawny scrambling, I say stay at base camp, where you can gaze up and learn something useful). Sure there may be no comparison for the first six weeks, in fact it is questionable whether the first six weeks of writing a book are enjoyable at all. But two years down the line, where do we find our two adventurers? I'll tell you.

Mountain Man is in the pub boring the pants off me with yet more tales from an increasingly insignificant episode more than 20 months ago, and I'm glowing like a demi-God, way past the nervous second chapter, half way definitely in sight and facing the very real prospect of eventually having written a proper book. Keep hold of those memories man, mind they don't flutter away on the winds of time. Me? I'll plump for the here and now if you don't mind.

I know I've used you Mountain Man, but I'm not guilty. After all it's not like you needed encouragement to tell your tale. Faced with that famous leather chair you always chose yourself as specialist subject. You started it, you were full to brimming if I remember rightly, ready to burst at the slightest invitation. I'd far rather listen and learn than compete in the verbal marketplace to sell my own brand. I already know what I think - why would I want to hear it again?

In fact the few times I do let rip are when I'm treading virgin territory as I speak, hacking away at a New Forest, hopefully with fellow adventurers, armed with nothing but a mouthful of swords. But people are so rarely willing to free their minds from the cultural casing, especially when others are around, they're so wary of throwing their brain into the melting pot, of offering it as nothing but ego-free imagination, as municipal intellect. And people are so suspicious of neutrality, of indifference to who comes up with an idea, so long as it's a good one. So like a circle of anonymous alcoholics the script rarely sways from one person's view, one person's monologue, a take-it-in-turn tedium which transports me anywhere but the conversation itself.

Such messages from the dead strangle the here and now here and now. The life, the potential, is squeezed out of each moment as we wallow in a desert of events already passed. ("What did you do last night?" "Oh, I talked about the night before of course.") These story tellers talk as if meaning belonged to each word and each word belonged to them. They tell the same stories in the same way, often to the same people. These actors are filled with terror, a fear of the strangeness of each new moment, so they try to make it as much like last night as possible. I'm suspicious of all confident speakers for as beer time wears on and their brain loses ground to an accelerating mouth, quantity throttles quality and the shouting match begins. Someone save us from such nights of the living dead.

And while we're at it, save us too from the expert. Of course such specialists need to operate in far off lands, but they so often fail to appreciate the journey that took them there. So instead of coming back to show us where they've been and how they arrived, they stand in the distance and bellow in a foreign tongue. Do they really think we're impressed? How could we possibly be? They may hanker for eccentricity, but I'm afraid most are plain dull.

Genuine insight, genuine imagination, needs neither brute force or devilish detail. Honesty and modesty will take us much further. And anyway in my experience it's rarely to one's advantage to divulge so much. I don't mean to be so awful – really I don't. But I haven't got the time or energy to think about how to make a better impression. I'm just writing a book - give us a break.

Now I know what you're thinking: "With uncommon humility that chap admitted he'd served us nothing but fleeting and unsubstantiated rhetoric, yet here we are, a dozen pages down the line, and we've tasted little more." Easy now, you're even starting to sound like me. I suspect you're already trying on a new life admired, and hey, I'm flattered (Oh, the sheer joyous abandon of writing with no editor and no right to reply. I urge you all to try it, really I do).

Well what can I say? I will talk about the act of creation, and I will talk about discovering beauty, but perhaps we might first look at some hard evidence staring out at us from the walls, for that way I hope you will see that my idea of beauty may not be so dissimilar to yours ("watch 'im, he's trying to blag it again".)

While art is not the only man-made carrier of beauty, it's lack of function certainly makes it the most pure, the most obvious, *potentially* that is. And while the question "What is art?" will always come clothed in controversy the moment it's uttered, a philosopher so preoccupied with the search for beauty must face it with nerves of steel, so read on and by all means be appalled and offended in equal measure, for I guess that's the point.

I put this question to Richard some time ago, and, with a bemused frown and polite pause, he replied: "Painting, innit", addressing me with the calm clarity one usually reserves for a child. And of course he's absolutely right, again.

Mozart offers countless moments of beauty caged within what is often a recognisable classical form. Shakespeare's genius too shines as bright as ever, despite what might at first glance appear to be a quite tortuous historical mode. So surely our love of the two geniuses comes from our wonder at the insight which drove them *from behind*, not the modish form in which it was presented (would we really be fawning over Tudor theatre if Shakespeare hadn't been born?).

The jaw-dropping beauty of a Van Gogh isn't found in that oily impressionism common to the era, or the fact we like to see flowers in a vase, millions of forgotten artists have produced that. And (just for you crazy fans of the modern sound) I guess you don't have to like the electric guitar to love Hendrix.

Genius will shine through the most obstructive formats, seizing Time's hands and pointing them at the stars, towards the universe, towards the universal. The best art reveals something profound about the human condition. It becomes a dialogue between artist and viewer, one spoken across time and culture, ignoring the format on which it is hung, or the subject it is *about*.

So if beauty lies not in the format or the subject, then might we see these as obstructions? Perhaps so, and I guess much art since the beginning of the 20th century can be characterised by a questioning of the carrier itself.

Abstract art, starting with the impressionists, attempted to present its subject in a suggestive way, which evolved into an exercise in distortion and then complete rejection.

We were invited to witness an artist's vision at its most pure, and I am certainly drawn to this endeavour, numbering many examples among my favourite works of art. But I would also number many others as among my least favourite. This may be because Darwinian selection and Father Time have yet to kill off the weedy imposters, and the good the bad and the ugly are still claiming equal space.

Abstract painting may have abandoned its subject but it was still brave enough to keep the format, so it could be judged on the wall right next to its ancestors. However, more recently art has it turned its deathly gaze on the very formats which once carried it so well, and it is this misleading mission from which much of my current frustration is born.

Shocking art reveals something shocking about the artist, or about us, and to my mind such sentiment can dwell with far greater intensity in the eyes of a portrait in plain oils than a bank of snuff movies flashing on a loop. Why do you think film directors pan away from the most shocking scenes? They are not hiding us from the awful truth, quite the opposite. They are revealing it to us in its full intensity, because they know full well that with scarce encouragement our imagination will happily plummet to depths of depravity which art in any format could never hope to represent. Representative *filmed* horror will always be left splashing in the shallow end.

I fear much modern art has lost sight of the original meaning of art, the point of art, that is to speak to the human soul. Many artists have seemingly abandoned the universal quest to reveal profound insights about the human condition. Like the global traveller who steps onto the first rung of many ladders, but fails to climb any of them, this new breed of mean-spirited self-indulgents have become fixated with creating a multitude of new formats. Yet so obsessed are they with the relationship between themselves and their work, on pushing the boundaries of art itself, that they often leave the boundaries of the human soul untroubled.

It once seemed that art was *about* art but *for* the people. Painters may have looked to the Heavens for a theme but they always looked to the earth for a viewer. Recognising we're all the same distance from the sun, they endeavoured to reveal the universal, to highlight the deepest parts of the human condition, to amaze and inspire, to light a spark of beauty in the hearts of those who bore witness.

But now it seems that while art may be *about* people, it is definitely *for* itself. Modern artists may look earthwards for their subjects, whether it be beds and bricks, TVs and tin cans, but I feel they're looking anywhere but Blighty for an audience. Perhaps they've been taught that the modern art lover has become immune to portraits, or landscapes, and now demands his art to be constructed from household products ("now where's me slippers – I love a good Constable me").

Clearly none of this would matter if the moment of beauty emerged alive, having heroically travelled that hallowed path from artist to art to audience. But I feel the art has stopped in the middle and is now looking at me, to see whether I'm among the chosen number who 'get it'. Why haven't I received my invitation to mirror their journey into my own soul, I wonder. I feel robbed, cheated, as if somehow my name's not down. Above all, the creations before me seem smug, rather satisfied with *themselves*, as if yesteryear's 'noble universal' has now been dismissed as some sort of dumbing down, some sort of cliche.

Ironically there are echoes here back to the days of the medieval religious state, where art was a gift from God and the artist his sacred messenger, with we the worthless rabble left to gaze in silent wonder at the privileged relationship being played out before our eyes - our reaction, our *opinion*, as relevant as that of the spiders hiding in our hair. Mercifully there existed such great creatures who could hide beauty right under the nose of their philistine commissioner, sending secret messages to an age way beyond their death. And when God faded away, the artist was finally given free reign to play Creator, his art was now the mirror and a whole new space created for we the audience, with a vital role to play in the realisation of beauty, now properly seen as a moment between audience and art.

But if this is so then why have we recently been hearing more about artists than their art? Noses in the air these quasi-religious fools are standing tall again. I'm not suggesting there is some new God to whom these modern artists pray, for I suspect the relationship is far less genuflection than masturbation. But the fear remains that like those dark dark ages, the audience, we *general public*, have once again been cast into the shadows with the spiders.

If art is not for an audience, not for *other people,* then why should it be supported by *other people,* either directly by attendance or indirectly through tax? Art cannot see empty galleries as a success – a glowing tribute to its high-mindedness. That's just art for art's sake. What should be a means has become the end, as if these conceited creations can stare at each other, their line of sight now left blissfully unobstructed by that damnable public.

There is no hilarious irony in leaving your public cold and nervous, feeling patronised and inferior, desperate to escape the space they had entered with such anticipation. How ironic that if when our galleries and concert halls are at their most accessible, when those centuries-old barriers of austerity are gradually being removed, their contents were to run in the opposite direction.

I do not think there is a beautiful idea that would suffer from being attached to a traditional structure, or indeed a form of any kind. But I suspect in many cases these artists knows only too well their limitations and are too scared to hang the vision on a familiar frame, preferring instead to lean on those four props of the talentless: controversy and confusion, gimmick and gratuity.

But if modern artists were really expressing their honest idea of pure beauty then how come their stuff looks so similar? From this attempt at rejection, new formats and new traditions are emerging: the white spaces, the lurid slogans, the video loops. And I fear the weaker artists are seeking solace in being part of these new movements, hoping to hide their ineptitude behind something bigger. They may affect some noble hari-kiri as they stick the knife in to their own heritage, but we all know there's no courage in suicide, and one suspects these marketing radicals are in fact conformist lemmings of the highest order, wholly lacking in the pure vision to which they deign to aspire.

But like Mozart and his forgotten cronies, there generally emerges one leader off whom the others feed, this baying pack of talent-free chancers glad to suck dry the lifeblood of a contemporary genius. For aren't parodies just that? Merely the rough shape of the victim's work, the mutilated body with its art ripped out, and aren't they all the worse for it? You wouldn't need to change many notes in a piece of Mozart for it to be almost unbearable, but it doesn't stop people trying.

What these people don't realise (or even worse, perhaps they do) is that you don't find Hendrix by learning the individual notes he played. You search for him by listening to the music and asking yourself *why* he played those notes, and you have found him when you can play other people's tunes *as he would have done*, playing *like* he plays, not *what* he plays. Ask yourself, which would sound more like Hendrix? Hendrix playing a cover version of a Mozart melody, or you playing a cover version of a Hendrix classic? I think you know the answer. Learn from the best by all means, but try looking for the artist and stop bloody copying his art.

I guess what I'm asking for is a bit more effort, a bit more substance and fewer in-jokes (in fact fewer jokes of any sort would be nice – how did artists ever come to imagine they were so funny, as if comedians were better-than-average painters.)

And please, much less irony and cynicism. It's so lazy, so *easy*. If you hadn't noticed we're actually living in the Cynical Age, cynicism is the tradition of our times, an era where honesty and modesty would surely deliver more impact, more shock value. A work of art, from whatever era, must act as the interface between the artist's world and ours, the middle of the journey, not the end. There simply has to be a search for beauty, an effort to move the viewer from beyond the canvas.

I fear this is gonna be a long night. It might even be the last, for what's this stumbling through the door? I know there's bits of the Good Book, especially in that first bit, where revenge is found in the name of the Lord – but you should see the state of Richard this evening. This could have been no accident, no drunken tumble, this smacked of pure Old Testament retribution, a right Old School kicking.

Who do you reckon? Sarah, on her own, *again*? To tell the truth she's never forgiven him for telling the Truth a few nights back, and then giving Suey the push, her partner in crime, well that might just have been the last straw. But Sarah? On her own, *again*? I'd never have thought our Nate had it in him, but him and Rats are thick as thieves these days. If our Nate got his personality back then I bet it wouldn't be long before he spilled the beans to his new buddy. Next thing you know Rats does a little digging job during his next father-son love-in and bullseye, a full-blown confession Your Honour.

I'm only guessing of course. Things are certainly moving on, and I fear Rich needs to brace himself for more. Let's face it, that night in the dark alley should have been the least of his worries and Nate was only supposed to be a walk on part. But I guess he's put in some good performances and someone's warmed to him. I fear this is gonna be a long night. It might even be the last.

I once defended my aversion to cinema by declaring that classical music provided all the fiction I need. The deeper that different works of art touch me, the more similar the experience becomes. Think of a football, with each black patch representing an art form, happily housing all artworks of that particular type. Most of them will sit happily on the surface, but a few will penetrate towards the centre, forgetting all boundaries as they move further and further away from their parental form, and closer and closer together with their new siblings, all heading for that warm core of perfection.

But while great works of art do have roots which meet way below their form, there are still important things to be said about art's various formats.

To me it is clear that music is the greatest of all art forms. It's freedom from subject (for any such ties it makes are voluntary, secondary) allows it to explore the greatest depths of emotion. It doesn't have to be *about* anything in the way other art does. We may be told that a symphony tells a story, but this knowledge is not central or even essential to our enjoyment of it. Even singing dissolves into rhythms and sounds, words we learn as we might a tune, rather than a story.

Music speaks to the human, the universal, and the most beautiful pays no heed to culture or epoch. And music has other privileged qualities. As explained before we can place a work of art on a line of reflection with the artist on one side and the viewer on the other. But with music there is another position between art and audience, and this is where the performer sits. This privileged being is far more than a canvas, merely required to present in obedient perfection the composer's intentions. It is they who revive the vision which might otherwise be left to die among a score of dots and lines. And because music needs to be played to exist, it allows a human to be performer and audience all at once, and I guess composer too if they are improvising.

Later I will talk of art having no meaning for the artist alone, but for now let's bask in this glorious exception. For at its moment of birth, of being played, music is also being heard, and enjoyed - time and space dripping away as mind, body and soul come together as one. Lucky souls indeed, towards whom I feel the greatest respect, and no little envy.

I think beauty can shine brightest on the least obstructive of formats, those which pay the least heed to culture or language, object or subject. So for the sake of controversy one might rank the following artforms as thus: music first, followed by painting, then poetry, literature, theatre and then cinema.

Before we go any further it is essential you understand this is a ranking by theoretical potential, not some observed average, although I'm sure you've suffered enough happy endings, drippy sunsets and cheesy guitar solos to realise this yourself. If bad art idealises its subject, then clearly the artform with the most subject is most susceptible to this criticism. Although every format has its tacky commercial end I still contend there are heights one can reach in music which are forever beyond the grasp of, say, cinema or even literature.

The list also travels from the universal at one end to the fashionable at the other. Music written hundreds of years ago is still able to raise hairs, moisten eyes and pit stomachs, but films, which were no doubt more popular in their day, often lose their potency in a matter of years, soon looking strange, foreign, even amusing.

Painting and poetry have become very familiar forms, their practitioners all too often suffering from that awful affliction *prettiness*, but their shapes and words have the potential to convey something far deeper and, after music, are next best able, I believe, to access the abstract, and the universal.

I placed literature before theatre, because while literature can conjure up all manner of visions in our mind's eye, theatre is largely restricted to scenes, human interaction and dialogue. However, while translation is possible, both formats are surrounded by weighty cultural barriers. Finally comes cinema, more for historical reasons than anything else. While visually it can be more 'spectacular' than theatre, it can never compete with a live performance and ultimately is far better suited to entertainment than beauty.

Which brings me on to the complex distinction between art and fiction, not least because it may at first seem as if all art is fiction, in as much as they can both be contrasted with fact. But I would argue that if fiction is merely real-life possibilities in a made-up order then to my mind it may as well be fact. We have real-life spy stories, and made-up spy stories. Are you really telling me their differences outweigh their similarities, that one is art and one isn't?

All stories, whether in a novel or a newspaper, can be seen as a warm stream of salient facts contrived from a cold ocean of indifference, a pattern in the commotion, a meaningful journey rewritten over indifferent time. And while this assimilation may give newspaper stories their dramatic sheen, it also grounds fictional stories as described in a reality they may do better to escape.

So does this mean cinema is artistically doomed by this obligation to be *about* something? Of course not, but more often than not this is the fate it chooses for itself. For nothing random happens in films, no statement left unanswered, no scene unexplained, no comment irrelevant; all is so tiresomely necessary to the plot – I sit down to what they tell me is a complex thriller and I feel I've been thrown into some concentration test, in which I will, come The End, be examined and scored according to how closely I was watching.

"I knew that would happen you know, I was so *not* thrilled by that thriller," beams the film bore in excitement to his friend. "Yeah well I got it in the first half hour actually," his smug mug of a mate replies. "Yeah? Well I had it down to a fucking tee when the opening credits started rolling, if guessing it was going to be a complete waste of my time is what you mean," I scream, to them, to myself, to my own head, the way we all do.

The mechanics of story-telling, where the reader or viewer is first drawn one way and then another, and in the end is predictably shocked by an unpredictable twist, is a craft to be learnt, entertainment, excitement, like a fairground ride. Add to this its covert employment as an imperialistic weapon in you-know-who's fight for global domination (baddies with foreign accents, the sanctity of faith and family, the strength of the little guy) and before you know it we're being force fed a great honking cheese monster.

Conspiracy theories aside, in this cash-obsessed industry the operator who delivers the most often to the most people will always make the most films. Now money is the measure of all things perhaps cinema cares not for its ranking in my list and after my tirade against the artist who cares not for an audience, one might think I should be more hospitable to an artform which proves so popular.

But my problem with cinema is that the need for mass popularity and financial success has crippled the resultant form. Where is the risk? Where is the shock? Where is the beauty? I go to see what is alleged to be the 'latest' film and within minutes I'm consumed with déjà vu. Instead of revealing the new, this sickly sludge just confirms the old, the same tales we fairies loved to hear as children, to send us to sleep without a worry in our little heads. They may have shoved a bit of shooting and shagging in the middle but we cry babies are still demanding a soppy ending before beddy-byes.

And if I haven't offended or appalled you yet, then brace yourself. To my mind it is clear that education must be the key: if we were properly introduced to the wonder of the arts while at school then perhaps we wouldn't buy such trash when we become adults. Kids are the biggest dreamers, choke full out their imagination-to-knowledge ratio is at its most potent, the mix at its richest. We must stop patronising them and we simply *must* stop testing them, binding their minds' poor feet as soon as they're able to walk, toughening up those soles and souls, ready for our world of work.

The current debate about tuition fees for higher education (I always wanted this book to date - I've noticed all the great ones do) is centred around what students can expect the Government to pay for, and what they should have to pay for themselves. But if philosophy and the arts and all that other lily-livered left-wing pinko nonsense was taught to our innocent children at a proper age, at a time when their minds were most open to imagining, to dreaming, to the abstract (and least open to bloody science and technology) then we wouldn't need to spend so much time and money teaching this freeloading toss when these students are older and fatally corrupted by commerce and fashion.

Our education from day one is seen as a ten-year apprenticeship for the world of work, which means the world of capitalism, as if money and the means to acquire it is the sole root of happiness, all we need for a fulfilled and meaningful life. But with a lifetime of pressure guaranteed, can't we just leave them alone for a few years? For if, at this fertile stage, our young minds were given true licence to run riot along the corridors of the world's greatest operas, unhindered by their parents' bitter fixation with snobbery and elitism, then we wouldn't need a liferaft of state subsidies and accessibility policies to drag us along in years to come – wild horses couldn't stop us.

I'm dreaming again, perhaps I should really keep some of this to myself, for I'm fully aware how completely unacceptable it is to talk objectively, forcefully about art. But if a former Philistine like me can get hooked then so can anyone, I'm just trying to share my fortune.

I just know we can do so much better then our current commercialised ideas of beauty, this emphasis on cuteness and curves, which pass by our slipping standards so easily. Wholly inadequate and quite derisory ideas of beauty are gulped down like free milk and biscuits, served up by money men with no interest or belief in the staggering potential of human beings. Our hazy lazy eyes no longer care that they're delivered prettiness, happiness and moral goodness, when what they paid for was art.

And we must rescue beauty from the fashionistas while we're at it – because sexually attractive is what they really mean. Genuine beauty is man made, not skin deep. It is the culmination of one person's journey into the higher realms of existence, not some silky fabric draped over a curvy female - that's just posh porn. Not that there's anything wrong with that of course, but I don't want you to think our journey will take us up the catwalk – you've definitely taken a wrong turn if that's where you're treading.

Quality would be so much higher if we demanded it, and at no extra cost to anyone, or anything. To those who continue to live life as a fairytale such standards will feel harsh and unpleasant, as they are forced to face in art what they choose to ignore in reality. But we must not give in to their childish demands, for such mindless idealism tells us nothing but lies.

For our good art, our good stories, will balance pattern with confusion, feature as many weeds as roses, the latter shining all the brighter in their proper context. Our heroes will have ulterior motives, and our women will be immune to love. Truth and bravery may not pay, just as cowardice and lies might just succeed. And most importantly the undeserving will achieve great things and the strong will not triumph all the time, although neither will the weak.

You might wonder whether such sentiments are in fact anti-art, you might insist that the creation of art *is* the very exercise in idealism at which I scoff, an escape from the human condition, and for many artists this is indeed so. But to my mind true art is profundity, insight, and terrible beauty, and that lies deep down in we humans, not in the circles of angels we imagine watch over us.

Absorb the relentless brutality of a Shostakovich symphony, or spend a disquieting half hour with a late Picasso – such men were invoking the tortuous and the terrifying, the violent and the perverse, decades before Hollywood started churning out its jolly jelly, squeezed to this day into those rabbit moulds we saved from our childhood parties.

Indifferent endings (just you wait for mine!) events with no consequence, injustice, randomness, the ascendance of mediocrity, the death of ambition, the unlikely withering of passion – these are insights into the human condition about which most fiction tells us nothing. But when so many Drama Queens live their life according to the moral structure of a Hollywood story, then perhaps we shouldn't be surprised when they demand the same in their cinema.

Sorry to interrupt but as we're nearing the end I thought it only fair to deliver some breaking race news. I've just heard that Rich keeps falling off his bike. Being the author and all I won't divulge my sources, but the word is he can't stop seeing Emma every time he gets in that saddle, every time he turns a corner there she is, standing stock still, fixed to the sodden concrete like ancient gum. Only this time he *does* brake, swerves to avoid her, and falls head first into the road, folding his face into a creamy mince. Seems they might not have touched him after all. So could there be a late runner in the race, a deathly message from the dead indeed? The question now is how the bookies will react, could there be a new favourite?

But I certainly wouldn't want any of this discussion to put you off art, in all its glorious forms, or make you over analyse what's in front of your eyes. For when all is said and done, art is always best divided into two categories, good and bad, and these are judgements you must make for yourself. Does it do it for you, or not?

The cliché 'beauty is in the eye of the beholder' tells us about the subjectivity of taste, usually in the amorous realm, but in an unintended way it may contain some deeper truth. It may tell us that real beauty, beauty authentically sought, is somehow a shared privacy. It needs the air outside to breathe, but its presence can only be felt while gazing out from our private universe. It exists as a mental state, in the eye of each who care to search *beyond* the public creation there for all to see. Artworks can all be 'looked at', but their beauty must be *beheld*, and this is essentially a private exercise.

So don't laugh at the solitary man frowning for minutes on end in front of a painting. At least he's giving it a go, and more fool you if you giggle on past without a second look. Last time I saw a Monet I stared at it for 15 minutes, or so I'm told by the museum assistant who yanked me out of my trance because I was dribbling down my chin. They thought I was special needs, and I guess they were right.

Beauty must make the journey from vision to creation to experience – it must die as it was born, in private - and then the magic is over, until the next person comes along. We must be lonely in that crowd. Real thought transfer can happen here, the ultimate

Trekky dream is not so far away, from artist to beholder, the beauty for which the creator strived living on way beyond his grave.

But don't stay there forever, and don't whatever you do get talking. You've come on your own remember. Now we've come so far it would be a tragedy to be lured towards that fetching finery, the wine reception regulars chattering away in the corner. For if there's snobbery in the art world then it exists in these patrons, not the artists, who'd much rather sink a couple of snifters in the bar with you than spend one second discussing their work with Gerald and his fund-raising bath buddies. The beer test remember.

Sure art needs audiences, and for a million reasons artists should be part of them too. But ask yourself why anyone would spend a lifetime admiring and not even be *tempted* to step inside. I'll not waste time preaching it's better to create your own art than ponder over someone else's. I'm just suggesting you make time and make a start, if only to settle the matter in your own mind. Who's watching?

W e're winding this up now, we're finishing finishing, it's time to get down to brass tacks. Let's talk about the process of creation.

Before this book I was all wasted energy, an uncontrolled series of thoughts followed me around, taunting me, daring me to turn and face them. So I decided, as a mental exorcise, to begin a journal, without logic or design, just to placate my ghosts, just so they could be caught, for isn't that the secret desire of every stalker?

But over time shapes began to form in front of my eyes, patterns would appear, quite beyond my conscious making. Once-isolated ideas took on a new lustre when placed alongside their new siblings, acting more like a family reunited than dinner guests just met. Recurring thoughts gained a gravitas they would have been denied had I not poured my memory onto paper. The log book itself started to generate its own thoughts, gaps needed filling, loose ends tying, and soon I was rearing and feeding a beast which grew stronger and stronger with each mouthful.

So if you wondered why we started with a walk, it was to provide an expansive sense of time and space, one we are rarely afforded by our high-rise micro lives. For when you feel ready to embark on a project you must think big, not just in terms of size but scope as well. If you think too narrow you'll have nowhere to turn but backwards when things begin to get tough. Far better to allow space to scout round a problem, for it may be more easily attacked from another angle. Single-minded focus is all very well for the digital simplicity of modern commerce, but we are searching for beauty remember, and this is a gold we may find in the most unexpected of places, and may miss altogether if we are not prepared to stray from the path.

If you have inspiration for a painting then get yourself a big old canvas. If you have a couple of melodies then imagine the symphony in which one day they may sit. If you have a good idea for a scene or an interesting character then dream of the novel in which they might star, and then write it with hooks at either end. Don't decide now what part it will play in the final cut, you have to be more ambitious, you have to have more faith in the value of, and your ability to, travel.

Don't get tied down by structure until you have a decent handful of inspiration to play with. Let your best ideas *tell* you the framework in which they will best sit, let the sound and feel of your words or brushstrokes or melodies tell their *own* story. Let existence steer essence, for you have no idea what will happen in your mind tomorrow.

You will never be able to tap an idea's true potential if you keep it in isolation so don't be scared to let it play with the other children, even the rough ones. They may beat it up, but so what? We cannot be sentimental about our ideas, remember, they're not ours as such anyway. And if one is killed then you simply adopt and start loving and feeding the killer.

What might begin as a defining theme will more often than not become subsumed into something you could never imagine at the time. Link roads built between towns can and will become settlements in themselves, and may in time outlive the towns they link, or not. Urban sprawl is no problem for there ain't no green belt in this metaphor. Have confidence in this process and such faith will reap fine rewards. For you'll be amazed how much work your children will do on their own if given enough time, enough space, and a big enough climbing frame to play on.

When it comes to crunch time choose carefully – choose that which you are best at, that which can best accommodate your most inspirational moments – those times when you have most felt to be the source of real quality, real class. And then set out on a long journey, for art is not all art you know.

Your creation *will* have a life of its own if properly nurtured, short bursts of evening inspiration will direct its shape. And you'll find there is nothing quite like rushing into the glorious unknown, that burst of artistic energy when you just *know* what you're doing is new, exciting, of genuine worth, and certainly an impressive candidate for the final piece. But the next day, basking in the glow of that glorious escapade, when it felt like you did a week's work in one day, superform asks you to relax, to play servant to yesterday's master, to buff down his nasty edges, fill in his gaps, to touch him up. You will and must take equal pride in the mundane, because when your project is done, and is ready to be made public, that bum note will always sound the loudest.

In time your adeptness and dexterity will improve, and the line between art and crafts will become blurred, as it is in the world's most beautiful creations. This is when superform is operating at its highest level, when our wonder cares not to distinguish between the Beauty and the Beast it rides, when all seems as one.

I'm not convinced you *have* to go through the bad times to reach the good, that's just a crappy cliché. But I once slaved away at this monster for a whole day, producing five hours worth of meaningless waffle which I knew would never make the final cut. In a fit of frustration I predictably turned to the bottle, and after a quick snifter decided to give it one last shot, and lo and behold produced an indispensable hour of gold. Would I have hit that rich seam at dusk if I'd spent the whole day gardening? I have no way of knowing for sure, but it did make me wonder whether I could be more effective in my work.

So I stepped back and analysed what qualities my most successful sessions shared and was able to isolate a creative urge, artistic adrenaline if you like, a feeling which in time I'd come to recognise as clearly as a hunger pang. I'll say it again, we simply must not take nine-to-five home. That's their world, not ours. I guess we can all know ourselves a little better.

But it's not all hard work and frustration. When you are well into your journey, when there really is no going back, you may also find yourself wanting even more out of life.

The gradual fermentation of the book has inspired in me a patience and confidence to embark on other creations, other big projects which grow at a similar pace. Thinking long-term has become a habit.

When I look back over my journey it seems I was far more disposed to hard work at the start, and I look back so fondly, and with such admiration on the tireless tenacity of that early pioneer. It seems I tackled with great relish some huge and complex barriers I'd certainly baulk at now. Surely, if I'd known it would have been so much work I would never have started?

Well it seems not, for when considering my *next* project, anticipating another 200 blank pages with next to nothing in the way of inspiration or direction I am once again filled with such excitement I can barely wait to start. Starting is as exciting as finishing, and there's nothing like the warm security of being right in the middle. You really can't lose. This has got to be right.

I thought this might be the end, but as far as I can see no-one's saying anything about his new look, this Weeping Man who makes the Weeping Woman seem rather foxy. Nate's staring right past him, Sarah's shouting nothing, Ratty shoots him the occasional frown, but that's it. They're acting like they all knew he would come in looking like that – seems like I'm the only that's surprised. Even Richard's taking it in his stride. For some reason I walk over to my old mate and take his jacket - I couldn't just let that scene of nothingness continue. If this is the last night then none of them seem particularly up for it – there's not a tuxedo in sight.

Like a pack of wildcats are they starting to play with their prey? Ratty, Nate, Sarah, Suey, Emma, me? – surely one of us will strike it lucky. But what really happened on *that* night? Year Zero? Can you remember? There were drinks, there was laughter, there was crying and then what? I'm not even sure Richard knows what he did, although Sarah certainly does. Thing is, something's not right here. I'm no detective, and this is certainly no detective story, but something's not right. There's not a tuxedo in sight.

But if you still don't believe me then consider an already established project in which you are forced to think long term, just to get you in the spirit of things. Wine-making might work, with the added bonus of cheap booze at the end of it, but perhaps gardening is a better example. The lack of immediacy which used to turn me off has now become its greatest appeal. Decisions I made months ago are now starting to produce results, and I just *love* the yearly cycle, the yearly circle. Nothing bends time like the seasons, and believe me, that's not the only the only metaphor growing in the garden.

For remember we are eventually here to give something back, superform dictates that a creation in full blossom must in some way inspire more creation, in oneself and others. We should look to nature, not only to emulate its subtlety and complexity, but perhaps most importantly its regeneration. Our art should grow as an organic lifeform, trunks, branches, unexpected ugly bits, all playing their part, justifying their place, and finally at their death producing seeds for a new life.

When you've written your novel write another, expand on a bit of it you particularly liked. Write that lucrative spin-off series. Get better, get different, never stop creating, but always have a project, always have a goal, and always finish it (or at least feed it to something bigger).

However, like all metaphors they become less plausible the further they're stretched. For plants have roots on which they rely, and our creations must not be so restricted. I wrote the first lines of this book many years ago and you won't find them anywhere. But the rest would not have followed had they not been written. It's a technique I first discovered when writing music. At first I thought it was somehow dishonest, or misleading, more a way to impress than to create. But I began to realise the beauty behind it.

Techno, for example, is built up of distinct tracks or layers, each taken up by an 'instrument', drums, bass, strings, piano, bleeps, vocals. Simple melodies repeat themselves on loops of varying duration and the song itself generally starts off sparsely, builds up to a crescendo, explodes into a spectacular middle bit, and then returns to its minimalist beginnings.

Much of the appeal of techno lies in this predictability, and this mathematical structure clearly lends itself to a methodical and evolving style of creation. One might start by recording a two-bar bass, which the computer then plays back to you in an endless loop in perfect time. Then you add a different yet complimentary melody on a different instrument and so the process continues.

But here comes the key bit. After composing all the layers I would delete the first. What remained blended together in a way I would never have orchestrated from scratch, mature harmonies which like it or not were composed by me. I may not of heard them in my head before I started, but they certainly arose from my own process, inspired by a secret melody, this venerable mute, sacrificed in full honour. I think this method can guide all manner of creation. Don't be scared of evolving, fusing, moving on, deleting – original ideas will always be there, not in black and white perhaps, but as silent partners they will prove priceless.

But however you rear your beast, it will need a mixture of inspiration as food and hard craft as maintenance. While I would discourage anyone from dictating its shape at the start, in time a shape or form is just what you will need, for it be presentable, for it to withstand the public gaze. For no matter how many roses you plant at its core, you cannot expect people to fight through a tangled barricade of brambles to find them.

So we need some sort of design, our public will need to be guided, not necessarily straight there, but they must feel they are progressing, getting nearer. You will gain immense pleasure from this landscaping, this time off, but don't let it's joys tempt you into spending longer there than you need. We must not let servant turn master, we must not let presentation hold sway over substance.

This book and it's parts are obviously my form. The length is a traditional one and it has a start a middle and an end. It even has a story - of sorts. But this is not it's raison d'etre. The world doesn't need another round up of politics, philosophy and art, and it certainly doesn't need a bunch of pissheads trying to kill each other. It's the moments of inspiration which give it meaning, give it life, and I reckon so long as there's a handful in each chapter then it's been worth it. But without these gems it really would be a waste of time, like the 'artist' who produces all form and no beauty, yet another watercolour seascape inspired by nought save convention and gutless approval.

Now don't get me wrong for I certainly don't dislike genuine craftsmen, those proud masters of form who present themselves as nothing else. I'd suggest it's a universal delight to see a pair of skilled hands at work: the speed, the accuracy, the near-alchemy as a smooth baby is delivered from a lump of chaos.

I just have a problem with those who sell pretty as beauty, and themselves as artists. For they propagate the traditional lie that for something to be art, for something to be beautiful, the craft behind it had to have been quite hard to do.

How many times have you heard people say to modern art: "I could have done that." So what! The question is how does it make you feel, do you *like* it? And if you don't then fair enough. If those abstract shapes leave you cold then so be it. But I'd suggest that artist is making a far more genuine attempt to connect with his public, to convey his idea of beauty, then that witless twat who's spent the last three months painting a World War bomber emerging from a fluffy cloud.

Now that's the sort of 'art' that leaves *me* completely cold. And yes, I too feel I could have done that, given time, but only as punishment. His dream, if he has one, is to trick someone into thinking his picture is in fact a photo. Yeah, whatever. I'll show him something which looks even more like a photo, it's called a photo.

But this book is not directed at the fakirs, it's more for those who see creation as something *other* people do, it's for those who believe the lies artists tell them, that some people are merely born to admire and applaud. But if the search for beauty still sounds rather daunting then lets see if this is beast best tackled from another side.

If our search for beauty is ever going to get off the ground we must also recognise the value of all creativity, of any kind. Making something from nothing according to an idea of your own is a process containing great power. Personally I find cooking to be the ideal example, and one which essentially allows for a lifetime of infinite improvement, for there's no judge as harsh as a taste bud.

And it satisfies on so many levels: Animal? We eat to survive. Social? Meals are among the best (and worst) ways to inaugurate, nurture and consolidate relationships. Recreational? An evening cooking with a bottle of wine is a lot of fun. Political? Profit-driven battery farming versus free range sustainability. Aesthetic? The colour and design of the final meal can be presented artistically. Logical? The essential aspect of timing involves considerable forward planning and multi-tasking. Managerial? A big meal may require the delegation of preparation. Scientific? What else resembles the laboratory more than a kitchen, with its Bunsen rings, measuring jugs and cooking tongs. Educational? You'll acquire a compendium of times and temperatures, based on a sophisticated knowledge of food type and density. And finally (like the moral of the day) temperamental? Less is always more, and patience and restraint will reap regular reward.

Oh yeah, and you also get to play with knives and fire.

But the point is, the search for beauty through creation will be immeasurably improved by getting in the habit of making things and making things up. We must stop buying, stop watching, stop talking. It really is time to start a project, however small. As a once great man once said: "It's not what you've got, it's the way you play it."

I believe any human creation can contain beauty, for beauty lies in the motivations of the creator, in the inspiration, not its vehicle. But if something is made with profit as its ultimate goal then I fail to see that it will contain much beauty (which of course is not to say that beautiful things cannot earn great profits). Consider what is actually made these days, literally *anything*, which doesn't have profit maximisation as its defining brief. This is why it's down to us. We must bring things into this world which are beautiful, and they will be even more so because their existence was inspired by a mind set free from the March of the Market, its vision shining ever brighter against that tawdry corporate backdrop.

But beware, they will try to stop you, they will insist you are wasting your time, that it's easier to buy their cheaper version, so you must be strong. And even if they turn out to be right in the short-term your skills will soon overtake those programmed into their machines. We must fill the world with things which simply cannot be justified by profit maximisation. We must not let them force their agenda upon us, we were here first. Never imagine capitalism as some insensate transparency, a mere system free of values. Look at who has benefited and continues to benefit. Success breeds success and the random circumstances of birth are almost everything. Their's is no blank canvas, no level playing field.

Step away for a while, leave them to it. What are you scared of? That they'll hunt you down and demand a note explaining your absence from the Mall this weekend? It's Saturday and you've gone back to work: not yours perhaps but definitely someone else's – it's the same ballpark. You must learn to walk away, to ignore their marketing pleas, to stare blankly at those sales staff. Get the bus home quickly, leave your shopping bags on the mall floor if you have to. Run, run! When I am fully engaged in writing this book, when all thoughts are directed towards it, then I see no higher life. To be creatively submerged in the search for beauty is to operate at the highest level of human existence.

However we will see that ultimately art cannot remain a private pursuit, any more than language would have evolved in a world containing just one person. The idea must travel from the inner to the outer world, but it cannot remain in that leaking studio. It needs time, it needs time's moments, moments spent with someone else, otherwise it remains in a state of suspension, lost in space.

There is a balancing act to be performed: the public gaze must in some way be written into our brief, but too much of this tricky ingredient and we are left with objects merely created to impress, and we all know what they sound and look like. The creation of beauty it seems is the master key that unlocks many doors, but the one marked 'guaranteed popularity' should remain closed. I know – it's hard, it's so tempting to take a peek, to feel that warm glow burning from the other side.

But it's a fake fire and can be flicked off as quickly as it is turned on. You'll never be in charge in that room and before long you'll be left in the cold and dark with nothing to show for it but a dirty cheque. The world of popularity is also the world of inevitable rejection, for as surely as the business will eat your food, will it one day shit it out.

So just what did happen that night? Year Zero? Do you know what Richard's just told me in the Hall of mirrors? 'I didn't do Justice you know – it wasn't me.'

Oh come *on* Rich. But I just knew he meant it, words may lie but eyes simply can't - and those black holes spoke the darkest of truths. And just when I thought this was going to be no detective yarn he showed me the evidence your honour. Sticky with his own blood, he handed me a screwed up receipt he's just found in the lining of his jacket, the *lining* indeed. And I saw the note with my own eyes, in *his* writing.

It said: "S killed J and she'll kill you too." A warning to himself from the past? Now that's pretty smart for anyone, let alone our Rich. I don't want you to feel too sorry for him, but he must have known for some time what was going to

happen last night. Whoever was there, that night of Old Testament caning must have been written in stone. He must have been in some state to decide to write to himself, to some future that would never recall the horrible truth he'd just heard, the truth he just knew was about to be beaten out of him. And that must have been some argument for her to admit everything. Why would she want him to know? It's rarely to one's benefit to divulge so much, and if you can count on anyone to keep it zipped it's our Sarah. What is she playing at? And more importantly how long has Miss Silent-but-Violent been stringing poor Rich along? Just what then *did* happen on that first night, Year Zero, the day Sarah accepted her mission? Richard's lifelong affair with Suey has cost him dear it seems: with no memory of the key moments he's been a pushover. Still, what do I care? Perhaps they *were* all there, that would certainly explain the lack of response, the lack of sympathy, the lack of words this long long evening. Trouble is, I've a feeling I'll never know.

Richard never really spoke about the events of Year Zero. I always put it down to first night nerves, but now we know why. He didn't speak because he can't remember, and when this dawned on the charming Sarah ... well the rest is history. Seems our Rich'll believe anything. I wonder what else she told him? I wonder what other parts of his-story she rewrote? I always told you someone else was having a go. Well whaddya know, I missed a key scene ... again! But apparently all good directors leave the scariest bits to the imagination. And anyway, what do I care.

If money is a poor motivator, then approval is not much better. And I reckon there's none quite as gutless as the 'artist' who creates in public. What type of person would want to share such secrets?

I suspect an inverse-snobbery gnaws away at the heart of those who demonstrate the creative process. Perhaps they're trying to debunk what they would have you believe is their passion, snubbed by the gang of private visionaries they'd so love to join. Those who can't - teach, right? (The cruellest of truths which so rarely applies to school teachers.) These public exhibitionists reduce art to a set of remembered tricks of the trade linked together by .. well, you decide: "Can we have any suggestions from the audience?" And don't those laughing lemmings lap it up: "Is that all it is, after all," they sigh with relief, egged on to this deathly conclusion by the grinning clown before them. But I warn you Mr Smiley, you kill art and you kill one of the clearest expressions of beauty. What price your dented ego?

For with each trick turned to impress, they fill another cup to throw on the hissing spitting souls of their audience, fading furnaces which should be stoking up a thirst for beauty. Workshops are all very well but I do so hope these shops do work. I hope people are indeed inspired to "try this at home", I do so hope they feel challenged by the unknown, rather than reassured by its opposite.

Of course there *are* tricks of the trade which can help us in the creation of beauty, but they must be treated as means, not ends. Being able to chop onions quickly does not make you a good cook, but I guess there isn't a good cook who can't. Clearly there are brushing techniques for painting, theories of scale and harmony to be learnt for music, ideas of suspense and character development to be grasped for fiction (yeah yeah, ha bloody ha, there's always next time).

Even the greatest of masters produced a formulaic catalogue of early work, an expression of academy style learnt months before their personal vision transcended the craft. But there are also artists who created genuine beauty without formal teaching and there are Grade A students who have never come close. Ideally we want the right amount from both sides, inspiration and perspiration, art and craft, one brick from one pile, one brick from another.

With superform as our guide, the wall will be strong.

So Sarah was the killer, they say it's worse from a mamma puss but I'm not so sure. So Sarah was being *very* clear after all. "I'm a killer," she told me one day, remember that? Now on any other occasion from any other person that would clearly have been something of a showstopper. I could have stopped the show there and then, but like an arrogant fool I failed to take my own advice. "I'm a killer," she told me one day, remember that? Typical rationalist I thought, an actor without a play, all essence, no existence, all means, no end. "Yeah okay Sarah, you're the killer – why not. And I'll be the detective if you like." But I wasn't a very good one for the truth was right there in front of my face, her words for once did not lie.

"Philosophy is about life, life is not about philosophy." How many times have I said that now? But just when I needed that mantra most I blew it. Still, what do I care? It's not like Richard's a saint otherwise, I held that watch remember.

Sarah listened to that crying until she could listen no more, but it never went away. The sound merely shifted from the outside (in which we are free) to the inside (from which we can never escape) a looping track burned into her personal stereo. Noise may need a listener, but one's sure enough.

And so I reckon the killing spree will continue, there's only one way to be sure of drowning out a sound, and that's to replace it with one just like it, but louder. My guess is she's still got her eye on Richard, and in that way I was half right. She's hoping Richard's tears will flood her head, the tears of a baby killer who never killed any babies, the father who never called anyone son, the son who never called anyone dad.

So Sarah was the killer and now I believe no-one (and believe me neither should you – don't say I didn't warn you). Truth has never been less important, has never meant so little. I always said Happiness and Beauty meant more, I always said words are the biggest liars of the lot. What matters now in our crying game? Winning of course. Winning is everything now, the truth won't out, not now, I probably wouldn't even tell you if I knew. What do I care? Truth leaves no trace, there is no past to refer to, only a history to be recorded and recalled, and that's a fiction we can all remember, if pushed.

Wow, this has sure been one long night, but that can't be it? This Silent Night can't have been the Last Sup. There must be one more. There has to be. But back out in publand still nothing is being said. They're acting like they all knew he would come in looking like that. And there's not a tuxedo in sight.

Finally we must make some space, and this is not at all easy. Like our visit to the gallery, we must essentially operate alone, in private. Because for every flash of brilliance there might be three or four flash in the pans by which we'd hate to be judged, and you may not even know at the time into which category each has fallen.

The artist in his ivory tower, churning out beautiful creations which he never makes public has stopped way before the finish line. But we must borrow some caution from this tortured soul, for when we eventually emerge we must appear resplendent in our new beautiful robe, and there will be no time for modesty then, false or otherwise. Real-life magic has occurred within the confines of those white turrets, and it's time everyone else got a good look.

And throughout your alchemic hibernation you must feel confident that your tower is a space well protected. While that home cannot be your home forever (for it's not actually yours – you'll see) it must be a safe haven while you're in residence. For we too will be tortured souls in private, with little time for anyone else, just like the eccentric artisans we so love to hate.

The creative process itself can be seen in terms of our inner and outer worlds. All art, all creation, must in the last instance have a public face, yet the process by which this comes about must, with equal necessity, be totally private. The creative process is about exploring our philosophical side, trying to answer Question B. It is about operating within the bubble's silky confines, and one simply cannot commit to this endeavour with one ear out for the doorbell.

If we are aware of an audience too early then too suddenly our dream is also for someone else, and like Sartre's 'other' we are suddenly and fatally reminded that our existence is made up of two worlds. You might fancy yourself immune to such lily-livered paranoia right now, but be warned. In time you will share this fear of the 'other', this Big Brother bruiser given unlicensed freedom to form a disfigured impression from one sleazy peep into your private show.

When creating I can quite grant Sartre his dramatic neurosis, for I have found that confidence becomes an act of brute force, especially when common sense points you in quite some other direction.

But remember, there is no shame in coming off-project for a while. It's giving up the dream for something else, someone else's, that will sentence you to a slow death. Sorry, but this was never supposed to be easy. If anything it's an antidote to easy, if easy be religion or nationalism or consumerism, or any other jism which allows you, encourages you, to stop thinking for yourself.

While the disjointed wasteful repetitive meanderings of the creative process are all justifiable from the inside (as our dreaming soul siphons off the cream, and pours away the rest) from the outside we will appear as a dribbling drunk, swallowing anything and everything, making a pathetic stab at the unattainable, a misguided ambition, redolent of the naked and the weak, and a world away from the resplendent Prince as we are one day to emerge.

This is a question of magic – for the creation of beauty, or rather it's public presentation in the final instance will be just that. Beauty is a kind of magic - it is our attempt at transcending the contingent mode into which we are born and can never escape. It is an illusion and an allusion, towards the universal and the essential, towards the eternal Father Time forever holds out of reach.

But don't get too down. The search for beauty will not condemn you to a lifetime of frustration, of the kind born from some pathetic uninformed idealism. We may be neither destined or designed for such endeavours, but we strive on nevertheless, safe in the knowledge that the search for beauty is the highest available mode of existence known to man, and in that search he gives meaning to a meaningless life. That the universal is philosophically beyond our reach is testament to the noble high standard we have set ourselves (and also because we've got to string this shit out for a lifetime remember). But along the way our attempts to find it will produce some offspring of which we can be justly proud.

The process itself however will never let us forget the power which existence holds over essence and the truth that practice makes success. As a famous golfer once said: "The more I practice the luckier I get."

The creative process may be the best going, but once you are fully involved you may begin to question just how far man has in fact stood up from his prehistoric squat. And you may consider that we only fancy ourselves Masters of the Universe because the inventions of a few amazing humans have made modern life piss easy. In fact never have I been more reminded of the contingent, random rabble of existence, the crazy complexity that rules the contents of my brain, the volatility of any persistence of identity and personality, as when I've been writing this book.

No my friend, you must never show your workings out, not this time. Like the magician who keeps his tricks up his sleeve, the creative process must remain shrouded in mystery and intrigue. For the sake of efficacy and ego there can be no viewing gallery. There will be much discarded material, for all great artists are also ruthless editors. But we wouldn't want the audience to see this process – we don't want to be associated with the detritus on the cutting room floor. And I would not want to gaze in on anyone else's. Imagine watching Beethoven compose his 5th, imagine hearing the weaker tunes he discarded, the corny melodies that didn't make the final cut. Prematurely exposed to the elements this work of genius would be tainted - without its topcoat it would fall to rags.

So if the outside is so damaging, then why can't we stay in the cutting room, you ask? Why isn't the search for beauty enough? Because superform commands that we must give back, we must share what we have learnt, others must benefit in the way we have. He demands we return the private to the public from whence it was inspired. Superform may guide us through the creative process, keeping us strong when we are weak, suggesting direction when we feel lost, breathing confidence over our most paranoid moments, but in the last he must be obeyed.

We must strive for excellence, and that is a judgement delivered from (and ultimately shared with) the outside. We can and must take our time, for we have just seen the fate of premature births, but we cannot remain pregnant for life. The world must keep turning, and when once we took a ride, so one day must we push. To reject in the end that which gave us so much in the beginning is to believe the identity myth, is to believe the lies we are told about our personality, is to see pride and prejudice in contingency and to imagine some privileged destiny in a community of chaos. That a process must be sustainable, i.e. takes no more than it gives, is a philosophical given, almost a defining quality of what a process *is*. For one which contributes to its own destruction will in the fullness of time become nothing.

Superform is one person we simply must answer the door to, and don't bother hiding, for this is the landlord stupid, and he has a key. So it seems the ivory tower was his after all and our tenure is up – apparently there's a growing waiting list, which is great for him and them, but now quite scary for us. Consideration of the audience is essential to the healthy delivery of our child, but after that it's a done deal. They'll never call once they've left home, and if anyone benefits then it won't be us they'll thank.

The child itself is our repayment to the society which got us pregnant: *we* were the ones in debt, no-one owed us anything. What a complex and mature manner to foster, returning the favour not to the past, but to the future. You capitalists may scoff at such a Hegelian view of a living breathing society but when a successful businessman enters the voluntary sector on retirement, declaring he wants to 'give something back', no one accuses him of falling foul of German idealism. Perhaps the riches for which we strive all these years eventually come to nothing in the end – and we all become a bit more philosophical.

But we must not be over keen to meet our public. Wait for superform's knock but ignore everyone else's, they're only bored, they only want to know because you've got a secret. You must play right to the whistle, for he will come and you will recognise the time.

We must show maturity and patience – no premature births now, for we all know about the 'prolific' artist, churning out cheese to clockwork deadlines. To me their work is rarely beautiful, and even when it is I feel it could have been so much better than these raw half-births before me, their tiny lungs gasping for air under the world's polluted gaze, but what's this? A slobbering queue of dummy-mummies, eyes rolling in puppy love for yet another mewling puking runt, their chapped lips salivating at the prospect of one more bestial kiss of life. And they almost devour this newborn weakling, in their pathetic attempt to keep the poor thing alive. But its lips taste the same as the last runt (again), the wine's been poured too early (again), and their addiction is not truly satisfied (again), and so quietly, obediently, they join the queue (again).

Who are these weird fans? Fanatical devotees certainly, dreaming of fictional characters and fictional lands as if they were as real as the countries they never visit and the people they never meet. And who is their production-line parent? - his pockets lined by twice-yearly bugger-offspring, sold into slavery for good hard cash. Like the garden shed producer of cheap plonk told me the other day: "You can always use the same ingredients, just so long as you change the label."

I on the other hand have no weird fans, or any fans at all come to that – I know a few who will catch me out of sympathy, (thanks by the way), but privately they will drop me again. This is going to be hard, real hard. No wonder I drink, and yes – it is cheap plonk. What can I say? I liked the new label.

So finally, what is this beauty we are aiming for? Clearly I can't provide an instruction manual for its creation, for essentially it is a feeling caught in time, a moment of intense wonder.

Beauty makes your hairs stand on end, it's that bit which demands your full brain, stops all thought and speech in its tracks – it can make you feel sick. It happened to Bach's contemporaries when they first heard his music, it happens centuries later when we hear it now, and it will happen again in years and years to come.

Beauty can only be felt by humans, and so beauty in a world without people makes no sense. This doesn't mean that nature cannot be beautiful, but it is beautiful by observation, not design. Beauty makes no sound when no-one's there to hear it and in a parallel world we may be wholly indifferent to sunsets and waterfalls, birdsong and rainbows – it is we who take beauty to nature, not the other way round. If it can be so indifferent to life and death then it's hardly going to care about looks.

Beauty is a human physical reaction, it may elude language's grasp, but then it eludes its lies too, and is perhaps all the more real for that. It can also be admired with great pride, not that secondary vicarious smugness with which we regard our sons and daughters, but proper pride in our own achievement. To see beauty in someone else's work, now that's a start, to create something which you consider yourself to be beautiful, well now you're cooking, but when someone *else* sees beauty in *your* creation, well life really does not get any better. As I said before, ignoring our ego will not make it go away, so really the question is *how* it is rightly indulged, not whether it is.

And remember, take a break, take a walk, use your hands, invent, build, refine. Superform is more than a dour disciplinarian, demanding you give back to society what you took on the tick. It can and must be applied to oneself, to the creation process, where you will find it a most generous and optimistic companion.

And once beauty has been created then the process starts again, with a new project, but this time with a process soaked in the champagne spray from that last victory. This is why we must finish, why we must reach the top of our ladder. This is why we must get on that podium, take that stage and face our plaudits. If we're only as good as our last then we need to deliver to know just how good that is, else we'll have nothing to build on, to learn from. The new form will not have become super, and you'll have been sent back to the start, without passing Go.

But once you've seen beauty you will want it more. Your inner world will become so saturated with success that it will season your every waking walking moment. You will see beauty in places you would never have thought to look. Life itself becomes exciting for you will realise that if it is we who bring beauty to art then we can bring it to the mundane also. The search for excellence becomes an attitude, a way of life. You should see my cheese on toast.

Now that's probably the closest I've come to defining beauty, and I hope the definition rings true. But if you haven't felt that bursting moment of intensity then I hope you have at least fallen in love. This book is not about love, but right now I see a parallel that can help those of you whose creative hymen has yet to be broken. If love be a universal theme, a heartfelt reaction common to all cultures in all centuries, the explosion when our inner and outer world's collide, then I beg you to accept there is a beauty which boasts the same qualities.

Sure, the vehicles of love – the letters, the handkerchiefs, the roses, the texts – may have changed down the years, as have the instruments, words and materials of art. But love is love and beauty is beauty, and it's that enduring human condition, human feeling, we're after. Man is never so noble as when he creates beauty. He never stands so tall above the world's waste line, its violence and corruption, its pretence and exploitation, as when he sets his mind to the timeless, the universal, the beautiful. It's what makes us really human, it's what gives true meaning to a life, and boy does it pass the time.

I don't want to sound too narcissistic here, but we can fall in love every day. However I'm now a little wary of this metaphor because there are many aspects of falling in love which do not apply. If rejection figures in our journey, then it's us who'll be doing the dumping, and any sacrifice will only be for our own better future. Some aspects of our search are more akin to tough maternal love, the sort found in the animal kingdom, although there are times when full-blown erotic abandon is a better model, as without shame we delve deep for the ultimate turn on, the moments which make those hairs stand erect.

Other languages have a choice of words for love. The fact that we English have just one may speak plenty about our culture yet leaves the concept itself strangely elusive, locked away in the closet no doubt. If we were honest there are many types of love; maternal, sexual, marital, filial, religious, political even, and one love can journey between any combination of these throughout it's life. Yet even to suggest such distinctions in this green and pleasant land is to commit an act of arch treachery, a tawdry attempt to cheapen man's greatest gift, as if each prefix was a tiny dagger striking at the heart of this most revered being. Still, you've gotta laugh.

But there have indeed been times when I've felt I'm losing my grip on a lover who was frankly out of my league from the outset: times when I've felt that this book was bigger than me, the goal it set for itself unattainable. There was a real beauty standing right next to me to which I would do no justice. It should have been a maternal love ending with the ultimate deed, the ultimate sacrifice. I should have surrendered control and left my baby to fend for itself in the outside world.

In its darkest moments it became something altogether different, a competitive destructive paranoid love, I feared the relationship would not end on my terms, and in fact I would be the one who was discarded, my dream in tatters, no book, no beauty, just memories of poison. But I soon realised that metaphors are there to serve reality, not shape it, and it was a little silly to imagine being dumped by a book. So one day I decided to take the reins, and while not afraid to let the beast turn this way or that if it so desired, never again would I let go, and so here we are. So I get on much better with the beast now, and I guess I'll be sad to see it leave, for we're really getting near the end. But it's raison d'etre is to be finished, published and criticised, and so it will be.

When you embark on your own journey, there's no doubt that an unhealthy period of self-indulgence, pretentious dreaming, and wild imagination is just what's needed to get going. But don't, whatever you do, think about the long journey ahead, for there will be bad times, times when you may feel your baby is playing up rather, and is the last thing you want to waste your time on.

So here's some free advice: I like to have three or four jobs on the go – one large and a few small fun ones, using the same creative creating skills but on a much shallower scale. I'd go mad without them. Just how *do* people survive with just their shitty job and their shitty TV, the dribbling dead waiting to die.

Sometimes you will hate the look of your growing baby, but you must have confidence that the ugliness resides as much in your gaze as the object upon which it falls. And in those times you will need some alternatives, some creative soma. Just don't, whatever you do, flick that ON button, because it will have quite the opposite effect on you.

For the power of art, and the process of engagement, is truly daunting – and this seems to have been translated into 'off-putting' for many people. This attitude exists as a frustrating flicker in my own life too. The frustrating flicker, which crackles in front of my vision, sucking the oxygen from my spare time, telling me that all things considered it might be better to let the screen do the talking. But TV belongs to the world of work.

It asks for the same deference, the same docility. We laugh obediently, half-heartedly, to make it through the day, and then come home, turn on a different screen, and laugh in the same way to make it through the night.

We need to step off the treadmill – we need something different, the search for beauty is the only way. The patience and discipline required may sound a bit too much like hard work, especially after a hard day at their work, but remember, it should be seen as a way of grabbing back our own time. But if one day you can't be bothered to continue the journey then in some ways you are half-way there, because you have understood the process. If all that separates you from your beautiful goal is time and effort, rather than understanding, then all indeed is well.

Can you take any more? Well, apparently Sarah hasn't eaten for a month, and that's the truth. Being the author and all I won't divulge my sources but is that sensible? Is that *possible*? What is happening with that girl? I knew she wanted an end but I didn't imagine it would be hers. Maybe that's why she spilled the beans to Richard, just so everything was out in the open. Sounds like the sort of closure claptrap she'd buy into. She looks okay though – a body many would kill for, die for even – but I didn't think *she* would. I wonder how long our lovebirds will last? Two of a pair alright, oddly suited in a homicidal way. But as any crossword fan will tell you there's no love in a novel, and there's certainly none in this.

So this really is it then. There'll be no tears for this is the beginning, not the end, this book you hold is where it all started, giving meaning to the years gone by, stretching back over time to when I wrote those first words, those ghostly lines you've never read. I acted like a writer, I wrote like a writer, I sat and shat like a writer, and it worked, for now I am one.

Good luck and good bye.

So this is it then, the final night, or so I thought. Seems I'm not the only one who's had enough. Here I stand, all suited and booted for the gripping finale and I've just had the shock of my life. The landlord we never spoke to of the pub we never named with the jukebox that never changed, each in turn providing audience, stage and backing music to our pointless little drama - but now? This is indeed a tale of bitter revenge, or French lager revenge might be better, for you should see what he's done to our pub, our club, our *home*. Never does essence leave existence so fast as it does after a refit. Such a brutal eradication of history would have lain beyond Big Brother's wildest dreams.

I blame Richard. I reckon he started it, with all that healthy living with the dad he never called dad. Just what *is* it about Dirty Dick? That trend setter, that Daddy Baddy. Do you recall? "Given it up mate, thinking of taking a bit easy," he explained to me, a bottle of House in one hand, tumblers in the other, the *proper* way to drink red wine. Remember that?

Someone's got to call time soon, or so I thought, and so they did, on the whole place. I had an ending planned, really I did, I was only joshing with all that stuff about indifference. But it won't work here, among the whiners and diners, the wine and the pine, the acoustics are all wrong. The Mondays won't like it, they won't like it one bit, too near to home for the breakfast bar brigade. Where's

the filth, where's the fear, where's the failure? And what the fuck are those *children* doing here?

Who'd have thought it, 200 pages of hatred, violence and death and I finally lose it over a question of interior design. Still, you've gotta laugh, I thought, as I ordered an ice-cold bottle of French beer. I've got no pride remember.

Talking about children, do you know where our merry gang are, do you know where they've gone? Surely they've not been signed up *already*! So I guess it's just us then, finishing as we started: me, this book, and you, whoever you are.

By the way, did you guess who the killer was? I must say it shocked me. As I said I never really planned any of this from the start. I wanted it to evolve as much as possible, and once up and growing I fancied myself the good parent, who sets boundaries, not rules, what *not* to do, not what *to* do. Description is always better than prescription after all, and a lot less effort, although there are times when I've just let it be, safe in the knowledge that whatever happened the cold season would kill it soon enough. Nothing bends time like the end of a novel. Perhaps the next one will be different, perhaps I'll get a better cast, a better story, a better ending.

So did you guess who the killer was? Thing is, strict betting rules apply here, and in the absence of a conclusive decision I'm afraid all bets are lost, accept mine of course. I was never betting on who'd kill dear old Dicks, how could I, he's a mate after all. Personally, I was betting on the other death match, the double header, and I guess we now know how that one turned round in the dying minutes. But as I said, words are liars at heart.

You see I was betting on Richard all along and I guess it's time I claimed my winnings. I've always been good at copying people's writing and believe me Dickie's scrawl is not the hardest – even *I* was a child once. (For some reason I walked over to my old mate and took his jacket - I told you it was a bit clever for our Rich, and I was right. Of course I'm right.) Thing is I really thought he deserved a break, if only to show him that we all need to believe in our selves, to believe in a self. And if for one second he could live life as the wronged victim then I'm sorry, I couldn't resist it.

So let's raise a glass to we humans, as we huddle together round our camp fires, shoved headfirst into a cold dark world offering no purpose save that which we poor shivering souls can bear to imagine for ourselves. And if we make up a jig or two to make it through the night, then you can't really blame us (altogether now, you *must* remember the house song. Come on you Greens!):

We're writing and fighting, we're skiving, we're driving
We're kissing and pissing, we're loving, we're lying,
We're skidding, we're killing, we're shitting, we're quitting,
We're drinking, we're sinking, now get some more in

(Repeat)

So did you guess, did you know who the killer was? Sarah may not be *the* killer but she'll always be *a* killer. She'll plot like a killer, plan like a killer, she'll still sit, spit and shit like a killer, I told her there'll be other stories, more scenes, more chances, we did a deal. I told there'd always be good parts for actors like her – that there's always a motive for the death of a husband. But she's frustrated, I know, she so wanted her ending – and perhaps she's gone elsewhere to find it. I don't blame her, I don't blame any of them really. Where are they? So it seems that *was* the last night after all, a quiet scene of ultimate indifference, even Richard took it in his stride. Oh well.

Head hung high I place my empty bottle on the metal bar I once called home and for one final time venture outside to the Hall of Mirrors, to the scene of Dear Dicks' pool of revelation. But I should have known, they'd chucked that too. All that remains is a summer festival prefab pisser and that damnable Demon sniffing and tugging at a skip full of horrors, a bonfire of broken wood and shattered glass, all that was left of our nest with no love. But I can see it's all still there, in kind, the office bar, the shaky stools, the piss-sheen bog, the exclusive jukebox, a dirty sleeve, a purpled wrist, a broken watch. What *is* it with that damn watch, it's face staring me stupid each night I forget to drink, hands pointing to the heavens, frozen in time.

And I'm doing something I haven't done for months. Crying? Hugging? Laughing? No, don't be daft, I'm wetting myself. I'm standing here at the place of piss and pissing my pants, a minute-long homage to the man whose gaze I held, whose hand I held, whose watch I held, fixed to the sodden mud like ancient gum. For some reason I begin to pull at our broken nest, but why? I know exactly what I'll find. But still I need to see the face. Damn those therapists but right now I need some closure.

And there it was, trapped beneath his favourite jukebox, lips made up like an Amsterdam transvestite, her last laugh slapped across his face in a colour I'd recognise anywhere.

Seems she got her man after all. I just hope it was worth it, Sarah. I so hope the crying's stopped.

So did you know who the killer was? I swear to you now, I've only just found out myself. This was never supposed to end this way, in fact this was never supposed to end at all. Perhaps some stories are just too strong, some Justice just has to be done.

And now I'm strangely jealous. What about me? They say we're only as good as our last, but that's real difficult for us novices, we fathers without a son, we killers without a kill, we believers without a God, we writers without a book. I guess we all have to live the dream, if only to get started. If only to get finished.

The End.

www.ingramcontent.com/pod-product-compliance
Lightning Source LLC
Chambersburg PA
CBHW051135020726
47501CB00005B/1520

* 9 7 8 1 8 4 5 4 9 1 4 6 8 *